Sebastian the Teddy-Bear

The Secret Portal

Book 1 in the 'Sebastian the Teddy-Bear' children's adventure fantasy series

Geoff A. Wilson

Copyright © Geoff A. Wilson (2022)

The right of Geoff A. Wilson to be identified as author of this work has been identified by him in accordance with the UK Copyright, Designs and Patents Act.

All rights reserved. No part of this publication may be reproduced, stored in a retrieval system, or transmitted in any form or by any means, electronic, mechanical, photocopying, recording, or otherwise, without the prior permission of the author.

kindle direct publishing

First published 2022
Kindle Direct Publishing (UK Office)
44 Ashbourne Drive
Coxhoe
DH6 4SW

Edited by Olivia J. Wilson

To Erik and Peli

About the author

Born in London to a British father and a French mother, **Geoff A. Wilson** grew up in southern Germany where he went to primary and secondary school. He is trilingual in German, French and English. He studied for his MA in Geography, Cultural Anthropology and Archaeology at the University of Freiburg (southern Germany), before completing his PhD in Geography at the University of Otago in Dunedin, New Zealand. From 1992-2003 he worked as a Geography Lecturer/Senior lecturer at King's College London, and from 2004-2019 as Professor of Geography (Emeritus Professor since 2019) at the University of Plymouth (south-west UK). Geoff became a world-renowned academic expert on questions about the resilience of human communities, more specifically about how rural communities cope with, and adapt to, change, disturbances and disasters. He has published over 100 academic articles on the subject and has written several books including *Environmental management: new directions for the 21st century* (with Raymond L. Bryant; UCL Press, 1997), *Multifunctional agriculture: a transition theory perspective* (CABI International, 2007) and *Community resilience and environmental transitions* (Routledge, 2012). Married and with one son, he lives in a small village on the south coast of Devon, UK. Geoff retired in 2019 to become a full-time writer. He specialises in psychological thrillers, short stories, children's fantasy books and dystopian novels. *Sebastian the Teddy-Bear: The Secret Portal* is his first novel.

Books by Geoff A. Wilson:

'Sebastian the Teddy-Bear' Children's fantasy series:

Sebastian the teddy-bear: the secret portal (KDP Publishing, 2022)

Sebastian the teddy-bear: the Viking curse (KDP Publishing, 2022)

Psychological thrillers/Psychological fantasy:

Depravity: a story about the darkness of the human soul (KDP Publishing, 2020)

Meltdown: the story of a tragic psychological collapse (KDP Publishing, 2021)

The dream: a psychological fantasy (KDP Publishing, 2022)

Dystopian fiction:

Pandemic: a dystopian story about what might have been ... and about what could still happen in future (KDP Publishing, 2020)

Crime thrillers:

Beyond evil: the story of one of the world's most vicious serial killers (KDP Publishing, 2022)

Short stories:

The machine (KDP Publishing, 2021)

Phil 81: a short story … about pheasants (KDP Publishing, 2022)

Check out Geoff's YouTube channel (you can find it under 'Geoff A. Wilson') where he talks in short videos about his book writing strategy and each of his books

Part 1

1

It was dark in the little village on the south coast of Devon in south-west Britain. A misty drizzle had drifted in from the sea, blanketing the houses huddled along the steep slopes in a damp spray that made the roofs glisten in the faint moonlight. In one of the houses, at the end of a cul-de-sac with detached houses and large gardens, family Gilbert had gone to bed. Their young son, 11-year-old Martin, was sleeping in his bedroom, a gloomy light from the standby switch of his laptop shimmering in the dark. His toy animals, a small white dog and a large brown owl, lay by his side, half covered by his duvet.

The creature entered the sleeping child's bedroom through a secret door underneath the bed. The creature slowly climbed onto the bed and switched on a tiny torch which he shone into Martin's face. The boy did not flinch and continued to breathe regularly in his sleep. The creature raised his arms and began to chant very faintly:

**UMMM MARISH GRANAFF GANG GOOL
RAST HEREBDYN IMMORTIS GRATTAN
URRR MAJORIM EXORBITUS THYSSUSS
DRRAM GARR NON RETURNUM SIC**

While he chanted, he placed his arms above Martin's head and put his face as close as possible to his. He could feel the child's breath, sense the smell of his hair and skin, and felt a deep sense of power. He concentrated intensively as he finished the last sentence of the incantation and placed his hands near Martin's eyes.

For a few seconds nothing happened, it was dead quiet. Suddenly a faint blueish light seemed to appear under Martin's forehead. It intensified and emerged from inside his head as a round marble-sized ball of light floated a few centimetres above his forehead.

In a few quick movements the creature had extracted a small glass phial from his coat and shoved the blue light into it, quickly closing the lid and placing the phial in his pocket. The light continued to glow faintly inside the phial. All the time the creature had continued to intently stare at the boy's face.

Martin had not moved during the whole procedure, but suddenly his face began to show signs of intense pain. With his eyes still closed, he emitted a loud groan, his whole body shuddered for a few seconds, and then he lay absolutely still. The only sound that could be heard was his regular breathing.

The creature left Martin's bedroom as quickly as he could through the secret door, clutching the phial with the blue ball of light tightly in his hands.

2

It was 7.30am and Mrs Healey, the headmistress of the primary school of the little village, was walking fast towards the school meeting room. The other teachers were already there.

"Apologies that we are convening so early, but as you know we have to discuss a matter of extreme urgency!", said Mrs Healey while she sat down at the top of the table and gazed into the tired faces of her fellow teachers. Suzanne St Austell, a fifty-something who had been a part-time teacher at the school for a long time, was sitting to her left and looked particularly glum.

"I come straight to the point", Mrs Healey said with urgency. "As you know several children from our village have fallen into a coma over the past few months. The health services were here again yesterday to complete tests on our water system and they have confirmed that there is nothing measurably wrong with our water. You may remember that a few weeks ago they also confirmed that it wasn't meningitis. In fact, they can't explain what is happening and why so many of our children have fallen into a coma, but understandably everybody is very worried, especially the parents."

Mrs Healey peered around the room and saw concern in the faces of her colleagues. Everybody knew what was happening and that no cause for the illnesses had been found.

"I have spoken to the board of governors of our school", continued Mrs Healey, and we have all agreed that the school should remain open as the cause of the children's comas does not seem to be linked to the school or threatens to be contagious in any way. Needless to say, however, we need to be extremely vigilant and you need to report any sign of illness in the remaining children immediately to me. Unless you have any questions, the meeting is herewith closed, and let's try to go about our day-to-day school business in as normal a way as possible."

The six teachers stared at each other but none spoke as everything had been said that needed to be said. Mrs Healey stood up and walked towards her classroom preparing the school materials for the day.

3

"Is he asleep yet?" Sebastian was sitting motionless on the chest of drawers in Erik's bedroom, glancing at the child in the dark.

"He should be", replied Teddy, "he switched off the light over 10 minutes ago."

Sebastian moved his legs and stood up, trying to avoid making any noise. Erik, a 12-year-old boy with long blond curly hair, seemed to breathe regularly and did not move. "He is definitely asleep", said Teddy, "finally we can stretch our legs!"

Sebastian and Teddy climbed down the chest of drawers, one drawer at a time. Luckily the drawers were half open and clothes were hanging out in Erik's usual mess, which made climbing to the floor easier. Teddy was quite a tall light brown teddy-bear with a pleasant face, brown button eyes, and wearing a rather fetching knitted blue jersey and matching trousers. In contrast, Sebastian was a rather small bear, only about the height of four tennis balls, with a sweet face and short arms and legs. He wore brown corduroy trousers and a checked blue shirt which seemed to suit him well. His short stature often made climbing up and down furniture awkward.

They both squeezed behind the chest of drawers and pressed lightly against the wall. A small door opened leading to a narrow passageway. Teddy flicked a switch and a dim light revealed a long narrow corridor that led to other parts of the house and beyond.

"Thankfully they have not yet put cavity wall insulation between the outer and inner walls of this house, otherwise many of our secret passageways would be obliterated!", remarked Teddy who always seemed to know a lot about these things. *What is cavity wall insulation?*, wondered Sebastian who had not been around for that long. There were still many things he did not know, but he was keen to learn.

Sebastian didn't like the narrow and dark passageways. The walls were damp and the ground slippery and occasionally mice and hairy spiders scurried along. He always wanted to rush through as quickly as possible and preferred to be above in the house where it was light and spacious. However, the rules prevented them from being around humans when they were awake, and Sebastian and his companions were under no circumstances allowed outside.

They came to an intersection in the passageway where two of Erik's other toy animals were standing. They had come from the secret passageway behind the living room. One was Bunny, a white rabbit with long pointy ears, red trousers and a green vest, and the other strangely named @@*^#, a small rice-stuffed green frog with bulgy round eyes, a red forked tongue, and white stitches around the edges which many found rather ugly. His name was unpronounceable (something like 'Atatxcfyuhg') which always caused a chuckle as it was linked to an 'accident' when he first became self-conscious when Erik mispronounced his 'name'. To be fair, Erik was only one and a half at the time and could not yet really speak properly. Sebastian had always felt lucky that Erik had given him a fairly 'normal' name.

"Hi guys, how is it going?", asked Teddy while slapping Bunny on the back. "We had to wait what seemed hours until Erik went to sleep. These days he reads for longer and longer before falling asleep, it was certainly easier when he was younger! We are very keen to stretch our legs after sitting for so long motionless on that chest of drawers. I don't know how you guys do it, but I am getting a bit too old for all this!"

"I know how you feel", replied @@*^#, "I often get such bad cramps from sitting in an awkward position while the humans are around that sometimes I just simply have to move! Luckily nobody has caught me yet, but it may just be a matter of time …."

"The worst, however, is that we have to return to the place where our human hosts have left us every morning and sit motionless so that our hosts don't realise we are alive!", grumbled Bunny. "It drives me nuts!"

Sebastian could well relate to this complaint as he had to find the exact spot where Erik had last left him every time Erik woke up, re-appeared from school, or came home after seeing his friends.

"Thankfully most of us live in households where humans are out of the house working or at school during the day and sleeping at night", said Teddy, "but I pity those who have old and retired human hosts who basically never leave the house! Imagine how much lying and sitting around motionless these poor animagi have to go through!"

They walked to an intersection of passageways that linked the house where Erik lived with neighbouring properties. A notice was pinned to the wall:

Council Meeting for animagi today
9pm in the great cavern
Please come along as we will discuss important

topics that will matter TO YOU ALL!

Sebastian looked at the poster and wondered about the term 'animagi'. "Teddy", he asked, "remind me again why we are called 'animagi?'"

"Did you not pay attention at school about animagi culture and history, Sebastian?", asked Teddy with a frown on his face. "Animagi, is an old Egyptian word meaning 'animals imbued with a soul'. The singular is 'animago'. The notion of animagi embodied Egyptian cultural and spiritual life, just think about all their deities that are half human and half animal, like jackal-headed Anubis, the cat-headed goddess Bastet, or hawk-headed Horus. Indeed, their pantheon of gods shows how important animals and especially animagi must have been to the Egyptians, and reference to us as 'animagi' probably dates back to the start of Egypt's rise around 2500BC. As you should also know from school, Sebastian, in the UK the word 'animagi' was probably first mentioned in the Great Decree of 1528 where it was accepted as the general English name we gave ourselves. I guess it is meant to reflect the fact that we come mainly in the shape of toy animals, such as teddy-bears, birds, dogs, frogs, and so on, but that we also come in many different shapes and sizes. Key is that the term animagi recognises that we have a 'soul', in other words that we are self-aware beings."

Sebastian was, as usual, amazed at Teddy's vast knowledge and pondered the logic of what Teddy had just said. He could see the reason for being called animagi, as they were just as alive as any human, animal or plant.

"Yes, I understand", replied Sebastian. "We are not just mere toys but real beings with feelings, attitudes and personalities and we can feel pain, sadness and joy."

"Indeed", argued Teddy, "and although the majority of animagi are probably still teddy-bears like me or dolls like Victorian or barbie dolls, increasingly there are now also animagi that are robots, plastic toys or other modern fancy stuff. It seems that each blockbuster movie such as Star Wars, Toy Story or Avatar generates a new batch of animagi!"

Teddy is right, thought Sebastian. *The range of toys shown in my favourite movie 'Toy Story', for example, with dinosaurs, toy soldiers, cowboys, Mr Potato Head, the dog with the spring in the middle, and all the other creatures, shows how many different potential animagi exist out there.*

"Hey guys we better hurry if we want to make it in time for the meeting!", said @@*^#. All four animagi made their way down the next passageway which branched off to the left and linked their house with the house of their neighbours. It led them further down below the cul-de-sac where Erik's house was located and into another maze of dimly lit corridors. They hurried along another passageway where they were joined by increasing numbers of animagi emerging from entrances that led to other houses in the neighbourhood.

"I wonder whether the council will allow Erik to become initiated soon, so that at least we don't need to bother any longer hiding from him or lying motionless for hours?", asked Sebastian.

"Yes, I think that might be on the cards, as he is now old enough to cope with it", suggested Bunny, "although fewer and fewer kids these days are allowed to become initiated."

"That's true!", retorted Sebastian, "I remember that at the last council meeting we had quite a discussion about the lack of newly initiated kids, although I can't remember now why this is happening." Sebastian felt quite proud that he had remembered something from the last meeting, as he often felt a bit overwhelmed by all the discussions, and still had problems focusing on difficult topics for any length of time.

"It's because fewer and fewer kids play with toys", Teddy reminded them, "they all just want to play with their stupid computer games and mobile phones, neglecting the likes of us more and more …."

"And in addition parents themselves are buying their kids fewer and fewer toy animals and dolls, going for the fancy electronic presents instead", added Bunny.

"Yes, that's the problem", sighed @@*^#, "they are just no longer interested in us, which also means so many of us are no longer becoming self-aware."

They all were silent for a while and thought about toys lying in children's bedrooms who would probably never become self-aware animagi. *There was, for example, this beautiful dark brown female teddy three houses down from Erik's house whose child owner just simply was not interested!*, thought Sebastian. Apparently she had just been left in a corner of the bedroom for weeks! But Sebastian wondered how the lack of attention paid by kids to toy animals and dolls was linked to their self-awareness, although he thought that the 'important topic' highlighted on the noticeboard was probably specifically about that issue.

4

"I think it will happen tonight", said Mrs Moluk, a member of the council and a beautiful old-fashioned Victorian doll with curly real human hair, a long dress and little black shoes.

"Yes, our reports show that 11-year-old Josh has given his toy bear increasing attention in recent weeks", replied Rigor Mortis, another council member who was a large penguin, white in front, black at the back, with a large long yellow beak and piercing black eyes. 'Mr Mortis' as he was known even by his closest friends looked rather distinguished and always had an air of aloofness about him that made many uncomfortable in his presence. But over the years he had proven to be an effective and efficient council member.

They both sat on one of Josh's bedroom shelves, peering down at the sleeping boy with the long blond hair. His brown toy bear with white patches on his paws was lying by his side. It was about 8.30pm and Josh had been asleep for a little while. They were just about to leave for the council meeting when suddenly Josh woke up with a start and switched on his bedside light. He still seemed very sleepy and almost surprised that he had woken up, probably by a dream. He sat up, grabbed his bear and hugged him closely to his chest whispering "my Hagelik!", fell back onto his pillow, and after a few seconds was sound asleep again with his bedside light still on. The bear started to stir …

"My, my ...", whispered Mrs Moluk, "I didn't think it would happen that quickly and especially while the boy was basically asleep! Let's get down from here quickly before the bear gets confused and wakes up the boy. It wouldn't be the first time that we have missed the crucial moment of an awakening, and we all know what can happen if the awakened animago is the one who then wakes up his host!" They climbed down the shelves, Rigor Mortis using his beak skilfully to lower himself from shelf to shelf and just reached the bear when he opened his eyes for the first time.

Mrs Moluk helped the bear to carefully wiggle out of Josh's embrace, held him firmly in her arms and stared into his eyes.

"Where am I?", the bear asked, looking confused from Mrs Moluk to Mr Mortis.

"Now, now ... Take it easy!", said Mrs Moluk, "a few deep breaths to get your bearings, just take it slowly. You are in Josh's bedroom and he has become what we call your 'human host'. He is the one who named you and, through his love, has imbued you with life. You have become an animago and Josh named you Hagelik."

Hagelik peered around the room dimly lit by Josh's bedside table. He saw the shelves with Josh's books, his toys lying all over the floor, and glanced at little Josh sleeping soundly right next to him half covered by his duvet, but he was still very confused.

"You have just experienced an 'awakening', Hagelik, and the name Josh has given you now stays with you forever", said Mr Mortis. "We have all gone through this and were all rather confused at the start. Take it easy as it takes a while to get used to being alive and being able to talk and walk. You will have plenty of time to get used to it as you are now bound to your human host until he dies."

What Rigor Mortis did not want to mention at this point was that animagi died when their human host stopped loving them, which was the major and saddest cause of death among animagi. Indeed, it was rare that animagi lived for decades to an old age like both Mrs Moluk and Mr Mortis. In some cases, animagi were linked to adult human hosts rather than children, like Mrs Moluk and Rigor Mortis, whose adult human hosts continued to love and cherish them.

"Unfortunately we are in a hurry, Hagelik", said Mrs Moluk as we have to go to a council meeting. So please come with us and we will explain more on the way, and you will also be able to meet some of your fellow animagi."

They quickly jumped off the bed, touched a hidden panel on the wall under Josh's bed and disappeared into the passageway.

5

Little Andrew was restless in his bed again. He was seven years old and had had severe problems falling asleep over the past few months. He had also begun wetting his bed again. His mother Rachel had changed the sheet for the second time that night and was now sitting at his bedside. Andrew was sobbing loudly, his head in her comforting lap.

"My little darling", said his mum caressing his blond hair gently. "Was it that nightmare again?"

Andrew's sobbing intensified when he brought back memories of the dreadful dream that had been haunting him for over a year now.

"Yes …", he murmured. "It's always the same dream, mum. I walk around with a book in my hand and a light that comes out of it kills everybody that I encounter. I can't stop it and all my friends are lying dead around me … and you … and dad …It's so terrible!"

Large tears ran down his cheeks, and he looked in despair at his mother.

What a strange dream he keeps having!, thought Rachel. *He has hardly begun reading books, and the ones he reads are innocent children's books. And he is not allowed to watch any of the evening movies with us on TV. Where does he get these ideas about killing people from? But then he has also had problems at school, beating other children, and his schoolmistress told me that he was afraid one of his schoolmates was going to kill him!*

"OK, Andrew, I have something that may cheer you up", Rachel said. "Dad and I were going to give it to you on your eighth birthday in two days, but as you are so miserable I will give it to you now. It might console you a little bit …"

Andrew could hear her rummaging in a box somewhere out on the landing. When Rachel came back she held a mid-sized toy animal in her hand: a toad with a red leather front, a blue back, and large globular eyes.

Andrew had stopped crying and stared at the frog. He had never shown much interest in toy animals, so his parents had not given him any as of yet. But Andrew seemed to connect immediately with the frog, holding him up and staring intensely into his globular eyes. The lifeless toad stared back with an empty look.

"Thanks, mum, I really like it. He can sleep right next to me and maybe he will keep the bad dream from coming back again!"

Andrew snuggled under his duvet, pulled the frog towards him and placed his head carefully on the pillow next to the frog. Rachel watched him for a few minutes, amazed at the sudden transformation of her son. The tears had disappeared and he fell asleep quickly, cuddling the toad in his arms.

6

"Quiet please!", shouted Mrs Moluk, but the noise in the great cavern where the animagi council meeting was taking place did not abate.

Sebastian and Teddy had been lucky to find a seat towards the top of the large arena. Sebastian peered around and, although this was not the first time he had been to one of these meetings, he was amazed again at how large the cavern was. Thousands of toys were seated in a large semi-circle facing a podium where ten council members sat behind a long desk. They had candles in front of them, microphones, papers and glasses of water. The cavern itself was dimly lit with electric lights attached to the large ceiling.

Sebastian remembered what Teddy had said earlier with regard to what an animagi was, and the council members probably represented a good cross-section of animagi community. Mrs Moluk was the only doll on the panel, there were also two elderly-looking teddy-bears, and Mr Mortis, the penguin, sat at the right far end looking distinguished and glum as usual. Sebastian recognised Mrs Moluk and Mr Mortis in particular as they were both also teachers at his school. Sebastian also recognised one old and odd-looking creature that looked like a witch with long straggly hair, a long pointy crooked hat, and a long-hooked nose. She was Mrs Hexybilla, another one of Sebastian's teachers in charge of lessons on animagi culture and history. One robot was sitting to the left of Mrs Moluk whom Sebastian did not recognise, but the strangest animago sat at the left far end of the table. He, or she?, looked just like a small tree or a large branch, with a few dry leaves covering the 'body' and moss covering the top of the 'head'. In spite of this, a face was clearly visible, as were limbs and deeply set dark eyes.

"Who is the animago on the left?", Sebastian asked Teddy.

"That is the appropriately named Mr Wood, a new member of the council", said Teddy.

Sebastian peered around the large arena again and marvelled at all the different shapes, odd forms and weird animagi sitting in the large arena. The oddest creature on the panel was, however, a human. Sebastian recognised her as Suzanne who, he had heard, worked with difficult children.

"What is a human doing on the panel?", asked Sebastian. Teddy replied that Suzanne was Hexybilla's human host, and that it was quite common for humans to be represented on animagi panels, again referring to the Great Decree of 1528 which had enshrined in Animagi Law the right for certain humans to be part of councils and panels. Sebastian knew that 'initiated' humans were closely involved in animagi affairs, but he hadn't realised that humans could also be part of the inner circle of animagi decision-making. Sebastian peered around the cavern again and saw that, indeed, a few other humans, mostly children, sat among the audience, none of whom he knew or recognised. *They must be part of the 'initiated'*, Sebastian thought, *what an honour it must be for them to be here!*

"Quiet please, thank you!", repeated Mrs Moluk who was chairing the meeting, forcing Sebastian to concentrate on the meeting itself although he was still pondering the constitution of the panel. "Many thanks to all of you for coming, especially to those who have come from further afield. We know how difficult it is for you to travel out in the open, even at this later time of day."

The noise in the large room quietened down gradually, although some latecomers caused a commotion trying to find the last empty seats.

"As you all know", Mrs Moluk continued, "terrible things have happened lately. Several children in this village have fallen into a deep coma and are currently in intensive care at local hospitals. The reason this matters for us is that they are all human hosts for animagi, and we don't know what long-term effects a host in a coma may have on their animagi."

A hush went around the large arena. Obviously many had not been aware of the link between the catastrophe that was befalling the human children and the possible danger to their animagi.

"What is even worse", Mrs Moluk continued, "is that several animagi of comatose children have disappeared! We have looked everywhere but they have completely vanished! At the moment we can't explain what is happening, but I would like to give the floor to an eminent visitor from London who will be able to shed a bit more light on the issue. Professor Pandanus, please …"

Mrs Moluk walked over to a large and rather obese panda bear with thick glasses, who was sitting in the front row facing the council, and ushered him towards a standing podium with a microphone.

"Hello everybody, and thanks again for coming to this meeting", began Prof Pandanus. He adjusted his glasses and shuffled some papers placed in front of him. "As Mrs Moluk said, I and my team of scientists" – and he pointed towards a handful of animagi sitting in the front row, all looking rather old and eminent – "have been invited here to investigate the possible link between human children falling into a coma and the disappearance of several of your fellow animagi. Let me mention first of all that the situation seems to be confined to your immediate area here, as to our knowledge, no other mass coma cases have been reported elsewhere."

Professor Pandanus' colleagues in the front row nodded, and several peered around the audience which was dead silent and tried to capture every word that was being said. Sebastian had the impression that the cavern light had grown dimmer and felt an increasing sense of unease and foreboding.

"Before I try to explain the limited evidence we have unearthed so far, let me start with a broader explanation about human-animagi relationships", continued Professor Pandanus. "As you should all remember from school, the relationship between humans and self-aware animagi probably started at the dawn of humanity, about 200,000 years ago. We have evidence of this through cave paintings depicting what might be cherished animagi, and through remains of animagi made of bone or stone found in several burial sites. Scientifically we speak of such a longstanding animagi-human relationship as a 'symbiotic' relationship. However, as you all know, this relationship is, unfortunately for us, rather one-sided, as our survival as self-aware individuals relies entirely on the well-being and love of our human hosts. If they stop loving us or if they die, or indeed if they fall into a coma, we die! Humans, on the other hand, seem unaffected by what happens to us. If one of us is accidentally destroyed in an accident or a fire, for example, humans do not seem to suffer major trauma, let alone die. We are still investigating the reason behind the children's coma cases, but it is difficult as there has not been any precedent to this in the past ..."

Sebastian looked at Teddy who stared with fascination at the speaker. *This is heavy stuff!* Sebastian thought! *Even the most eminent scientists don't seem to know what is going on!*

"Yet, there is another reason why myself and my colleagues are here", continued Professor Pandanus. "Many of you may not be aware that you are actually very lucky here in the village, where you have some of the largest underground caverns in the UK, situated just below human settlements and therefore easily accessible and, most importantly, unknown to non-initiated human beings! You may know that one of the key parts of the rite of initiation of humans into our world is for them to swear secrecy with regard to the existence of our caves, caverns and meeting places."

Sebastian craned his neck and looked at Suzanne on the council bench and some of the other humans sitting in the audience. Many other animagi also looked at them, and the nearest human to Sebastian, a girl of about 12, peered self-consciously around her evidently feeling the stare of hundreds of pairs of eyes.

"The existence of these caverns is not only important for this splendid meeting hall, which is one of the largest animagi meeting places in the country, but also for the location of our biggest repository of archival and library information related to us animagi. I guess that you hear a bit about that at school, and some of you might have even visited parts of the archives, but probably few of you will know that one of the caverns not far from here contains most of the prized knowledge associated with human-animagi relationships over thousands of years! Indeed, there are probably hundreds, if not thousands, of shelves stacked high with often unique parchments and old books about our history, not dissimilar to some of the human repositories in similarly safe locations around the world. We have, for example, written information on papyrus scrolls about animagi dating back to the time of the early Sumerians and Babylonians thousands of years ago, as well as a fairly complete collection of manuscripts relating to the Egyptian dynasties from between 2500-500BC. You may also be curious to hear that this vast amount of information has begun to be digitised by a whole team of animagi archivists, but you can imagine that they have only scratched the surface so far as each item needs to be scanned individually which takes a long time with the hundreds of thousands of documents held here."

Sebastian was amazed. He remembered Mrs Hexybilla talking briefly about the archives at school, and they even took a 'field trip' into one part of the archives with her, but he had not comprehended at the time how vast the archival collection was and that their village was, therefore, rather special.

"I and my team will be based here for a while, working closely with your chief archivist, Mrs Hexybilla and her team, to see whether our archival information holds any clues to what is happening here at the moment." Professor Pandanus sighed deeply at the thought of the amount of work that awaited them. "We are particularly interested in finding out whether historically anything like this has happened before and, if yes, whether we can learn something from that experience. But as I said, considering this is a manual rather than a digital task, it will take a while. What we also want to investigate is whether historical data gives us any further ideas about how human-animagi relationships work. A key question we have all asked ourselves from the moment of self-awareness is, of course, how the love of a child can imbue us inanimate objects – 'toys' – with life and a consciousness? How does the material we are made of" – and at this moment Professor Pandanus pinched his flabby synthetic fur – "become a living and feeling organism? Of course we have done plenty of work on this question at my institute in London already, but the archives here might again help us further, as it is a medical, moral and philosophical question that has preoccupied us since the dawn of human-animagi relationships."

Yes, Sebastian had always wondered, *how come that we are living beings although we do not seem to have a nervous system, a brain, blood or bones?* He looked at Teddy who had an injury on his foot where straw was partly hanging out. "Teddy does that injury hurt?", Sebastian asked cautiously?

Teddy listened intently to Professor Pandanus, but glanced briefly sideways towards Sebastian and to his foot and said: "Yes, of course it hurts! I had this for a while and I need to see a doctor soon as it does not appear to heal properly."

How can this hurt if it is only straw inside Teddy?, Sebastian continued to wonder, but realised that his questions were, for the moment, leading him nowhere.

Professor Pandanus' talk had come to an end and Mrs Moluk thanked him profusely. "My fellow animagi", she said, "now you have heard some of the scientific evidence behind what is happening although, as you will now be aware, we have probably more unanswered questions than solutions at the moment. Let me close this meeting with a word of warning: we strongly suspect that the coma of the children is in some ways linked to actions taken by one or several fellow animagi. One animago in particular, Garglethroat, might be involved …"

A loud gasp went through the audience; they all clearly recognised that name. *Now we are getting to the real gist of the meeting!* thought Sebastian.

"… As I said, Garglethroat might be involved in this matter", Mrs Moluk continued. "You may have heard that he recently escaped from our maximum-security prison located in a cavern not far from here where he was on death row for his earlier illegal attempt to take over this council by killing two of our most esteemed councillors."

Sebastian remembered the case of the killed council members only faintly as he had only just become self-aware at the time, but he certainly remembered the news reports about Garglethroat's escape! In a daring coup, Garglethroat and three of his fellow inmates, who were also part of his gang, had killed their guards and escaped through a tunnel dug behind their cells.

"I therefore urge all of you to be extremely vigilant!", cautioned Mrs Moluk, "as Garglethroat and his gang are extremely dangerous and probably armed, and we suspect that they are still in this neighbourhood. Please continue to work and to go to school, but please do not hesitate to report any activities that seem out of the ordinary or suspicious to any member of the council. We have been elected by all of you to the council positions we hold, and it is our responsibility to keep all of you safe. This is also true for all the initiated humans among us", and Mrs Moluk looked at Suzanne and the humans in the audience. "If you see anything suspicious among your fellow humans that could have an impact on us toy beings, please also report back to us immediately. It is only by working together that we can solve the crisis we are facing!"

There was a deadly silence in the large cavern, as the audience slowly came to terms with what they heard.

"You will, of course, wonder why we can't get rid of nasty and dangerous animagi like Garglethroat by influencing his human host", Mrs Moluk continued. "As those of you who are familiar with animagi law dating back to the 1528 Great Decree, we animagi are not allowed to harm or influence our human hosts. As much as we would like to sever the link between Garglethroat and his human host – who is a severely disturbed person currently locked up in a cell in a maximum-security psychiatric ward – we are not in a position at this stage to influence his relationship with Garglethroat who he, unfortunately, still appears to love very much. Worst of all for us, the fact that this human, Andrew Billings, is in a highly protected psychiatric ward, means that Garglethroat can currently roam around at will and at any time in our village. So, for the moment, we see no other solution than to capture Garglethroat and his gang and to put them back into prison where they belong!"

Mrs Moluk closed the meeting, but her voice was almost drowned out by the chatter of the audience. Everybody had a panicked look on their faces, and the name of 'Garglethroat' now hung in the air like a deadly spell.

7

Lucy was about 10 years old and lived a few streets away from Erik's house. As usual, she placed her three favourite toys next to her, a small yellowish teddy-bear called Barney, a doll with silky white hair named Penny, and a little brown dog called Woof. All three had been animagi for quite some time, but Lucy did not know that as she had not been initiated by the animagi council. She switched off the light and went to sleep.

Thirty minutes later a dark shape entered Lucy's room through one of the passageway doors under her bed. It was entirely dark in the room, only a slit of light from underneath her bedroom door cast the room in a pale glow, and the faint sound of a dog barking could be heard through the half-opened window.

The creature climbed carefully onto her bed and greeted the three animagi. "Hello, are you ready?", the creature asked.

"Yes, sir", Barney, Penny and Woof answered in unison.

"OK, go into the passageway and I'll meet you there in a few minutes", said the creature. "Under no circumstances should you come back into this room while I perform the incantation, do you understand?"

The three animagi looked frightened and scuttled off the bed as quickly as they could without waking Lucy.

"And have your money ready as we discussed!", hissed the creature.

Barney, Penny and Woof had already prepared their bags which contained their belongings for a long journey and the money for the creature. They disappeared into the passageway and closed the entry door behind them.

The creature stood next to Lucy and watched her intently. He then lit a small candle and placed it on the bedside table. He closed his eyes, raised his arms and began to chant very faintly:

UMMM MARISH GRANAFF GANG GOOL
RAST HEREBDYN IMMORTIS GRATTAN
URRR MAJORIM EXORBITUS THYSSUSS
DRRAM GARR NON RETURNUM SIC

While he was chanting he placed his arms above Lucy's head and placed his face as close as possible to hers. He concentrated intensively as he finished the last sentence of the incantation and placed his hands near Lucy's eyes.

For a few seconds nothing happened, the candle flickered slightly in a draft coming from the window. The dog had stopped barking outside.

A faint blueish light appeared under Lucy's forehead, intensified and emerged from inside her head as a round marble-sized ball of light that floated a few centimetres above her forehead. In a few quick movements, the creature had placed the blue ball of light into his small glass phial which he placed into his pocket. Lucy's face showed signs of intense pain but she did not wake up. She emitted a loud groan, her whole body shuddered for a few seconds, and then she lay absolutely still.

The next morning at 7am Lucy's mother entered her room. "Come on Lucy, it's already seven and you have to go to school!", she shouted. "Did you not hear your alarm clock?"

As Lucy did not move, her mother went to the bed and gently shook Lucy, but there was no response from the child. "Lucy! Lucy!", shouted the mother with a panicked look on her face. She shook her again, this time more intensely, but Lucy's body lay limp in her mother's arms. "Oh dear, Lucy, please, no, no …!", said the mother with tears running down her face as she realised that Lucy was in a coma.

8

A few days had passed. All the talk in the animagi community was about Lucy, the latest child to have inexplicably fallen into a coma, and the disappearance of her three animagi Barney, Penny and Woof. Sebastian was particularly sad about Barney's disappearance as they were both in the same school class, and Sebastian counted Barney as a close friend. *But, come to think of it, Barney had acted strangely the last few weeks, he seemed more withdrawn, and had begun to stand by himself during breaks,* thought Sebastian. The animagi council had repeated its warnings about vigilance, and everybody had begun to look at each other with increasing suspicion. Who was behind these strange cases of children in comas, and why was it happening?

Sebastian was sitting in his final school lesson for the day, *Animagi Culture and History*, taught by Mrs Hexybilla. Their school was in one of the caves not far from the Great Cavern where the council meeting had been held, and comprised several classrooms in individual alcoves on the side of the cave. Sebastian was not really concentrating on Mrs Hexybilla's lesson which was on 19th century animagi cultural artefacts, and his mind continuously drifted to all the things that had happened over the past few weeks: children in a coma, Garglethroat escaping from prison, and the visit by the eminent scientists from London who were deeply ensconced in their work on ancient books and papers in the archives.

Finally the school bell rang and Sebastian was relieved that the lesson was over. He had intended to walk back with @@*^#

and Hagelik, little Josh's new animago, but both had somehow already walked ahead and disappeared into the maze of corridors and passageways linking the school with individual houses in the village.

Sebastian packed his books and trundled along, not really sure whether he wanted to go back to Erik's house yet, as probably none of Erik's other animagi were likely to be at home to play with. In addition to Erik's animagi, Erik's dad, Godfrey Wilkinson, also had his own animagi, namely Teddy, who had been Sebastian's best friend from the moment of his awakening, and also Bunny and Ugah. The latter was a toy from a bygone and much less politically correct age – a so-called 'golliwog' toy, about 40 centimetres tall in the shape of an African human, with a black face and black frizzy hair, and wearing long stripy trousers. Sebastian had lately particularly grown fond of Ugah, but knew that there had been a lot of talk about the implicit and explicit racism associated with 'golliwogs' and that they had long disappeared from toyshops in the UK and elsewhere. Although from Sebastian's perspective there was no evidence of racism in their animagi community, sometimes Sebastian thought that Ugah felt a bit out of place, and that he was rather shy and chose his words carefully when he spoke. *But there was no need to feel self-conscious with all the different animagi shapes and forms present even within their small community!*, thought Sebastian. *Think about Mr Wood from the council who looks like a dead branch and how he must feel, or indeed @@*^# with his ugly white stitches around his froggy frame!*

Sebastian continued to walk along slowly. He was a bit bored. *So what to do if nobody is home?*, Sebastian wondered. He was by himself in one of the passageways leading to Erik's house when he caught a glimpse of a trapdoor in the roof of the corridor. *Hey, strange!*, he thought. *I wonder why I had not seen this before? Does this lead to another passageway above this one? I guess we are usually walking in a group along here and chattering away, so no wonder we don't pay much attention to our surroundings!*

A set of steps were cemented into the wall, leading to the trapdoor. Sebastian peered around him, saw nobody, and started the short climb to the trapdoor. A small handwritten label said:

Warning! Emergency exit.
Only to be used in case of fire or danger.
To open, turn red handle to the left.

Sebastian knew he should not open the trapdoor but he could not resist. He turned the handle to the left, expecting to emerge into another passageway. Instead he looked out onto the surface with a view over the pathway on the edge of the cul-de-sac road leading to Erik's and neighbouring houses. The trapdoor led to the outside!

Sebastian knew that animagi were strongly advised not to go outside for reasons of their own safety and not to startle uninitiated humans. Indeed, this was one of the first rules they were taught after their awakening. He remembered Mrs Moluk lecturing them at the time of his awakening with a very serious tone in her voice: "Imagine what would happen if uninitiated humans saw an animago moving about? It would create chaos, fear and probably acts of violence! The only reason we have successfully lived side-by-side with humans for millennia is that we have precisely stayed away from the surface and that only a few initiated humans know about our existence and way of life. We have to keep it that way for future generations, so no venturing outside unless absolutely necessary! In addition there are, of course, other dangers out there, especially vicious pets such as cats and dogs who would not hesitate to maul or kill us."

Mrs Moluk's harsh voice still rang in Sebastian's ears as he scanned the street and the bit of garden he could see. *I have never really been outside other than when Erik is playing with me*, thought Sebastian, *and only on a few occasions did Erik take me with him on a holiday where I was mostly in the car or indoors.* Indeed, only those animagi who needed to travel from community to community or further afield, like Professor Pandanus, had to use the surface, but very often these were intricately planned journeys that involved initiated humans taking animagi in their cars or luggage.

Sebastian looked down the passageway. It was still eerily calm and nobody seemed to be coming along the corridor. *Come on!*, thought Sebastian, *I'll just go outside briefly, have a look and come back immediately. I am sure there is no harm in this!* And while he was thinking this, he had a last look up and down the road to make sure no human was in sight and jumped out into the open, leaving the trapdoor open, just in case.

Sebastian quickly followed a low stone wall and disappeared into the densely planted garden that Godfrey, Erik's dad, had planted. Sebastian inhaled deeply, smelt the fragrance of the trees and shrubs and felt the damp earth under his paws. *What a great feeling to be outside and to smell fresh air for a change!*, he thought. *How can they ask us to be cooped up in houses, underground corridors and caverns all the time when there are all these wonderful things to be seen, felt and smelt outside!*, he wondered. *Maybe they should loosen their policy with regard to our use of the outdoors a bit more?*

Sebastian followed a narrow grassy path that Godfrey had left between clumps of trees. He marvelled at the different plants, colours and shapes of the trees and shrubs planted by Godfrey. *This is rather beautiful!*, he thought, and realised that much work and effort by humans went into gardening.

Suddenly he heard a rustle behind him. He turned around but saw nothing. A rustle again, this time a bit closer… *What is that?*, wondered Sebastian, *probably a bird?* He walked forward carefully but there was no further sound. In fact, the garden had become eerily quiet and Sebastian realised that the birds had stopped chirping and singing.

Sebastian turned around again and suddenly saw a flash of grey move towards him at incredible speed. *Benny, the neighbour's cat! I had completely forgotten about him!*, realised Sebastian. He saw Benny's angry face, his ears bent backwards in aggression, and his claws outstretched and clearly visible. *Oh no!*, thought Sebastian, *this is the end! How can I escape from this?* Benny was now just a few meters away and began to pounce, his mouth with jagged teeth clearly aiming directly at Sebastian's short neck, his claws targeting his chest. It all happened so quickly that Sebastian barely had time to move. Benny's open mouth was just centimetres away from Sebastian's face … when suddenly everything stopped.

Sebastian had closed his eyes when Benny pounced, thinking these were the last moments of his short life. But after a few seconds nothing happened. Sebastian carefully opened one eye, then the other, and stared straight into Benny's angry face suspended motionless in the air just before Sebastian. *What is going on?*, wondered Sebastian. *Why am I moving while Benny seems to be stuck in mid-air?* Sebastian turned his head slightly and saw that the trees and bushes had stopped rustling. Nothing at all seemed to be moving except for himself.

This is just totally weird, I don't understand what is going on!, mused Sebastian. He carefully moved forward and touched Benny's nose gently with his front paw. The nose felt soft and moist, just as he would have expected, but Benny did not move at all. Sebastian moved forward again and started touching Benny's body hanging in mid-air. Benny's fur felt soft and smooth, but his body did not budge. Sebastian walked a few paces, ducked a bit to avoid Benny's outstretched back claws, and slowly moved away, constantly looking over his shoulder to check that Benny was not moving. Benny still hung in mid-air, his claws grotesquely outstretched towards... nothing.

As if in trance, Sebastian slowly moved back along the garden path and the side of the road towards the still open trapdoor. There he just stayed and peered around him. The whole village seemed to have stopped. Cars on the distant village road were all motionless, a few people in the distance were also not moving at all. *What is this?*, Sebastian asked again. *It's not just Benny and the garden here, but the whole world seems to have come to a standstill! Is this some kind of joke someone is playing on me?* But just as he was asking this, he saw Benny suddenly being propelled forward clawing at the empty space in front of him, where Sebastian had been standing just a short while ago, and crashing with full speed into a bush ahead of him with a loud meow. Sebastian could not supress a smile when he saw Benny's predicament, but he also knew that he should not linger as Benny was likely to get his senses back very quickly, and Sebastian was still visible where he was standing. From the corner of his eye he also saw that the cars moved normally again and that the few people in the distance had continued walking as if nothing at all had happened.

Sebastian quickly jumped into the hole, rapidly closed the trapdoor behind him, and within a few seconds he was back in the passageway. He could feel his heart pounding, was rather breathless and had started sweating. Nobody was around, the corridor was still quiet and empty. Sebastian walked back towards his classroom realising that he had just escaped a terrible and sudden death, but he had no idea what had just happened…

9

"Gimme that frog!", shouted the little boy into Andrew's face.

Andrew was holding his blue and red frog close to his chest. "No!", he screamed at the boy.

Hearing the commotion, two of the boy's friends approached and looked down at Andrew who had been pushed to the ground by the boy. Andrew tried to get up.

"I want your frog!", repeated the boy, and started pulling one of the frog's arms.

You're beginning to decidedly get on my nerves, boy!, thought the frog.

Andrew was holding on to the frog's other arm, threatening to pull the frog apart. But Andrew could hold on no longer, the other boy, who was probably ten, was too strong and Andrew was only eight. With a cry of despair Andrew let go of the frog. The release came so suddenly that the boy pulling the frog fell backwards on the ground. His friends laughed. "Shut up, you idiots! At least I've got the frog!", said the boy, looking at the shiny red velvet on the frog's underside with pride.

Andrew got up and moved towards the thief. He was not going to give up that easily, and his frog had become very precious to him. *What will I do without my frog at night?*, he thought. *Thanks to him the nightmares have gotten better and I can finally sleep again. I need him back!* But he could see no way to get his frog back. The other two boys now also crowded around the boy with the frog, protecting the attacker.

Just as Andrew was about to give up, he saw something strange. The thief was holding the frog towards his neck, cuddling and stroking him. But Andrew thought he saw a movement … the frog's arm was rising ever so slowly. Suddenly the boy shrieked and tossed the frog away. "He pulled my ear!", the boy shouted, "I tell ya, he pulled my ear!"

The other boys laughed again, looking at the frog lying motionless between Andrew and them.

"You can have your bleedin' frog back!", shouted the boy. "I ain't want nothin' to do with a toy like that who can move!", and he brushed his shoulder with his hand as if to get rid of the memory of what had just happened. "Leave him be, boys!", he told his friends. "His toys are as weird as himself!", he said, pointing at Andrew.

Andrew quickly grabbed the frog back and held him close to his chest. *You wait and see!*, he thought. *One day I'm gonna get you and your friends!* He stared intensely at the frog and wondered whether he really had seen the frog move. *Maybe you are even more amazing than I thought…?* He walked away from the group of boys as quickly as his pride allowed, not daring to look back.

10

Sebastian was still stunned and disoriented about what had just happened. He walked slowly back towards his classroom, hardly noticing the last animagi who were leaving school on their way home. Mrs Hexybilla was just leaving when she saw Sebastian who looked rather pale and disoriented.

"Oh dear! Sebastian! You look like you've just seen a ghost! What's the matter, my little bear?", she asked with a worried voice.

Sebastian was still so in shock that he found it hard to speak. He sat down at a school desk in front of Mrs Hexybilla as his legs felt wobbly.

"I just had the weirdest thing happening to me, Mrs Hexybilla!", he said. "I am not sure if you'll believe me if I tell you …."

Mrs Hexybilla looked astonished at Sebastian, but her curiosity had been aroused. "Try me!", she said encouragingly.

Sebastian told her what had just happened, how he had found the trapdoor, ventured outside although he shouldn't have, the story with Benny suspended in mid-air, and time seemingly standing still. When Sebastian had finished, Hexybilla peered around her anxiously to check whether anyone else may have overheard Sebastian's story, but both the classroom and the corridor outside were empty.

"That is quite some story, Sebastian!", she exclaimed. "Come with me. I was on my way to the archives and there is something I want to check. I think you may be ready …."

They followed a few corridors that led them away from the school cavern deeper under the village. Although Sebastian had been to the archives before with Mrs Hexybilla, he still found all the various passageways they had to negotiate confusing. There were no signs or anything to indicate where they had to go.

After a short while the passageway suddenly widened and they stood before two large massive wooden doors with intricate engravings etched in what looked like gold and silver. Sebastian remembered from their previous school outing to the archives that the letters on the door said 'Animagi Archives', but they were written in a language he did not recognise.

Hexybilla took a plastic card out of her coat and swiped it on a device to the right of the door. Slowly and with a loud groan the two doors opened automatically, revealing a spacious cavern with several shelves from top to bottom covered in old books and parchments. A stale musty smell greeted Hexybilla and Sebastian as they entered. Sebastian wondered again at how many parchments and books must be stacked away in this repository and stared in awe at the piles of paper on each shelf.

To their right, Professor Pandanus and his colleagues sat around a large table covered in stacks of papers and parchments. Prof Pandanus briefly waved at Mrs Hexybilla but immediately looked back at the parchment in front of him, which he was analysing with a large looking glass. *They must be checking the manuscripts for hints about the children in coma as Professor Pandanus explained at the meeting*, thought Sebastian. *I wonder whether they have found something yet?*

To his surprise, Mrs Hexybilla walked straight past the shelves towards the back wall of the cavern where Sebastian saw another set of doors which were at least three times larger than the front doors. He did not remember having seen these at their first visit. Indeed, Mrs Hexybilla and her class had spent the whole morning just in the front cavern which at the time had already seemed vast enough.

Hexybilla looked back over her shoulder to make sure that the front door of the archives was closed and that nobody had followed them in. The professors still sifted through the papers in front of them, ignoring both Hexybilla and Sebastian. When she was satisfied that they were alone she said: "What I am about to show you not many animagi have seen, let alone young and inexperienced animagi like yourself, but your story puzzles me and I have the feeling that we need to check something out together which might shed some light on your experience with Benny the cat."

Sebastian just nodded as he was unsure what to expect. *Where are we going, and why is Mrs Hexybilla taking me there?*, he wondered.

This time Hexybilla did not use a swipe card but a number code to make the gigantic doors open. They slowly opened with an even louder groan and creak than the front doors. At first Sebastian could not see anything, as the light behind the doors was rather dim. But when his eyes had adjusted to the faint light, he could not believe his eyes. The giant doors had opened to another cavern, a gigantic vast cavern that was so high the ceiling could not be seen, and so wide and long that no walls were visible. All Sebastian saw were endless shelves with more stacks of paper, old parchments, ancient books, leather-bound manuscripts and even ancient papyrus rolls. Sebastian could not believe his eyes! *Wow!*, he thought, *I would have never thought that we had such vast caves under the village and, indeed, such large amounts of archival material to fill such a space!*

"What you see here, Sebastian, is the accumulated animagi knowledge of thousands of years. Although there are a few other archives like this around the world, I believe ours might be the largest and contains the oldest documents of all. As Prof Pandanus said at the recent meeting, we are indeed lucky to have such vast cave systems under this village that provide enough space to store so much information! Indeed, the floor we are standing on is actually below sea level!"

Sebastian was still awestruck at the sheer size of what he saw. "I bet not many animagi have seen this, Mrs Hexybilla!", he exclaimed.

"Indeed, Sebastian", replied Hexybilla, "you are one of the few pupils to have had the opportunity to see this. Come with me …"

They made their way past the first shelves, then turned right, then left, then straight, then left again … and soon Sebastian had lost all sense of direction, and all he could see were more shelves, more books, and more manuscripts piled sky-high on the surrounding shelves.

"We suspect that many of the books, parchments and manuscripts held in this archive, were saved by monks from various monasteries around England, before their dissolution by Henry VIII between 1536 and 1541", said Hexybilla as they walked ever deeper into the recesses of the archives.

"How do you know your way around this so well?", asked Sebastian.

"Well my dear bear, it's over 30 years of working in these archives that makes you know almost every shelve, even if there are so many!", replied Hexybilla.

They walked on for at least ten minutes, and still there was no end in sight in either direction, when Hexybilla slowed down and started looking at the numbers inscribed on the corners of each shelf.

"We are getting nearer, it must be just around the corner from here", said Hexybilla. "Ah, here we are …", and she pointed towards a shelf to their right. She climbed up a steep ladder, leaned to the right, and pulled out a very large ancient book bound in reddish, faded leather. "Here, Sebastian, help me with this please …", and she handed the book down to Sebastian who could barely hold it as it was so large and heavy.

"Strange!", said Hexybilla, "it looks as if someone has recently handled this book, and it wasn't me! Look, there are strange marks in the dust on the cover that almost look like having been made by the end of flippers, and the book hadn't been fully pushed back into the shelf as it was not quite flush with the neighbouring books!"

Hexybilla looked down the row of books on the shelf where the book had been, but could see no other evidence of tampering. Together they placed the book on one of the reading tables near the shelves.

Sebastian looked at the cover of the book which said 'Animagarostantla Radisovatra'.

"What does the title mean?", asked Sebastian.

"This ancient book is written in pre-English animagi language that is more similar to Egyptian or Latin", Hexybilla explained. "We know that the book dates from about 1500 before the Great Decree in 1528 enshrined in law that all animagi books should be written in English, which is why it is mainly written in pre-English animagi language, although some passages are in English. Its title basically means 'The Chronicles of Animagi Lore', and the book is one of the most precious held in the archives. This is why I am particularly annoyed that someone other than me seems to have tampered with it recently!"

Hexybilla put on her reading glasses and started turning the pages. All the pages in the book were handwritten in black ink and the paper felt very thick. Each page started with a beautiful intricately drawn large first letter, often with pictures of climbing vines and strange creatures.

"Now ... where is it?", wondered Hexybilla, "I swear I saw something linked to your story in this book a while ago when I first came across it", she said. "Ah, here it is. I'll translate for you."

Hexybilla peered intently at the page she had opened and spoke haltingly as she had to think how to best translate the ancient language into current English: "... there will come a time when a young animago will recognise the power he holds to unleash ... I am not sure how to translate the next bit ... maybe, 'the control of time'...."

Hexybilla looked expectantly at Sebastian to see whether he made the connection with what had just happened with Benny the cat. Indeed, Sebastian began to understand why Hexybilla had insisted on showing him this specific book.

"The prophecy foretells the coming of this young animago who will hold the key to Animagana and who will free the beings trapped within ...", she continued.

"What prophecy, and what is 'Animagana'?", asked Sebastian.

"Well ...", hesitated Hexybilla, and scratched her long, crooked nose. "The prophecy is something many of these old parchments talk about. It refers to the coming of an animago with special powers who, as we have just heard, holds the key to Animagana. Animagana, is a fictitious place in animagi culture and history believed to be a kind of heaven for all animagi, but the sources are unclear and contradictory on this. The answer is, therefore, that I am unsure as to what Animagana refers to. It could be a real or imaginary place."

"But what is this?", shouted Hexybilla suddenly, making Sebastian jump. "Look Sebastian! The key page on what Animagana is has been ripped out of the book!", and she showed Sebastian the serrated edge near the binding that showed that a page had been taken. "This confirms it: someone has indeed tampered with this book recently!", she said with anger in her voice.

Hexybilla licked her finger and turned to the next page. "Let's see what else it says: This animago will use the power to fend off evil, to help those who have sold their souls, and to reunite Animagana with the real world of animagi. The one the prophecy foretells will be familiar with the secret spell and will be able to use it wisely ...."

What does this all mean?, wondered Sebastian, *I really don't understand most of it.* Hexybilla seemed to confirm this: "This bit does not make much sense to me, I must admit, and even less so the next bit of text which uses different characters and which I can't even translate:"

UMMM MARISH GRANAFF GANG GOOL
RAST HEREBDYN IMMORTIS GRATTAN
URRR MAJORIM EXORBITUS THYSSUSS
DRRAM GARR NON RETURNUM SIC

As Hexybilla began reading this passage, occasionally glancing at Sebastian, Sebastian felt an increasingly strange feeling in his head, as if his brain was being ripped apart. He had the impression that his very soul was being torn out of his head and raised his hands to his temples in agony before Hexybilla had finished reading the passage.

"Wait … stop!", he shouted.

"Sebastian, are you alright?", Hexybilla asked, realising that Sebastian had suddenly turned pale and had slumped forward.

"N…n…no", stammered Sebastian, "I was just suddenly feeling very ill in my head when you read out that last sentence. I feel better now …"

Hexybilla looked anxiously at Sebastian but saw that his face had regained some colour. "I can only guess that this text passage talks about 'immortality' and 'not being able to return' to something or somewhere, but this is a language I don't recognise!", argued Hexybilla with a frustrated sigh. "But let's just think again about the prophecy and the foretelling of an animago who can unleash the 'control of time'", suggested Hexybilla. "Isn't this what you just described to me happened out in the garden?"

"I guess so", replied Sebastian, still massaging his temples gently, although he was not sure at all. "But that would mean that I am the one the prophecy refers to?", he wondered. "That can't be! I am just a little teddy-bear whose host is Erik and who goes about his life just like any other animago in this community!"

"Yes, you are probably right", suggested Hexybilla, "although I think we need to meet regularly, and you have to inform me about any other such occurrences as soon as possible. Please promise me!"

"I will, Mrs Hexybilla, I promise I will!", answered Sebastian, and he was very relieved that at least one other animago knew his story and could probably help him if it happened again.

"There is one more interesting point this ancient book mentions", said Hexybilla as she turned a few pages, "and the other reason I brought you here is that you might be able to help me to solve this issue. I have already talked to Professor Pandanus and his team about it and they will, of course, also help, as this is the main reason they are visiting. But I think you should also enrol the help of Teddy for this as he is such a bright animago! You should also tell him about what just happened to you out in the garden."

"That is a good idea, Mrs Hexybilla", replied Sebastian, and he looked forward to telling Teddy about his adventure with Benny.

"Here is the passage I want you to look at and help me find out what it means", said Hexybilla, while pointing at the text in the book. "For some reason this one is written in English":

Seven deadly sins
Seven sinful stories
And seven monsters to unlock

**Seven ways to expire
Will unravel the mystery
To Animagana's world
By taking away the souls
Of the weakest of all**

**But, behold animagi
Of unspeakable temptations
And no turning back
Without reverse wisdom**

"Wow!", exclaimed Sebastian. "That sounds really interesting, but what does it mean?"

"That is exactly what I would like you, Teddy and Professor Pandanus to find out as there is clearly a link here with 'Animagana' and, possibly, also with your time-freeze adventure", replied Hexybilla while she closed the book with a loud dusty bang which reverberated through the gigantic cavern.

11

Godfrey Wilkinson, Erik's dad and one of the initiated humans, had told his 12-year-old son to meet him in the living room of their spacious detached house.

"Hi Erik, how was school?", asked Godfrey.

"It was ok", said Erik, the answer he usually gave to this rather boring question.

"I have something important to discuss with you", said Godfrey, "so you better sit down, and let's just switch off the TV for a moment." Erik had been watching 'Family Guy', one of his favourite programmes, and pressed the 'pause' button on the Sky remote control.

"Now listen well, Erik, as this is very important and might come as a bit of a shock!", warned Godfrey.

Erik leaned back on his favourite sofa and wondered what this was all about.

"This is about your toy animals, Erik", continued Godfrey, "you know Sebastian and @@*^# whose name I can never pronounce." Godfrey waited for a reaction from his son, but Erik looked at him waiting for further explanation. "Well … this is difficult …", hesitated Godfrey, "to cut a long story short, your toy animals are actually alive, in other words they can move and talk and think!"

Erik looked at his dad and said: "Is this a joke, dad, or what? What are you talking about?"

Godfrey had been warned by the animagi council that this was the normal reaction of all human hosts who were suddenly told that their toys were alive and self-conscious.

"OK, just relax Erik, and don't panic at what will happen next", said Godfrey. "Come in guys!", he shouted, and in walked Teddy, Sebastian, Ugah, and Mrs Moluk.

Erik sat on the sofa with his eyes and mouth wide open and could not utter a word. His toy animals – as well as Teddy and Ugah, who were Godfrey's animagi, and Mrs Moluk from the animagi council – had just walked into the room by themselves and stood in a circle in front of the sofa!

"Well done Mr Wilkinson", said Mrs Moluk, "I'll take it from there", and she moved a bit closer to Erik looking into his stunned eyes. "I am Mrs Moluk", she introduced herself, "and the others you of course know as it was you who named them over the years."

Erik stared at Sebastian, Ugah and Teddy. "What? … what? …", he stammered, not knowing what to make of this.

"Hi Erik", said Sebastian, "I am pleased to finally make your acquaintance in person after so many years! I could always speak, walk and think since you named me yourself, but we were not allowed to show you as you had not been initiated."

"What Sebastian is talking about", interjected Mrs Moluk, "is that only so-called 'initiated' kids like yourself have the privilege to be told about their toy animals who we call 'animago', or 'animagi' for plural. The reason we have decided to initiate you now, with the help of your dad", and she nodded in acknowledgement towards Godfrey, "is because your animago Sebastian might be a rather special little bear, and because we feel you are now ready to be involved with animagi matters. I will explain why later, but first just get used to the fact that you can converse with your animagi."

In the meantime, Teddy, Sebastian and Ugah had climbed onto the sofa and sat on Erik's lap, smiling at him. "Hi, Erik", they all shouted, grabbed his right hand and shook it.

"Hi", said Erik timidly, as he was still stunned by what he saw. "But how come you can walk and talk? You are just stuffed toy animals?"

"Well, even for us that is still a mystery", explained Mrs Moluk, "but be aware that we feel pain like you and need our sleep just like humans. In other words, other than the way we look and the stuffing inside us, we are very much like humans."

Erik slowly awoke from his stupor and looked intently at his animagi. "That is incredible!", he said, "if I had known earlier, I guess I would have treated you kindlier all these years!"

"Believe me Erik", Mrs Moluk said, "you have actually been one of the kindest human hosts and as far as we know you have always treated your animagi with care and respect. This is also one of the reasons why we have chosen to initiate you. Indeed, evidence increasingly suggests that the personality of the human host is also somehow transferred to his or her animago. This means that nice, friendly, patient and well-balanced kids are likely to have animagi that also show these characteristics. Whereas nasty, angry and badly behaved children often have animagi who may themselves be very bad characters. You certainly seem to be one of the nicest kids in the village, so it is an honour for us to welcome you among the initiated children."

Although Erik did not fully understand what Mrs Moluk had told him, he was pleased to hear that they all thought that he was a nice kid. Godfrey and Mrs Moluk quietly left the room as they realised that Erik now needed some time alone with his animagi.

In the meantime Bunny, one of Godfrey's other animagi, had also entered the room. He obviously had been told about Erik's initiation, but, contrary to the others, he seemed a bit reluctant to greet Erik. For a while he stood in the middle of the room, watching the other animagi huddling around Erik.

Why is Bunny not joining us on this joyous occasion?, wondered Sebastian. *He has been acting strangely lately, kind of withdrawn. I wonder what he is up to?* But Sebastian's attention was quickly drawn back towards newly initiated Erik.

"Erik, can I ask you a favour?", wondered Sebastian.

"Well, yes of course Sebastian", replied Erik. Sebastian felt a strange warmth around his heart hearing his name addressed to him in person for the first time by the one who had named him.

"Could we watch some of my favourite movies together, as I always had to look at these when you and your mum were in bed and I was usually too tired myself?", asked Sebastian.

Erik had expected a slightly more profound request after all these years of unknowingly living together as self-conscious beings, but he cheerily replied: "Yes, of course Sebastian, which movies did you have in mind?"

"Well, we have to watch 'Toy Story' first as I know this is also one of your favourites, and then 'Gremlins', although it's a bit old-fashioned now, and of course also the various 'Narnia' movies with speaking animals, and 'The never-ending story', and …"

"Wow!", interrupted Erik, "you really seem to know your movies, Sebastian! Sure, we can start right away as it gives me a good excuse not to do my homework!"

Erik seemed well at ease with the animagi now, who all snuggled up to him while he selected 'Toy Story' from the many movies stored on their Skybox. He pressed 'play' and they all started to watch the movie.

Godfrey and Mrs Moluk were listening outside the half-closed living room door, and Mrs Moluk seemed very satisfied with how Erik's initiation had gone. "Good work Mr Wilkinson, that has gone quite smoothly, and Erik will be such a great addition to the group of initiated human beings! You can be very proud of your son!", she said. "We will wait a bit before we tell him about what has been happening lately in the village, and as you know the poor boy will have to take in quite a lot, I'm afraid! Did you also hear that another child from the village has fallen into a coma, Lucy, and that her three animagi have disappeared: teddy-bear Barney, doll Penny, and little dog Woof? We need to be extra vigilant with Erik, as his bond with Sebastian is a particularly important one for us."

Godfrey had heard about the other coma case and felt very sad about it, but he did not fully understand what Mrs Moluk alluded to with regard to Sebastian. Nonetheless, he was happy that Erik's initiation had gone smoothly and that he could now finally talk openly about animagi-related matters with his son. Godfrey was indeed very proud of Erik, as he watched his son with Sebastian on his lap and the other animagi sitting next to him, all laughing at Woody's antics in 'Toy Story' trying to hide the fact from their boy owner that Woody and the other toys were 'alive'.

12

"This just can't carry on, Mrs Billings!", shouted the headmistress of Andrew's school. "He is eleven now and in his first year of secondary school, but his behaviour has been appalling! As you know he has again beaten up another child who had to go to hospital to get stitches on his lip and cheek, and he continually disrupts class with swearing, lude comments and outright nasty behaviour towards his fellow pupils."

Rachel Billings looked down, too embarrassed to look the headmistress in the eyes. Andrew was sitting next to her, very restless and seemingly absent-mindedly gazing out of the window. In his arms he was clutching his toy frog.

"Andrew!", his mother shouted. "This is your future we are discussing! How can you not pay attention! Tell us why all this is happening and why you are behaving so badly?"

Andrew stood up, too tense and uptight to sit down. "They all hate me!", he shouted. "All the kids and all the teachers, they just hate me! The one I beat up tried to kill me! I had to hit back hard!"

"That is not true, Andrew!", replied the headmistress, "and you know it. Barnaby, the child you attacked, is one of the most mild-mannered and nicest kids in our school. He would not hurt a fly. The kids watching you fight said that you just attacked him out of nowhere, you were not even provoked!"

"That…that…that is a lie!", stammered Andrew, all red in his face now and sweating. "You're all against me!"

"You see Mrs Billings what we have to deal with! We just can't cope anymore! I fear that Andrew has to be expelled from school as this is the third time we are meeting over a serious assault incident. We just do not have the ability to deal with disruptive children like Andrew at our school. I am afraid that you have to look elsewhere now for a school place."

Rachel Billings did not reply. She knew it was futile to argue and, in the end, the headmistress was right. Andrew's behaviour had become so unpredictable, even at home. And now that he was 11, he was getting stronger and had also started threatening her and her husband. She stared at Andrew with a bewildered look. *How can he be my child?*, she wondered. *Nobody in my family is aggressive or has been badly behaved like this! Even the doctors we have seen seem puzzled as to why Andrew is behaving so aggressively.*

Rachel grabbed Andrew's hand firmly and pulled him behind her. The headmistress opened her mouth to say something, but thought the better of it and kept quiet. There was nothing else to say.

Back home Rachel locked Andrew up in his room. "I can't cope any more Andrew!", she sobbed. "I am locking you in as I need a bit of rest now. All this shouting with the headmistress has made my head spin. So just lie down in bed and rest a bit, I'll unlock your door again for supper."

Andrew stood in front of his locked door and heard his mother's footsteps receding. *They all hate me!*, he thought again, *even my own parents. But we won't let this continue for much longer!*, he thought, looking at his frog.

He threw himself on the bed and flung his schoolbag across the room. It landed with a loud crash on his laptop on his desk.

He did not care whether the computer had broken. He looked to his left where his red and blue toy frog was lying. The frog had grown over the years and had started developing a bit of a paunch. The surface of his leather also seemed to have taken on a slightly slimy sheen, and his eyes were no longer dead but had a vivid reddish colour.

"You're the only friend I have!", said Andrew to the frog.

"I know!", replied the frog, turning his head and looking at Andrew.

"I still don't understand why you can talk and why you seem alive", said Andrew, "but that's the best thing that has happened to me. You're the only one who understands me!"

The frog remembered all too well when he had suddenly come alive. It was during a night, when Andrew was about eight. A storm was raging outside and Andrew had woken up very scared. He had shouted for his parents, but nobody had come. He had turned towards his frog, cuddled him and said: "You are the only one I love! I hate everybody else!" At this moment the frog had come alive. He remembered turning his head and staring intently into Andrew's eyes, who seemed to understand what was happening.

"What name will you give me?", the frog had asked with a gargly voice filled with phlegm.

"Hey! You can talk!", Andrew had said. "That's neat! Your voice sounds all gargly, like you've swallowed some slime down your throat, so I'll call you Garglethroat!"

Since that night, about three years ago, they had grown closer and closer. Garglethroat did not yet want Andrew to know it, but he had influenced Andrew's aggressive behaviour by cajoling him to beat up kids and be nasty to his mum. He heard Andrew's parents chiding him for misbehaviour at school, and one day Garglethroat and Andrew had tortured one of his schoolmates who had come home to visit. There was blood everywhere, and on Garglethroat's insistence Andrew had hurt the boy very badly. This was the last time Andrew had received a visitor. After that incident Andrew and Garglethroat kept entirely to themselves, concocting ever more vicious plans about how to kill and maim other humans, how to steal money from Andrew's father's wallet, and how to play-act 'nice kid' when he wanted something from his mum.

"They will expel me from school", Andrew said looking maliciously at Garglethroat.

"You had it coming mate!", replied Garglethroat, "with the way you treat your schoolmates and your teachers I am actually surprised they didn't get rid of you earlier!"

"Maybe you're right", said Andrew. "I think I am done with school now. My parents will never find a place that will accept me."

They both lay side by side on the bed, looking at the ceiling, and wondering what would happen next.

13

Sebastian, Teddy and Hexybilla were sitting at a table, deep in the giant back room of the archives. They had the riddle in front of them, copied from the ancient book Sebastian and Hexybilla had recently looked at:

Seven deadly sins
Seven sinful stories
And seven monsters to unlock

Seven ways to expire
Will unravel the mystery
To Animagana's world
By taking away the souls
Of the weakest of all

But behold animagi
Of unspeakable temptations
And no turning back
Without reverse wisdom

"With everything that's been happening lately I have the feeling that we need to understand and solve this riddle as quickly as we can", said Hexybilla. "I somehow have a feeling that something really bad will happen soon …"

Teddy and Sebastian nodded in agreement. They had already filled Teddy in about Sebastian's adventure with Benny, swearing him to secrecy. Hexybilla had also told them about the latest coma case among children in the village, further emphasising that every day counted if they wanted to understand what was happening.

"Professor Pandanus has made some progress with regard to other important documents held in the archives", Hexybilla continued, "but he confirmed that what we have in front of us is probably the most important clue with regard to the children in coma. He told us to go ahead and that he will join us a bit later."

"OK, let's do this methodically, line by line", Teddy suggested.

They looked at the first line of the riddle.

Seven deadly sins

"It is pretty obvious what 'seven deadly sins' means", suggested Teddy. "If I remember rightly from what I have read, the seven deadly sins are also referred to as the seven cardinal sins, and are an important aspect of early Christian ethics about human's age-old tendency for self-centeredness and selfishness. The sins are …. let me get this right … wrath, greed, sloth, pride, and …." Teddy scratched his chin as he could not remember the last three.

"They also include lust, envy, and gluttony", added Hexybilla.

"That's right, thanks Mrs Hexybilla", acknowledged Teddy.

Sebastian was not sure what they were talking about, but was again amazed at Teddy's knowledge of such things. He could not remember learning about the seven deadly sins at school at all, at least not yet.

"So somehow the first clue is about these sins, and I suspect that the way the archives are organised methodically should be linked to this", suggested Teddy.

"OK, that's a possibility", said Hexybilla. "Unfortunately the organisation of the archives is not as logical as you might think, as this was all done probably in the 16th century when most of the materials were moved from the various monasteries in England. Let's have a look …"

They walked from their table to the first rows of shelves. Although labels written in ink and old-fashioned English were present at the corner of each set of shelves, as Hexybilla had suggested, the books and manuscripts did not seem to be organised alphabetically, nor were they ordered chronologically. The shelf next to them, for example, just said 'phials, trinkets and goblets used for alchemical procedures'. Teddy looked at one book with the title 'Glass phials and Nostradamus alchemy: a treatise in three volumes'.

"OK, this shelf has clearly nothing to do with the seven deadly sins!", he remarked.

"Let's split up and each of us should look at a different section", suggested Hexybilla, and they all went into different directions, noting the different shelf labels on their notepads.

After two hours of roaming around the archives – Sebastian got lost at least three times – they reconvened at their table comparing their notes.

"I have a lot of different information about animagi history, culture, art", said Hexybilla, "but nothing that suggests a specific shelf about the seven deadly sins."

"I have found one book on 'envy' dating back to 1645 written by a certain Lucrucius, whoever that was", said Teddy, "but I found this more by accident as it was in a section on 'animagi and human relationships'. What about you Sebastian?"

"I am afraid I found nothing useful as I spent most of the time trying to find my way back to here", admitted Sebastian. "I got lost too often …"

"Well, we haven't really gotten very far", sighed Teddy, "and this is only the first line of the riddle!"

They were sitting gloomily around the table when Professor Pandanus appeared. They quickly filled him in on their lack of progress so far. Prof Pandanus scratched his big panda head and mumbled: "seven sins … archives … seven sins … art! Yes, of course, the seven sins were not only important with regard to Christian writings and morals but also played an important part in European art history. Indeed, beginning in the early 14th century, the seven deadly sins grew in popularity as a theme among European artists, especially German painter Hieronymus Bosch whose various paintings of oil on wood referred to the acronym 'SALIGIA' for the Latin name of the seven deadly sins, namely superbia, avaritia, luxuria, invidia, gula, ira and acedia. Maybe it is a painting by Bosch we should be looking for rather than a book or manuscript?"

Sebastian suddenly thought that he remembered having seen something linked to what Professor Pandanus was talking about. "Saligia, Saligia", he mused, "this somehow sounds familiar but I can't quite remember where I might have seen reference to it."

The others looked expectantly at Sebastian.

"Think, Sebastian, think!", Hexybilla encouraged him. "You know that probably lives depend on us solving this riddle!"

Sebastian closed his eyes and tried to retrace his steps through the archives followed by Teddy, Hexybilla and Professor Pandanus.

"The problem is that I was lost for most of the time and didn't know where I was!", he said with a frown. "It might be best if we just walk towards roughly where I was in the archives and I may remember where I saw reference to 'Saligia'."

Sebastian tried to retrace his steps through the endless rows of shelves, dimly illuminated by distant lights on the ceiling of the vast cavern. *First I came from here, then I had turned left from that row of shelves, then I remember passing this reference to Nostradamus, whoever that was, then I think I must have gone here ...* Slowly, Sebastian weaved his way through the maze, at times stopping, thinking, and even backtracking when he was not sure that he recognised the shelves. They gradually made their way towards the far-left corner of the vast hall, as a wall began to be visible to the left. *That's right, for a while I remember seeing the wall to my right as I was walking back towards the others, so the wall now being on my left now is OK,* he thought. He passed a few more shelves and the vast back wall of the cave began to be visible, as a dark murky featureless wall first and then, as they got closer, as a stone wall with a few shelves and some areas of barren crudely hewn rock.

"I have never been in this part of the archives!", admitted Hexybilla, "although I am meant to be the animago expert regarding this vast hall."

Teddy looked at the labels on the shelves which seemed to be reduced to only one letter now: A, I, G, I, L, A again and then S. "Wait a moment!", he explained, "I think I've got it!", and he walked back in the reverse direction along the row of shelves straddling the back wall: S A L I G I A! "Here it is!", he shouted, this must be the shelves linked to the first line of the riddle.

All four animagi walked along different shelves and looked at the books.

"Not one book or manuscript in my shelf is linked to the seven deadly sins!", shouted Hexybilla so the others could hear. "What about your shelves?"

"Nothing!", came the simultaneous answer from the three others. "My books seem to be all linked to early mathematical riddles, nothing about the seven sins!", shouted Professor Pandanus.

Sebastian had also not seen anything in the shelves that seemed relevant to their enquiry. By chance he looked beyond the shelf at the back wall of the cave, and that is where he saw it ... A large painting. He walked towards it and realised that it was an oil painting about the size of a door, painted on wood. It was stuck firmly to the wall. The painting showed seven circles surrounding a large circle in the middle. Each circle was filled with grotesque and hideous beings, some half human and half animal. There was a lot of blood and guts to be seen and dead bodies were lying everywhere. Each circle had a label, starting with 'superbia', followed by 'avaritia', then 'luxuria', 'invidia', 'gula', 'ira' and 'acedia'. *The seven sins!* thought Sebastian. The centre had no label but seemed to show the culmination of the 'sins' in a gruesome bloodbath of bodies, shapes and creatures.

"I think I've got it!", shouted Sebastian, and the others quickly came rushing towards him. "Look at the painting! I think it shows the seven sins", he exclaimed.

Professor Pandanus immediately took out his large looking glass and exclaimed ecstatically: "Yes, Sebastian, that's it, well done! And look at the bottom right corner: 'H.B.' for Hieronymus Bosch. The painter closely associated with the seven deadly sins!"

"I wonder whether this is an original", asked Teddy as they all peered closely at the different circles shown on the painting. "If yes, it must be worth a fortune!"

"I couldn't tell without further analysis", said Professor Pandanus, "but key is to find out how this painting could now help us solve the riddle. Yes, we have a link to the first line of the riddle, but what does this painting tell us that we don't know already?"

They all started looking for further clues, touched the painting for hidden gaps or holes, followed its edges to see whether it was indeed a door and looked intently at the writing on the painting itself. But there was nothing that revealed any more than suggesting it was a painting associated with Bosch and that it showed the seven deadly sins.

"Ok", said Teddy. "At least we have found something clearly linked to the first line of the riddle. Maybe the other lines will help us further?"

"Right! Let's go back to our table and start all over again with the second line", suggested Hexybilla. "At least it will be easy to find this painting again as it is in the far-left corner of the giant cave."

14

After a good twenty-minute walk Sebastian, Teddy, Hexybilla and Professor Pandanus were back at their table again. One of Professor Pandanus' colleagues had left sandwiches and drinks for them, and they all realised that the stale air in the archives and their concentrated search had made them very hungry and thirsty. They looked at the second line of the riddle:

Seven sinful stories

"I think I may be able to help with this one", said Hexybilla while chewing on a cheese-and-ham sandwich, "as it may be linked to my speciality – animagi culture and history. I thought about this line of the riddle since Sebastian and I looked at it for the first time and it initially did not make much sense to me, but now that we have found at least some explanation for the first line this makes more sense to me."

They all looked at Hexybilla expectantly.

"As you will remember from school", Hexybilla continued, "animagi lore is as complex as that of humans, with several creation myths, legends and, indeed, rather nasty stories abounding. One such myth actually relates directly to the seven deadly sins we just talked about. Come with me …."

They walked for several minutes to a shelf with the label 'Animagi Myths and Legends'.

"My favourite part of the archives!", explained Hexybilla, and swiftly propped up the nearest ladder against the shelf and extracted several old-looking books, some larger than others, but all looking very ancient and comprised of old handwritten pages similar to the *Chronicles of Animagi Lore* Sebastian and her had looked at together recently. They swiftly walked back to their table and Hexybilla opened the first book.

"This is one of the oldest animagi books we know", Hexybilla explained. "It is called the 'Original Ledger' and relates a story from thousands of years ago about animagi clans fighting each other to death as they begrudged each other's successes with regard to knowledge, weaponry and territory."

"'Envy'!", Teddy shouted immediately, "one of the seven deadly sins!"

"Indeed!", replied Hexybilla, "so 'envy' is the first of the seven sins that appears in animagi lore. The next one" – and she looked at a second much smaller, but equally ancient-looking, book – "is entitled 'Gradina' and is a bit more recent than the first one. It tells the story of one animago who had amassed a vast fortune and power and who was meant to have a seemingly endless sexual appetite. As a result, he had his nearest male enemies slaughtered and subjugated their wives and daughters into his vast harem. Needless to say that he found an untimely end as he was betrayed by one of his servants who killed him while he was raping one of his young victims!"

"Lust!", exclaimed Professor Pandanus and Teddy simultaneously.

Hexybilla, continued her chronicle of animagi legends, with the next book dealing with greed, through the example of an animagi community that was never satisfied with what they owned, and the following with wrath through various examples of violent anger perpetrated during what seemed to be a particularly tumultuous time in animagi history between about AD400 and AD800. The following story about pride from the 12th century particularly upset Sebastian – a wealthy animagi doll with human-like features who felt she was the most beautiful animago ever to roam this earth – and he began to realise that the story of his fellow beings, if these legends and myths held any truth, was a much darker and sadder one than they had learned at school.

Hexybilla pulled out the last two books from her pile which looked more recent. The first one, written in the 17th century, suggested that many animagi had become too accustomed to an 'easy' life, scavenging on human ingenuity and inventiveness rather than developing cultural and technical artefacts of their own. "In other words", said Hexybilla, "this author probably rightly argued that 'sloth' had become all too common among animagi culture – a problem that we are still struggling with today."

The others nodded in approval as the theme of laziness and over-dependency on human culture and inventions had marred recent animagi history.

"The final deadly sin, gluttony, is unfortunately another by-product of this cultural decline", continued Hexybilla. "This last book" – and she pointed towards a fairly modern-looking tome that looked more like an academic study than a book of legends and myths – "is a recent study about increasing obesity among animagi. Just as in the human world, lack of exercise, reliance on more and more electronic gadgets and endless availability of sweet foodstuffs are to blame but also, as the author implies, gluttony!"

Sebastian thought about the many overweight and obese animagi in his school alone, and completely overweight Professor Pandanus shifted uneasily on his seat not daring to look anyone in the eye.

"So if my analysis is correct", said Hexybilla, "here we have the sequence of deadly sins through the lens of animagi history of myths and legends: envy, lust, greed, wrath, pride, sloth and gluttony."

"But how does this help us with the riddle?", wondered Sebastian.

They sat in silence thinking about Hexybilla's analysis.

"Let's assume Mrs Hexybilla's analysis is the correct interpretation of the second line", said Teddy, "then this must be somehow linked to the Hieronymus Bosch painting we just discovered. Could it, for example, mean that the sequence of the seven sins in animagi lore is linked to a sequence of actions we need to perform with regard to the painting? I suspect the secret to Animagana lies within or behind the painting!"

They immediately set out again on the long walk past the endless rows of shelves towards the back left corner of the cave where the Bosch painting hung on the wall. When they reached it, the seven circles on the painting started to make more sense as they could directly relate them to the gruesome stories they had just heard about animagi lore.

There is the one showing greed or 'avaritia', another one showing sloth or 'acedia'... all with the Latin names of the sins on each of the circles, thought Sebastian and he let his paw gently touch the painting.

"Ok", suggested Teddy, "maybe let's press on the circles in the sequence of the animagi lore of the seven sins and see whether anything happens."

Teddy gently pressed the circle with the heading 'invidia' for 'envy', followed by 'luxuria', 'avaritia', 'ira', 'superbia', 'acedia' and 'gula'. Nothing happened …

Professor Pandanus and Hexybilla tried the same, touching slightly different parts of the circles, but still nothing happened.

"We may be barking up the wrong tree after all!", grumbled Teddy.

"I think we are on the right track", said Professor Pandanus. "What does the third line of the riddle say?"

And seven monsters to unlock

"So the first line of the riddle told us where to go, the second may have told us the sequence of what to do with the painting, while this third line has the term 'unlock' in it, so I think this one may be the instruction of where to press on the painting!", suggested Professor Pandanus. "As Mrs Hexybilla knows, the book was written in 1545, so the authors knew about this painting which was produced sometime around 1500."

"Seven monsters … let's see …", Professor Pandanus continued and pulled out his large looking glass again and scrutinised each of the seven circles on Bosch's painting. "Yes, here they are …", he said, pointing with his panda paw at a clearly visible monster in each of the circles depicting the seven sins. "So let's press on the monsters in the sequence Mrs Hexybilla suggested earlier", and Professor Pandanus put his paw on the first monster – an evil-looking dragon-like creature

– in the first circle in Hexybilla's sequence entitled 'invidia' for 'envy'.

For a short moment nothing happened, but suddenly a small area around the dragon moved inward with a loud audible click. Professor Pandanus looked expectantly at the other three animagi.

Teddy came forward and pressed on the monster shown in the circle 'luxuria' for 'lust' – a half-human half-animal beast with a large forked tongue hanging out – and again a small area around the monster retracted back with a click. They did the same with the other circles, each showing a different type of monster in different parts of the circles until they came to the last one: 'gula' for 'gluttony'.

"Come on Sebastian, you press it!", said Hexybilla, and Teddy lifted Sebastian up so he could reach the last circle. Sebastian pressed on a dreadful-looking slimy toad, and the area around the toad moved back into the wall with a click. Again, nothing else seemed to happen when suddenly a much louder click was to be heard and the whole painting began to swivel vertically around its middle axis. The four animagi saw that the painting had been covering a massive stone door, at least 50 centimetres thick, which now stood open.

Behind the door a small cave was visible, dimly lit by a faint light in the ceiling. It was completely empty. Just a few footmarks were visible on the dusty floor …

15

13-year-old Andrew did again not sleep well. He woke up. It was entirely dark in his bedroom. He thought back at the events of the day. After several dreadful rows with his mum Rachel over Andrew's behaviour, Andrew's dad had finally decided to leave the family. "I can't stand it anymore!", his dad had said when he slammed the front door after looking at his son for a last time. Andrew did not even blink and had gone back to his room immediately, listening to his mother sobbing in the kitchen.

Andrew turned to the side, trying to get back to sleep when 'it' happened. He heard a voice in his head. But it wasn't just any voice; it was Garglethroat's gargly voice.

I know you can hear me!, the voice said.

Andrew jumped up and switched on his bedside lamp. He looked at Garglethroat who was, as usual, lying next to him, half covered by Andrew's blanket. Garglethroat had grown even fatter and slimier over the past few months. He had a nasty smile on his face.

You can hear me in your head Andrew!, said Garglethroat without moving his lips.

"How can that be?", asked Andrew with a puzzled look. "Can I also communicate with you without speaking?"

Sometimes I can hear your thoughts, replied Garglethroat in Andrew's head. *I think it works when you are thinking about me, which is quite often. Try it!*

Andrew closed his eyes and clenched his fists, concentrating hard on thinking something for Garglethroat. *I think you are amazing!*, Andrew thought. *Can you hear my thoughts?*

Yes, I can! See, it isn't that difficult, thought Garglethroat. *I think we can also communicate over longer distances as I seem to hear some of your thoughts when you are out of the house.*

Andrew cuddled Garglethroat very hard. *You are even more amazing than I thought! What would I do without you?* Without giving a further thought to his father, Andrew fell asleep again.

16

Sebastian, Teddy, Hexybilla and Professor Pandanus looked aghast at the empty room at the back of the archives.

"What is this?", asked Professor Pandanus, "there is nothing in here, absolutely nothing!"

They walked along the walls and looked for hidden doors or entrances, they touched the wall to see if there were any further secret passages, but they found nothing. Teddy looked at the footmarks on the floor that were already there when they had entered. It looked as if there were four different sets of marks, one of a relatively large animago with short claws on his feet, and three of smaller animagi, possibly teddy-bears or dogs. The footmarks led to the middle of the room where there was evidence that four animagi had stood there for a while and changed position several times, but then only one set of footprints led back to the door behind the Bosch painting.

"How strange!", Teddy remarked. "It looks as if four animagi went in but only one came out again!"

They all looked at each other unsure what to make of all of this. After solving at least parts of the riddle they had expected to find more than just an empty room with a few footprints.

"There is clearly nothing of interest to us in here for the moment", said Hexybilla. "I suggest we clear any sign of us having been in here, in case the animago who left the footprints comes back."

As they left the room they all wiped their footprints so that only the old ones in the middle of the room were left.

"Yes, that looks good", said Sebastian, "you can't see any evidence now that we were in there."

"How do we close the door", asked Professor Pandanus, leaning against it but it was so heavy that it would not budge.

"Let's try pressing the monster images in reverse", suggested Teddy, "maybe this will lock the door?"

They pressed the monsters in the seven circles of the Bosch painting. At first nothing happened, but then with a loud groan and a big bang the door closed again. Bosch's painting was again flush with the cave wall and nothing suggested that this was a door.

They made their way back through the archives to their table.

"Although we have achieved a lot today", said Hexybilla, "I am still not clear what this all means. How is that back room we discovered linked to Animagana, let alone to the prophecy possibly linked with Sebastian?"

"We still have a few hours left, and Sebastian has more flexibility now that Erik has been initiated, so let's look at the rest of the riddle. Maybe the clue is in the next paragraph", suggested Teddy.

They looked at the riddle again and the first line of the next paragraph:

Seven ways to expire

"What does 'expire' mean?", asked Sebastian naively.

"It's another word for 'dying', Sebastian", explained Hexybilla. "A rather strange word to use …"

"I think I may be able to help here", said Professor Pandanus, "as I think this is linked to our investigation of archival sources about the children in coma", and he took out a wad of paper full of scribbled notes. "Let me see ...", he continued, shuffling through his papers. "Ah yes, here it is! This is a summary of notes from a shelf towards the front right of the archives labelled 'Death'. At first we thought this was not relevant to our investigation, but I think there is a link. Let me explain: In animagi lore, as in human myths and legends, death plays a very important role. After all this is probably why many humans and animagi are religious in one form or another ... The unexplained nature of death and what happens thereafter. Our investigation of several old animagi books and manuscripts suggests that animagi lore talks about six key forms of 'death' or, in the words of the riddle, of how to 'expire'. The 'Book of Doom' from 1510, for example, lists the following: disease, decapitation, dismemberment, disembowelling, poisoning and hanging. You can see that some of these have natural causes, especially for 16th century authors, including disease, while all the other five are human- or animagi-inflicted causes of death common in the 16th century. Now, what is particularly interesting in the context of our riddle is that the seventh 'death' is listed as 'lethargus' or 'coma' in English."

Sebastian, Hexybilla and Teddy looked at each other. *Clearly Professor Pandanus is onto something here!* thought Sebastian.

"This suggests", Professor Pandanus continued, "that coma was seen as a form of death in ancient time, although the manuscripts refer to coma as not a 'real' death but a 'quasi-death'. This suggests that they saw coma as a half-state between life and death, where part of the soul has left the body but where the 'essence' of the soul still clings to life and is, therefore, particularly potent. The manuscripts suggest that people in coma were, therefore, often venerated in the past as beings that could mediate between the world of the living and the world of the dead."

"This is really interesting, Professor Pandanus", said Hexybilla. "Possibly the key to Animagana is linked to coma as a form of 'death', as the riddle implies."

"If the soul of a person or animago in coma is seen as something really powerful, could it be that the soul unlocks something?", wondered Teddy. "Could it open a door or a gate to Animagana? I think that's what the rest of that paragraph in the riddle suggests:"

Seven ways to expire
Will unravel the mystery
To Animagana's world
By taking away the souls
Of the weakest of all

They all stared intently at the five lines.

"OK, if Professor Pandanus and his colleagues are right, the first line points to coma as a form of death and the power of the soul of humans or animagi in a coma", said Hexybilla. "So if we assume that 'coma' and 'soul' are key in the first line, the rest starts making sense: people in a coma, in the case of our village and, for some unknown reason, human children, will unravel the mystery to Animagana's world'."

"I don't think it is a surprise that it is children who are in a coma because their souls have been tampered with", argued Professor Pandanus. "Look, the answer is in the next two lines:

'by taking away the souls of the weakest of all'. By nature, children are weaker as they are still growing and their 'souls' – if of course one believes that souls really exist – may be equally weak and easy to 'steal'. I guess the cut-off age is somewhere between the age of 14 and 15, when children's adult consciousness starts to form."

"OK, OK", said Teddy, "I can see the logic in what you are saying, but that still does not explain how 'souls' could be stolen from children, leaving them in a coma as a result?"

Again, they sat around in silence for a while, as Teddy's cautionary note had highlighted that they had not fully understood the riddle.

"Wait a moment!", said Sebastian. "Mrs Hexybilla, do you remember when you read out to me that other passage from the *Chronicles of Animagi Lore*, that book 'Animagaro…something Radi…something' that you could not translate because it is in a funny language?"

"Yes, I remember Sebastian", replied Hexybilla. "You are referring to the book 'Animagarostantla Radisovatra'. What has that got to do with our discussion about souls and children in coma?"

"Well, Mrs Hexybilla", said Sebastian, "remember that I had one of the strangest feelings when you read out that strange passage, as if my brain was being squeezed and my soul torn apart. I nearly fainted …"

"That's right!", replied Hexybilla, "now I remember. You turned as pale as a ghost and nearly fell off your chair."

"Well, that's it then!", exclaimed Teddy. It may be that the secret incantation unlocks the soul, especially that of vulnerable children. Where is that incantation Mrs Hexybilla?"

Hexybilla rummaged in the pile of papers in front of them and found it.

"Here it is", she said, "but I am rather reluctant to read it out if what we think it can do is true!"

They all glanced at the four lines without daring to read them aloud:

UMMM MARISH GRANAFF GANG GOOL
RAST HEREBDYN IMMORTIS GRATTAN
URRR MAJORIM EXORBITUS THYSSUSS
DRRAM GARR NON RETURNUM SIC

Even just reading the lines made them feel a chill coming through the caves, and they thought they heard thousands of manuscripts and parchments on the shelves rustling in unison, like the tortured souls of the village children in a coma.

"OK, let's assume we are right and this incantation somehow unlocks the souls of individuals and opens some kind of a gate or portal", said Professor Pandanus, trying to refocus on the task in front of them. "What about the last paragraph of the riddle?"

But behold animagi
Of unspeakable temptations
And no turning back
Without reverse wisdom

"It clearly tells us of 'unspeakable temptations' and that there is 'no turning back'", he continued. "Unspeakable temptations about what, and no turning back from what? And what does 'reverse wisdom' mean?"

"I suspect this is linked to the portal to Animagana", said Hexybilla. "Unfortunately the page in the *Chronicles of Animagi Lore* referring to Animagana has been ripped out. Sebastian and I found this out when we went through the book."

Both Teddy and Professor Pandanus were very disturbed by this news.

"Is there no other ancient book that could tell us what this legend of Animagana is about?", asked Teddy. "Clearly there must be something very attractive there, if someone is willing to put children into a coma for the sake of extracting their souls!"

"Yes", added Professor Pandanus, "and why did that individual need to put so many children into a coma? And what about all these animagi who have disappeared from the village recently?"

"There are still so many unanswered questions", relied Hexybilla, "but I think we have made very good progress today, so I would like to thank all of you, also you Sebastian, for helping to solve at least part of the riddle in front of us. We will look further into the question about Animagana over the next few days, and I will ask my dear friend Mr Rigor Mortis to help us, as he is also an expert on the archives. Indeed, he seems to have been doing his own research here lately as I have seen him here several times over the past few weeks. I will particularly ask him to organise a 24-hour guard for the Hieronymus Bosch painting, so that nobody tampers with it or, indeed, tries to get into that back room."

They all agreed that this would be a very wise course of action and that Mr Mortis was the ideal person to be in charge of security issues.

"In the meantime", Hexybilla continued, "please feel free to go in and out of this cave as you see fit, as you are now all part of a select group who know more about the riddle, the prophecy and the fate of our village children than anyone else. Sebastian, I will give you the code for the door to this part of the archives, so that you can come in at any time, but please be careful not to get lost! Professor Pandanus, this is also true for your team of experts. I will, of course, also inform the members of the council about what we have found today and there may be further instructions coming from them over the next few days."

Sebastian felt very proud to be part of such an exclusive group, and he was already planning to have a look at further books and manuscripts held in the archives over the next few days. *Maybe I'll find the answer to what Animagana is and why it is seems to be so important?*, he wondered.

17

Rigor Mortis was furious! He slammed the door to his school office with a loud bang. He had just come back from an extraordinary council meeting where Hexybilla had told them about their discovery of the cave behind the Hieronymus Bosch painting. She also reported that there were signs that someone else had been in the deepest recesses of the archives and had tampered with the key book containing the prophecy and the riddle, the 'Animagarostantla Radisovatra' or 'The Chronicles of Animagi Lore'.

Within a few days they have found what took me nearly a year to solve!, he thought. He took the crumpled page he had stolen from the *Chronicles of Animagi Lore* out of his pocket and looked at it with an angry frown on his penguin face.

"If only I had taken the entire book! What an idiot I am", he shouted and put his flippers around his head in despair. *But I guess I wanted to make sure that nobody saw that evidence had been taken from the archives, but I was playing it too safe!*, he lamented. *The only thing they don't seem to know is what the cave behind the Bosch painting is for and how to actually open the portal to Animagana. He, he, he ... that's because it is explained on the page I ripped out, and as far as I know there is no other such reference to Animagana in any of the other books or manuscripts in the archives!*

Rigor Mortis looked down at his expensive clothes and the Swiss-made Rolex watch on his wrist. He was dressed in a very expensive-looking gold-embroidered cloak with matching shoes and a cap made of rare black polar bear fur. He saw a reflection of himself in the mirror on the side of his desk and he thought he looked rather distinguished and dashing!

All of this I can only afford with the money I have made by selling entry to Animagana through the portal to animagi willing to pay the price, he continued his self-criticism. *I could have never afforded any of this on my pitiful teacher's salary, and my position on the council is a purely honorary one with no payment whatsoever!*

He looked at his Rolex watch which alone was worth several thousand pounds.

I will have to move very swiftly now to complete and cash in on the last portal openings. Luckily I still have a few animagi lined up for transfer to Animagana, and the one who has just approached me looks particularly keen and promising.

He laughed out loud. *The best thing*, he continued speaking to himself, *is that Hexybilla has asked me of all people to actually guard the Bosch painting and to make sure that no unauthorised person gets in! Ha! The fools! That way at least I can continue to control the portal for a little while!*

But he still felt deeply angry and depressed, as he knew that his spell of riches was coming to an end. *How disappointing after all the work I have put into this!*

There was a knock on his door. He did not expect anyone at this late hour, who could it be? He slowly walked to the door and opened it a little, when the door was pushed back straight into his face. In front of him were two hideous-looking characters holding a blindfold …

18

Hidden in the deepest recesses of the animagi cave system of the village, Garglethroat was sitting on a stone throne covered in red velvet. Garglethroat had become very fat and looked even more disgusting compared to the past when he was still with Andrew. His skin was slimy, and he seemed to perspire constantly with droplets of sweat dripping from his red velvet front. He had deep red-black bulgy eyes that were constantly oozing a thick liquid, with crusts of pus accumulated around their edges. He wore no clothes, but his fat paunch hung over the front of his body covering his smelly private parts.

Three of Garglethroat's henchmen – who had been part of his gang recently escaped from prison – stood in a semi-circle around him, looking rather scared.

Garglethroat shouted at them with his dreadful voice that sounded like a deep gargle mixed with saliva and phlegm from deep inside his body: "You idiots! How long do I have to wait for you to get me some meaningful information about the archives and the portal?"

Garglethroat's henchmen stared down at their feet, not daring to look into Garglethroat's rheumy and slimy eyes. Ori Fisse, one of his men, was a disgusting-looking animago in the shape of a bulldog. His host, a rough kid from the village who was involved with drugs and was on his way to becoming a serious alcoholic, had often mistreated him, with the result that Ori Fisse looked much the worse for wear with large holes in his fur and bits of stuffing hanging out in various places. As a result, Ori Fisse had a bad limp and was always in pain moving about. Skeleto, a skinny plastic skeleton about 40 centimetres tall, stood to Ori Fisse's right and looked particularly scared. Gremlin, a little monster-like creature with strong arms and stout legs, glanced worryingly at Ori Fisse, fearing the worst as he had witnessed many of Garglethroat's rages.

"We've been out of prison for over three weeks now, and still you haven't found anything, despite the fact that we had received clear information that a portal existed somewhere here in the village!", Garglethroat continued, fuming. "Remember how lucky we were to be incarcerated with that fellow animago who seemed to know a lot about Animagana and that the portal was somewhere around here! And remember also how we slaughtered him after he gave us the information!", said Garglethroat with a raucous laugh. *I think Andrew also enjoyed that kill when I passed him my thoughts when I slit the fellow's throat!* remembered Garglethroat.

Ori Fisse, Skeleto and Gremlin laughed with Garglethroat at the memory of how they had chopped off the fellow's head with a crude self-made blade. They were glad that the tension between Garglethroat and them had slightly abated through their joint memory of the murder.

"Don't you want to attain immortality as the parchment predicted?", continued Garglethroat. "Don't you want to sever your link to your stupid hosts who define how long you will live? Remember when our hosts die we die, how unfair is that? I have a special bond with my host Andrew, but I don't want to die when he dies which may happen sooner rather than later! The portal mentioned by that bloke in prison will lead us to

Animagana where we can finally live our lives independently from our human hosts and away from all these animagi rules and restrictions that have made our lives such a misery so far!"

Ori Fisse, Skeleto and Gremlin nodded in unison.

"OK!", said Garglethroat, "Ori Fisse, you continue monitoring the entrance to the animagi archives closely, as the solution to Animagana and the portal clearly lies there, and report anyone going in and out to me immediately. We obviously know that this stupid and fat Professor Pandanus and his team of no-hopers are already in there, but you also said that the archivist Hexybilla recently took a young animago in there … Sebaldus … or something like that was his name?"

"It was Sebastian, boss!", replied Ori Fisse. "He is a young and relatively inexperienced animago and we don't know why he was allowed into the archives with Hexybilla. I could not follow them in, so I don't know what they discussed. We also heard that there was an extraordinary council meeting this morning, but we don't know what the discussion was about. Maybe about the archives?"

"OK, Ori Fisse, continue checking what this Sebastian fellow is doing, and report back to me regularly. We may be onto something here …", commanded Garglethroat.

"Yes, boss", replied Ori Fisse and left the cave.

"Now let our distinguished visitor in, Skeleto", said Garglethroat pointing at the cave door, "we have left him waiting long enough."

Skeleto opened the thick door and guided Rigor Mortis in. He had a blindfold wrapped over his eyes, and was led by Skeleto into the room who removed the cloth. Rigor blinked as his eyes gradually adjusted to the dim light in the room. He approached the stone throne and stared Garglethroat square in the face.

"What is the meaning of this abduction, may I ask? How dare you?", shouted Rigor Mortis with an air of aloofness.

Garglethroat's henchmen had moved closer in case Rigor Mortis tried to attack Garglethroat.

"Don't be scared, Mr Mortis ...", said Garglethroat impatiently. "We have heard that you may know something about a portal leading to Animagana, which is why I wanted to see you. I am interested! But if you don't give us the information I need I am not sure you will get out here alive again. The blindfold was an insurance for us so that you don't reveal our location if I let you go, but you need to give me a good reason not to kill you here and now and add all this expensive stuff you are wearing to our collection of stolen goods!"

And another one who seems to know about the portal and Animagana!, thought Rigor Mortis. *What a day this has been! But maybe I can actually use this situation to my advantage?*

"OK, I can see that I haven't got much choice considering that I am at your mercy", replied Rigor Mortis. "So, I'll be frank with you and make you a business proposition."

Garglethroat shifted his fat slimy body a bit to the left and let out a gigantic fart. The smell wafted over towards Rigor Mortis who pretended not to notice.

"I have found the portal to Animagana", said Rigor Mortis.

The cave was deadly silent, the only movement was the slight flicker of the candles lighting the room.

"You have found what?", shouted Garglethroat. "How is that possible if animagi scholars over the centuries have failed to find it?"

"They have been looking in the wrong places, Sir", replied Rigor Mortis, "and indeed for the wrong type of portal. It needed a lot of research by someone like myself who has unlimited access, and knows the archives very well, and who is sharp enough to make the connection between several seemingly unconnected bits of information."

Garglethroat's interest was clearly aroused, as he shifted his weight forward and stared Rigor Mortis straight in the eyes. "So what deal are you offering?", he asked.

"I have heard from your men that you are interested in finding Animagana", said Rigor Mortis. "As you already know, legend has it that animagi lose the connection to their human hosts by crossing into Animagana and become immortal … the dream of many of us who are frustrated by the tedious dependency we have on humans who have to continue loving and cherishing us so that we can continue living, and also by our dependency on our hosts' wellbeing for our own survival. What an unfair relationship!"

"So what's in it for you? Why offer me the deal and not just go yourself?", asked Garglethroat with a suspicious look on his toad face.

"Because apart from immortality some of us weaker animagi also expect a certain quality of life, and that can only be achieved with money!", replied Rigor Mortis. "You must be extremely wealthy from the riches you and your gang have accumulated over the years, so I offer to sell you the information about the portal for you to use as you see fit. When I go to Animagana myself I am sure I can make good use of the riches I have accumulated to ensure a good quality of life."

Garglethroat looked at Rigor Mortis who stood in front of him with his expensive clothes and watch, and saw an animagi who was clearly keen on money, status, and wealth.

"OK, I am interested", replied Garglethroat, "so give me the information you have and I'll see what I can do."

"Not so fast, Sir", said Rigor Mortis. "I will need some assurance that you will let me go and that you will pay me handsomely. No money, no information about the portal! So this meeting could be the start of a long-term business relationship with you, but I will only divulge the last bit of information once I have my reward stashed safely away!"

Garglethroat realised that Rigor Mortis was no push-over, and that he would have to give in to his demands at least for the moment. He could always deal with Rigor Mortis later once he had all the information about Animagana he needed.

"Very well then", conceded Garglethroat. "We will try and agree a sum of money and then take it from there. What about one thousand pounds?"

Rigor Mortis stared deeply into Garglethroat's eyes. "You must be joking, Sir! You can do better than that! My Swiss watch is worth more than that", he replied. "I was thinking more about hundred thousand pounds!"

Garglethroat smiled and spat out a big wad of phlegm against the wall to the right of where Rigor Mortis stood. The phlegm seemed stuck to the wall but then gradually started oozing downwards, leaving a glistening trail of slime as it slowly made its way to the cave floor. He laughed and replied: "You must be joking, mate! No information is worth that sum even if it brings immortality! Skeleto, blindfold this guy again and take him back to where he came from so that he has time to redo his sums!"

Rigor Mortis was manhandled by Skeleto and Gremlin from behind and blindfolded. He had no time to reply, but the fact that Garglethroat had not ordered him killed suggested that his offer was nonetheless being considered.

But now that so many seem to know about Animagana and the portal I am quickly running out of time, he thought, while he was escorted out of the cave and up the maze of passageways.

19

Sebastian was sitting by himself in the archives perusing a few books that Hexybilla had placed in front of him which might mention Animagana. She had confirmed that Professor Pandanus and his team had found sources that suggested that any animagi crossing over into Animagana would lose the link to their human host and, even more importantly, would gain immortality. They sought further confirmation of this by looking at every possible book or manuscript that could be linked to the myth.

Hexybilla had also informed them that the council was keen to look into the matter of the riddle and the hidden chamber behind the painting, and that they had appointed Mr Mortis to guard the painting and the cave behind it. Sebastian was relieved at this decision as he had always been told that Rigor Mortis was an animagi with the highest level of integrity. *Indeed*, thought Sebastian, *he is both one of my teachers and a member of the council and one cannot have many more institutions vouching for someone than that.*

Sebastian was flicking through a rather boring book that seemed to have nothing to say about Animagana. By coincidence he was near a shelf not far from the Hieronymus Bosch painting.

Suddenly he heard a sound. The archives were dim as usual, so it was hard to see. The entrance to the chamber was hidden by several rows of shelves, so Sebastian stood up and peered around the corner to see whether anyone was approaching. He was relieved to see Rigor Mortis making his way straight towards the Bosch painting and was just about to shout a greeting when Sebastian saw that Mr Mortis had three other animagi with him. Sebastian recognised them as Lucy's animagi, Barney, Penny and Woof. They looked scared to death and seemed rather pale.

What is this?, wondered Sebastian, *I thought we and Mr Mortis were the only ones allowed in here, so what are Lucy's animagi doing here with Mr Mortis?*

He stopped still half hidden by the shelves and observed Rigor Mortis peering around him as if to make sure nobody was watching. Sebastian was even more intrigued by this behaviour, and decided to hide further behind the shelf where he could just see the Bosch painting.

Rigor Mortis told Barney, Penny and Woof to be quiet and started pressing the seven circles on the painting in the same sequence Teddy had identified a few days earlier. The painting and the door behind it started swivelling around its axis, and Rigor Mortis let the two animagi into the small cave.

This is getting stranger and stranger!, Sebastian thought. *I should tell someone immediately as the deal was to guard the chamber, not to go into it!*, but there was nobody around. Sebastian knew that Professor Pandanus and his colleagues were somewhere, but last time he saw them they were at the opposite end of the vast cave.

Sebastian could not resist the temptation and walked towards the half open door. Half hidden by the door he peered inside. He saw Rigor Mortis standing in the middle of the small cave, exactly on the spot where they had seen the footsteps end the first time they had entered the chamber. *The footsteps match*

Mr Mortis' feet!, Sebastian realised. *It is him! He is the animago who has also solved the riddle of the chamber! And we have entrusted him with guarding the chamber. Oh no …!*

Sebastian did not know what to do. He knew he should call someone immediately but he was too curious to see what Rigor Mortis was actually doing in the chamber.

Rigor Mortis took a small glass phial out of his expensive vest. It shimmered blueish in the dim light. He opened the phial and said to Barney, Penny and Woof standing next to him: "Be ready as you will only have a few seconds once I release the content of this phial."

The three animagi crowded next to him, still very scared, but it looked as if they had rehearsed this part before. Rigor Mortis opened the phial and threw its blueish transparent content into the air. He then calmly intoned:

UMMM MARISH GRANAFF GANG GOOL
RAST HEREBDYN IMMORTIS GRATTAN
URRR MAJORIM EXORBITUS THYSSUSS
DRRAM GARR NON RETURNUM SIC

There was a sound like a hiss and what looked like a tear began to open in the air in front of him. Mr Mortis used his flippers to enlarge the tear and Sebastian thought he heard something in the distance … dim music and raucous laughter! He could only see darkness through the tear …

Barney, Penny and Woof slipped through the tear and disappeared. Barney had looked back just before going through the tear, and Sebastian thought he could detect some indecision in Barney's face. But it was too late. Only a few seconds later the tear seemed to close all by itself.

Rigor Mortis stood there for a few seconds as if checking that no evidence was left about what had just happened, and then quickly turned around towards the door. Sebastian just had time to jump aside before Rigor Mortis could see him and hide behind the first set of shelves near the door.

Rigor Mortis performed the reverse sequence of pressing the seven circles on Bosch's painting and the heavy stone door closed with a loud crunch. He quickly made his way through the shelves and walked towards the exit of the large cave.

I have just seen how he activated the portal to Animagana!, thought Sebastian. *The incantation we saw in the 'Chronicles of Animagi Lore', so now we know what it's used for, but what was the blue shiny light in the phial he used? I need to find out!*

Sebastian quickly followed Rigor Mortis who could still be seen in the distance walking briskly towards the exit.

20

Rigor Mortis walked fast. He clearly had somewhere else to go and Sebastian found it hard to keep up without being seen.

I have to tell someone about what I have just seen!, he repeated to himself, but Professor Pandanus and his team were still nowhere to be seen, and Mrs Hexybilla did not appear to be in the archives at the moment. Few animagi used mobile phones for communication as there was no reception in the passageways and caves.

Rigor Mortis left the archives and Sebastian had just managed to sneak through the doors before they closed without being seen by Rigor. They walked through the maze of corridors, past the school and past Erik's house towards the top of the village. Although a few animagi were walking or standing around in the passageways, Sebastian had no time to talk to them for fear of losing Rigor Mortis. They all looked surprised at him as he walked past them, breathing and panting heavily as he tried with his short legs to keep up with Rigor's much longer stride. Rigor Mortis turned into a narrower passageway leading to a house. Still he had not noticed that he was being followed.

I know this corridor!, thought Sebastian. *It leads to the house where 11-year-old Josh lives and where his animago, Hagelik, was just 'awakened' a few days ago.* Hagelik had joined Sebastian's school class and had started socialising with Sebastian and Teddy.

Rigor Mortis cautiously opened a small door and disappeared through it, leaving the door open. Sebastian followed carefully and peered through the door. It led into a dark room and all he could see was the shape of a bed above the doorway. There was no sign of Rigor Mortis, so Sebastian quickly went through the door and slowly walked to the edge of the bed.

This must be Josh's bedroom!, Sebastian thought, as he saw the shelves with Josh's books – lots of Harry Potter books and also the Pullman trilogy about Lyra and 'dust' among many others – and the floor was littered with toys of different shapes and sizes.

Rigor Mortis was still nowhere to be seen so Sebastian peered over the edge of the bed. There he saw one of the most frightening sights he had ever seen: Josh was in bed sleeping while Rigor Mortis sat right next to his head, peering intently at Josh's face with his dark black penguin eyes and placing the end of his flippers gently near Josh's eyes. Rigor pulled out the glass phial he had just emptied in the secret chamber and began a slow incantation:

UMMM MARISH GRANAFF GANG GOOL
RAST HEREBDYN IMMORTIS GRATTAN
URRR MAJORIM EXORBITUS THYSSUSS
DRRAM GARR NON RETURNUM SIC

There it is again! thought Sebastian, *the same incantation Rigor used in the chamber with the portal! But why is he using this now and why is he peering so intently at Josh?*

Suddenly a giant blueish light began to appear under Josh's forehead, intensified and emerged from inside his head as a round marble-sized ball of light that floated a few centimetres above his forehead.

Oh no! realised Sebastian, *this is how he extracts the substance he used to open the portal. It is the soul of children he puts into his phial, the bastard, and this is what puts them into a coma! I have to stop him ...*, and Sebastian jumped onto the bed, ready to pounce on Rigor Mortis.

But before Sebastian reached Rigor, who was just about to shove the blue light into the phial, a dark shape suddenly came flying from one of the shelves, jumped onto Rigor Mortis' shoulders and threw him off the bed onto the floor. The still empty glass phial skidded across the floor and came to a halt in front of a toy fire engine.

"Hagelik!", shouted Sebastian, "well done! Wait, let me help you!", and he hurled himself towards Rigor who tried to wrestle Hagelik off his back. Hagelik had his paws tightly wrapped around Rigor's throat, yelling "You bastard! What have you done do my host?"

Sebastian jumped onto Rigor and tried to hold his flippers, but he was too small and weak. With a flick, Rigor threw Sebastian towards the bedside table, rolled over and started crushing Hagelik with his weight. Hagelik groaned and had to let go of Rigor's throat, panting for air. Rigor quickly got up and kicked Hagelik hard with his clawed foot. Hagelik yelled in agony.

Rigor Mortis quickly climbed up the bed again towards Josh. The blue ball of light still hovered above Josh's forehead but had begun to move back towards the skin. Rigor quickly snatched the ball of light, jumped off the bed, grabbed the glass phial lying on the floor and put the light into it.

"You two will pay for this!", shouted Rigor.

Hagelik was still lying in pain on the floor, while Sebastian was recovering from having banged his head on the bedside table. Rigor Mortis picked up a golf club lying under Josh's desk and walked towards Sebastian, his black eyes glistening angrily.

He raised the club, intent on killing Sebastian with one hit. *This is the end!* thought Sebastian, closing his eyes … when suddenly the door to Josh's room opened. Josh's father stood there in his pyjamas shouting "What in the world is going on here? What is all this noise?", while his hand searched for the light switch.

Rigor dropped the club and in a dash shot under the bed and disappeared through the door leading to the passageway.

Josh's father switched on the light. Josh was lying in bed, seemingly sleeping, the room was the usual mess with toys all over the place and Hagelik, Josh's teddy-bear, was lying motionless on the floor. There was another small teddy-bear lying on the floor which Josh's dad did not recognise, but he paid no further attention to Sebastian.

"How strange!", said Josh's dad, "I could have sworn I heard something!"

He peered around for a last time, but as all seemed quiet he switched off the light and closed the door behind him.

Sebastian waited a few seconds before asking Hagelik whether he was ok.

"Yes, I am fine", Hagelik replied. "What was Rigor doing to Josh?", he asked anxiously.

Sebastian filled him in as best he could about what had happened in the archives and how Rigor had taken Josh's soul to use for the portal.

Hagelik was aghast. He looked at Josh, his host, and began to cry. "Is there anything we can do?", he asked.

"I am afraid there is nothing we can do for Josh", said Sebastian, "and we can't risk waking him up as he is not initiated and the shock of seeing his animagi suddenly alive could be too much for him! The only thing we can do is to report this as quickly as possible to members of the council. Come quickly and we'll try to find Mrs Hexybilla!"

They had a final look at Josh who seemed to be sleeping peacefully, his chest going up and down indicating that he was breathing regularly. But Sebastian knew that Josh was either already in a coma, or would be soon once Rigor used up Josh's soul to let through the next batch of animagi to Animagana.

21

Sebastian and Hagelik quickly made their way down the passageway from Josh's house. Sebastian was very keen to talk to Hexybilla after all he had found out, and to denounce Rigor Mortis. *What a traitor!*, Sebastian thought, fuming with rage.

They turned a corner in a dimly lit corridor when they saw two individuals crouched over another one who was lying on the floor. The creature on the floor was Rigor Mortis, he looked unconscious. Stooping over him were Garglethroat's henchmen Ori Fisse the bulldog, and Skeleto the plastic skeleton. When they saw Sebastian and Hagelik, they immediately picked up the wooden clubs with which they had assailed Rigor Mortis and ran towards them.

Sebastian and Hagelik did not hesitate one moment, turned around, and started running down the passageway as fast as they could. The ground was slippery and they had to watch their step as they turned a sharp corner into another set of passageways Sebastian did not know. Hagelik could smell the foul bulldog breath of Ori Fisse behind him and thought their pursuers were getting closer.

Sebastian chose a turn to the left, then to the right, in the hope of eventually finding a passageway with other animagi who could help them. But suddenly he had to stop abruptly. The passageway in front of them was blocked … by cavity wall insulation!

"Damn cavity wall insulation!", Sebastian swore. "Hagelik, there is no way around it, we are stuck!"

Ori Fisse and Skeleto had quickly caught up with them.

"Ha, my little bears, it looks as if there is no way out from here!", shouted Ori Fisse releasing a spray of spittle from his bulldog mouth. "Come here little ones!", he teased, "and let me smash you with my club!"

Sebastian stood with his back to the cavity wall insulation material which felt smooth and foamy against his shoulders. He dived past Ori Fisse who hit the ground with his club just where Sebastian had been standing a second ago. Ori Fisse brandished his club again and hit Hagelik over the head, who collapsed on the floor.

Sebastian made the mistake of looking back towards Hagelik, which allowed Skeleto to block off his escape route. Skeleto raised his club, Sebastian tried to duck and slip through Skeleto's spindly plastic legs, but the club hit Sebastian hard on the back. He cried out in agony. A second blow hit Sebastian's head and he lost consciousness …

22

Sebastian woke up in a daze. He was in small cave, chained to the wall by his hands and feet. Hagelik was lying next to him, still unconscious.

Where am I?, wondered Sebastian, peering around him. In the corner he saw another shape chained to the wall that looked like a penguin. *Rigor Mortis!*, thought Sebastian. *I am chained in a small room with the traitor!*

"What are you looking at?", asked Rigor Mortis, and Sebastian saw that a small trail of stuffing oozed from a wound on Rigor Mortis' head. "You are the two animagi who attacked me in Josh's bedroom!", he realised. "What's your name?"

"I am Sebastian and this is Hagelik", Sebastian replied pointing towards Hagelik's still unconscious body. "I am one of your pupils at school. I sit in your 'Morals and Ethics' class", replied Sebastian, and he thought what an irony it was that the traitor was the one teaching them morals and ethics! Sebastian also saw the expensive clothes Rigor Mortis was wearing and in particular the expensive-looking watch on his wrist. *And it looks as if you also fit at least two of the deadly sins, Mr Mortis!*, Sebastian thought. *Greed and pride!*

Sebastian could no longer hide his anger. "I know all about you, Mr Mortis!", he shouted. "Not only did we try to stop you from taking Josh's soul, but I have also seen you enter the chamber with the portal to Animagana and let Barney, Penny and Woof through. You bastard!"

Rigor Mortis was flabbergasted. *There is yet another animago who seems to know all about me and Animagana, this is really the end!*, he thought with a loud sigh. "Well Sebastian, as you seem to know all about me there is no sense in hiding the truth from you! We are in Garglethroat's cave and I don't think he will let us out alive! He is after this ...", and he pulled out the phial from the pocket of his expensive coat. "Once he has this, and once he knows about the secret incantation for the Animagana portal, our lives are worth nothing! And as you also seem to know about all this, Garglethroat now has three of us to torture, so he will get what he wants in the end anyway!"

Rigor Mortis stared at the phial and suddenly looked mortified. It was empty!

"Damn, it must have spilled when these two thugs attacked me!", he shouted. "We have lost the essence of Josh's soul! This is not good as we now have nothing to bargain with!"

"So what will happen to Josh?", asked Sebastian, "will he stay in a coma?"

"Not that I care!", replied Rigor, "but the answer is no. Josh will be ok. It is only when the essence of the soul is activated at the portal in the secret chamber that it is consumed and can't return to its owner, leaving him or her in a coma. Wherever the essence of Josh's soul was spilt in the passageway, it will find its way back to him quickly. He will probably wake up with a headache, but nothing more ... Lucky boy! But I am about to meet another animago in about half an hour who has already paid me handsomely for a passage through the portal to Animagana and who will guide me to another human child where I can get his soul ... that is if Garglethroat lets me."

What a despicable character!, thought Sebastian. *He does not care at all about the pain and hardship he has caused to the kids in the village and their parents! And he is planning to snatch yet another soul from a poor kid within the next hour! All he seems to think about is himself and how to further enrich himself with the Animagana portal. Greedy bastard!*

Hagelik was stirring next to Sebastian and held his head in his paws. "My head ... my head ...!", he moaned.

Sebastian looked at Hagelik and saw that the club had left a wound on Hagelik's head where white stuffing was oozing out. Just as he was about to tend Hagelik's head, the door to the cave opened and in came the most disgusting creature Sebastian had ever seen. Garglethroat squeezed his fat toad body through the narrow entrance, leaving a trail of slime behind him and on the door. He was followed by Ori Fisse and Skeleto who both grinned maliciously at the three captives.

"Hello again, Mr Mortis!", Garglethroat said with his gargly voice. "I see you brought some company!", and he glanced viciously at Sebastian and Hagelik. "As you will have gathered, we have refused your new offer to sell us about the key to the Animagana portal. I am pretty sure we can extract the secret from you for free! You should have accepted my original one-thousand-pound offer after all!"

One thousand pounds for the key to Animagana! To Sebastian this sounded like a fortune.

"Anyway, no time to dither!", shouted Garglethroat. "Skeleto, please accompany Mr Mortis to my room and I am sure we will find a way to get the information we need. I am keen to leave this place and start a new life in Animagana! Ori

Fisse, get rid of these two!", and he pointed at Sebastian and Hagelik.

Sebastian now got really scared. Should he tell Garglethroat that he also knew about the secrets of the portal to Animagana? *But Garglethroat will kill us anyway*, thought Sebastian, *so it doesn't really matter! Such a shame to die now, just after Erik has been awakened! I think we would have had a great time together!*

Skeleto led Rigor Mortis, whose flippers were still tied together, out of the room. Ori Fisse approached Sebastian and Hagelik with a deep grin on his face. He pulled out what looked like a giant meat cleaver. Hagelik was sobbing loudly next to Sebastian. Ori Fisse stood in front of Sebastian and raised the meat cleaver above his head, he was going to split Sebastian in two. *This time this is it!*, Sebastian thought and closed his eyes. He thought he could hear the swish of the cleaver being thrust towards his head ... he kept his eyes closed expecting a terrible pain to come as his head was split in two ... but nothing happened!

Sebastian waited a few seconds then carefully opened his eyes. Ori Fisse still stood in front of him and had lowered the cleaver which was just centimetres from Sebastian's face, but Ori Fisse no longer moved. In fact, he was standing still like a statue. Hagelik had also stopped sobbing and seemed frozen in a foetal position next to Sebastian.

It has happened again! thought Sebastian. *Time has again frozen just when I was about to die!*

Sebastian remembered how quickly Benny the cat had come back to life after his first time-freeze, so he did not hesitate for a moment. As Ori Fisse was so close to him, Sebastian bent forward and, despite the chains wrapped around his hands, managed to untie the keys that dangled from Ori Fisse's belt. As Sebastian leaned forward towards the keys, he could smell the foul stench emanating from Ori Fisse's bulldog body and the smell coming out of his mouth.

Sebastian quickly opened his and Hagelik's chains. They were free! Ori Fisse was still not moving. The difficult part was to drag Hagelik's heavy and limp body along the ground towards the door which still stood open. Sebastian pulled hard, using all the power his short arms and legs could muster. He peered over his shoulder towards Ori Fisse. *It can't be long now before time starts again!*, Sebastian thought, but Ori Fisse had not moved yet.

Just as Sebastian had reached the door and dragged Hagelik's inert body halfway through the entrance, Ori Fisse began to stir, was carried forward by the thrust of his meat cleaver, and almost fell over. Ori Fisse peered around him and seemed rather confused. The chains in front of him were empty! He peered towards the door and saw Sebastian dragging Hagelik out of the doorway. He lunged towards the door.

Sebastian had just managed to drag Hagelik, who was also beginning to stir, across the doorway when he saw Ori Fisse dash towards the door. He quickly released Hagelik's paw, jumped towards the door … and closed it in Ori Fisse's face. But it was not yet locked! Ori Fisse pushed hard at the door and was clearly stronger than Sebastian.

"Hagelik! Quick! Help me close this door!", shouted Sebastian as Hagelik was now fully awake and peered totally confused around him. After a few seconds Hagelik put his weight against the door which helped to shut it. Ori Fisse still pushed hard from inside the cave, swearing loudly. While Hagelik was holding the door, Sebastian tried to work out which of the keys fit the door. He tried one, but it was the wrong one. Another one also did not fit.

"Quick Sebastian, I am not sure how much longer I can keep that door closed!", shouted Hagelik.

The third key fitted and Sebastian locked the door with a loud creak. They both slumped to the floor exhausted. Behind the door Ori Fisse could be heard banging at the wood and cursing.

"What happened, Sebastian?", asked Hagelik. "One moment I was about to be cleaved to death, the next I am outside the door with you without chains and you have Ori Fisse's key!"

Sebastian filled him in quickly and also mentioned that this had happened to him once before. "I don't know how I do it, Hagelik", said Sebastian, "but it seems every time I am in mortal danger this time-freezing kicks in. It has now saved me twice!"

They followed the passageway but did not know at all where to go as this was a part of the cave system completely unfamiliar to both. In the distance they could hear loud shouts and a terrible cry of agony. Rigor Mortis!

"Come on, Sebastian!", urged Hagelik. "Let's go the other way. We have to get out of here!"

Sebastian knew that what Hagelik suggested was the right course of action as they were still in mortal danger if Garglethroat caught them. After all, he had just ordered them killed! But his curiosity won the upper hand again.

"I just want to find out what they are doing to Rigor Mortis", he told Hagelik, "but you can wait here, and if I am not back in three minutes you make your way back to Mrs Hexybilla and you tell her the whole story! Don't forget to mention that I saw Mr Mortis taking Barney, Penny and Woof through the portal."

"Yes, but …", replied Hagelik, but Sebastian had already moved towards the passageway where the terrible sounds had come from.

Sebastian did not have to walk far. In front of him a door stood ajar, and he could clearly hear Rigor Mortis' cries of pain. He also recognised Skeleto's raspy voice and Garglethroat's dreadful gargle. A third animago was with them in the room laughing.

"I have told you the code for the archive doors, the code to enter the secret chamber in the archives, and the secret incantation you need to open the portal!", shouted Rigor Mortis in agony, "and you have written it all down! I have also told you what to do to extract a child's soul and which child would be the next most suitable for the procedure of extracting a soul! What else do you want from me?"

"Indeed!", Sebastian heard Garglethroat say, "it seems we have all the information we need boys! Kill him!"

"Please no! Sir! Please!", begged Rigor Mortis. "I still have plenty of information that will be valuable to you…Please, listen! I can tell you …"

Sebastian heard a loud swish, and Rigor Mortis abruptly stopped talking. A loud gargling sound could be heard, a final sigh, and then …silence. Rigor Mortis was dead.

Sebastian ran as fast as he could back to Hagelik.

"Phew, you're back!", shouted Hagelik, "I was just about to leave."

Together they ran along the passageway, never looking back, with the agonised cry of Mr Mortis still ringing in Sebastian's head …

23

"It only took a few minutes to extract all the information we needed!", said Garglethroat with a large smile on his face. "This guy was even more of a coward than I thought!", and he nudged Rigor Mortis' lifeless body with his slimy foot.

Together with Skeleto and Gremlin he walked over to the neighbouring cave. The door was locked and they could hear Ori Fisse shouting and cursing inside.

"What is going on here!", shouted Garglethroat. "Skeleto, open that door quickly!"

Skeleto turned the key and out came Ori Fisse, fuming with rage.

"Where are they, the little bastards!", he screamed, looking down the empty passageway.

"What do you mean Ori?", asked Garglethroat with a deep frown on his face. "Are you saying the two animagi escaped?"

"Well ... master ...boss ...emmm...yes, they escaped", admitted Ori Fisse with a very embarrassed look on his face. He did not understand what had happened. One moment he was about to kill the smaller of the bears with his meat cleaver, and the next they disappeared into thin air and his cleaver only hit air.

"You are saying that you did not manage to kill two young animagi chained in front of you???", screamed Garglethroat.

Ori Fisse looked down in shame, not daring to look up. *I am dead!*, he thought.

Garglethroat had already grabbed a large knife which he always carried on his belt and was about to kill Ori Fisse, when Skeleto held his arm saying: "Wait boss! I don't think we have time for this as the escape of the two animagi means that they probably know about our plans. Who knows? They might have even overheard us killing Rigor Mortis?"

Garglethroat was still holding up the knife, his face red and convulsed with rage. After a few seconds he admitted: "You are right, Skeleto, we now need to hurry as the portal to Animagana may not be available to us for much longer. I don't know how much the two animagi know about all this, but let's not take a chance! I'll pack our most valuable and easily transportable treasures. Thankfully I already have one valuable item on me", and he looked at his fat wrist which now sported Rigor Mortis' dashing Swiss Rolex watch.

"We also need to meet up soon with the animago Rigor Mortis mentioned who has already bought his passage to Animagana", said Skeleto. "Luckily it was also easy to extract from Rigor Mortis where they were about to meet in about half an hour!"

Ori Fisse sighed with relief that Garglethroat's attention had been deflected away from him, and looked at Skeleto with gratitude from preventing Garglethroat killing him there and then. But he was also sure that Garglethroat would not forget about his failure to kill Sebastian and Hagelik...

"You three go on and find the animago Rigor Mortis mentioned who will lead us to the next human kid ready for extraction of his soul", snarled Garglethroat. "We need this to get through the portal. Here is a copy of the incantation Rigor Mortis passed us, and here is the phial in which you need to put the essence of the kid's soul. Be careful, it no longer has a lid." He gave Skeleto, Gremlin and Ori Fisse a crumpled sheet of paper containing the information Rigor Mortis had just given them. "I'll meet you at the entrance to the archives, but be quick!"

24

Sebastian and Hagelik had rushed through the passageways as fast as they could, always fearing that they were pursued by Garglethroat's henchmen. After a while they merged into corridors that looked more familiar to them and began to make their way towards their school.

"I have to tell Hexybilla about all this immediately, even if it is very late and she is likely to be asleep", Sebastian told Hagelik. "But I think we need to move fast, as Garglethroat and his cronies are likely to make their way to the secret chamber immediately!"

"I better check on my host Josh and see whether he is ok", said Hagelik. "I'll meet you again in thirty minutes in front of the archives?"

"OK", replied Sebastian, "but hurry! We then meet in Erik's bedroom as I also want to make sure he is ok."

Sebastian made his way to Hexybilla's private cave. Like all council members with initiated human hosts – Sebastian remembered from the council meeting that Suzanne was Hexybilla's host – she did not need to be around her host like others with uninitiated hosts, and was allowed her own accommodation near the animagi school.

Sebastian knocked at her door and Hexybilla opened, looking very sleepy. Sebastian noticed that she was not wearing her crooked witch's hat and that she had a large bald patch on the top of her head.

"Sorry to disturb you so late at night, Mrs Hexybilla", said Sebastian, "but I have matters of the utmost importance to discuss with you."

Hexybilla let Sebastian in, and Sebastian recounted the dramatic events of the day, starting with him surprising Rigor Mortis in the secret chamber with Barney, Penny and Woof, him and Hagelik witnessing the extraction of Josh's soul, their imprisonment and escape from Garglethroat's cave and, most horrific of all, the murder of Rigor Mortis.

"Before he was killed", Sebastian continued, "Mr Mortis revealed that children only fall into a coma once the essence of their soul – a blueish marble-sized ball of light – has been used to open the portal. As Josh's soul essence was spilt before it could be used, we assume that he is OK. Hagelik is just checking whether Josh is fine."

Hexybilla was stunned by all the revelations. Within a day Sebastian had found all the missing information they needed. Now they knew how souls were extracted, why children fell into a coma, and how to open the portal. And they knew who the traitor was who, for money, had sold a passage to Animagana to gullible animagi customers.

"And we all trusted Mr Mortis!", she said with deep sadness in her croaky voice. "What a disaster! As Garglethroat now also has all this information we need to move fast. I am sure he and his henchmen are keen to go to Animagana as quickly as they can and to extract the soul of another kid. I have to raise the alarm and inform the other council members immediately. This will not be easy as they will all be asleep, some with uninitiated hosts staying in houses a distance from here. If only we had mobile phones like humans, we could alert everybody much more quickly, but they are no use here without reception!"

She stared Sebastian deep in the eyes. "You have done very well, Sebastian, and in the name of the council I thank you for all you have found out. Based on your second time-freeze experience, which allowed you to escape from Garglethroat's cave, I am increasingly convinced that you may be the animago the prophecy in the 'Chronicles of Animagi Lore' talks about. Remember what we read recently, but which now seems like eons ago? 'There will come a time when a young animago will recognise the power he holds to unleash the control of time': doesn't this now make sense to you? And remember that the prophecy also foretells 'the coming of this animago who will hold the key to Animagana and who will free the beings trapped within'. You now indeed hold 'the key' to Animagana, Sebastian!"

Mrs Hexybilla is right!, Sebastian thought. *It all seems to be coming together. Am I really the animago this age-old prophecy is talking about?*

"But what about the bit on 'freeing the animagi trapped within Animagana'?", asked Sebastian. "How would I achieve this if I don't go to Animagana myself, which I have no intention of doing?"

"That I don't know, Sebastian", replied Hexybilla, "but the way things have been going I am sure we will find out soon!"

Hexybilla put on her coat and hat and walked off to inform the other council members of what had just happened. "You go home Sebastian and get some sleep!", she shouted. "And make sure Erik and your animagi companions are ok!"

25

Ori Fisse, Gremlin and Skeleto quickly made their way to the meeting point where Rigor Mortis had been due to meet his next customer for the portal to Animagana. Skeleto looked at his watch. They were just on time for the meeting. They stopped just before the intersection of the passageways where the meeting was planned.

"I'll go on my own first", said Ori Fisse, "as the animago is expecting Rigor Mortis and not us. What's the name of the animago again who was due to meet Rigor?"

"In his last death throws Rigor Mortis said that his name was Bunny, Ori", replied Gremlin. "Rigor Mortis said his host is an old guy called Godfrey Wilkinson and he has a son, Erik, who is about 12 I think."

Ori Fisse moved forward alone and peered around the corner. There was Bunny, looking very nervous, sporting a small bag that Rigor Mortis had obviously told him to pack with all the things he needed for the passage to Animagana. Bunny looked at his watch when he saw Ori Fisse turning the corner.

"Are you Bunny?", asked Ori Fisse.

"Yes, and who are you?", asked Bunny.

"Rigor Mortis has been briefly held up and has sent me to meet you and to extract the human child's soul. Rigor will meet us at the archives."

Bunny stared suspiciously at the rather disgusting-looking bulldog animago who had slimy spittle dribbling from his mouth. "That's not part of the deal!", Bunny said, "I was meant to meet up with Mr Mortis!"

"Suit yourself!", said Ori, "but that's it for Animagana for you, my friend, as we have plenty of other customers who have already paid up and are ready to go", and he started walking back towards the intersection of passageways.

"Wait!", Bunny shouted. "I guess it's OK if you promise that we will meet Mr Mortis soon."

"OK", replied Ori Fisse. "Just let me get my two helpers", and he whistled loudly. Gremlin and Skeleto turned the corner and joined them.

Bunny felt increasingly nervous. *Who are these animagi and why have Mr Mortis' plans changed?*, he wondered. He was increasingly unsure about what he was doing. *Is going to Animagana really what I should do?* Bunny asked himself. *But I have already paid Mr Mortis the handsome sum of five hundred pounds, which took me years to steal in small instalments from this naïve idiot, my human host Godfrey! And although Godfrey has treated me well and has always loved me, I nonetheless always felt out of place in this so perfect household with all these bright animagi who always made me feel rather inferior!* He thought about Teddy in particular, who he had grown up with but who he liked less and less. *Pompous Teddy with all his brains and knowledge, and he always has an answer to everything! And then this little git of Sebastian came along who is equally pompous and arrogant! And I want to be free of my human host, not to die when Godfrey dies who is already pretty old after all! Animagana will offer me freedom to do what I want and to live forever!*, Bunny was thinking himself into a fury, while he observed the three animagi who crowded around him.

"Now tell us where the human kid is to get the essence of his soul!", commanded Ori Fisse.

"Why do you need to do that now?", asked Bunny. "Can't we just go to the Animagana portal Mr Mortis mentioned?"

"It doesn't work like this, mate!", Skeleto said. "No soul, no portal!"

"OK", conceded Bunny. "The kid I suggested to Mr Mortis is Erik, Godfrey Wilkinson's son."

26

Sebastian had gone back to Erik's house and had woken up Teddy, @@*^# and Ugah. Bunny was nowhere to be seen. Hagelik had joined them soon after, confirming that little Josh seemed OK and that he was still fast asleep. Sebastian had filled in Teddy and the others about what he had witnessed.

"We better look out", Teddy had immediately replied, "as these bastards will surely be after you, now that you know all their secrets!"

"Yes, I am very scared!", admitted Sebastian, "but I think Mrs Hexybilla and the council should be able to protect us from Garglethroat and his henchmen and also secure the portal to Animagana."

"I sincerely hope so!", said Teddy as they walked along the passageway to Erik's room.

They all entered Erik's room through the door near his chest of drawers. Erik was fast asleep as it was about three in the morning. They did not want to wake him up as he had to get up early for school in the morning.

The five animagi made themselves comfortable on Erik's chest of drawers where they could see each other as well as Erik, in case Garglethroat's animagi made a move tonight. But it was very dark in Erik's room, and it did not take long for Hagelik and @@*^# to fall asleep, and Ugah also started nodding off pretty quickly.

Teddy looked at them. "Let them go to sleep", he said to Sebastian, "as long as we are awake, we and Erik should be safe."

The minutes passed. Everything was silent. Sebastian thought back about the past day. He could still not erase the dreadful cries of pain of Rigor Mortis just before he died. *Nobody should witness something like this!*, he thought. *But then he brought it on himself by betraying all of us and the council. Greed and vanity won over responsibility and honour!*, Sebastian mused. *How sad!*

Sebastian felt very tired. *What a day this has been!*, he thought. *Maybe if I just close my eyes a little bit? Teddy will surely stay awake and keep watch* ... and he nodded off into sleep. Teddy, sitting next to him, was already snoring loudly…

27

Bunny led Ori Fisse, Gremlin and Skeleto into Erik's bedroom. All was dark. They could see the shape of the child in bed, breathing regularly. They could also hear a loud snore from above the chest of drawers.

Ori Fisse ventured into the centre of the bedroom and looked up. In the dark he could just make out the five shapes of Sebastian, @@*^#, Teddy, Hagelik and Ugah. All were asleep. He waved to Gremlin, Skeleto and Bunny to come forward and whispered: "All clear, they are asleep. I think it is the same two bears up there who just escaped from our cave, but I can't quite make them out in the dark. Anyway, first things first …! Bunny, you wait outside as you don't want to see this! Gremlin and Skeleto, at the sign of any movement from up there", and he pointed at the chest of drawers, "you kill!"

Ori Fisse made his way to Erik's bed, climbed up, and placed his face right next to Erik's. He pulled out the crumpled bit of paper from his pocket and switched on a tiny torchlight attached to his key ring.

I better get this right, he thought, *or Garglethroat will kill me! But under torture Rigor Mortis gave pretty clear instructions about how it's done.*

He put his bulldog paws gently against Erik's forehead and began the incantation:

UMMM MARISH GRANAFF GANG GOOL
RAST HEREBDÝN IMMORTIS GRATTAN

URRR MAJORIM EXORBITUS THYSSUSS
DRRAM GARR NON RETURNUM SIC

A blue light emerged from Erik's forehead. Ori Fisse quickly grabbed it and put it into Rigor Mortis' phial, making sure he held it upright as it had no lid. As he climbed down the bed the phial clanged against one of the metal posts of Erik's bed.

Sebastian woke up with a start. *I have been asleep!*, was his first thought. He peered around sleepily and at first could not see anything, but then he saw it: a faint blue light was moving away from the bed … and it was held by someone!

"Ori Fisse!", Sebastian shouted, "he has stolen Erik's soul! Quick wake up!"

The four others woke up with a start, but it was too late. Ori Fisse, Gremlin and Skeleto had already disappeared into the passageway. Sebastian could hear some rummaging just outside the door to the passageway.

"Quick!", he shouted, "they are blocking off the door to the passageway!"

Teddy, Ugah, Hagelik and @@*^# quickly climbed down the chest of drawers, @@*^# slipped and fell from the last drawer but was uninjured. He swore loudly. Sebastian was already at the door to the passageway, but it was blocked.

"Quick, let's go to the living room door to the passageway!", shouted Teddy, "we have to catch them before they get to the portal! Erik will be in a coma otherwise!"

They heard a stir behind them. Erik was awake!

"What is going on, guys?", Erik asked, "what's all the commotion about?"

"No time to explain, Erik!", shouted Sebastian. "Come with us if you don't want to end up in a coma!"

Erik did not understand at all but jumped out of bed immediately. He knew about the coma cases in the village and the dreadful state the kids were in, all now lying in intensive care at local hospitals. He had also known Lucy well, the latest coma victim who lived just a few houses down the road.

They rushed towards the living room, where Teddy opened the door to the passageway.

"It's gonna be a tight squeeze Erik!", Teddy warned, "but you should just fit in."

Erik squeezed through the tiny door. Thankfully he was quite slim and not too tall yet and he just fitted through the entrance. They hurried down the passageway leading away from Erik's house. Gremlin, Ori Fisse, Bunny and Skeleto already had much of a head start and were nowhere to be seen.

"We know where they are going!", said Sebastian. "To the archives, quickly!"

Erik was amazed at the intricate maze of passageways. Although Teddy had told him a lot about the animagi world since his awakening, this was the first time he was down in the passageways. They felt damp and clammy and were poorly lit. In most places he had to crouch down or even go on his knees to pass. Intersections seemed particularly tight. They squeezed through what seemed an endless labyrinth of passageways, Erik's hands and knees were already muddy and dirty. But he did not have a clue where they were going and why they were in such a hurry …

28

Erik and the five animagi arrived at the doors to the archives. They were closed. Erik looked in wonder at the two large massive wooden doors with their intricate engravings etched in gold and silver.

"They are already in there!", shouted Sebastian, "we may be too late!"

Sebastian took out the swipe card that Hexybilla had given him and opened the doors. Still no sign of Garglethroat and his henchmen! They rushed past the shelves in the front cave of the archives. Nobody was around, it was too late at night for Professor Pandanus or any of his team to be working. Hexybilla was still busy somewhere else contacting the council members across the village.

They arrived at the second set of doors. Even to Erik who was taller than the animagi these looked gigantic. Sebastian used the secret number code he had been given and the large doors slowly swivelled open. They rushed through the gap and ran towards the far-left corner of the vast hall where the Bosch painting guarded the entrance to the Animagana portal.

We will be too late! We will be too late!, agonised Sebastian. *If Garglethroat and his animagi get through the portal before we reach them Erik will fall into a coma!*

After what seemed like an eternity they were near the Bosch painting, completely out of breath. Erik could not stop marvelling at the vastness of the cave and all the ancient books and manuscripts on the shelves. But he realised too that there was no time to ask questions. He also sensed that they hurried partly because of him and that something terrible would happen if they did not catch up with Garglethroat and his henchmen.

"But what will we do if we catch Garglethroat and his gang?", asked Teddy. "They are bound to be armed and we have nothing with us?"

"I don't know", said Sebastian, "but we have to stop them at whatever cost, for Erik's sake", and he glanced at Erik who looked increasingly puzzled about what was happening.

They reached the Bosch painting. *Nobody is guarding the painting as Rigor Mortis had been the one in charge of security!*, realised Sebastian. *Nobody is there to help us ...*

The door to the portal chamber was half open. They carefully looked inside and just heard Garglethroat mumble the last sentence of the infamous incantation Sebastian had now heard all too often:

... DRRAM GARR NON RETURNUM SIC

The bluish speck of light – Erik's soul – was already visible floating in the middle of the room. Below it Garglethroat, Ori Fisse, Gremlin and Skeleto were standing, staring expectantly at the blue light. The lidless glass phial was lying discarded on the stone floor.

"But there is a fifth animago with them!", exclaimed Sebastian. "Bunny! What is he doing here?"

A swishing sound could be heard and a large tear had begun to open, just like the first time when Sebastian watched Rigor Mortis perform the incantation. Ori Fisse pulled the edges of the portal further apart so that Garglethroat's fat bulk would fit through.

"Bunny, you traitor!", shouted Sebastian, and darted forwards into the chamber.

Teddy tried to hold him back, but Sebastian already had too much momentum. He stumbled and fell to the ground.

Garglethroat had already gone through the tear, followed by Gremlin. Only Bunny and Skeleto still stood there, surprised by Sebastian's sudden appearance.

"Take this, you damn nuisance!", said Skeleto and threw a dagger at Sebastian.

Sebastian jumped out of the way and the dagger flew past him ... straight into Ugah's leg who cried out in agony.

Skeleto pushed Bunny through the tear and followed him instantly. The tear began to close ...

"Too late! We are too late!", cried Sebastian, pounding the stone floor with his fists.

"Quick, let's follow them!", shouted Teddy. "It may be the only chance to save Erik from falling into a coma."

They all watched Erik who had suddenly put his hands to his head and started crying out in agony. "My head! My head! Help me ...!", he begged.

The tear closed further ...

"But we don't know what will happen if we get through the portal with Erik", said Sebastian breathlessly. "Will Erik be OK on the other side?"

"We don't know", replied Teddy, "but if we do nothing the portal will close and we will have no further chance of getting through. Erik will fall into a coma within the next minute or so!"

Without hesitation the five animagi darted forwards towards the portal. Hagelik supported Ugah who was limping badly, while Teddy and @@*^# helped Erik who felt weaker and weaker by the second.

Sebastian meanwhile was at the portal, trying to pry the sides open a bit more for Erik to fit through. Again he could hear the faint sound of music and raucous laughter coming through the hole. He could feel resistance from the edges of the tear, a strong force that was willing the portal to close. Sebastian struggled to prevent the portal from closing further. Teddy came to his help and together they managed for a few seconds to stop the edges of the portal pulling in further.

The others pushed Erik through the portal, threw Ugah into it, and @@*^# and Hagelik also dove through. Teddy was losing his fight against the portal closing and with a rapid movement let his body fall through the portal. The tear was now only a few centimetres wide, Sebastian was still hanging on to one of its sides. In a last desperate movement he swivelled his body around and jumped through the portal.

The portal closed with a swooshing sound. The room was empty, and only their footprints could be seen on the dusty floor …

Part 2

29

Sebastian felt as if he was sucked into nothingness, a black void leading nowhere. For a while it seemed as if he was floating. Then he suddenly fell onto something soft and slimy. He had fallen onto Garglethroat!

"What the hell!", moaned Garglethroat, and threw off Sebastian with a flick of his toad arm.

"They followed us! They dared follow us!", shouted Ori Fisse.

Sebastian peered around him. They were all lying on the floor in a muddled heap of bodies. They were in a small wooden room. From a distance, music, laughter and the tingling of glasses could be heard.

"You fools!", croaked Garglethroat. "This is your death sentence! Get them!", he commanded his henchmen.

Ori Fisse and Skeleto were the first to get up. Sebastian and the others were still lying on the floor, still too stunned by the passage through the portal. Sebastian looked at Erik who was lying motionless on the floor. *Oh dear! Is Erik in a coma?*, thought Sebastian. *Has our desperate action to come through the portal failed to save him?*

A blueish glimmer was shining above Erik, increasingly congealing into a small marble-sized blue light. It hovered briefly above Erik's forehead. Ori Fisse lunged at the light, attempting to catch it in his paw, but he was too late: the light entered Erik's forehead, was briefly visible under the skin, and then disappeared into his skull. Erik opened his eyes and peered around him, wide awake.

It worked!, realised Sebastian. *It seems Erik has been saved!* But he was watching Ori Fisse and Skeleto draw daggers from their belts. *We are certainly not saved yet! How many weapons do these guys have?*, wondered Sebastian, looking at Ugah's rather nasty injury inflicted by another one of Skeleto's weapons.

Ori Fisse and Skeleto were just about to hurl themselves onto Sebastian, when the door to the room suddenly opened. They immediately hid the weapons behind their backs.

"Well, well, well…! What have we here?", said a rather obese-looking animago in the shape of a large bird with a large black and orange beak. His feathers were ruffled and he wore an apron coated with remnants of food of various unappetising colours. Worst of all, he smelled of alcohol that wafted over to Sebastian and the others in a vile smelling cloud.

"… and more visitors from the world of humans!", said the creature. "How many more are there to come? Money, money, money for us! So, the more the merrier!"

He stepped forward unsteadily and helped them onto their feet. He found it difficult to pull up Garglethroat due to the frog's excessive weight.

"Well, this one will have to get up by himself, hick!", and he roared with laughter. He shouted at the open doors: "Hey, fellas, we have more visitors from the human world! This time it's a whole crowd of eight … nine …wait… ten who've made it! Is that even a human among them?", he asked pointing at Erik who was slowly getting up.

"I can't believe it!", he continued to shout at his invisible audience behind the door. "They have even brought a human being!"

He stared at Erik for a long time with his deep penetrating eyes.

"I am Bertenwanger, but everybody here calls me 'Callisto'", he said. "I am the owner of this distinguished establishment!"

They recoiled from his foul alcoholic breath. They had never seen such a disgusting creature before!

"Where are we Mr Callisto?", asked Teddy.

"Forget the 'Mr', mate!", replied Callisto. "Here we are all very informal. Some might say too informal … Ha, ha, ha!", and he slapped his chunky bird legs while laughing.

"You are indeed in Animagana, which is, I guess, where you wanted to be? Didn't you?"

Nobody replied as they were less and less sure whether they wanted to be here.

"You are in my beautiful pub called the 'Jolly Roger', the best and liveliest establishment for miles around and, most importantly, the place where your portal seems to exit!"

A commotion could be heard outside the door, as some of Callisto's fellow animagi tried to peer inside. "A human … they brought a human …!", was a phrase uttered by several of them.

The animagi crowd looked as bad in shape as Callisto, in tattered clothes, with ruffled fur and feathers, dirty velvet skins, grotty coats, hair coated with grease, and smelly breaths.

What place is this?, wondered Sebastian. *These animagi are nothing like the ones we know from home!*

"Right! First things first!", said Callisto. "Let's relieve these gentlemen of their weapons! I thought I saw a flicker of a blade when I came in, from that bunch over there!", and he pointed at Garglethroat and his men.

Five of Callisto's stout-looking animagi sporting rather vicious-looking sabres with intricate ornaments on their grips moved forward and faced Garglethroat, Skeleto, Gremlin and Ori Fisse.

"Not so fast my dear Sir!", shouted Garglethroat. "Who gives you the right to disarm us?"

"You've got some cheek, mate!", shouted Callisto. "You are in my pub … uninvited … and I have the right to do whatever I want in here! Get their weapons!"

Garglethroat realised that they were outnumbered and gave a sign to his henchmen to give up their weapons. Sebastian breathed a sigh of relief. Several daggers were collected from Garglethroat's gang.

"And what have we here?", said Callisto, pointing at Garglethroat's Rolex watch. "You better pass this immediately to Mr Callisto, my friend!", he said menacingly.

Callisto's animagi crowded around Garglethroat, sabres raised. Garglethroat had no option but to give up the watch he had stolen from Rigor Mortis. Garglethroat looked furious and could hardly restrain his anger.

Maybe there are some things I am beginning to like about this place!, thought Sebastian, and saw that his companions also smiled.

"Look, Callisto!", said one of his men. "We have also found this in this fellow's pocket", and he pointed at Ori Fisse.

"Let me see!", said Callisto, looking at a piece of crumpled paper. "This looks like instructions about the portal from your world to ours, including a secret incantation! Now this could be worth something in the right hands, couldn't it fellows!", and he turned towards his animagi who nodded in agreement.

Garglethroat stared at Ori Fisse with murder in his eyes, but did not dare speak up in front of Callisto and the others. *Your time will come!*, thought Garglethroat with a fierce look in his dark bulgy eyes.

"OK, now that this is sorted, let's go downstairs and have a drink!", shouted Callisto leading them out of the room. "It may be your last one for a while! Ha, ha, ha…"

Oh dear! That sounds ominous!, thought Sebastian. *What have we let ourselves in for by crossing into Animagana? But at least Garglethroat and his henchmen are now disarmed and they also lost the code to the portal!*

30

Sebastian stood on the landing with Callisto and the others outside the portal room. He was peering down into the main bar area of the pub, where rough-looking animagi stood at the bar or sat at tables filled with full and empty glasses and bottles. Everybody seemed to be drinking, most looked drunk, and some were even slumped over tables after too much drink. Some stood and swayed together arm-in-arm, singing badly and loudly "Yo-ho-ho and a bottle of rum!" Some wore eye patches and sailor's caps and hats, and almost all wore sabres on their belts. Sebastian could smell the fumes of alcohol wafting towards them.

Callisto led them downstairs towards two of the few empty tables.

"I think we better go now, Mr Callisto", said Garglethroat. "Many thanks for your hospitality."

"Sit!", said Callisto with a commanding voice that did not leave room for any opposition.

They grudgingly sat down, Sebastian and his fellow animagi and Erik at one table, and Garglethroat and his henchmen at the other a few tables away. Several of Callisto's animagi, sabres at the ready, sat with them.

"Let me introduce you to one of our old salts while I get you a round of drinks", said Callisto to Sebastian's group, encouraging one of the animagi on the neighbouring table to join them. It was a very old and worn-down looking bear, with a black patch over his left eye, a wooden leg below his right knee, and a large black hat which was wider than long with a skull and crossbones picture on the front.

"Hello folks, my name is Gunpowder Jack", said the old animagi. "Are you the new batch of animagi who have just come through the portal?"

"Yes, Sir", replied Teddy. "Can you tell us where we are and what is going on here?"

"Well, you are in Callisto's Jolly Roger pub", Gunpowder Jack replied. "Hasn't he told you?"

"Yes, he has", said Sebastian, "but who are all you guys?"

"Well, little bear, I thought that's pretty obvious!", said Gunpowder Jack. "As the 'Jolly Roger' name of the pub implies, we are pirates! All of us! Jolly Roger is the name for the skull and crossbones which is our trademark", and he peered around the bar pointing at his fellow animagi.

Callisto came back with several bottles of rum and small glasses encrusted with old gunge and indescribable remnants from previous drinking sessions.

"Here folks, have a drink!", he shouted with a raucous laughter. "You'll need it!"

Sebastian had never drunk alcohol before and pushed the glass away.

"Drink!", shouted Callisto.

Sebastian carefully poured a bit of rum into his glass and put the dirty glass to his mouth closing his eyes. The liquid seemed to be on fire and burned the whole inside of his body. He glanced up with watery eyes, panting heavily and coughing.

"There is one who obviously never tasted rum before!", said Callisto and joined his fellow animagi who all laughed at Sebastian's predicament.

Teddy, Ugah, Hagelik and @@*^# also had a swig of rum and they all cringed at the taste and high alcohol content. Erik looked reluctantly at the full glass in front of him. He also had never drunk spirits before. Reluctantly he took a sip and, like Sebastian, started coughing and wheezing and his eyes started watering.

"Ha, ha, ha!", the pirates laughed, obviously enjoying the fact that their hosts were not used to alcohol.

Matters were very different on Garglethroat's table, where a second round of drinks had already been poured, and where Garglethroat and his henchmen clinked classes with Callisto's men. Only Bunny appeared very subdued, just nipping at his rum, and glancing with a worried look towards Sebastian's table. *What have I done?*, he wondered.

Having partly recovered from his first sip of rum, Sebastian peered around him. The drinking, singing and chanting at the bar seemed to have increased. At a corner table, one animago was looking the worse for wear, his face increasingly pale. He swayed from side to side and started vomiting onto the table in front of him. His body slumped forward, with his face lying in the green bile slowly dripping from edge of the table …

"Look at them!", said Gunpowder Jack, "you must think what a rotten bunch we are!", at which point he took another large swig of rum.

"I can't see any of the other animagi from our village who must have come through the portal recently", remarked Teddy. "Do you know where they are, Gunpowder Jack?"

"You mean the other lot who came through the portal up there like yourselves?", asked Gunpowder Jack, pointing at the room with the portal. "Well they've already been sold to the slave traders!"

"Slave traders?", Teddy, Sebastian and Hagelik asked in unison.

"Yes", said Gunpowder Jack. "You lot are quite valuable as slaves. It's been great for us that so many of you have come through recently ... a nice little money earner for us lately, I must say", at which point he took another even larger swig of rum.

"Now you've heard it!", said Callisto who had come back to their table. "I'm afraid that's the fate that awaits you, that's why I said that this could be your last drink for a while!"

Sebastian and his companions were stunned. *What is this place where there does not appear to be any law and order, and where animagi like ourselves are sold as slaves?*, thought Sebastian. *It just can't be!*, and tears began to well up in his eyes.

Teddy was just about to console Sebastian, when a fight broke out at the next table. Two sombre-looking pirates brushed glasses and bottles from the table with a flick of their arms and drew their sabres.

"You dare say in front of everybody that at our last raid I took more of the loot than I deserved?", said one of them, a one-eyed ferret with a large scar running down half of his face.

"Yes you did!", replied his opponent, a black bear with a large golden ring hanging from his left ear and a scarf tied around his head.

The ferret lunged at the bear, his glistening sabre held high. The bear parried what would have been a mortal blow, and thrust his blade towards the ferret's arm. The ferret jumped aside but his opponent had cut a deep wound in his arm and greyish stuffing began to hang out. The ferret stared at his arm and the bear used the brief moment of hesitation to lunge at him again, thrusting his sabre deep into the ferret's stomach. The ferret looked at the bear with eyes, wide open, grey stuffing coming out of his mouth, and sagged to the floor... dead.

The pirates, including Callisto's men, had gathered around the scene, but everything happened so quickly that nobody had had time to intervene. They all stared at the dead ferret on the floor.

"Well I guess he deserved it!", said Callisto. "You were probably right that he took more than his due share at the last raid", looking at the bear who was cleaning his sabre with one end of his scarf.

"Yeah!", replied the bear. "C'mon lads! Drinks for everyone!", and they all went back to their tables as if nothing had happened. The ferret was still lying on the floor, dead, and with eyes wide open ...

Sebastian and his companions were stunned and did not dare to move. They had just witnessed a blatant murder and nobody seemed concerned! *Our lives will really not be worth much in this place!*, thought Sebastian with fear in his eyes, and he could see that the others thought exactly the same.

Sebastian glanced over at Garglethroat's table to see how they had reacted to the murder. But Garglethroat's table was empty! Garglethroat, his henchmen and Bunny had used the turmoil to escape!

At the same moment Callisto had also realised that four of his prized slaves had disappeared. "Damn!", he shouted, "the fat frog and his lot have made a runner!", and he quickly ordered five of his men to follow them. "Don't let them escape! They are too valuable on the slave market!"

That's what we should have done!, thought Sebastian. *But it's too late now!*

Indeed, Callisto's men had surrounded Sebastian and his companions. "We better get this lot down to the hold, before any more escape", said Callisto, "but first I need a word with this one ...", and he menacingly pointed at Sebastian.

"What to do you want from him?", asked Teddy protectively.

"None of your business, my friend!", replied Callisto. "You ... come with me!", and he roughly grabbed Sebastian by the arm and dragged him towards the bar.

Sebastian glanced back at his companions with a scared look on his face. *What does he want from me?*, he wondered. They sat down at a quieter corner of the bar where Callisto grabbed another drink without offering one to Sebastian. He searched with one hand in one of the pockets of his filthy apron and took out the crumpled note with the incantation he had taken from Ori Fisse.

"I have the impression you seem to know a lot about the portal, little bear, am I right?", asked Callisto.

Sebastian felt that it was not worth beating about the bush and replied: "Yes, I guess I do."

"OK, tell me what the writing on this bit of paper says and how it is linked to the portal?", urged Callisto, putting a hand at the grip of his sabre.

Sebastian understood the subtle hint and told Callisto about the incantation and that it had to be read out both to extract a soul and to open the portal. "But I am not sure that it works that way for going back to the human world", he also conceded.

"The riddle we looked at back home clearly said that there was 'no turning back'."

Callisto scratched his stubbly head. "Is that so, is that so?", he mumbled. "Alright then! Copy this piece of paper for me and make sure there is no mistake!", and he passed Sebastian a small sheet of paper, a pot of ink and a quill.

Sebastian remembered what had happened when Hexybilla had started reading out the incantation when he felt a strange feeling in his head, as if his brain was being ripped apart and his very soul was being torn out of his head. *I will have to be very careful when handling this text! After all it seems to be cursed!*, he thought.

"Am I meant to write with this?", wondered Sebastian pointing at the quill and ink.

"That's all we have here!", shouted Callisto. "Now get on with it, and beware! I am watching you!"

He can't read or write!, Sebastian realised. *This may be our chance!*

He began to carefully copy the text from the incantation, making sure that he paused regularly so that the text did not affect his soul. *How had Rigor Mortis done it?*, he wondered, *reciting the text so many times! He must have found a way so that the incantation no longer affected him!*, thought Sebastian. At the same time he also tried to memorise the secret text. *This may be our only way back out of this place!*, he thought.

UMMM MARISH GRANAFF GANG GOOL
RAST HEREBDYN IMMORTIS GRATTAN
URRR MAJORIM EXORBITUS THYSSUSS

DRRAM GARR NON RETURNUM SIC

He peered over his shoulder and saw Callisto watching him intensely. He copied the first line, and started feeling a pain in his head. He stopped until the pain eased a bit. Then he copied the second line. The pain increased. He paused again.

"Get on with it!", urged Callisto, "we haven't got all day!"

A drunk pirate was shouting further down the bar and threw an empty glass at the barkeeper. While Callisto briefly peered towards the bar, Sebastian quickly changed the words 'majorim exorbitus' in the third line to 'majorum exyrbitus' in his copy. Callisto looked back. *He hasn't noticed!*, rejoiced Sebastian. *With these words changed the incantation will hopefully be useless to whoever tries to use it!*

When Sebastian had finished copying the paper his head was throbbing with pain. Strangely, the pain had not increased after the third line, suggesting that the changed words had already made a difference. Callisto quickly grabbed the sheet of paper, stuffed it together with the original sheet into his pocket, and took Sebastian back to his companions.

31

They were quickly escorted towards the entrance of the pub. Sebastian informed his companions that Callisto had forced him to make a copy of the secret incantation from Ori Fisse's sheet of paper. He also explained that Callisto could not read or write and how he had used a distraction to cheat Callisto by changing two of the words in the third line.

"Well done, Sebastian!", whispered Teddy, "that was smart thinking!"

As they walked, Sebastian was also desperately trying to repeat the incantation he had memorised: *umm marish granaff gang gool, rast herebdan ... or was it herebdin ... immortis grattan, urrr majorum exirbitus ... wait! That's the change I have made in the copy! What was the original ... majorem? ... majorim? ... exorbimus?... No! No! ... It's too complicated, it's slipping away!*

Sebastian looked in despair at Teddy, but Teddy was distracted by the view they had from the pub door. As they stepped outside they could not believe their eyes. The pub was located on a slope above the shore of what looked like a vast ocean which seemed to stretch endlessly into the distance. The pub was in a small clearing, there were a few outhouses but no other buildings or settlements could be seen. Dense forest surrounded the clearing with trees taller than any Teddy or Sebastian had seen before, lianas and epiphytes hanging from their thick trunks and branches. The air was moist and humid and smelled sweet and damp, and the sound of hundreds of exotic-sounding birds could be heard. The pub was on a large bay that in the distance was flanked on either side by high mountains which were covered by what looked like large glaciers. Dense forests covered the slopes right to the edge of the ice.

On the shoreline below the pub an intricate wooden pier had been built, where three wooden three-masted sailing ships were anchored. The pier was covered in piles of crates, vats, wooden barrels, ropes of different shapes and sizes, and fishing nets. Animagi bustled about, putting goods onto wooden horse carts. Cursing and shouting could be heard as one of the ships was being readied for departure, with sailors up in the masts preparing the sails, and large quantities of goods hauled on deck.

While marvelling at the view, Sebastian still kept trying to remember the incantation, but it was slipping further and further from his mind: *umm marish granagg ... granadd ... granatt ... No! It's useless, now I can't remember even remember the first line!*, he conceded angrily.

Sebastian and his companions were taken down to one of the ships that was ready to sail.

"Hello Callisto!", an old gaunt ferret-like animago with a long black beard and a tattered pirate hat greeted Callisto. "It looks like you are bringing me more slaves to sell? Your portal seems to be spitting them out like a horn of plenty regurgitates gold coins! Welcome on my ship the 'Black Falcon'."

"Hello Capt'n Blackbeard", replied Callisto. "Yes, I hope that these ones will fetch even more than we got for the last bunch! Look what we have here", and he pushed Erik forward towards Blackbeard.

"My, my ... a human!", the captain replied. "It's been a while since I've seen one of those, I must admit! And what a good-looking young specimen he is! He will fetch handsomely at the market, I can guarantee that."

Erik felt very scared and recoiled from Blackbeard's touch.

"Don't touch him!", shouted Sebastian, and pushed himself in front of Erik.

"Oooh, a feisty little one ...!", shouted Blackbeard. "I will teach you to pay your captain more respect!", and he raised his sabre towards Sebastian.

"Hold on, Blackbeard!", intervened Callisto. "You don't want to damage our goods, do you? They are worth nothing dead!"

Blackbeard grudgingly lowered his sabre and looked at Ugah's injured leg. "What about this one, is he worth anything with that injury?"

"I can still walk, Sir!", replied Ugah quickly. "It has already started healing."

"Get them into the hold!", shouted Blackbeard to two of his heavily armed sailors. "And you lot be ready to set sail, we are leaving!"

Sebastian and his companions were led away.

"I have one more thing for you to sell, Blackbeard", said Callisto, and he took out the new sheet of paper with Sebastian's copied version of the incantation. "I have extracted the information about how to use this from one of our captives. This is the secret incantation one needs to open the portal. It has to be read aloud when stealing a soul and when opening the portal. I have the original I confiscated from the animagi when they arrived through the portal, and you try to sell this one to the highest bidder at the slave market. Whichever human is interested in crossing back into the human world will need knowledge of this incantation. I trust that you will extract the best possible price for this, but keep the knowledge of how to use it for yourself until you sell! You can see that if this information gets into the wrong hands it could be a disaster!"

Blackbeard grabbed the sheet of paper and put it into his coat pocket.

"Don't worry, Callisto!", he replied, "I'll get you a good price as usual. Set sails!", he shouted to his crew, "we're off!"

32

"I have never seen a mess like this one!", shouted the paramedic. The woman was lying in a pool of blood, her throat slit. A large kitchen knife lay next to her. Detective Ralph Roberts looked at the 16-year old boy sitting at the edge of the pool of blood, his hands around his knees, one hand still holding the phone with which he had just rung 999. Andrew had buried his head in his knees and did not dare look up. He was shaking all over and sobbing.

"Why did you kill her?", Detective Roberts asked with a disgusted look on his face. "She was your mother!"

"They all hate me!", replied Andrew. "My mum was the worst of them all! She wanted me dead ... dead ... dead! The voice told me to kill her by slitting her throat."

"Which voice?", Roberts peered around at his men with a questioning look.

"The voice in my head. It keeps telling me what to do."

"And you always do what the voice tells you to do?", asked Roberts.

"Yes, always! The voice has always been right!"

Andrew looked into the corridor leading to the kitchen. A shape with a blue back and red front could be seen rushing from one room to another, but only Andrew had seen it.

"You will have to come with us, son!", said Detective Roberts. "We will take you to the police office first for questioning. A psychiatrist will also be present and ask you questions. You have the right to remain silent, but it may be good if you could give us the name of your family lawyer."

"A lawyer …?", Andrew asked with a frown, looking up for the first time. "We can't afford a lawyer! Look at the dump of a house we live in, we can't even afford decent accommodation since my dad left us three years ago!"

Detective Roberts had been briefed on the way to the crime scene. He knew that Andrew was living alone with his mother and that his dad had left them because he could no longer cope with the violent outbursts of his son and with his wife constantly trying to cover up for Andrew. *Social services had their eyes on this family for a while*, Roberts thought, *but they obviously underestimated the situation. Now look at the mess! As Andrew is 16 now I suspect that he will never be released from wherever the institutions will put him. Looking at this, I hope they lock him up for good!*

One of the police constables lifted Andrew off the floor and handcuffed him. His mother's blood was dripping from his backside and elbows. When they escorted him out towards the waiting police van Andrew glanced back at his mother's body with a face showing deepest sorrow.

33

Sebastian and the others were thrown into a dark and damp cabin with a low ceiling, located somewhere in the hold of the ship. The heavy wooden door closed behind them with a loud clank as the door was locked. It took them a few seconds to adjust to the dim light that came from a single candle in one of the corners of the cabin. Suddenly they heard a moan.

"Is there anyone there?", asked a barely audible and hoarse voice.

Sebastian and the others stared at the darkest corner of the cabin where they saw a pile of rags lying on the floor. *But the rags are moving!*, thought Sebastian, *it's a human!*

Not knowing what to expect, they cautiously moved towards the creature lying on the floor. It was a very old-looking man dressed in dirty and torn rags and chained with hands and feet to the wall. The man was blind as both his eyes had been gouged out and only empty sockets were visible.

"Who is there?", the man asked.

"We are animagi who have been imprisoned here with you", said Teddy. "Who are you?"

"My name is Brother Arnulfus", said the man with a barely audible voice. "I have been imprisoned here for a long time, sometimes I think that Captain Blackbeard has forgotten about me!"

"Why are you locked up, Brother Arnulfus?", asked Sebastian.

"Because I have tried to escape when they were going to sell me at the slave market", replied Arnulfus. "After my third attempt they gouged out my eyes as a punishment."

"This again confirms what a cruel place Animagana is!", said Teddy with anger in his voice.

"No, not the whole of Animagana", replied Arnulfus. "There are some communities that are actually quite reasonable and where law and order does exist!"

"We are relieved to hear that", replied Teddy, "as our first impression of Animagana is not a very good one!"

"Yes", interjected Sebastian, "we have just witnessed a murder in the Jolly Roger pub!"

"That does not surprise me!", said Arnulfus, "The Jolly Roger is one of the vilest places in the whole of Animagana."

They felt a sudden jolt and the cabin started swaying from side to side.

"I think the Black Falcon has just set sail", remarked Teddy.

"Sit down my dears and tell me your names", said Arnulfus. "I think we have plenty of time for a yarn until we reach the slave market, our destination."

They introduced themselves and also mentioned that Erik was with them, a human child.

"A human!", Arnulfus replied with sadness in his voice. "My oh my! The poor child!"

Erik took a deep breath. Everybody they met seemed to pity him for being there. *That doesn't sound good at all!*, he thought.

As Arnulfus appeared trustworthy enough they told him how they had arrived in Animagana and what had happened at the Jolly Roger pub. Arnulfus listened intently and threw up his arms in sadness. "I bet you expected something different than this dreadful place, even, as you said, you didn't come here voluntarily!"

"Yes", said Sebastian. "All the books we looked at in the ancient archives seemed to portray Animagana as some kind of wonderland, almost like a paradise."

"Well", replied Arnulfus, "that's what we all thought when we decided to come here, as indeed all animagi and humans you will meet here at one point came here voluntarily, expecting to find some kind of paradise."

"But what has attracted humans and animagi to Animagana in the first place?", asked @@*^# who had been rather quiet so far.

"I guess it's different motivations for humans and for animagi", replied Arnulfus who seemed quite pleased about all the questions and the distraction they were providing. "Let's start with animagi. You will know that in Animagana animagi lose the direct connection to their human host, which is the main reason most animagi have come here. In the human world, when their hosts died they died, which didn't seem right at all."

Brother Arnulfus paused briefly, allowing Sebastian and his companions to digest the information he was passing them. The ship started swaying a bit more from side to side, suggesting that they were now sailing in the open sea.

"But for humans coming to Animagana like myself the motivations have been different", Arnulfus continued. "For most of us it meant escaping from something or someone. But humans have not fared well here, as we were always in a minority. Nonetheless, as for animagi, the result of coming here for us humans has been immortality, and for some this provided enough reason to come here. In other words, we never grow old!

Old people like myself were old when we arrived here, I have not aged one day since arriving here!"

"So how old are you?", asked Hagelik.

"I am 477 years old!", replied Arnulfus.

Sebastian and his companions were stunned.

"477 years! But that's impossible!", exclaimed Teddy.

"… and I am not the oldest by far although I am older than most", continued Arnulfus. "The pirate animagi you have encountered, for example, are all a bit younger than me and came over to Animagana as one group in 1687, when the English pirate captain of their ship was about to be caught by the French. From what I heard, they had a portal to Animagana on their ship and they also must have had some knowledge about the secret incantation needed to extract souls and open the portal. They ransacked one of the Spanish settlements in the Caribbean, kidnapped all the children they could lay their hands on, and sacrificed them for their souls to come here. I am not sure whether human pirates also came over with them, but legend has it that their ship was found years later, a ghost ship with tattered sails and covered with children's skeletons. Obviously the children had all fallen into a coma after their souls were taken and died soon after, as nobody was looking after them!"

"So what about yourself, Brother Arnulfus?", asked Sebastian. "What made you come here?"

"Well, Sebastian", replied Arnulfus. "Mine is one of the saddest stories of all. I came here from England in 1537. Does anyone want to venture a guess as to why this was an important year in English history?", he asked in a schoolmasterly voice.

"1537 ... 1537...", mused Teddy. "Yes, I know. Could it be linked to Henry VIII's reign and the dissolution of the monasteries?"

"You are right, Teddy", replied Arnulfus. "I was a monk in the Monastery of Glastonbury in south-west England when it was dissolved in 1537 by Henry VIII, hence my title of 'brother'. But what a tragedy this was! You may know that monasteries during the Middle Ages and even into the 16th century were the repositories of most animagi and human knowledge."

Sebastian remembered what Hexybilla had said about where most of the old parchments, manuscripts and books had come from that were located in the archives in the village: from the dissolution of the monasteries!

"Most of the books stayed in the human world and were saved by being placed in vast archives, maybe like the one you mentioned earlier in your village", continued Arnulfus. "But some books, including their monk owners and their animagi made their way to here, just before their monasteries were destroyed by Henry VIII's men. The saddest part is that we willingly sacrificed young apprentice monks, mere children aged between 10 and 14 years, to extract their souls! Can you believe that! None of us is proud of that, but as you will know Christian history is full of such horrific deeds!", at which point he sighed deeply and crossed himself looking at the ceiling with his empty eye sockets.

"The result was one of the largest exoduses of humans and animagi to Animagana, possibly in their thousands! Over the ages a few more humans made it to here, depending on whether they could get hold of the sacred incantation and knew the location of a portal. However, the fate of most humans on

Animagana has been a very sad one indeed, and I feel sorry for Erik who is with you!", he said with sadness in his voice.

"So you know the secret incantation needed to extract souls and open the portal!", said Sebastian hopefully.

"My dear bear!", replied Arnulfus, "that was 477 years ago! I can barely remember what happened yesterday, let alone a weird incantation in a language none of us knew or understood!"

Sebastian's shoulders slumped down in despair. *Here goes my last hope for remembering the incantation!*, he thought. *We will never get back to our world!*

"So, anyway", continued Arnulfus, "we all hoped for a better immortal life by coming here. For us monks it was the hope to be able to recreate our monastic life away from the clutches of King Henry VIII and his henchman Thomas Cromwell, while for the pirate animagi it was to be a new life without their human hosts and without the English man-o-wars breathing down their necks. But look at what society we have created! As you have seen in the Jolly Roger, the pirate animagi have become, or maybe just continued to be, a bunch of good-for-nothings, without law, order, morals and anything to live for. The only thing they seem to be interested in is drinking and pillaging nearby communities! Our monastic communities, led by both humans and animagi, have fared slightly better, but many have also disappeared over the ages. So while we never age, many of us, humans and animagi, have nonetheless died, killed by each other just as that poor animago you saw killed at the Jolly Roger earlier! Several have committed suicide. As for humans on Animagana, while we human monks were in our thousands when we arrived here with much hope between 1536 and 1541, we are now just maybe 250 or so who are left. Of the many animagi pirates who came here, the death toll has even been more severe, with just about 50 left now, most of which you saw at the Jolly Roger drinking themselves into oblivion!"

He paused and glanced gloomily at the floor with his empty eye sockets.

"On top of this", he continued, "nobody seems to be able to procreate on Animagana, nobody ever had children, not even the animals and the beasts of the forest! This place is dead and sterile! And don't ask me how the forest beasts got here, because some are very large and dangerous and could not possible fit through one of the portals!"

This place is truly dreadful!, thought Sebastian. *Why would anyone volunteer to come here?*

"As you will have guessed", Arnulfus continued, "many animagi and humans were very disappointed about Animagana as it was not at all the paradise they had hoped for. In the absence of law and order, many communities rapidly started fighting each other for the meagre resources that could be found. Indeed, many communities were obliterated soon after they had been established. In the end, only the most ruthless and vicious animagi and humans survived, maybe with a few exceptions of very remote communities that managed to cut themselves off from the rest, or that tried to live by monastic or other virtues. As a result, many wanted to go back to the human world as quickly as they could. But for the ones who had knowledge of the secret incantation and who knew where portals were located, the only way to do this was to find human children whose souls could be extracted!"

Sebastian remembered Professor Pandanus mentioning that the extraction of souls only seemed to work with children whose souls were still being 'formed', mainly with children younger than 14 or 15 when children's adult consciousness started to develop.

"The unfortunate outcome has been the killing of almost all human children who had made it to Animagana", continued Arnulfus with deep sadness in his voice, "and you can imagine that at certain periods there was a veritable spree of child slaughter! Children were just kept like cattle, ready for the slaughter! As you know they were not killed outright, but their souls were taken, the animagi and humans who wanted to return fled back to the human world, and the children here were left in a coma, never to awake. Although I hear that several comatose children are meant to still exist in Animagana, most were simply killed after it became evident that the animagi who had used their souls were not coming back. As far as I know, the last large exodus of animagi from Animagana, using human children's souls, was over one hundred years ago. I think there has not been one single escape from Animagana since, as there are basically no human children left whose souls would offer an escape route back to the human world. In addition, even if some of the animagi who have been here for a long time were to go back to the human world, I am sure they would die instantly as their human hosts back in the human world will have been long dead! So most of us are pretty much stuck here, immortal but with no children of our own and in most cases, nothing to live for."

Sebastian and the others sat there in stunned silence. The story of Animagana was even worse than they had thought.

Erik started sobbing. "I am dead...dead...dead!", he said, realising the inevitable fate that awaited him and holding his head in his hands. Teddy and Sebastian went over to console him, but they knew there was nothing they could say. *Erik is in terrible danger*, thought Sebastian, *we must do everything to protect him! He might be the only living child in the whole of Animagana at present!*

"Is there anything we can do to protect Erik from being sacrificed for his soul?", asked Sebastian.

"I'm afraid not", replied Arnulfus. "As you can gather from my account, he will fetch a very high price at the slave market, and I fear that someone will try and extract his soul as quickly as possible as there are plenty of humans who would like to go back to the human world and possibly some of the recent animagi arrivals whose hosts might still be alive back in the human world. Whether they would survive the transfer back to your world after such a long time is anyone's guess, but for Erik there is nothing you can do at the moment!"

"Can't you use your time-freeze trick, Sebastian, to get us out of here?", asked Hagelik who was the only one to have witnessed Sebastian's secret power when they were imprisoned in Garglethroat's cave.

"I'm afraid it doesn't work like that, Hagelik!", replied Sebastian. "I only seem to be able to do it when I am in mortal danger, and I can't control it at all. I can't just will it to happen, that doesn't work! And even if I could do it here and now, what good would it do if we haven't got access to a guard with keys?"

The ship was suddenly swaying harder from side to side.

"The seas are getting stormier it seems", remarked Arnulfus.

"Maybe we should all lie down and get some rest", suggested Teddy, as they were exhausted after Arnulfus' story of Animagana.

Sebastian suddenly realised how tired he was after everything they had gone through the last few days. He lay down in one corner of the cabin and closed his eyes. Although his mind was spinning at the thought of the two murders he had witnessed, and at the thought of travelling through the portal to the dreadful place Animagana appeared to be, he immediately fell asleep.

34

Hexybilla had convened an urgent meeting of the animagi council. They were sitting in one of the meeting rooms at the animagi school.

"Thanks for making it at such short notice", she said, greeting all the council members, "and thanks to Professor Pandanus for joining us again. As you know we could not react quickly enough to the dreadful news Sebastian had brought us after his imprisonment in Garglethroat's cave. I tried to contact you as quickly as I could, but we were already too late to protect the entry to the secret cave with the portal. Erik has been kidnapped, his soul probably extracted and he has possibly been killed. In addition our most important animagi who knew all about the portal, especially Teddy and Sebastian, have disappeared, together with Bunny, @@*^# and Ugah, and our newly 'awoken' fellow animago Hagelik. I suspect it is not a coincidence that, with the exception of Hagelik, all of these have come from the Wilkinson household."

"What do you think happened to them?", asked Suzanne, the only human on the council.

"We don't know, Suzanne, we don't know", replied Hexybilla. "We can't tell whether they used the portal at all, whether they are hidden somewhere, or whether Garglethroat has captured them."

"What is the latest on Garglethroat and his men?", asked Mr Wood, sitting stiffly and uncomfortably in his chair.

"We have found his lair deep in the recesses of our cave system", replied Hexybilla, "but it was empty! So we don't know what happened to them and whether their disappearance is in any ways linked to that of the others."

"What about the body you found?", asked Professor Pandanus.

The room was silent for a moment as the council members pondered the recent news that a body had been found in one of Garglethroat's caves.

"I can confirm that we have found the body of Mr Mortis", replied Hexybilla morosely. "He had been savagely tortured before he was killed, just as Sebastian had reported to me. Sadly we also know that Mr Mortis was the traitor in our midst, the one who secretly investigated how the portal worked and who sold entrance to Animagana to gullible fellow animagi for money. In the end, he was a truly despicable character who betrayed our trust and maybe he deserved the fate that in the end awaited him!"

The council members nodded in agreement.

"But I have at least one bit of good news!", exclaimed Hexybilla. "Sebastian informed me that Mr Mortis said that children whose souls have been taken only fall into a coma when the essence of their soul has been used to open the portal. In the case of 11-year-old Josh, Hagelik's human host, his soul had not been used as Rigor Mortis had 'lost' it from his phial. I am very pleased to report that it appears that Josh's soul did somehow find its way back to its owner, and, as a result, Josh woke up the next morning as if nothing had happened. He was very sad, though, to realise that Hagelik had gone!"

The council members breathed a sigh of relief.

"As we don't know whether Garglethroat is still somewhere here and whether he has aspirations to use the portal, I have ordered the portal to be guarded by at least three trusty animagi day and night. What we still can't control, though, is further harm to human children in the village. At least we know that there have been no further cases of children falling into a coma in the past few days. Maybe these dreadful events have now come to an end!"

"If Erik, Sebastian and all the others have gone through the portal, Mrs Hexybilla, is there any way we can communicate with them or even help them come back?", asked Mrs Moluk, the council chair.

"Let me answer this one if I may", interjected Professor Pandanus. "Myself and my team are doing our utmost to find more information about Animagana and how the portal works. Thanks largely to Teddy's and Sebastian's help, we now know the incantation and how to use it, but unfortunately the crucial page about Animagana had been ripped out from the 'Chronicles of Animagi Lore' by Mr Mortis and we still have not been able to find it, although we searched his room from top to bottom. As we speak, my team are analysing further manuscripts and parchments in the archives to see whether there is any more information on Animagana and how to come back from it. But it may take time to find that information, and whether we can relay this to our friends who might have crossed over into Animagana I can't say at this stage."

"Thanks you very much, Professor Pandanus, for that update", said Hexybilla. "Unless there any further questions I hereby close the meeting. We will report back as soon as we know more about our vanished companions."

35

Garglethroat, Ori Fisse, Skeleto, Gremlin and Bunny had dashed out of the pub as quickly as they could when the brawl started. Luckily everybody was so distracted that they had a good head start before they saw the doors to the pub opening behind them and five of Callisto's men running in their pursuit.

Like Sebastian and his companions, Garglethroat and his henchmen were stunned at the scenery that greeted them. They had never seen such wide-open spaces in their lives, but they did not have much time to stand and stare at the wide vista in front of them.

"Quick to the forest!", croaked Garglethroat and they climbed the steep slope above the pub to the nearest trees. Garglethroat was struggling, as his severe obesity meant that he was not very fit. After a short while he was sweating profusely and panted as they scrambled up the slope. Callisto's five animagi were catching up quickly.

Garglethroat and his group made it into the forest. The trees were gigantic, taller than any trees in the human world, with thick lianas and epiphytes hanging from the massive trunks. The undergrowth was very thick and comprised of tree ferns, large succulent plants that looked carnivorous with remnants of fat insects swimming in slimy pools in their luscious petals, and giant mushrooms that towered over their heads. Garglethroat had difficulty making his way through the dense growth and got stuck several times. Ori Fisse and Skeleto pushed and pulled him as fast as they could, but they heard Callisto's men approaching fast.

"They're catching up, boss!", said Gremlin with a worried look over his shoulder. "And we have no weapons…"

Garglethroat groaned. He could not keep up that pace for much longer, and he knew that without weapons they would not stand a chance against Callisto's severely armed men. They reached a clearing and Garglethroat sat on a rotten log, completely out of breath. Callisto's five animagi burst out into the clearing, sabres raised.

"Give up! You haven't got a chance against us!", shouted the one in front, a tall lanky rabbit with an eye patch over his right eye.

Garglethroat was just about to admit defeat and be led back to the pub when they heard a rustle behind them. A group of about ten animagi burst into the clearing, heavily armed and looking even more ragged than Callisto's men.

"Stand back Callisto's men!", the animago at the front of the group shouted. "These animagi are ours!" and he pointed at Garglethroat and his companions.

Callisto's men looked worried as they were clearly outnumbered.

"For now you win, Mephisto!", shouted one of Callisto's men, unsheathing his sabre, "but Callisto will not be pleased that you have deprived him of the money these animagi will be worth at the slave market!"

"I don't care about Callisto!", shouted Mephisto. "Now get away from here before we kill you all!", at which point Mephisto's men brandished their sabres and started shouting.

"And you lot", he said pointing at Garglethroat and his companions, "come with us! Tie them together and give the fat toad a hand as he looks exhausted already!", he ordered one of his men as they moved off deeper into the forest.

"Who are you?", asked Garglethroat.

"We are slave traders on our way to the slave market at Raupenburg", replied Mephisto.

Here, join the other ones who are for sale!", and he pushed them towards a sorry-looking bunch of five bedraggled animagi in chains guarded by another five of Mephisto's men. "You are a nice addition to our batch of slaves to sell, ha, ha, ha! But you better be good walkers, as it's a seven-day hike!"

I am in a real pickle here, thought Garglethroat. It was not the first time he began thinking about going back to the human world with whatever means possible. He already hated this place! With all the turmoil, he had not thought once about Andrew since coming to Animagana, but for the first time for a long while he missed the mental communication with Andrew Billings. *Andrew can you hear me ...Andrew?*, he thought … but there was no reply.

36

The Black Falcon had sailed through a severe storm, with the ship swaying dangerously from side to side in the gigantic seas, and Blackbeard had to reduce sail to a minimum storm rig. Standing in the driving rain behind the helm, Blackbeard swore as the storm was losing them valuable time. *I hope we make it on time to the slave market at Raupenburg!*, he thought. *I know that we can make a fortune, especially by selling the blond human boy!*

After a day and a half the storm had finally abated and the settlement of Raupenburg, located on a small sheltered cove at the foot of one of the gigantic mountains guarding the entrance to the large bay, came into view.

"We've just made it in time! We will be arriving in half an hour!", shouted Blackbeard to his crew. "Get the prisoners on deck and make them look good! I want them to look spick and spam for the slave auction!"

Sebastian and his companions were dragged on deck, but the crew had left Arnulfus chained in the hold. It took Sebastian a while to adjust to the glaring daylight after several days in the near darkness in the hold. He held his paw above his eyes to screen out the sun and peered towards the coast. A settlement came into sight, comprised of a few shabby-looking huts perched on a steep slope with a muddy road leading in and out. A central square was visible, teeming with people. Several wooden platforms were visible in its centre crammed with what looked like chained up animagi.

The Black Falcon hat hastily docked at one of the few available spaces along a semi-derelict wooden pier.

"Quick! Quick!", shouted Blackbeard. "Get them to the square; they might have already started the slave auction!"

Sebastian and his companions were quickly pushed ashore, guarded by five sturdy and heavily armed crew members and followed by Blackbeard. They rapidly made their way up the steep slope on a muddy road which was deeply rutted by hundreds of footprints and cartwheel tracks. Sebastian's feet got stuck repeatedly in the mud, in places he sank in to his knees. *This is not just mud!*, Sebastian realised. *The road is also covered in turds and puddles of piss! We are walking through the local toilet!*

Teddy, Ugah, @@*^#, Hagelik and Erik had also realised what they were walking through, and they all put their hands in front of their noses to protect themselves from the pungent stench emanating from the excrement they waded through.

A group of female animagi dolls stood at the side of the road, scantily dressed in pink dresses and wearing a large amount of rather shrill make-up. "Well, hello boys!", said one with a teasing and luscious voice looking at one of the ship's crew. "You want to have some fun?", at which point she slightly raised her dress showing a rather fleshy and not very inviting upper leg.

"I would, love, if I had time!", replied the crewmember glancing at Blackbeard behind him, "but we have to take this bunch to the slave auction. Maybe later!"

The dolls laughed and flicked their eyes at the other sailors, hoping for business after they had delivered their prisoners.

"Who were they?", Sebastian asked Teddy. "I have never seen animagi behave like this before!"

"You don't want to know, Sebastian, you don't want to know!", replied Teddy and looked mysteriously at Sebastian.

I still have so much to learn!, thought Sebastian again, as Blackbeard's sailors pushed them further up the road.

They reached the main square where their guards had to carve a passage through the standing crowds to reach the wooden platforms in the middle. As Sebastian had suspected, the platforms were full of chained-up tattered and tired-looking animagi, most of whom were covered in rags, and none looked respectable. Guards with whips stood at the corners of each platform, herding the prisoners closer together to make room for the last arrivals. Blackbeard and his men found one last empty patch on one of the platforms and chained Sebastian and his companions to the nearest post.

Erik was put in front of the group and peered around him with a scared look on his face. He towered over most of the other prisoners who were all animagi of different shapes, sizes and ages. *No other human is being auctioned, I am the only one!*, he thought with dismay.

It took a little while for the last prisoners to be tied up and crammed onto the last empty spaces on the platforms. There was a lot of shoving, pushing and swearing, both from the prisoners themselves and the guards. Whips were cracked repeatedly, forcing the prisoners to huddle together ever more tightly.

The audience was comprised entirely of animagi who all looked rough and ready to start bidding at the slave auction, but Sebastian also spotted three animagi standing on the edge of the square who looked and behaved differently. They wore tattered robes similar to the ones Arnulfus had been wearing. One was a large brown bear with a big nose and large round brown eyes. He seemed to be staring straight at Erik and said something to his neighbour.

"I wonder who these are?", said Sebastian to Teddy, pointing at the three.

"They look like animagi monks to me …", replied Teddy and glanced nervously to one of the guards with a whip who looked menacingly at them with a finger over his mouth telling them to be quiet.

I hope the monks will buy all our group!, thought Sebastian, *as the other lot look terribly threatening to me!*

A large bull-shaped animago with a long sabre encrusted with what looked like precious stones stood up on top of a tall barrel. "Welcome to Raupenburg and this month's slave auction!", he shouted with a loud booming voice. "Most of you know the rules, but for those who don't, here they are: the killing of prisoners is forbidden during the auction. Once you have purchased your slaves you can do whatever you like with them!" Laughter erupted among the crowd. "You can buy as many slaves as you want and you can bid as often as you want", continued the bull-shaped animago. "The only currency we accept is silver and gold coins as usual, but I remind you that no pigs or cattle are accepted as payment!" Again the crowd laughed out loud. "We will start with Platform One."

Platform One was the one next to where Sebastian and his companions stood. It was covered in a mixture of animagi, some young, some old, some looking in better shape than others. Three animagi on Platform One standing just opposite Sebastian stood out, and Sebastian saw that they stared intensely at him and his companions. They appeared younger and fresher than the other animagi and somehow looked familiar to Sebastian. One was a small yellowish teddy-bear, the other a doll with silky white hair, and the third was a little brown dog who looked particularly forlorn.

One is my friend Barney from school!, realised Sebastian, *and the others must be Penny and Woof! They are all Lucy's animagi!*

Sebastian nudged Teddy and pointed at the three animagi. Teddy turned his head and could not hide his surprise recognising them. "Oh dear!", he whispered. "The three most recent animagi to disappear from our village! The young girl Lucy is their human host who was the latest to fall into a coma!"

Sebastian waved his paw slightly to show to Barney, Penny and Woof that he had seen them. They seemed absolutely terrified. *I bet they didn't imagine Animagana to be like this when they decided to come here with the help of Mr Mortis!*, thought Sebastian. *The traitors! Because of them their host Lucy is in a coma!* But he still somehow felt sorry for them.

The auction on Platform One began and trade was brisk. Potential buyers had looked around the group of animagi on the platform, some had inspected them close up by feeling their arms, gaping into their mouths and checking whether they had any signs of disease. They had done the same on Sebastian's platform and on Platform Three. Pundits bid for either one or several animagi, and some of the younger and healthier-looking ones seemed to invite bidding wars between several pundits. The most expensive one on Platform One, a large gorilla-shaped animago, fetched one gold and two silver coins, paid by a sturdy-looking older animago who looked like a farmer. Barney,

Penny and Woof were bought by a female monkey-shaped animago for two silver coins.

All prisoners who had been sold off were whisked off the platform quickly and taken away by their new masters. Barney, Penny and Woof stared at Sebastian with despair in their eyes. *Will I ever see them again?*, wondered Sebastian.

The animagi monks standing at the edge of the crowd had not moved, nor had they bid for any of the prisoners.

The sale on Platform Three, to the right of Sebastian's platform, proceeded along similar lines. This time the most expensive sale was for three slightly worn-out Victorian dolls who looked like the female animagi who had greeted them on the muddy road and who fetched two gold coins. The buyer was a seedy-looking stoat-shaped animago who rubbed his hands and salivated heavily after he had won the bidding.

"And now to our most prized asset for sale today!", shouted the bull-shaped animago on the barrel who was orchestrating the auction. He pointed at Erik. "A human child sold by Captain Blackbeard on behalf of Callisto, the owner of the Jolly Roger pub we all know so well! Needless to remind you that we haven't had a human child for auction for a while and how valuable they are for reasons you all know!"

Erik, who had been standing at the edge of the platform visible to all, took a few steps back and grabbed Teddy's paw. He was stoically supressing tears, but could not hide his fear.

"Callisto has put a minimum of ten gold coins on this one!", continued the auction master. "Who wants to make a first bid?", he asked peering around the audience who had begun to crowd around the platform, all peering at Erik.

"Ten gold coins!", shouted a sturdy-looking bear at the back of the crowd.

"Eleven!", came the immediate reply from the other side of the audience.

"Thirteen!", shouted a small weasel-shaped animago who could barely be seen.

"Fifteen!", cried one pushing his way to the platform.

There was a brief silence as other pundits looked at their purses and counted their coins.

"Twenty!", shouted a large lemur-shaped animago with lanky arms and legs who stood right next to Erik.

"Twenty gold coins!", shouted several in the audience. "We haven't seen a price like this for quite a while!"

The lemur peered around with a confident look on his face. The crowd remained silent. Erik looked terrified at Teddy.

"Forty gold coins!", came a shout from one of the huts with a balcony fringing the square.

The crowd looked up and saw a large lion-shaped animago wearing a black hat and a purple robe that looked like silk. A large golden sabre hung from his belt, thick gold rings adorned the digits on his right paw.

"Leonidas!", shouted the lemur. "You outbid me again! I'll get you next time!", and he walked away with a furious look on his face.

"Forty gold coins for the blond human child, forty gold coins!", shouted the bull-shaped animago on the barrel. "Do I hear more than forty gold coins?"

The crowd was silent. Evidently this was a very large sum of money.

"Nobody can afford to outbid forty gold coins!", shouted the sturdy bear who had opened the bidding. "The boy is yours, Leonidas!", and the rest of the audience acquiesced.

"Don't let him take me away, please!", begged Erik looking at Teddy and Sebastian. "You know what will happen to me! They will take my soul and leave me in a coma! Help me!"

"I will try my best", replied Teddy calmly.

Leonidas had made his way down from the balcony, followed by a retinue of what looked like servants. *He must be very wealthy!*, thought Sebastian. *You wonder how he has made his fortune in such a wretched place!*

Leonidas approached the platform and looked at Erik. "A fine-looking specimen you are!", he said, "well worth the expense! Men, chain him up and put him in my cart!"

Teddy pushed his way forward to the edge of the cart and stared Leonidas straight in the eyes. "Sir!", he said, "we are Erik's companions, and it would greatly help Erik if we came with him! He is very distraught!"

"Very distraught!", laughed Leonidas inviting his servants to laugh with him. "I bet he is, as he probably knows how rare and valuable human children are in this place! Who is in your group and what have you got to offer?"

Teddy pushed forward Sebastian, Hagelik, Ugah and @@*^#.

"We have only just arrived on Animagana", Teddy explained, "and are much fresher than most of the animagi for sale here."

"Ey, watch it!", said an old animago rabbit standing next to Teddy. "We ain't that bad!"

"We can offer various skills", continued Teddy continuing to look at Leonidas, "including ...", and he knew he had to make up something fast to persuade Leonidas, "including intelligence, a good ability of problem solving, we can read maps and are overall well educated."

"Ha, ha, ha!", roared Leonidas. "And you think these skills will come handy here on Animagana? Here we need strong animagi who can lift logs and kill the wild beasts of the forest, not intellectuals who sit behind desks!"

"I am strong!", said Hagelik flexing the muscles of his arms.

"OK, you look as if you could lift a log!", conceded Leonidas, "and obviously you too!", he said pointing at Teddy. "What about this golliwog? He looks a bit damaged if you ask me?", and he pointed at Ugah's leg injury.

"Oh that is healing already", said Teddy, "and Ugah is also very strong, as is Sebastian, despite his height", and Sebastian stood on his toes to make himself look taller.

"And what about this one?", asked Leonidas pointing at @@*^#. "What ugly seams this frog has!", and they laughed loudly as he pointed at @@*^#'s white stitches around the edges of his body.

"He is very fast and very reliable!", replied Teddy, making up answers as quickly as he could.

"Very well then!", said Leonidas who seemed to be in a good mood after his successful bidding for Erik. "Blackbeard! How much does Callisto want for this lot?"

Blackbeard still could not believe how much Erik had fetched, as he was looking himself at a percentage of the sale, so he was in good spirits and not too bothered about how much

Erik's companions would fetch. "They're yours for another gold coin, Leonidas", he replied.

"Deal", replied Leonidas, "what's one other gold coin if you have already spent forty!", and he laughed again out loudly.

Erik breathed a large sigh of relief and looked gratefully at Teddy. Although he still felt very scared, he felt much better knowing that his companions would come with him. They all knew that, once separated, it would be very difficult for them to leave Animagana again together. They were quickly led from the platform and the auction resumed for the remaining animagi on their platform.

"I have another piece of merchandise you might be interested in", said Blackbeard while approaching Leonidas, and he showed him the paper with the copy of the incantation Sebastian had made.

"What's that?", asked Leonidas, and Blackbeard explained what it was.

"Lead them to the cart!", ordered Leonidas pointing at Erik and his companions.

Leonidas' servants pushed them along the muddy road towards an empty two-wheeled cart with metal bars on the side, a straw covered wooden floor, and two large oxen draught animals.

Just before being shoved into the cart, Sebastian peered behind him and saw that Leonidas had bought the sheet of paper, but he could not see how many more gold coins changed hands. Sebastian also caught sight of the animagi in monk's clothes at the edge of the crowd who continued to stare intently at them. It almost seemed to him that the large brown bear with the big nose and the large round brown eyes stared directly at him and nodded his head slightly.

"Leonidas has also bought the secret incantation from Blackbeard", Sebastian told Teddy and Erik. "I think it's the copy where I falsified the two words, but I am not entirely sure!", he conceded.

"OK, we need to watch that", replied Teddy as they made themselves as comfortable as possible on the straw in the cart.

37

"He has been at it all night again!" The warden in the *South Devon Maximum-Security Psychiatric Hospital* looked at the small TV screen in front of him. "This is one of the worst episodes he's had for a while!"

His colleague came over to look at the screen. The grainy image showed Andrew Billings slamming as hard as he could against the walls of his padded cell. He was wearing a straight-jacket which meant that his arms were tied closely against his body. But he had full use of his legs. As he picked himself up from the floor he ran as fast as he could the short distance to the nearest wall and smashed into it. The rubbery wall surface threw him back onto the floor near the middle of the cell.

"Open the sound so that we can hear what he is shouting", said the second warden with a mischievous tone in his voice. Neither of them had much sympathy for Andrew Billings, who was the most vicious and violent patient they had.

"You are all against me!", shouted Andrew. "He says everybody wants to kill me! Everybody always wanted to kill me!"

"Here we go again!", said the first warden. "The same litany ever since he's been here since he was 16. Remember, that's exactly what he said after he had slit his mum's throat just after they brought him here five years ago. Although, who is the 'he' is always referring to?"

Andrew had stopped throwing himself at the wall and was now sitting in the middle of his cell. For safety reasons his cell was empty, except for a small foam mattress which Andrew hat tossed into the corner. He sat still, mumbling.

"What's he saying now?", asked the second warden. "Turn up the sound!"

The first warden turned the sound knob to maximum as Andrew was talking quietly to himself, almost whispering. "Garglethroat … Garglethroat … where are you? It's been days now since I last heard from you. You're the only one who I can communicate with! Where are you? Are you dead?"

"Garglethroat?", asked the first warden. "What's this all about? He has never mentioned a 'Garglethroat' before?"

"Yes, that's new", admitted the second warden. "Maybe we should tell the doctor? Luckily all this is permanently being recorded, so the doctor can see by himself … Billings really is acting weird today!"

Andrew had stopped mumbling and sat still in the middle of his cell, his eyes closed. The wardens quickly got bored and turned their interest towards the monitors showing other psychiatric patients.

38

The cart had been travelling the whole day, and night was beginning to fall. Sebastian's group had quickly left the village, flanked by Leonidas' servants on foot on either side of the cart, and led by Leonidas who was riding a small horse. Three other armed animagi had joined them who were part of Leonidas' retinue.

The road had taken them out of Raupenburg and had followed the flanks of the high glacier-covered mountain towering over the bay. Dense forest had swallowed them up as soon as they left the village. Sebastian and his companions had stared out through the bars in amazement at the landscape and the dense vegetation. They were not used to being out in the open, having lived most of their lives in subterranean passageways and caves. Their senses were almost overwhelmed by the intense shades of green, the fragrant smell of the epiphytes, and the chirping and screeching of forest birds. On several occasions larger animals such as lizards, toads, snakes and even a flying squirrel had crossed their path. At one point they heard what must have been a rather large animal crashing through the undergrowth not far from them, and Leonidas' servants had looked rather ill at ease, but no animal could be seen.

The road had quickly narrowed to a path that was just wide enough to take their cart. On three occasions large branches and a fallen tree had to be cleared off the path by the servants, while Leonidas' armed men stood guard with their sabres drawn.

They are clearly fearful of the animals in this forest!, thought Sebastian. *I wonder what fierce beasts roam these woods?*

When it was getting dark, they stopped at a small clearing. A round fireplace full of charred logs could be seen in the middle, suggesting that the clearing had been used many times before by travellers. Leonidas' men busied themselves setting up camp, cutting firewood and carrying water in leather buckets from a nearby stream.

Leonidas walked over towards them. "How are my new slaves doing?", he asked with a large grin on his lion's face. He was clearly pleased with his new purchases, despite the high price he had paid.

"We are OK, thanks", replied Teddy, rubbing his back which was hurting after lying on the straw on the hard wooden floor of the cart for too long.

"Where are you taking us?", asked Sebastian.

"You animagi will be working in my gold mine", Leonidas explained. "I am actually quite pleased that you five come in different shapes and sizes, as I need some to carry heavy loads and help shoring up the tunnels", and he pointed at Hagelik in particular, "while you small ones will be able to creep into the tiniest cracks to get to the smaller seams of gold", and he looked at Sebastian and @@*^#. "My gold mine is the largest on Animagana and the reason I am very rich. I have been very lucky! The mine is still two days travel from here, so you'll have to make do with this cart for a little while!"

"What about me?", asked Erik, "will I also work in the mine?" Erik remembered that one of his favourite documentaries on the *National Geographic* channel was one about gold diggers in north-west America. *Maybe I wouldn't mind help finding some nuggets!*, he thought hopefully.

"What's your name, son?", asked Leonidas, and Erik told him his name.

"Well Erik", Leonidas continued, "I have other plans for you. I haven't paid forty gold coins to waste you in my mine, as workers don't last very long down there!", and he laughed, looking at Sebastian and his animagi companions. "Guards, take Erik and tie him up to that tree so that I can watch him more closely!", Leonidas commanded.

Erik was taken from the cart and pushed towards a large tree whose trunk was covered in a strangling fig that was gradually squeezing out the life of the wooden behemoth. Leonidas' guards sat Erik in front of the tree and tied his hands behind it. After they had eaten a meal that consisted of a broth interspersed with chunky bits of salty meat and coarse bread, the group quickly settled down to sleep. Leonidas was the only one with a tent-like cover. His guards and servants had taken out coarsely woven sleeping mats and nestled around the fire as best they could. As they were still relatively high up on the flanks of the gigantic mountain the night was rapidly getting chilly.

After the guards had let them out briefly to go the toilet, Sebastian and the others made themselves as comfortable as they could on the straw in the cart under thin blankets provided by the servants. They quickly fell asleep.

39

Sebastian awoke to the sound of rustling next to their cart. He opened his sleepy eyes, and took a while to make out a shape hunched over Erik in the silvery light of a full moon. It was Leonidas!

Sebastian gently nudged Teddy, and it took a while to wake him up without making too much noise. "I think Leonidas is trying the incantation on Erik!", whispered Sebastian. "All he wanted is to extract Erik's soul, he doesn't care at all about Erik! They are all the same here on Animagana, they are all bastards!"

Teddy was finally awake and looked intently at the scene unfolding before him. "If it's the copy you made with the two wrong words it should not be able to harm Erik. No need to try and wake Erik up as it would only get us into major trouble!"

Sebastian agreed. "Try and memorise the words, Teddy, as we may need the incantation", he suggested. "You take the first two lines I take the last two. Shame we haven't got anything to write on us!"

"OK!", replied Teddy.

Leonidas was now positioned directly over Erik's sleeping body. He held a small glass phial in his left paw. He stared Erik straight in the face and started the incantation:

UMMM MARISH GRANAFF GANG GOOL

Erik stirred slightly, but did not wake up. Teddy tried hard to memorise the words.

RAST HEREBDYN IMMORTIS GRATTAN

Erik seemed to wake up and put his hands to his head. Something was hurting him. Teddy had already forgotten some words from the first sentence.

Here we go! thought Sebastian, *the next sentence is key! Let's see what happens!*

URRR MAJORUM EXYRBITUS THYSSUSS

Is this my modified version of the incantation?, wondered Sebastian, as he could not remember the correct words. He desperately tried to remember what the correct two words were: majoram? majorim? majorem? exarbitus? exorbitus? exerbitus? *It is just too difficult a language to memorise, we will never manage!*, thought Sebastian frustratingly. *But I think it's the wrong incantation.*

Erik had already woken up after the first two sentences had been uttered, but he had been prepared after what Sebastian had told him about the two replaced words. Still, he could not prevent himself from putting his hands against his head at the end of the second sentence as the pain in his head was indescribably strong. He thought his head would burst! Interestingly, after Leonidas had read out the third, wrong, line of the incantation the pain almost vanished instantaneously. Erik could pretend with more conviction to still being asleep.

Leonidas completed the incantation:

DRRAM GARR NON RETURNUM SIC

Everything was silent. Erik pretended to be snoring. The silvery moon peered through the dense canopy of giant trees. Drips could be heard falling from nearby ferns and branches. Nothing happened. No ball of blue light came out of Erik's forehead. Leonidas knew something was wrong!

"What the hell!", he roared, waking up everybody. Erik pretended to wake up with a start when he heard others stirring.

"Blackbeard and Callisto have sold me a dud incantation! The bastards!", shouted Leonidas as he got up. "I'll get them! I'll get them!"

"Erik is alright! Erik is alright!", whispered Sebastian, "Yippee! My little trick worked!", he said proudly and Teddy patted him on the back in acknowledgement.

Leonidas quickly gathered his men around him. "Change of plans!", he shouted. "After this disaster we need to find the correct incantation! It looks alright on the sheet of paper, but some words must have been changed or swapped. I remember others mentioning that the incantation has to be absolutely right both for the extraction of a soul and for passing through the portal. Without the proper wording Erik is pretty useless to us! I hope I have not wasted forty gold coins!", and he glanced over at Erik who was watching them with apprehension.

"So we need to make a little detour via the monastery", Leonidas said to his companions. "But I suspect we will not be very welcome there after what happened last time!", he said with a sigh.

"I wonder what that means?", said Sebastian to Teddy, "but at least we have forced a change in itinerary. That can only be good as I am not ready to work as a slave in a gold mine!"

"Yes, well done Sebastian, and well done Erik for playing the part", replied Teddy.

"Did you manage to memorise the first two lines of the incantation, Teddy", asked Sebastian.

"Wait!", said Teddy, "it was Umm Marish Granadd Gong Guul … or was it Umm Darish Branaff Gang Geel …? Oh dear! I have already forgotten. What about you?"

"Rast Herepton Immortus Grettan … or something like that for the third sentence!", replied Sebastian, "but I am not sure either, and I can't even remember the original two words that I replaced in that sentence anyway. It's useless without pen and paper!"

"At least it sounds as if the monastery we are going to may have the solution anyway. And they're bound to have pen and paper, or at least quill and ink!", said Teddy.

40

Suzanne St Austell was late for her appointment with Prof Hedley from the psychology department at the local university. First she had been at the extraordinary animagi council meeting where Prof Pandanus had been introduced and Mrs Moluk warned them of the threat posed by Garglethroat, and then there had been an emergency at the local care home where she worked part-time as a carer for children with severe psychological problems. She was at the university because she also did a part-time Masters degree in psychology on top of her duties as animagi council member, her care job and having a family with two children, one of whom was still at home. Not surprisingly, at times Suzanne found it difficult to juggle the demands between all these time-consuming activities.

By chance, the psychology department at her local university was one of the best in the country, with an excellent reputation for research and teaching, and she had so far enjoyed every part of the course. She was now in the final stages of her four-year part-time degree and had begun working on her dissertation.

She was breathless when she reached Prof Hedley's door, as she had just run up two flights of stairs. She composed herself, caught her breath, slightly adjusted her long blond hair and knocked at the door.

"C'mon in", shouted Prof Hedley, not looking up from his computer. He was checking his e-mails. "Have a seat", he said without looking at who had come in.

Suzanne sat down and pulled some papers out of her bag while Hedley was tapping away on his keyboard. "I'll be with you in a sec", he mumbled, "just need to finish this urgent message."

Suzanne looked at the back of Hedley's head. She was unsure whether she found him attractive, but she liked him a lot in a professional sort of way as he had given her very useful and patient advice on her dissertation so far.

Hedley finally swivelled his chair around. "Ah, Suzanne, how are you?", holding a hand towards her. "How is the methodology for your dissertation coming along?"

"Thanks for seeing me", replied Suzanne. She knew how busy these profs were, always flitting from one conference or research project to another. They barely seemed to be in their offices, with the ubiquitous access to the internet now making working 'on the move' ever easier. "I think I have narrowed down the case study I would like to focus on."

"Excellent!", replied Hedley. "I think your research question sounds really fascinating and the choice of the right institution to use as case study is crucial. Remind me again what you are exactly trying to do?"

"As you may remember from my last e-mail and our recent conversation, I have narrowed down the research question towards a critical analysis of rehabilitation programmes for severely mentally deranged and ultra-violent psychiatric patients. My interest stems largely from the fact that I work with psychologically severely disturbed children in my part-time job, and I would like to research something for my dissertation that will have relevance for what I am doing now and that might also benefit my patients."

"Yes, that makes a lot of sense", replied Hedley, swivelling his chair slightly and playing with a pen in his right hand. "What theoretical approach were you going to use?"

"At our last meeting you recommended looking at Garringer's work on violent versus accommodating methods in rehabilitation. I found his articles on the importance of warden behaviour, patient cell infrastructure and visitor time impacts very interesting. He is obviously of the school of thought that violent psychotic criminals can be cured through a combination of institutional and family or friend-related enabling processes. So I would like to test this in more detail by looking at two or three inmates in a maximum-security psychiatric ward. The methods would mainly involve qualitative approaches through in-depth interviews with the patients themselves, the wardens and senior prison personnel in charge of the main policies and approaches used to treat the patients."

"That sounds fine to me", replied Hedley. "So, which institution did you have in mind?"

"First I thought about St Cyrian down on the coast that has dealt with violent psychopathic criminals since the late 19th century, but initial enquiries suggest that there might not be enough patients to choose from, and the hospital director also only sounded mildly interested. St Cyrian would have been handy with regard to travel as it is close to the village where I live and also has links to the care home where I work, but I don't think I can use it for the planned research if I don't have the full support of the director of the institution. So I approached the director of the South Devon Maximum-Security Psychiatric Hospital, and he seemed very keen on the research. He also mentioned a few patients who would fit the type of respondents

I am looking for and he also promised me the cooperation of the wardens. So, all of that looks quite promising ..."

What she did not tell Hedley was that she also knew Andrew Billings, one of the most infamous patients at the hospital, and that she was interested in interviewing him under the disguise of her dissertation topic. She knew Andrew through her eldest son, now at university, who had been a classmate of Andrew at the village primary school. The thought of her son at primary school briefly brought back memories of Andrew's already very odd behaviour as a young boy, especially the occasion of his only visit to her home. After briefly playing with her son without showing much interest, he had suddenly hidden behind the sofa shouting at them: "All you want is to kill me! He says that's why you brought me here!" He had hugged his toy frog closely to his chest and seemed to murmur into the frog's ear while staring at Suzanne and her son with abject hatred.

After that, Andrew had never again been allowed to visit her home, although Suzanne continued to eagerly follow Andrew's gradual slide into increasingly violent psychotic behaviour, culminating in the brutal murder of his own mother when he was only 16 years of age. Suzanne had known Rachel, Andrew's mother, reasonably well, had spoken to her at length at the time when Andrew's father felt compelled to leave the family due to Andrew's increasingly erratic behaviour and his mother's seeming reluctance to acknowledge what was happening. Suzanne remembered feeling very sorry for Rachel at the time and that she, like most other parents in the village, had no solution to offer as to what Rachel could do to help her son.

Who would have thought that shortly afterwards all this would culminate in Rachel's horrific murder?, she thought. *I guess Andrew's sad story partly sparked my interest in psychology. As an initiated member of the animagi community, and especially as host to an interesting animago like Hexybilla, I have been particularly interested, from a psychological perspective, in Andrew's strange and very intense relationship with his toy frog Garglethroat. Indeed, we now know what a nasty animago Garglethroat has turned out to be! Is there a relationship between Garglethroat's aggressive and murderous behaviour and Andrews'? These are the questions that really interest me from a psychological research perspective, but for obvious reasons I can't discuss these with Professor Hedley. He would think I have gone mad myself if I told him about the animagi world below our feet, and that he and his children probably also have talking and reasoning animagi running around in passageways under his house! If he knew that I even sit on the animagi council in our village!*

"Well done Suzanne", replied Hedley, bringing Suzanne back abruptly to reality. "I don't see any methodological problems regarding the choice of that institution, and it's also not too far for you to drive. Can you please make sure that you submit an ethical approval form, as there will be a lot of ethical issues associated with accessing potentially vulnerable patients? You also need to fill in a risk appraisal form to make sure that your own safety is always considered when you talk to patients. I suspect that for the very violent ones you will be separated by a pane of glass or a safe partition?"

"I have not yet checked that", replied Suzanne trying to refocus on her dissertation, "but from my experience, these maximum-security hospitals never allow researchers face-to-face contact with patients. There are always separate cubicles or partitions and you tend to communicate via a telecommunication system. Effectively it will be a bit like the scene in the movie 'Silence of the Lambs' where Jodie Foster talks to Hannibal Lecter down in his secure cell ..."

They both laughed at the thought of the movie that had made psychotic murderers more popular and interesting than probably any other movie.

"I will let you know, and you will need to sign both the ethics and risk forms anyway, so we will have another opportunity to talk about this", continued Suzanne. "Even if I have to see one of the patients face-to-face, there will be constraints like straight-jackets, and a warden will always be in the room with me. Don't worry, as I am already quite used to dealing with violent psychotic people in my job ...", *although they are kids, and here I'll be dealing with violent grown men like Andrew Billings!*, she thought, but did not want to alarm her dissertation supervisor further.

After a final acknowledgement by Hedley that she was on the right track Suzanne got up and shook Hedley's hand. He was back at checking his e-mails even before she reached the door ...

41

Garglethroat was struggling to keep up with Mephisto's gang. They had walked solidly for four days through the dense forest, with the narrow path winding through swamps, deep gullies and past treacherous ravines. Increasingly Garglethroat, who was not fit at all, had started stumbling, slipping and falling over, often accompanied by raucous laughter from Mephisto's men.

"The fat toad is increasingly holding us up!", one of Mephisto's men shouted to the front when Garglethroat was lying face down in the mud again. "Why don't we just kill him and be done with it?"

"That might be the best idea!", replied Mephisto from the front. "We can't afford to miss the next slave auction in Raupenburg. We need the money! Give him one more chance tomorrow, if he can't keep up we'll cut his ugly head off! For now, it's time to make camp anyway as the sun has already set."

Garglethroat was leaning against a large tree, panting heavily. *I won't survive another day like this!*, he thought. *I am totally exhausted! We have to try to escape tonight otherwise I'll be dead by tomorrow!*

Under guard, Ori Fisse, Skeleto, Gremlin and Bunny were helping Mephisto's men gather firewood. "The boss will not make it much longer!", whispered Ori Fisse to Skeleto while they were out of earshot from their guards. "We have to do something sooner rather than later!"

"I agree!", replied Skeleto. "I am pretty exhausted myself, especially as they haven't given us much food the last four days."

"Look what I managed to nick yesterday from one of the guards who had fallen asleep!", said Ori Fisse showing Skeleto a mid-sized dagger with an intricately carved bone handle. "Thankfully I overheard the guard tell another that he thought he lost his dagger in the swamp, which is the reason why they haven't searched us! I say we act tonight!"

Back at the camp, everybody was huddled around the fire as the nights in the woods were damp and chilly. A full moon presaged a clear sky which meant that this night would be even colder than the previous one.

Mephisto's guards tied up Garglethroat, his henchmen, Bunny, and their other five animagi prisoners as usual, and wrapped them up in blankets a few meters from the edge of the fire. Ori Fisse was the furthest away and could barely be seen in the dim light. He whispered their escape plan to Garglethroat who fully agreed with him that it was either tonight or never, as he would not last another day. Bunny was kept in the dark as Garglethroat and his men trusted him less and less.

Gradually the raucous laughter and drinking of Mephisto's men died down as one man after the other went to sleep. As usual, one was standing guard near the fire. Exhausted as he was Garglethroat had fallen asleep immediately, and Skeleto, Gremlin and Bunny were also asleep quickly. Ori Fisse forced himself to stay awake but he closed his eyes pretending to be sleeping. The camp was quiet and only the crackle of the dying fire could be heard.

After a while Ori Fisse opened one eye carefully and glanced at the guard sitting opposite him across the fire, his face lit by the embers. *He looks pretty tired too!*, thought Ori Fisse. *I bet he'll be asleep pretty soon!* And indeed, a few minutes later the guard was slumped slightly forward, snoring loudly. Ori Fisse wiggled his arms, but it was difficult as they were tied and he had been wrapped tightly into the blanket. After what seemed an eternity he finally managed to grab the bone handle of his dagger, and after another few minutes he had managed to position it in such a way that he could begin cutting the ropes that tied his bulldog paws together. He felt the rope break with a snap. His paws were free! He quickly untied his feet, woke up and freed Skeleto and Gremlin, and moved towards Garglethroat who seemed to be completely hidden in his blanket like a freshly-wrapped new-born baby.

"Garglethroat! Garglethroat! Wake up!", Ori Fisse whispered into Garglethroat's ear shaking him gently.

Garglethroat woke up with a moan, dark rings under his bulgy eyes suggesting deep fatigue. The guard was still fast asleep. Nobody else was moving. They struggled to get Garglethroat on his feet as his legs were so tired.

"Stay here, boss, and leave this to us!", said Ori Fisse and Garglethroat slumped back onto the blanket.

Ori Fisse quickly moved behind the sleeping guard and slit his throat with a quick jerk of his dagger. Big white stuffing came out of the gaping wound, and Ori Fisse had his hand on the guard's mouth so that his final croak remained silent. Ori Fisse quickly grabbed the guard's sabre, passed his knife to Skeleto, and they made their way to Mephisto's tent pitched between two large tree trunks. There was a guard in front of the tent, but he was also asleep. With a quick and agile fling of the sabre Ori Fisse chopped off the guard's head which rolled a few meters down the slope towards the fire, stopping just short of a group of three other sleeping guards.

Ori Fisse and Skeleto quickly moved into Mephisto's tent. The tall lanky rabbit was sleeping in a large bed with red drapes and fluffy pillows. He had taken off his eye patch and a dark hole was visible where his right eye had once been.

"Mephisto sleeps in style!", Ori Fisse whispered to Skeleto pointing at the large bed, "while his prisoners sleep on the damp forest floor!"

With a quick move he pressed his sabre into Mephisto's chest. Almost simultaneously Skeleto had cut Mephisto's throat. Mephisto had not uttered a sound.

They collected Mephisto's ornately decorated sabre and the weapon of his dead guard, passed a sabre to Gremlin, and quickly proceeded to kill the seven other guards, none of which had time to react or utter a sound. However, while killing one of the last guards, Gremlin stumbled over a flask of rum that skidded with a loud noise into the fire. The last two remaining guards woke up with startled looks on their faces and quickly drew their sabres.

"What is going on? Mephisto! Mephisto!", shouted the first one, while the other guard stood back-to-back with his companion.

"Mephisto won't help you, neither will the others!", shouted Ori Fisse. "They are all dead! You've messed with the wrong people by capturing us!", at which point Ori Fisse, Skeleto and Gremlin charged. Bunny had woken up and watched the butchering unravel in front of his eyes.

The first guard parried what would have been a deadly blow by Ori Fisse, while the second guard threw himself at Gremlin. Skeleto helped Ori Fisse to quickly dispatch the first guard with a deadly cut to his head. But Gremlin struggled to defend himself against the heavy sabre blows of the second guard. He was forced backwards ... and stumbled over a firewood log. Gremlin's sabre flew out of his hand as he tried to cushion his fall with both arms. The second guard did not hesitate a second and split Gremlin in two with one sabre blow. But he did not have enough time to turn around and face Ori Fisse and Skeleto who attacked him from behind with sabres raised. They simultaneously struck the guard on the head and on the right shoulder. He slumped forward, mortally wounded, and fell into the fire ...

Garglethroat had watched the battle scene unfold before his eyes. He felt a brief pang of sadness at Gremlin's death who had been a trusty and loyal companion, but at the same time he was also very proud of his men. Although Gremlin was dead, the three of them had killed fifteen animagi!

Bunny had looked on in stunned silence. *These guys are so violent and don't hesitate to kill! I don't think they'll keep me alive for much longer. What have I done? Why did I join them?*

The five remaining animagi prisoners were huddled together in panic. Still tied together they were now at the mercy of Garglethroat and his two remaining henchmen.

"What shall we do with these, boss?", asked Ori Fisse.

"Just leave them as they are", said Garglethroat. "We can't take them, as they would hinder our progress and probably even try to kill us! Let's just leave them tied up here, there is no way they can escape. We'll go into Mephisto's tent and get a good night's sleep and hopefully find something better to eat than the rubbish they have given us the last four days. And then I guess you all know where we are going!"

For the first time since coming to Animagana, things looked a bit brighter for Garglethroat and his remaining two companions. Bunny, however, was less sure about his fate.

42

Godfrey Wilkinson, Erik's dad, was desperate. It had been five days now since Erik had disappeared without leaving a trace. The police had been involved as usual in cases like these, but Godfrey could only tell them that Erik had suddenly disappeared from his bedroom. He had not mentioned that two of Erik's toy animals, Sebastian and @@*^#, had also disappeared, and that three of his own, Teddy, Ugah and Bunny, were also missing. Neither could Godfrey tell his wife, Alathia, the full story, as Alathia had never been initiated to the Animagi world. It was particularly hard for Alathia not knowing what had happened to her only son, and she had taken time off work due to severe depression.

Hexybilla had invited Godfrey to attend all the meetings in which the latest disappearances were discussed. They gathered in one of the larger caves where Godfrey, who was quite tall, could sit in more comfort. Suzanne, the sole human member on the animagi council, was sitting next to Godfrey. They both knew each other well through their involvement with the animagi world. Most other council members were also present, as was Professor Pandanus.

"How are you feeling, Godfrey?", asked Suzanne.

"Pretty rough! Thanks for asking, Suzanne", replied Godfrey. "Do we know more about what happened to Erik and the missing animagi?", he asked addressing the council.

"We are pretty certain now that Erik and the five animagi who disappeared with him have used the portal to go to

Animagana", Hexybilla replied. "We are also pretty convinced that Garglethroat and some of his companions used the portal to escape from here. This seems to be confirmed by the fact that no further cases of child comas have now been reported for nearly ten days, and that nobody has reported a sighting of any of the missing."

"If that is the case, how can we help Erik and his companions to come back to this world?", asked Godfrey. "Is there any way we can communicate with them?"

"Obviously we can't send someone over to help them, as each time it would necessitate extraction of another child's soul", said Hexybilla. "But Professor Pandanus and his colleagues have made some progress with regard to the process of coming back from Animagana. Professor Pandanus, please …"

"Thanks Mrs Hexybilla", Professor Pandanus said while standing up and addressing the council members. "Although we haven't found a second copy of the 'Chronicles of Animagi Lore' where the crucial page had been ripped out, we are beginning to puzzle together what is needed for the return from Animagana to the human world. Let me start with a word of caution first, though. This manuscript in front of me, dated from 1904", and he held up a smallish black book with coarse yellowed pages bound in thick leather, "suggests that the last return from Animagana occurred in 1899, from a portal located in Paris, France. It explains that these returning animagi had only recently crossed into Animagana, similar to our disappeared animagi from this village, which meant that their hosts were still alive and that there was, therefore, no risk to their lives of coming back. Most importantly it mentions that upon the return of the animagi through the portal, children who had fallen into a coma all over Paris woke up seemingly unharmed."

The council members were elated at this piece of news and looked at each other with smiles on their faces.

"At last a bit of good news!", said Mr Wood. "There may still be hope for our animagi, and for Erik, if we can somehow get them back."

"Indeed …indeed!", continued Professor Pandanus. "But again I need to warn you that things will not be easy. The book also gives a brief description of Animagana in the late 19th century, and the picture they describe is not a pretty one. They described it as a lawless place of individual colonies of animagi and a few humans fighting each other over meagre resources. Food was scarce, violence and murder were ubiquitous, and most inhabitants seemed to be stuck in a pre-modern world without much technology, education or knowledge. In other words, they described it as a dangerous and primitive world!"

"My poor son!", sighed Godfrey, "how will he be able to survive in such a world?"

The council members looked at Godfrey with sympathy and felt very sorry for the plight of Erik.

"Yes … it will be tough for him and the others to survive", acknowledged Hexybilla, "but there is another problem for Erik, and I think we need to acknowledge that: if they want to return to here, and I am sure we are all assuming that is their intention, how are they going to extract the essence of a human child's soul to get back through the portal? Inevitably it will mean that somebody will have to be sacrificed, and I can't imagine that there are many human children on Animagana …"

It suddenly dawned on Godfrey in what dreadful danger his son was, but he left his fears unspoken. He peered around at the council members and saw that they were all thinking the same.

"There is another matter we need to consider", said Hexybilla. "We can't assume that Garglethroat will not also try to come back to our world, although I am sure we all agree that it would be better if he stayed in Animagana forever!"

The council members nodded in agreement.

"I have, therefore, convened a small task force, led by Suzanne, to look into the matter how best we could rid our world of evil murderers such as Garglethroat", Hexybilla continued. "Suzanne, have you made any progress since our last meeting?"

"We have had a few discussions", said Suzanne, "but have not come up yet with a concrete plan other than killing Garglethroat and his henchmen as they emerge from the portal."

"As you know, Suzanne, our animagi constitution prevents us from doing that", said Mr Wood. "Like humans, we have our laws and they clearly state that an animagi like Garglethroat has to be tried in a court and sentenced. The only option is, therefore, to capture him again and put him and his men into prison."

"… like we did a few years ago", replied Suzanne, "and look what happened: Garglethroat escaped from our maximum-security prison where he was on death row after killing two of our most esteemed animagi councillors! In the process they also killed one of the prison guards! We need to find another way to get rid of him!"

Inwardly the council members all agreed, although they knew that murdering Garglethroat was not an option even if a legal exemption could be made.

Suzanne looked firmly at the council. "Our task force will think about further options and we will report back at the next meeting."

"Many thanks, Suzanne", said Hexybilla. "May I close the meeting by saying that we wish Godfrey all the best and hope that he will see his son very soon."

Godfrey thanked Hexybilla for inviting him, but deep inside he knew that he might never see his son again.

43

Leonidas' fury had not abated overnight. He had thrown Erik back with the others into the cart and they had set off early. At one point the narrow path divided and after a brief discussion with his companions Leonidas took the path to the left, back towards the coast. As they gradually climbed downhill the forest got even thicker and lusher. They were all plagued by swarms of what looked like giant mosquitos with rather nasty stings. Sebastian and his companions were constantly on the lookout and swatted as many of the flies as possible, but some managed to sting them leaving rather large swellings on their arms and legs.

After a few hours, the humidity in the forest became almost unbearable and the trees seemed to be closing in and letting very little sunshine through. Sebastian and his companions were exhausted from the fly-swatting and were drowsing on the straw-covered floor of the cart.

Suddenly they heard a very loud roar not far from their cart. Leonidas' men immediately drew their sabres and took up a defensive position.

"Sabrejaws!", shouted Leonidas. "I hope it's only one!"

Their trek had come to a halt. Everybody peered anxiously into the dense undergrowth were all was suddenly eerily still. Only the rustle of a few leaves could be heard ...

Without warning a giant beast, about the size and weight of a rhinoceros but with four large sabre-sized teeth jutting out of its hideous mouth, attacked two of Leonidas' men standing next to the cart. The two guards had no chance and were killed instantly by a flick of the sharp canines that tore large gashes into their sides and bellies. Leonidas and his remaining guards and servants hurled themselves at the beast, sabres and daggers drawn. One guard managed to gouge the flank of the sabrejaw with his sabre, but was killed immediately by a flick of one the beast's large clawed paws. However, the beast was now bleeding profusely from the gash on his side and limped badly, not being able to put any weight on his front paw. Leonidas repositioned himself quickly and before the sabrejaw could injure him with his large teeth, buried his sabre to the hilt in the animal's stomach. The beast let out an ear-numbing roar of agony, and caught Leonidas arm with his jaw, hurled him around, and threw him like a sack of beans into the undergrowth.

But Leonidas' guards now had the upper hand, with two standing on the beast raising their sabres for a final deadly blow. Just as they wielded their weapons to strike the beast, a loud crash could be heard. A second sabrejaw emerged from the undergrowth. Leonidas' servants started to run down the path, while the last remaining two guards turned towards the sabrejaw. But they had no chance. With a flick of his paws the sabrejaw killed the first guard, while he mauled the second guard with his teeth.

Leonidas was nowhere to be seen or heard. Sebastian and his companions clung to the bars of the cage on the cart, unprotected and weaponless. The two sabrejaws turned towards them, their large bluish tongues hanging out salivating.

"That's it! We are done for!", shouted Teddy. "Move to the middle of the cage, maybe the metal bars will protect us!"

Their hopes were short-lived. The second sabrejaw jumped on the wooden roof of the cart which began to sag under its enormous weight. The first sabrejaw put his head next to the bars in anticipation of the cart falling apart. The roof caved in and the sides of the cart came apart. Both sabrejaws jumped towards Sebastian and his companions, mouths wide open. Sebastian and the others put their arms in front of their heads for futile protection and closed their eyes ... and ... nothing happened.

Sebastian opened his eyes. Time was frozen. Both sabrejaws were suspended in mid-air like Benny the cat in what seemed like an eternity ago. Sebastian was getting used to this situation and acted quickly. His companions were frozen in their last positions, eyes closed and arms in front of their heads. He hauled them out of the remnants of the cart one-by-one, knowing that he did not have much time. He had spotted a large tree with climbable branches about ten metres away and deposited his four friends below the tree. While it was easy to carry @@*^# and Ugah who were not too tall, Teddy was heavier and Hagelik even more so. But the one most difficult to drag along was Erik, who weighed much more than any of the others despite being a child. Sebastian only managed to drag Erik a short distance from the cart.

Just when Sebastian had managed to push and heave Erik a few metres, time suddenly unfroze and the two sabrejaws crashed into the now empty remnants of the cart. They peered around, puzzled and dazed.

Sebastian's companions began to move. Erik looked around him confused.

"Run, Erik, run!", shouted Sebastian, and Erik got up immediately and ran towards them as quickly as he could.

"Up the tree behind you! Quickly!", he shouted, letting Erik, who was very fit and sporty, climb past him, and pushing Teddy towards the first reachable branch. It took them a little while to understand what had happened, especially Erik, Teddy, Ugah and @@*^# who had never experienced Sebastian's magic gift, but when they saw the two sabrejaws gather their wits, turn around, and rush towards them, they did not hesitate to grab whatever branches they could get hold of and climbed as high into the tree as possible. Hagelik was the last one. He was grabbing the branch Sebastian and Teddy were standing on when the first sabrejaw reached the tree, stood on its massive hind legs and stretched out its neck. The sabrejaw opened its mouth and just as it was about to close on Hagelik's legs, Sebastian and Teddy had managed to pull Hagelik up onto their branch. The sabrejaw's mouth closed with a loud 'clack', showering them with drops of fetid saliva.

Both sabrejaws circled the tree, grunting menacingly. But at least Sebastian and his companions were safe as the sabrejaws were too heavy to climb trees.

"Phew! Well done Sebastian!", said Teddy, patting Sebastian on the back. "This is becoming a habit!", Teddy said, "me thanking you for saving us! I can see now what you mean by 'time-freeze'! At one point I was about to be eaten alive by a sabrejaw, while at the next point I was at the bottom of this tree ten meters away! Amazing!"

"Yes, thanks a lot!", replied Ugah while rubbing his still injured leg, and the others also thanked Sebastian profusely.

"But now we are stuck here!", said Sebastian. "We are not saved yet!"

One sabrejaw still circled the tree, staring up at them with blood-shot eyes. The other rummaged in the undergrowth and dragged out Leonidas' limp and unconscious body. The beast was just about to stick its large fangs into Leonidas' torso when a long javelin flew through the air, penetrating the beast's flank by at least fifty centimetres. The beast howled in agony. Another javelin hit it in the front leg, while his partner was pierced by two javelins and three arrows simultaneously. The second sabrejaw collapsed on the ground with a large puddle of blood forming around him, while the other sabrejaw disappeared into the undergrowth with a mighty leap.

"I think they've had enough!", shouted a booming voice. "Finish the one lying on the ground! The other one won't come back for a while, but be vigilant!"

A large brown bear with a big nose and large round brown eyes came into view, followed by two other large animagi. They all wore monk's robes.

"The animagi from the slave market!", said Sebastian. "What are they doing here?"

"Hello there!", shouted the brown bear looking up at Sebastian and his friends. "Are you alright? I am Brother Konrad, these are Brother Regulus and Brother Bonifacius", he said pointing at his two companions.

"Yes, thanks Sir!", replied Teddy. "But you came just in time!"

"You may remember us from the slave market", said Konrad, "we saw you being bought by Leonidas and decided to follow you. Especially because of this one …", and he pointed at Erik who had climbed high up into the tree. "This boy is indeed very valuable, as you will by now have realised!"

"Thanks a lot for saving us from the beasts!", shouted Erik. "I hope you're not also after my soul like all the others?"

"No, we're not, boy. I can assure you of that!", replied Konrad, and Erik gave a big sigh of relief.

Maybe for the first time I can trust somebody here in Animagana?, Erik wondered.

While Sebastian and his companions climbed down the tree, Regulus and Bonifacius were crouched over the limp body of Leonidas.

"He's alive, but he is in bad shape!", said Regulus. "I guess we have to take him with us, despite him being such a vile character?"

"Yes, indeed", replied Konrad. "As you know it is part of our oath to help all fellow animagi and humans, whether they are slave traders or not! Put him onto our cart!"

Regulus and Bonifacius walked back on the path and came back with a large cow-like beast behind them that was pulling a covered cart. They hauled Leonidas' body onto the cart and invited Sebastian and his companions to sit on the cart.

"You better rest as you must be exhausted after all you have gone through!", said Konrad.

"Where are you taking us?", asked Sebastian.

"To our monastery near the coast. It is another two days march from here, but we should be there by sundown tomorrow."

Sebastian and the others made themselves as comfortable as they could. Sebastian glanced at Leonidas' body next to him and started searching his pockets.

"What are you doing?", asked Teddy.

"I am looking for the piece of paper with the wrong incantation on it, the one he used on Erik!", explained Sebastian.

But it was nowhere to be found! *Maybe it got lost in the fight with the beasts or maybe Leonidas had thrown it away in fury after he realised it had not worked!*, thought Sebastian disappointed.

44

By the end of the day, Sebastian and his companions and the three monks had made good progress, although the path they had taken was even more narrow and windy than the path from Raupenburg. At times, Brother Konrad had the cart unloaded and carried over fallen trees, narrow passages, and large potholes. Sebastian and the others slept whenever they could on the cart, helped by the gentle rocking motion.

As the sun was setting behind darkening clouds, Brother Konrad picked a relatively level spot near a stream for their night's camp. After helping with the gathering of firewood and preparing a simple meal, they all sat together near the fire. Leonidas was still unconscious and had been placed under a blanket on the cart.

"We haven't had much opportunity yet to talk", said Konrad, "as the path is rather treacherous and requires our fullest attention, as you have seen. Tell me a bit about yourselves."

They had already introduced themselves after the fight with the sabrejaws, and now told the three monks how they got to Animagana and why they were there in the first place. They also warned Konrad about Garglethroat, who was somewhere on the loose since escaping from the Jolly Roger pub, and who was probably keen to get hold of Erik's soul to keep the option open to return to the human world.

"We have not yet got a good impression of Animagana", admitted Sebastian, "and we all would like to go back to our world as quickly as possible. But we know that this is virtually impossible as we would need to extract a soul from a human child, just as Leonidas had tried with Erik last night."

Sebastian told the three monks about how he had falsified the copy of the incantation and that this had saved Erik's life.

"That was smart thinking!", said Konrad with an appreciative look at Sebastian, "but I guess you were also a bit lucky that Callisto had not given the original piece of paper to Blackbeard to sell!"

"Yes, Konrad, that is very true!", replied Sebastian.

"What about yourselves, where do you come from originally?", Teddy wondered.

Konrad made himself more comfortable in his seat. "Well, that is a long story! We came here as monks as part of the dissolution of the monasteries in England in 1537 and …"

"We have heard that story!", interjected Sebastian, "by someone called Brother Arnulfus who we met on the Black Falcon."

"Ah, Arnulfus!", said Konrad, "we know him well, although I have not seen him for a while. How is he?"

Sebastian told him about Arnulfus imprisoned on the Black Falcon, how he had told them in detail the story of the monks from his monastery, and that his only way of escape was probably to be sold at the slave market.

"What a sad story", said Brother Bonifacius, "we should help poor Arnulfus."

"Indeed we should!", replied Konrad, "another deed to put on our to-do-list."

"Tell us about your monastery", asked Teddy.

"When we all came here in 1537, animagi as well as a few human monks, we had not covered ourselves in glory, as

Arnulfus probably already told you. Many of us came from a large monastery north of London in a town called St Albans. There we had sacrificed several young monks for their souls and left them to their fate in a coma – and eventual death – to get through the portal to Animagana, a despicable act if you ask me! As a result, many of us wanted to redeem ourselves by recreating at least part of the monastic life we were used to, and especially by helping others in Animagana as much as we could. That's why we built the monastery where we are taking you tomorrow. It's also called St Albans, in memory of the place where many of us came from. But, judging from your story, what will be of most interest to you is our 'scriptorium', the large library we built in the centre of the monastery that contains all the old books, manuscripts and parchments we had managed to save from the destruction of the monasteries back in England. And you will see that we rescued quite a lot! The answer you are seeking as to how to return to your world might be held in the scriptorium. We shall see!"

Sebastian and his companions looked excitedly at each other.

"And you know where the portal is located in this monastery?", asked Teddy.

"Yes, we know the room where it is, but I think it has not been re-used since we arrived here in 1537", replied Konrad. "I will show you where it is when we are in the monastery. But let's go to sleep now, we still have a lot of travelling to do tomorrow."

45

After the slaughter of Mephisto's gang by Garglethroat's men, Bunny felt less and less at ease. He was utterly scared that the same fate could befall him at any time. *But I don't have much option for the moment other than to follow them!*, he thought as they trudged along on the muddy path. *But at the first occasion I will give them the slip, otherwise I'll be dead!*

It had taken Garglethroat, Ori Fisse, Skeleto and Bunny several days to make their way back to the clearing where the Jolly Roger pub stood. Garglethroat had never walked so much in his life and struggled to keep up with his much fitter companions who often had to help him over fallen trees lying over the muddy path. They now stood at the edge of the clearing overlooking the pub.

"You look like you've lost some weight, boss!", said Ori Fisse trying to cheer up Garglethroat.

Garglethroat stared back at him with an inscrutable look full of anger. "My weight is none of your business, mate!" Ori Fisse looked away and kept quiet, Bunny smiled inwardly.

They watched patrons going into the pub relatively sober and walking straight, and others coming out completely drunk, swaying from side to side and often vomiting as soon as they passed the doors.

"What a sorry bunch these pirates are!", said Garglethroat. "We should not have a problem at all to overpower them!"

They waited a while hidden behind bushes. Suddenly they saw an obese large bird with a large black and orange beak coming alone out of the pub. He walked slowly uphill towards them to an outhouse where beer barrels were stored.

"Callisto! There he is!", said Garglethroat. "Over to you boys!"

Ori Fisse and Skeleto quickly made their way down to the outhouse, while checking that nobody else was coming out of the pub. They entered the small building, and after only a few seconds dragged Callisto in front of them. Ori Fisse was holding a large dagger under Callisto's sagging throat. They quickly pushed him towards the bushes where Garglethroat and Bunny were waiting.

"So we meet again!", said Garglethroat, "but this time under slightly different circumstances!"

Callisto tried to speak but only emitted a gargle as the dagger partly choked his windpipe.

"I could kill you here and now", said Garglethroat, "but if you tell me where the sheet of paper with the incantation for the portal is that you stole from us, I will let you live!"

Callisto slowly raised his right arm and pointed towards the right pocket of his coat, still struggling to breathe with the dagger held tightly under his throat.

"There is a good boy!", said Garglethroat teasingly and took the crumpled piece of paper from Callisto's pocket.

"Yes, that's the one, boys! We got it! Now we only need to find Erik, grab his soul, and we have our insurance policy to get out of this nasty place! So, next question Callisto: do you know where Erik is? Have you already sold him at the slave market?"

Ori Fisse slightly released the pressure on the dagger so that Callisto could speak. Callisto cleared his throat and spat out a large gob of phlegm. "Captain Blackbeard sold him and his companions at the slave market to a fellow called Leonidas. They were going to be taken to Leonidas' gold mine two days walk from the slave market, I believe."

Garglethroat gave Ori Fisse a quick sign and Ori Fisse slit Callisto's throat with a slice of the dagger. Callisto's limp body slumped to the ground. Bunny was shocked again at how callously another animago had been murdered by Garglethroat's men, but he tried not to show any emotion.

Garglethroat folded the piece of paper with the secret incantation and slipped it into a small leather pouch. *I hope this will keep it safe and waterproof!* he thought and tied the pouch around his neck with a leather strap. *I am sure we will need the incantation sooner than we think!*

Garglethroat and his companions stayed close to the forest edge and made their way towards the pier where the Black Falcon was moored up, swaying idly in the midday breeze. Captain Blackbeard was sleeping in a hammock near the ship's helm, two sailors were sleeping in the shade on deck, and four others were playing cards while copiously drinking from a large bottle of rum. Brother Arnulfus was still in chains somewhere in the hold.

Garglethroat and his men managed to board the ship without being seen by the drunken card-playing sailors. They quickly made their way towards Blackbeard who was snoring very loudly. With his now familiar thrust of the dagger under Blackbeard's throat, Ori Fisse woke him up indicating that he should stay quiet.

Blackbeard looked very surprised. "What the…!", he said with a suffocated sound, "I thought you were long gone!"

"Well, we're back, mate", said Garglethroat nonchalantly, "and I have a business proposal for you. If you and your men sail us beyond the slave market to Leonidas' gold mine we will give you a share of our takings and let you go unharmed. If you say no, Ori Fisse will slit your throat! And believe me, he's had a lot of practice at making a clean cut lately …!"

Ori Fisse and Skeleto chuckled. Bunny did not dare look at the scene.

"Well, I haven't got much choice at the moment, have I?", replied Blackbeard. "But the seven of us here on the ship plus the four of you are barely enough to sail a ship like the Black Falcon. We normally take at least twenty sailors."

"We'll just have to do with what we have, Captain", said Garglethroat with a voice that did not invite any contradiction. "Make ready to sail … and no tricks, Blackbeard! We will keep a close eye on you!"

Blackbeard got out of the hammock and shouted orders to his seven sailors to ready the ship for departure. Ori Fisse hid the dagger behind Blackbeard's back but remained ready to strike any second. The sailors looked surprised at the four newcomers but did not question Blackbeard's orders as they were used to having to obey at short notice.

"Skeleto, you go into the captain's cabin and secure as many guns as you can", ordered Garglethroat. "We might need them to keep these guys at bay!"

Skeleto disappeared under the hold and came back a few minutes later with his skeletal arms full of muskets.

"No guns, boss", Skeleto remarked, "only muskets, but I think I got them all and I have checked that they are all loaded."

Ori Fisse took one musket and stood back, aiming at Blackbeard. Now the crew looked up and started drawing their sabres.

"You better drop your weapons and do as your captain has ordered!", shouted Garglethroat. "We will not hesitate to shoot your captain at any sign of insurrection and then shoot all of you!"

Ori Fisse and Skeleto relieved the crew of their sabres. The sailors grudgingly loosened the moorings and started setting the sails as the Black Falcon slowly edged away from the pier.

"Just in time, boss!", shouted Skeleto, "Look!", and he pointed towards the pub where a group of at least ten pirates were running towards the pier.

"Wait Blackbeard!", the pirate running out in front shouted as he reached the pier. "Where are you going? You were not due to sail until tomorrow?"

Blackbeard did not reply as he felt the tip of the musket press into his lower back. The Black Falcon was now in the middle of the harbour and started turning towards the narrow entrance. The sailors raised the lower topgallant sail on the main mast which caught the wind with a loud whoosh and propelled the ship forward. Within a few minutes the Black Falcon was out of the harbour, all sails raised, and making its way towards the open ocean.

Meanwhile more than twenty pirates had gathered on the pier. "We have just found Callisto's body near the outhouse!", shouted one. "His throat has been slit!"

"What is going on? And why is Blackbeard sailing away?", asked another. "Something funny is going on, I tell you …!"

"If Blackbeard has anything to do with it, he will pay!", shouted a large bear who was the captain of the Dark Raider, the second sailing ship moored to the pier. "Ready my ship and we'll try to apprehend them and find out what is going on!"

"Aye, aye, Captain Muguruza, let's catch the murderers!", his sailors shouted back as they rushed towards the Dark Raider.

46

Sebastian and his companions and the three monks awoke in the middle of the night to the clap of loud thunder. Every few seconds flashes of lightning were striking trees not far from their camp. Just as Sebastian was about to check with Teddy whether they were safe, it started raining very heavily. Within seconds they were all drenched.

Brother Konrad came running towards them, his feet sloshing in the rapidly forming puddles. "All of you, go into the cart quickly, unless you want to get chilled to the bone!"

They pushed the still unconscious body of Leonidas aside to make more room in the cart, but they could barely squeeze inside. Erik had to crouch in one corner and hold his legs against his chest to give the others enough space.

"What about you and your companions' Brother Konrad?", asked Teddy. "You'll get soaked!"

"Don't worry about us!", replied Konrad, "your wellbeing is more important than ours."

These are really the first genuinely well-meaning and nice animagi we have encountered in Animagana!, thought Sebastian. *They really want to help us! Maybe we have a chance after all to return to the human world.*

Suddenly the rain changed to hail. Marble sized clumps of ice pounded the camp, some bouncing back several metres into the air before finally landing on the ice-strewn ground. The flimsy cover of the cart was barely able to protect Sebastian and his friends from the onslaught. Konrad, Bonifacius and Regulus had quickly sought cover under a large tree on the edge of the small clearing and glanced forlorn at the sky in their soaked cloaks. After a few minutes the hailstorm stopped as suddenly as it had started but was replaced again by heavy rain.

"We should set off in the dark while the path is still passable", shouted Konrad over to the cart. "If it continues raining like this, the streams that cross the path between us and the monastery will become impassable."

They quickly gathered their soaked belongings and made their way down the path in the dark. The monks could not light a torch due to the pouring rain, but flashes of lightning showed them the way. After a while a pale moon was visible through gaps in the clouds and etched the forest in an eerie light that helped them make out the edges of the muddy path. The cow-like beast pulling the cart with Leonidas' body increasingly struggled to keep its footing. It often slipped and the three monks had to use all their strength to prevent the cart from toppling over the side. Sebastian and his companions used their blankets to protect themselves from the pouring rain, but after a while the fabric was soaked and offered little protection from the elements.

What an awful place Animagana is!, thought Sebastian. *Pirates, murderers, wild beasts, horrendous storms and muddy paths! How I miss Erik's house, my school and even the spider-infested passageways in our village!*

After a few hours walking in the continuous rain and after several near-accidents with the cart, dawn was beginning to break. The clouds had darkened again and the rain had intensified, large rain drops splashing onto the already soaked path that was increasingly turning into a small stream itself.

Several times they had crossed small but evidently swollen streams crossing the path. At one point they all had to hold on to the cart so that it did not get swept away in the murky water. Brother Konrad looked increasingly worried.

After another hour the group came to an abrupt halt. They stood on the edge of a steep riverbank in front of a raging torrent about twenty metres wide. The torrent flowed fast and large waves were breaking in its middle where the water flowed fastest. The river was filled with broken trees and branches, and the current was so strong that the riverbank was being eroded rapidly with large chunks of earth and rock falling into the water.

"As I feared!", lamented Konrad. "These streams swell quickly when it is raining that hard. There is no way we can cross it here and we might also have to temporarily abandon the cart. Brother Regulus, how is Leonidas?"

"He still has not regained consciousness, Brother Konrad", replied Regulus. "We have tended his wounds inflicted by the sabrejaws and we have stemmed further stuffing from oozing out, but we need to get him to the monastery quickly if he is to survive."

"You stay here with him Brother Regulus, while we make our way to the ford upstream, but we might lose a whole day doing this", said Konrad. "We will send for help as soon as we reach the monastery. Hopefully the rain will have stopped by then so that we can get the cart across the river."

Sebastian gaped at the dense vegetation covering the riverbank and dreaded having to walk through the undergrowth without a path.

Konrad looked at the bedraggled and soaked group in front of him. "I'm sorry about this, but we will have to make our way upstream along the riverbank without a path. There is a ford upstream which we occasionally use in heavy weather, but I am not even sure if that will be passable in this weather."

They trudged on for several hours through the dense undergrowth, climbing over dead trees, getting snarled in thorn-covered vines, slipping on wet mats of moss and constantly having to watch their step so as not to twist a foot or break a leg. It was still raining hard and they were drenched to the bone.

After what seemed an eternity, Konrad stopped and looked across the stream. "This is the ford. The river is a bit wider and shallower here, but as you can see there is still a lot of water, so we will have to be very careful. Brother Bonifacius, Hagelik and Teddy, please help me find a long vine that we can use to hold on to while crossing."

They fanned out into the wet forest and after a while came back with a long green and supple liana. Konrad tied one end of the liana to a large tree and the other around his waist and cautiously walked into the river. Although he was a tall bear, the water soon reached his waist and he found it difficult to keep his balance in the raging torrent. He lost his footing and quickly was carried away by the water, but the tightening liana allowed him to quickly regain the edge of the river. On his second attempt he walked a bit upstream and managed to stay on his feet until he reached what seemed to be a slight elevation in the middle of the river.

"OK, I can stand here safely, the water is a bit shallower here", remarked Konrad. "Hagelik and Teddy, you come over to me and that way you can hold the liana from here while I try and cross to the other side."

Teddy and Hagelik joined Konrad who held the liana tightly to ease their passage. They then secured Konrad from their vantage point in the middle of the river. Konrad was again nearly swept away but just managed to stay on his feet, and after a few large strides he reached the other riverbank, hauled himself up the steep eroding bank, and tied his end of the liana to a tree. Now the liana acted like a tightrope to which they could hang on to while crossing. As Sebastian, Ugah and particularly @@*^# were too short to cross the river by themselves, brother Bonifacius put them in his knapsack, tied it around his shoulder, and crossed the river behind Erik who made sure that he held on tightly to the Liana until he had reached the other side.

"Well done everybody!", said Konrad. "There are a few more streams to cross, but none will be as big and swollen as this one, so we should be able to reach the monastery soon."

It was still raining hard, and dark clouds seemed to stretch to the horizon, suggesting no end to the deluge.

47

Wet and exhausted Sebastian and his companions and the two monks reached the edge of the forest just before dark. It was still raining very hard. In the distance St Albans monastery could be seen, standing on a large clearing surrounded by dense forest above a cliff by the sea. It looked more like a castle than a monastery. It was comprised of several buildings surrounded by a rampart. Although it did not have a moat, there appeared to be only one entrance with two large wooden doors and a small bridge leading to it. Some of the buildings had small turrets on the side. The main building looked like a church and had large stained windows through which the flicker of candles could be seen. The monastery's steep tiled roofs glistened in the rain. Tilled fields were evident in the clearing where the monks grew corn, barley, wheat and horticultural products. A waterwheel was turning slowly, with small irrigation channels leading to some of the fields. As it was getting dark and still raining very hard, no monks were visible outside the monastery's ramparts.

Brother Konrad knocked on the large wooden gate. A small porthole opened and a guard peeked through. Recognising Brother Konrad he opened the gate immediately.

"Welcome to St Albans monastery!", said Brother Konrad, evidently relieved that they had finally completed their journey. Fellow animagi brethren came running out of the main building to meet the group. They all greeted Brother Konrad with evident joy. Konrad quickly gave orders to some of them to immediately go back along the path and retrieve Brother Regulus and injured Leonidas.

Among the group surrounding them, one figure stood out: a young human boy, about 12 years old, tall and slim, with black hair and dark eyes and wearing a monk's robe. He stood transfixed and stared at Erik. He moved forward through the crowd, walked straight to Erik and held out his hand. "Hello, I am Sylvester. I am 477 years old but I look like twelve!"

Erik was soaking wet, so tired he could barely stand and very hungry, but for the first time on Animagana he laughed out loud. *Another human boy! And he looks about the same age as me, although he is 465 years older!* he thought, and shook Sylvester's hand vigorously.

"Indeed! You don't look 477! I am Erik and these are my companions Sebastian, Teddy, Ugah, Hagelik and @@*^#. We have just come from the human world through the portal in the Jolly Roger pub. We were sold for slaves in Raupenburg, and the animagi who bought us tried to steal my soul, but thankfully Brother Konrad and his fellow brethren saved us and brought us here."

"I am so pleased to see another human!", said Sylvester, "and especially a young boy! That's great!"

"I think our companions are very hungry and tired", Konrad interrupted, "so I have to briefly interrupt this welcome and show them the refectory and their sleeping quarters. Let's get you some dry clothes first of all."

They were led to a side entrance of the main building where a young monk passed them simple cream-coloured monks' robes. For the first time since the whole ordeal began back in their village, Sebastian and his companions could get out of their wet and dirty clothes. Teddy's knitted blue jersey and matching pants were not only wet but also torn in several places, while Sebastian's brown corduroy trousers and checked blue shirt had large holes and were covered in mud. While Hagelik's and Erik's robes looked rather short, @@*^#'s robe seemed to have swallowed him up and neither his feet nor his ugly white seams could be seen.

"Well, that's an improvement!", said Teddy looking at @@*^#, and they laughed loudly as they gaped at each other in their robes.

They were quickly taken to the refectory where the monks were just starting dinner. There were about fifty of them, all animagi, seated along wooden benches. Candles lit up the large room which was at the centre of the main building. Piles of food stood in front of them, ranging from freshly baked bread, large jugs of mead, baskets filled with what looked like lamb chops, and heaps of baked potatoes. Sebastian and his companions were seated at one end of the table and realised how hungry they were. Erik was sitting next to Sylvester. They all tucked into the food in front of them without need of an invitation. They were ravenous ...

"This is great!", said Erik to Sylvester while gnawing on a lamb chop.

"Yes, it's brilliant having met you, I have so much to tell and show you!", replied Sylvester.

"My dear brethren!", shouted Konrad to his fellow monks, while tapping a glass to tell them to stop chattering and indicating to Sebastian and his companions to continue eating. "I am delighted to welcome the animagi Sebastian, Teddy, Ugah, Hagelik and @@*^# and the young human boy Erik to St

Albans monastery. They have just recently come through the portal in the Jolly Roger pub and have had quite a rough time in Animagana so far! So let's show them that there is also a nice side to this world, and I invite all of you to show them as much courtesy as you can and to answer all questions they might have. We will be spending a bit of time in our scriptorium as they are keen to investigate ways to return to the human world ..."

A hush went through the refectorium.

"Yes, I know this is rather unusual, as to my knowledge the last transfer back to the human world was over a hundred years ago! But be aware that they did not come to Animagana voluntarily, so we need to respect their urge of wanting to go back home."

The monks nodded and looked with great interest at Sebastian and his friends.

"As you know, these five animagi are not the first ones to reach us recently. We already have eight other animagi who arrived through the Jolly Roger portal recently, and we presume they are from the same place as you", and he gazed at Sebastian and his companions who had suddenly been distracted from their food.

"That's interesting!", said Teddy to the others. "Now we know the fate of at least eleven animagi from our village, also counting Barney, Penny and Woof who were sold at the slave market."

"Yes, but we don't know how many animagi disappeared from our village through the portal, or did Hexybilla tell you, Sebastian?", asked Ugah.

"No she didn't, or at least I can't remember", replied Sebastian. "I guess we should try and get as many animagi back as possible with us though the portal!"

"I have sent out my monks to search for the other animagi you mentioned and buy them back from whoever purchased them from the slave traders. Let's hope they can find at least some of them."

"Thank you so much for everything you are doing for us!", said Teddy looking gratefully at Konrad.

"But there is also a word of warning to you all to be extra vigilant", said Konrad also addressing his fellow monks. "A fellow from Sebastian's world named Garglethroat also made it through the portal with some of his henchmen and an animagi traitor named Bunny. We hear that they are very violent, that they don't hesitate to kill, and that they might be keen to extract the soul of a human boy as a means for them to get back to the human world. So we are tripling the number of guards near the main doors and on the ramparts, just in case …"

Erik and Sylvester looked at each other, knowing how lucky they were to be protected by Brother Konrad and his fellow monks.

After a wonderful dessert comprised of a mixture of freshly picked berries and fruits from the forest topped with a thick cream, Sebastian and his companions were led to their sleeping quarters high up in one of the turrets. They were allocated in pairs to their rooms which were basic monks' cells with two beds, a small stone washbasin with a large jug of water, and a crude wooden table with two chairs. Large leaded windows looked out over the main square in front of the refectory towards a large dark round building that towered over all the others.

"What's this building?", Teddy asked Brother Konrad.

"That's our library, the scriptorium. That's where we will go tomorrow to search for the incantation and the secret for you to get back to your world."

48

They had been sailing for several hours. The Dark Raider was slowly catching up with the Black Falcon. Although Skeleto and Bunny helped to hoist sails and unfurl ropes, Blackbeard realised that their skeleton crew was insufficient to sail as efficiently and fast as possible. Standing behind the helm, he peered over his shoulder and estimated that at their current speed the Dark Raider would have caught up with them within the hour. Ori Fisse and Garglethroat still stood behind Blackbeard watching his every move. Ori Fisse pointed a musket directly at Blackbeard's back.

I am not sure whether I want Captain Muguruza to catch up with us or not, thought Blackbeard. *If they catch up, there will be a fight and many of us, including myself, might be killed! If we escape we are still at the mercy of the fat toad and his henchmen! So it's a no-win situation really! But there is not much I can do at the moment anyway, not with a musket pointing at me, so let's just see what happens ...*

Garglethroat had also realised that the Dark Raider was catching up. Although dusk was approaching and nightfall might help them escape, Garglethroat anxiously gazed at the sky to see if the weather might come to their rescue first. Low grey clouds drifted over their heads, but there was little wind and a misty drizzle descended upon the already wet planks and gangways. Sails started flapping for lack of wind and the ship's pace had markedly slowed down. The sea which had been rough earlier was now quite smooth.

Within an hour they will catch us!, thought Garglethroat, and in a hand-to-hand combat we will be outnumbered, especially as Blackbeard's men will quickly turn against us!

Blackbeard's sailors were indeed eyeing them with increasing suspicion, glancing hopefully at the approaching Dark Raider which was now only about one kilometre behind them. Muguruza was clearly visible behind the helm, looking in anticipation at the Black Falcon. But with darkening skies, dusk began to fall quickly. A thick fog had set in, enveloping both ships in grey wisps of clouds.

"We will lose them!", shouted Muguruza to his crew. "Hoist the last shred of sail, we have to catch them before the fog closes in!"

The Dark Raider was now only ten ship lengths away, it seemed inevitable that the Black Falcon would be caught within the next few minutes. Garglethroat looked increasingly anxious at the approaching ship and gave Ori Fisse a sign to press the tip of the musket harder into Blackbeard's back. "We have to go faster, Blackbeard!", he shouted. "If they catch us you will be the first one to die!"

Despite the cool mist, Blackbeard was sweating profusely. With a worried look he glanced at the flapping sails and the futile attempts of his crew to eke out the last bit of speed in the failing wind. Wisps of fog still swirled around the ships, allowing the odd glimpses of the pursuing Dark Raider. But quickly dusk had given way to a moonless pitch-black night. Only the bow lights of the Dark Raider could be seen, slowly approaching.

"I have an idea!", said Garglethroat. "Blackbeard, have one of your men light the stern light!"

"But that will show them where we are, boss!", remarked Ori Fisse. "Would it not be better to hope for the fog to close us in and then disappear out of sight in the dark?"

"Trust me …", replied Garglethroat.

49

Erik and Sylvester shared one of the monks' cells. Although Erik was dreadfully tired, he was very curious about Sylvester's story. "Tell me more about yourself, Sylvester", urged Erik.

Sylvester was already lying in bed but had expected Erik to ask him about his background. "I came with the monks from St Albans monastery in the human world where I had just started as a novice. I came from a humble family of candle makers, and my parents were glad when the monastery agreed to take me on and cover all my board and lodging. But soon after I had started, Thomas Cromwell, Henry VIII's chief minister in charge of dissolving England's monasteries and redistributing their wealth, destroyed all monasteries in England. It was a dreadful time for us! It was utter chaos! Nobody knew what was going to happen and what would become of us, and we were particularly worried about the loss of thousand-year-old knowledge stored in the monasteries' libraries and scriptoria. That's when Brother Konrad and his fellow monks decided to use the portal and escape to Animagana."

Erik thought about the story that Arnulfus had told them on the Black Falcon and how worried he had also been about the potential loss of knowledge.

"We had all the information we needed about where the portal was located in our monastery and how to use it from the then recently published 'Chronicles of Animagi Lore', which your group must have also used to come here to Animagana", continued Sylvester.

"I don't know much about it", replied Erik, "but I think that's the book that Teddy and Sebastian used to find the secret incantation for coming here. We can ask them tomorrow."

"The main problem was that the monks needed to extract the essence of human children's souls to get here, and that posed a huge moral dilemma for the monks. They knew that they had to sacrifice several, if not all, their novices in order to get the monks to Animagana together with their belongings and precious books and parchments. It meant that one human child's soul enabled the passage of only one or two monks into Animagana before the portal closed again. After a lot of praying, and just as Thomas Cromwell's men knocked on the monastery's gates, the monks decided to go ahead. They extracted the souls of their novices and came to Animagana. But only a few human monks made it, it was mainly animagi monks who managed to escape."

"How come you survived, Sylvester?", asked Erik.

"I knew what was happening to my fellow novices and friends and was very scared. The night of the soul extraction, I hid in a cupboard and watched the dreadful scene unfold in front of my eyes. I knew that the novices would never wake up again from their comas as there was no intention by the monks to come back to the human world in the near future. They knew that they would be hunted down, and possibly killed, by Thomas Cromwell's men. I followed one of the older monks to the portal and as he went through I slipped through behind him, just as the portal was closing. When we arrived on the grassy slope that was here before the monastery was built, the first thing I got was a thorough spanking, and it was argued that my selfish action had prevented another monk from escaping from the clutches of

Henry VIII's men! But I shouted back that I was not nearly as selfish as the monks themselves who had killed several innocent children just to get themselves into safety. That shut them up for a while, and they left me alone after that. But our escape hung over my relationship with the monks here for the last 465 years, and at times I still wonder whether they have not regretted that I made it safely to here without sacrificing my soul for one of their fellow monks. And I have been trapped in this stupid and useless child's body ever since, which means they still treat me like a little kid although I am basically as old as they are!"

Sylvester and Erik were quiet for a while, digesting the sad story of the monks' escape to Animagana and Sylvester's predicament. Erik understood the moral dilemma the monks had faced: on the one hand they felt compelled to save the accumulated knowledge of millennia and also themselves, but on the other hand their actions had to be based on the selfish decision to sacrifice many children to make the passage to Animagana possible. He also understood that Sylvester had been in an awkward situation ever since.

"So I have always had a difficult position here in the monastery", continued Sylvester. "I curse my body that does not age and that makes me look like a young boy, although my mind is that of an old man who is rather tired of having lived 477 years. Yet the monks still treat me like I am a novice!"

Sylvester sighed in exasperation and glanced over to Erik, but Erik had fallen asleep …

50

It was pitch black. Before the fog had closed in, Captain Muguruza could clearly see the outline of the Black Falcon just a few ship-lengths in front.

"The fools have kept their stern light on!", exclaimed Muguruza. "That will make it easy for us to spot them, even in this fog!"

"Shall we open fire, Capt'n?", asked the sailor next to him.

"No", replied Muguruza, "we can overpower them with our crew and we don't want to damage the Black Falcon. All men to your posts, ready for boarding!"

The light in front of them had changed course slightly and was moving steadily ahead, but they were gradually catching up. They were now only about two ship-lengths away. The fog was so thick that nothing could be seen except for the light. After a few minutes they seemed to be on top of the light, but still no ship could be seen. The crew of the Dark Raider was standing at the bow railing, grappling hooks and weapons at the ready, daggers between their teeth and sabres raised.

They were now on top of the light which seemed surprisingly low.

"It's just a dinghy!", shouted Muguruza in anger. "They put the light on a dinghy, while they sailed away in the dark! We've lost them!"

51

Brother Konrad led Sebastian and his companions to the scriptorium in the large building at the centre of the monastery. While Sylvester had gone his own way and was going to meet up with Erik later on, Brothers Bonifacius and Regulus also accompanied them. They walked past large shelves covered in books and manuscripts saved from the dissolution of the monasteries in the 16th century. Monks were sitting on high stools writing with quills and ink on parchments, etching intricate engravings on book covers, or colouring in fanciful letters at the start of book chapters. Some monks looked irritated at the newcomers but quickly resumed their work.

"I will show you our copy of the 'Chronicles of Animagi Lore' that we saved from St Albans monastery in the human world", said Konrad. "We'll see if it is similar to the copy you saw back in your world."

They climbed a rickety wooden spiral staircase to one of the top floors of the scriptorium. Large books were stacked in narrow wooden shelves covered in dust.

"As you can see", said Konrad, "this section has not been used for a while", and he blew off the dust of a large book he pulled off the shelf. It was a copy of the 'Chronicles'.

Sebastian and Teddy got very excited as this was their chance to see a copy of the incantation they had so desperately tried to memorise. Sebastian looked expectantly at Teddy who smiled back.

The book looked identical to the copy Sebastian had seen in the archives of his village. Brother Konrad indeed opened the book at the page with the incantation:

**UMMM MARISH GRANAFF GANG GOOL
RAST HEREBDYN IMMORTIS GRATTAN
URRR MAJORIM EXORBITUS THYSSUSS
DRRAM GARR NON RETURNUM SIC**

"Here it is!", exclaimed Sebastian with excitement. "Careful Brother Konrad not to read it out aloud, as it immediately causes headaches and dizziness! Look, Teddy, 'majorim exorbitus', the two words I replaced which saved Erik's life", he said proudly and Erik looked at him with renewed gratitude. "Let's also see the passage with the riddle we solved."

Brother Konrad flicked a few pages and showed them the familiar riddle written in English:

**Seven deadly sins
Seven sinful stories
And seven monsters to unlock**

**Seven ways to expire
Will unravel the mystery
To Animagana's world
By taking away the souls
Of the weakest of all**

But behold animagi

Of unspeakable temptations
And no turning back
Without reverse wisdom

Teddy explained to Konrad how they had solved most of the riddle, bar the last two sentences, and told Konrad about the page that was missing.

"Brother Konrad", asked Sebastian, "most of the book is written in pre-English animagi language which we can't read, do you happen to be able to read and translate it?"

"Yes", replied Konrad. "At St Albans monastery we were trained to read the old animagi language. If I remember correctly, because it's been a while since I have opened this book, the most important passage is here and says: 'There will come a time when a young animago will recognise the power to unleash the control of time. This young animago will hold the key to Animagana and will free the beings trapped within. This animago will use the power to fend off evil, to help those who have sold their souls, and to reunite Animagana with the real world of animagi. The one the prophecy foretells will be familiar with the secret spell and will be able to use it wisely."

"Yes, I remember this is what our village witch also told me", said Sebastian, "and she even thought that I was the one the prophecy related to!"

The room went deadly silent as Brother Konrad looked at Regulus and Bonifacius.

"You mean to say", said Konrad after a while, "that you have the skill to freeze time?"

"Well ...", replied Sebastian rather unsure how much he should reveal, but Erik gave him a reassuring look. "I've now had three occasions when I could freeze time. Each time I was in mortal danger and had no control over what I was doing. But it saved my life and that of my companions every time."

Brother Konrad peered again at his fellow brethren. "Could it be …? Could it be…?", he mumbled. "We have been talking about the prophecy ever since the 'Chronicles od Animagi Lore' were written, but never quite understood what it meant. Based on your story and the fact that you seem to have the power to freeze time, maybe you are indeed destined for something great, little bear! Let's look again at what the prophecy says: 'There will come a time when a young animago will recognise the power to unleash the control of time.' So, yes, that fits your description. 'This young animago will hold the key to Animagana and will free the beings trapped within.' This one is more difficult to interpret but maybe you are meant to take the animagi back home who recently came through the Jolly Roger portal? 'This animago will use the power to fend off evil, to help those who have sold their souls, and to reunite Animagana with the real world of animagi.' You have already used your power to fend off evil, against both evil Garglethroat in your world and against the beasts of the forest here in Animagana. But I am not sure what 'reunite Animagana with the real world of animagi' means. 'The one the prophecy foretells will be familiar with the secret spell and will be able to use it wisely.' Again, you know the spell, you have even manipulated it wisely to save Erik. All seems to fit Sebastian! Maybe you are the one the prophecy foretells!"

Again the little room was silent as Konrad's incisive analysis started to sink in.

"It seems to make sense", said Teddy after a while. "But the problem is that, first, we don't know whether the incantation works the same way for going back and, second, that we can't extract a human child's soul anyway without killing one!"

"Yes, that is a quandary!", acknowledged Konrad, "and while we might be able to find out about the incantation, I can't see a solution to extracting a human child's soul, unless we sacrifice either Erik or Sylvester, which is, of course, completely unthinkable!"

Erik breathed a loud sigh of relief and was also glad Konrad had given his full assurance that his new friend Sylvester would never be touched.

"But what we do have here, and as I mentioned back in the forest", continued Konrad, "is a portal back to your world. In fact it is in the basement of this scriptorium. However, to my knowledge nobody has ever used it other than when we arrived … but it was only an empty field then of course! I will show it to you on the way out."

"What about the page that had been torn out of our copy of the 'Chronicles' back home and that we could never find?", wondered Teddy.

Brother Konrad flicked the sheets in the book and found the page Teddy referred to. "OK, let's see whether this will give us a clue. Hmmm… it says a bit more about Animagana, interestingly referring to it as a 'paradise'! Rather misleading wouldn't you think? Ah … and this bit is probably of greatest interest to you. If my interpretation of the ancient language is correct, it confirms that humans can come back from Animagana any time without risk to their lives, but animagi can only go back if their hosts are still alive. It says here that 'if the human host has died, the animago who returns will die immediately upon stepping through the portal'."

"This explains why virtually no animago has gone back to the human world over the centuries", suggested Teddy, "as they would have known that they would not survive the transfer back as their human hosts would have been long gone."

"Yes", said Konrad, "and this explains why none of us animagi monks ever went back, as by the time we might have wanted to go back, our human hosts in St Albans would have been long dead."

Konrad focused back on the text. "It also confirms that souls of human children are reinstated if their animagi come back. This suggests that through the act of going back an animago takes the soul of his or her human host back with them. I suspect that the children in coma from your village you mentioned should re-awaken if we could get all of you recent arrivals back through the portal."

Sebastian thought about all the poor human children from their village and how they might never wake up from their coma.

"The passage in the book also says that while the incantation can be used in all portals, the incantation you used will automatically take you back to the original portal you used in your village", Konrad continued. "In other words you can use any portal on Animagana to get back to your portal in the village by using the incantation you know. This means that our portal should in theory be able to take you back directly to your village."

"And ... ah here!", exclaimed Konrad. "It says that returning from Animagana is difficult and refers back to last part of the riddle we already know:"

But behold animagi
Of unspeakable temptations
And no turning back
Without reverse wisdom

"It is clearly that last part which we need to understand if you were ever to have a chance to return to the human world. Brothers Bonifacius, Regulus and I will ponder this a bit further as there are a few other manuscripts we could consult, but I think we have probably done enough for now. You must be starving!"

They were indeed rather hungry again as they had passed most of the morning in the scriptorium and breakfast had been rather early. Lunch was awaiting them in the refectory.

"I will show you the room with the portal on our way to the refectorium", said Konrad, and he led them towards the basement of the scriptorium. Contrary to the intricately hidden portal in the archives of their village, the portal room in the monastery was behind a simple and unlocked wooden door covered with bookshelves on the walls. There was nothing special about the room and it seemed to be in use as part of the library.

"Most monks don't even know what lies in this room", thought Konrad aloud as he led them out towards the refectorium.

52

Leonidas opened his eyes. He was in a small room that looked like a monk's cell. A skinny stoat-like animago in a monk's robe was sleeping on a chair next to his bed. Leonidas moved his legs but a sharp pain forced him to lie still for a moment. He looked down his body and saw bandages in several places. Gradually his memory came back: *The last thing I remember was being attacked by sabrejaws ... and then nothing! The monks must have found me and brought me back to their monastery.*

Slowly he eased his body out of bed without waking up the sleeping monk. He looked out of the window of his cell, down towards the courtyard situated in front of a large building. Konrad and his fellow monks, as well as Sebastian and his companions, were just coming out of the scriptorium and made their way towards the refectorium, together with several other monks streaming out of other buildings. Another young boy, about Erik's age, was walking towards them. Together they walked fast towards the large building, trying to get out of the pouring rain. *They've also made it out of the forest alive!,* Leonidas thought. *And there is that blond human boy whose soul I should have extracted! I still don't understand why the incantation didn't work. I wonder who that other boy is who walked with them?*

Leonidas carefully opened the unlocked door to his cell. The corridor outside was empty. He held his side which was still painful underneath the bandages. *I need to get out of this monastery, the monks will imprison me here once they realise that I have recovered. I need a disguise!*

He went back into the cell and looked inside a wardrobe behind the door where he found a plain monk's robe with a hood. He put it on, slipped out of the door and walked slowly down the corridor towards a narrow spiral staircase. *Nobody is around. They must all be having lunch in the refectory*, thought Leonidas. He went out of the building, making sure he was not seen by the few monks visible on the ramparts. A guard stood in front of the main monastery gates, trying to shelter from the rain under a small wooden roof. Leonidas ducked behind a barrel. He grabbed a fist-sized piece of wood and threw it beyond the guard. It landed with a loud 'clunk' on something hollow. The guard left his post and walked through the mud towards the noise. Leonidas quickly went to the gate, opened the unlocked small side door and slipped out of the monastery unseen. He watched the monks on the ramparts make their rounds and covered the open ground as quickly as he could. The fields around the monastery were empty, drenched in rain. Leonidas made his way towards the edge of the forest as fast as his aching body would allow. He was free …

53

Hexybilla woke up with a start. Someone was banging repeatedly at her bedroom door. Still half asleep she put on her nightgown and her slippers and shuffled to the door. She opened the door a slither and saw a pale-looking Professor Pandanus breathing heavily, urging her to let him in.

"I apologise for waking you up in the middle of the night", said Professor Pandanus, "but we have just found something of the utmost importance that you must see. Can I come in?"

Hexybilla let him in and they sat down on a sofa on the side of a fireplace with still smouldering logs. Professor Pandanus pulled out a vellum cloth wrapped around a smallish rectangular object. He removed the cloth and showed Hexybilla a small black book with a white skull on its cover. Hexybilla read the cover written in pre-animagi language: The Book of Death. Professor Pandanus took the book back and opened it on a specific page. He was breathing heavily and was clearly very distressed.

"Read this passage, Mrs Hexybilla, and you will see why I and my colleagues have become very frightened! As this book was rescued from the monastery dissolutions in the 16th century, I think it might provide an alternative explanation as to why Henry VIII dissolved all English monasteries and their libraries. I don't understand why it ended up in our archives, but I think we need to destroy it immediately."

Hexybilla put on her reading glasses and began reading the passage Professor Pandanus had pointed out. As she read her eyes widened, her breathing accelerated, and she let out a loud gasp of exasperation.

"Oh dear me!", Hexybilla sighed. "You are right, we need to destroy it immediately! I hope it will burn!", and she threw the book into the embers. For a short moment nothing happened. The book was lying on the red-hot logs, seemingly unaffected. But after a while green smoke began to ooze from the book and a ray of green light was visible between the pages. The book suddenly erupted into flames, and a faint hollow scream could be heard that sounded as if it came out of the book itself! Hexybilla and Pandanus stood up frightened and moved away from the fire watching the book being consumed by the flames. The whole room was filled with green smoke and the smell was truly disgusting. Hexybilla and Pandanus ran to the door and opened it wide, letting the smoke dissipate into the passageway. Gradually the smoke eased. Only a pile of greenish ash was visible in the fireplace.

54

Garglethroat peered behind his shoulder into the dense fog. The light of the dinghy had quickly faded away as they had made a sharp ninety degree turn. The darkness had swallowed up the Dark Raider.

"I am pretty sure we lost them", said Garglethroat and Blackbeard nodded reluctantly.

Blackbeard had somehow hoped Captain Muguruza would catch up with them and maybe even free them. *Garglethroat's trick with the dingy unfortunately worked!*, he thought. *No chance that they will catch up with us now in this fog and darkness.* He felt Ori Fisse's presence behind him with the musket pointing at his back, as he steered the Black Falcon by compass on a north-westerly course.

Blackbeard's sailors had observed the recent developments with increasing apprehension. They knew they could not get close to their captain as Ori Fisse would shoot Blackbeard in the back, but they also thought that Garglethroat and his two henchmen would be no match for them if they attacked all at once. They were unsure what to make of Bunny who stayed in the background, had helped the crew with some of the sailing tasks, but had seemed reluctant to join in with Garglethroat and the two others from the beginning.

"We will wait for the right opportunity", whispered one of the sailors to his mate standing next to him. "They will have to sleep sometime!"

Just at this moment Ori Fisse let out a big yawn. He was indeed rather tired as he had pointed the musket at Blackbeard since they set sail and had to be vigilant throughout. Blackbeard steered along the coast. Noticing Ori Fisse's tiredness, Garglethroat gave Skeleto a sign to take over from Ori Fisse.

"I am also getting rather tired", complained Blackbeard, "I have been behind the helm non-stop for over sixteen hours now! I am not sure I can do this much longer!"

"Shut up, you ruddy ferret!", shouted Garglethroat. "You will stand behind the helm as long as I say, and I don't care if you drop dead or not!"

Garglethroat and Ori Fisse took a nap for a few hours while Skeleto watched over an increasingly tired Blackbeard who had to clutch the helm to support his tired legs. Four of the six sailors were also asleep, while the other two crewmembers were busy handling the sails while continuously watching Skeleto.

Blackbeard kept looking at the sailors as he did not dare peer behind him to check whether Skeleto was still pointing the musket at him. After a while the two sailors stood up and stopped tending the sails. They stared at Blackbeard and motioned to him to turn his head. Blackbeard turned around and saw that Skeleto was asleep, the musket resting on his skinny upper thighbones. Skeleto was snoring. Garglethroat and Ori Fisse seemed also fast asleep. Bunny was nowhere to be seen.

"Now!", whispered Blackbeard to the sailors who quickly woke up their four sleeping fellow crewmen.

They rapidly made their way up towards the upper deck where Blackbeard was standing, wooden clubs in hand. They passed a club to Blackbeard who tiptoed towards Skeleto. He raised the club and was about to strike Skeleto's skull when a loud bang from a musket disrupted the silence. Blackbeard collapsed, a bullet hole in his forehead. Ori Fisse was holding a smoking musket pointed at the other sailors. Skeleto had woken up with a start and Garglethroat rubbed his sleepy eyes.

"Get them!", shouted the sailor standing in front, and all six dashed towards Garglethroat and his men, clubs raised.

Skeleto killed the sailor rushing towards him with a well-aimed shot to his chest. Garglethroat had reacted quickly and passed a freshly loaded musket to Ori Fisse, while grabbing hold of another two muskets himself.

The remaining five pirates had slowed their attack, surprised by the quick reaction of Garglethroat and his two henchmen. Ori Fisse used this slight hesitation, stepped back, jumped the railing behind him and used his higher vantage point to shoot another sailor. Garglethroat also took a well-aimed shot at a pirate who rushed at him with his sabre raised. Garglethroat's shot tore off half of the pirate's head and his limp body collapsed in front of Garglethroat, spilling his stuffing over the deck. The remaining three pirates were now in a panic and hesitated even more to go forward. Having used up all their musket shots, Ori Fisse and Skeleto moved forward, sabres in one hand, daggers in the other, and with a few well-aimed strikes killed all three sailors.

Garglethroat looked at the seven dead pirates piled up in front of them. "Good job, boys!", he commended Ori Fisse and Skeleto. "But we now have a problem in that we can't sail the ship. I don't know how the sails work and neither do you!"

"We'll try to manage, boss", replied Ori Fisse. "Maybe Bunny can help us?"

Just as he was speaking Bunny emerged from behind the ship's forecastle where he had been hiding during the fight.

"Where have you been all this time?", asked Garglethroat. "I have the impression you are avoiding us!"

"Sorry I could not help with the fight", replied Bunny. "I was asleep."

Garglethroat looked suspiciously at Bunny. "I am no longer too sure about your commitment, Bunny!", said Garglethroat. "Are you still with us?"

"Yes, of course", replied Bunny, but he did not say it with much conviction. "But I am getting rather sick of Animagana, I must admit, it is not at all how I expected it to be. All we've had to do so far was fight for our lives all the time. There is no comfort here, just basic survival, and the animagi we have met so far are in rather bad shape!"

Garglethroat, Ori Fisse and Skeleto did not reply, silently agreeing with Bunny's assessment.

After a while Ori Fisse spoke up: "Bunny is right, boss! Skeleto and I have also begun to wonder whether it wasn't a mistake coming here. Although we are outcasts back home in the human world, I am not sure that we will make it here for very long. I wouldn't mind going back to our world and trying my luck there."

"You wimps!", shouted Garglethroat. "After all this effort of going through the difficulties we faced getting here, you now want to go back?"

"Remember, boss, that only a few days ago you were at the end of your tether and nearly dead", said Ori Fisse forcefully. "It was only thanks to Skeleto, myself and Gremlin that you survived from the clutches of Mephisto, don't forget that!"

Garglethroat looked threateningly at Ori Fisse and put his hand to his sabre, but eased off after seeing both Ori Fisse and Skeleto ready to draw theirs. Ever since arriving on Animagana Garglethroat had felt a sense of unease and even slight panic. *I can't communicate mentally with Andrew anymore!*, he thought. *It must be the fact that we are in something like a parallel universe here in Animagana, and our thoughts don't seem to be able to breach the gap between the two worlds. I hadn't realised that I would lose contact with my host, and I must admit that I find this very hard! I wonder how Andrew is getting on in that dreadful lunatic asylum without being able to contact me? I need to know whether he is alright ...*

"OK, I see your point lads!", said Garglethroat, without revealing what his true motives were to return to the human world. He would not admit to anyone – not even his henchmen – how closely connected he felt to Andrew Billings. "If we could lay our hands on that young boy Erik and extract his soul I may also be tempted to go back to our world. But I am afraid that we have other problems at the moment as we somehow need to get this ship safely ashore and find Leonidas' gold mine where Erik and his companions were taken."

Ori Fisse, Skeleto and Bunny nodded in agreement. Garglethroat took the helm, checked the latest north-westerly bearing and told his men to lower as much sail as possible to make steering the large ship easier for a crew of just four.

While Bunny, Ori Fisse and Skeleto made their way precariously up the slippery rigging, the Black Falcon made its way slowly north-westwards through the thickening mist. No land was visible through the thick fog as darkness enveloped the ship.

55

After their research in the scriptorium, Konrad had taken Sebastian and his friends to the refectory. One monk took Konrad aside. "I am afraid I have bad news, Brother Konrad", said the monk looking guilty. "Leonidas has escaped. He woke up while Brother Subenius was asleep by his side, and he somehow managed to slip out of the monastery unseen!"

"It is up to Leonidas if he wants to leave us, Brother Grandolfus", replied Konrad, "he is not our prisoner. But it is worrying that the guard did not see him get out of the monastery. I will double the guards and tell them to be extra vigilant, especially with this nasty animago Garglethroat on the loose who Sebastian and Teddy mentioned. But let Leonidas be. He will struggle to make his way alone back to his goldmine, which is several days walk from here through dense forest infested with sabrejaws."

"There is also some good news", continued Grandolfus. "The monks you sent out to repurchase some of the animagi from Sebastian's village, who were recently sold on the slave market, have come back. They have managed to buy six of them. Three, called Barney, Penny and Woof, cost a fortune to buy back, but you had said that no expense should be spared."

"That is good news", replied Konrad, "and I don't care how much it cost us. At least they are safe for now. Where are they?"

"They were exhausted after the long trek through the forest and are all asleep", said Grandolfus.

Konrad went back to Sebastian and his companions and told them the good news about their six fellow animagi. He sat them next to the eleven other animagi from their village who had been rescued earlier by the monks, making it seventeen rescued animagi altogether. They looked eagerly at Sebastian and his friends, but all looked rather shy and lost. Apart from Barney, Penny and Woof, Sebastian did not know any of them, but Teddy knew some from sight.

"We are so glad to see you here", said a small white dog named Snowy. "We have been so lucky to end up here in the monastery, but overall we really have not enjoyed being here!"

The other animagi from the village nodded in agreement. A large brown owl called Uhu looked at them with her big brown eyes: "Yes, and we really regret the deal we struck with Rigor Mortis who brought us here and that we betrayed our human host, a young boy called Martin who is now in a coma. All this money we spent to come to this dreadful place! And greedy Mr Mortis who lied to us about this being a paradise!"

Everybody agreed as they recounted their stories how they got to the monastery and how the monks had saved them from the slave traders. Teddy remembered the boy Martin who had fallen into a coma and vaguely knew Snowy and Uhu. He told the others about Barney, Penny and Woof and the three other animagi from their village who had just been rescued by the monks.

"That now makes 17 animagi from our village plus us five, so 22 overall", calculated Teddy. "If we could somehow all find our way back home we could save the majority of children from their coma."

"But how will we get back to our world?", asked a small tiger called Tigger.

"Well, that's the problem!", said Teddy. "Without the essence of a human child's soul we are stuck in Animagana forever! Think about the monks who have been here for 477 years! None of us wants to end up immortal in a world like this."

"But are you saying that there is no way out of here?", asked Snowy.

"Yes, that's what I am effectively saying", replied Teddy, "unless any of you is willing to sacrifice either Erik or Sylvester to harvest their souls?"

They all stared down not daring to look each other in the face. They all knew that there was no way they would ever sacrifice one of the human children. They knew they were stuck in Animagana, possibly forever!

56

After struggling with ropes and halyards, and scrambling up and down the rigging with only a faint light from the ship's lantern, Garglethroat and his crew had reduced the sails on the Black Falcon to a minimum. The ship slowly made its way north-west. The dense fog still prevented them from seeing the coast, and only the north-westerly compass bearing kept them more or less on course.

"This fog is really a nuisance!", swore Garglethroat. "From the maps Blackbeard had in front of him I can't make out at all where we are! I don't know how far the coast is, or where we are in relation to Leonidas' mine marked on the map."

Dawn was breaking slowly and Garglethroat and his men at least began to see parts of the ship, but the fog was still so dense that visibility beyond the Black Falcon was zero. As there was no wind the sea was dead calm, only a very light breeze inflated the main sail on the mizzen mast they had left rigged.

"Should we maybe just drop the drag anchor and wait for the fog to clear, boss?", asked Ori Fisse.

"I don't know where the drag anchor is, do you?", asked Garglethroat. Ori Fisse stayed quiet.

A faint sound could be heard in the distance, a regular hum, like waves crashing onto rocks. Garglethroat stretched his fat neck trying to see anything beyond the bowsprit of the Black Falcon, but the fog muted the sounds and enveloped everything in a white shroud. The hum grew louder.

"What is it?", asked Skeleto.

"I am not sure!", replied Garglethroat. "It could be waves breaking on the distant coast ... but I don't really know. We better steer away from the noise until we can see something."

Garglethroat turned the helm hard portside and the Black Falcon slowly turned by ninety degrees. Bunny stood at the foot of the Bowsprit, peering into the white mist. Suddenly a black shape appeared on the starboard side. "I think I can see a dolphin or a whale!", cried Bunny, "or ... wait... it's not moving ... it's a rock! Rock starboard! Hard to port!"

Garglethroat threw his bulk against the helm and turned it portside as fast as he could. Ori Fisse and Skeleto had both rushed to the sides of the ship and leaned over to look out for rocks.

"Another rock on starboard!", shouted Skeleto. "Large rock on portside!", shouted Ori Fisse. They could now hear loud breakers crashing against rocks everywhere around them.

"There is no way out of this, boss!", shouted Ori Fisse. "Rocks everywhere ... and it's getting narr...."

The Black Falcon struck a rock hard and threw all four animagi off balance. The ship lurched to the right with a mighty splash, straightened again, then lurched left and hit another rock with a loud screeching sound. Garglethroat and his men heard how the wooden hull of the ship was being smashed to pieces, while in the ship's hold Brother Arnulfus was thrown to the floor, still chained and with no way of escape. And still the Black Falcon sailed on through the maze of razor-sharp and jagged rocks, propelled by the mizzen sail which they had not been able to take down in time.

Suddenly the ship hit a large rock head on. Garglethroat and his men were thrown forward. Bunny lost his balance and fell over the side of the ship into the foaming water beneath. Garglethroat hung on to one of the halyards, but another mighty shock went through the ship as it hit the next rock. The Black Falcon rolled onto its portside, but this time she did not recover and started tilting more and more to the left.

"To the lifeboat! Quickly!", shouted Garglethroat, as all three now hung on for dear life.

Ori Fisse scrambled towards the lifeboat that already hung precariously over the side of the ship and unclipped the boat from its davits. He made sure that his dagger remained clipped to his belt, but he had left his sabre behind. The lifeboat fell ten metres and crashed into the sea. Ori Fisse jumped behind the boat and hauled himself inside. Garglethroat and Skeleto had managed to reach the side of the sinking ship. A sudden jolt of the Black Falcon propelled them forward and they both fell head first into the water. Ori Fisse had grabbed an oar and quickly rowed towards them. The Black Falcon loomed directly above them, tilting further and further. Ori Fisse pulled Skeleto aboard the lifeboat, but they could not lift Garglethroat's heavy bulk over the gunwale. Neither had managed to keep their sabres.

"Hang on to the boat boss, we need to get out of here very quickly!", shouted Ori Fisse, peering over his shoulder and watching the mass of the Black Falcon tilting towards them. The ship now leaned almost ninety degrees, her portside impaled on a large jagged rock. The ship made a final lurch and splashed into the sea with a loud bang, barely missing the lifeboat. Rigging and spars showered the lifeboat, hitting Ori Fisse and Skeleto who rowed away as fast as they could, Garglethroat hanging on to the side with all his remaining strength.

They finally managed to extricate themselves from the cordage, masts, rigging and debris, and rowed out into open water. The Black Falcon had now almost completely turned, the hull sticking out of the water with its barnacle-encrusted keel glimmering in the emerging sunshine. A gurgling sound could be heard as the hull rapidly filled with water. The ship's bow started disappearing, water oozing from every porthole and broken window. It did not take long for the ship to tilt upright, with only its stern sticking out vertically and gliding into the abyss.

Finally I am free!, thought Brother Arnulfus as his cabin was engulfed by water and the ship took him down into the depths. On the surface gurgling water and debris was all that was left of the Black Falcon.

Garglethroat, Ori Fisse and Skeleto watched in awe, they were particularly surprised at how quickly the ship had vanished.

"Wow!", exclaimed Ori Fisse. "That isn't something you see every day! It just shows what rubbish sailors we are! One minute we have a ship and the next it's gone. Just like that!"

After a lot of effort and swearing they hauled Garglethroat over the side of the boat.

"You really need to lose some weight, boss!", said Ori Fisse while pulling hard.

Garglethroat was about to reply when they heard a sound. "Help me! Help me!", a faint voice could be heard in the distance.

"Bunny! It's Bunny!", shouted Skeleto, as they all looked in the direction where the shouts came from. "Over there! He is clinging on to a broken spar!"

They rowed over to Bunny who looked exhausted, hanging on to the spar with the last of his strength, and pulled him inside the boat.

"Thanks guys!", said Bunny, "I thought I would go down with the ship! Luckily this spar saved my life."

Dripping with water and completely exhausted Garglethroat checked the little leather pouch that hung around his neck with the copy of the secret incantation. It seemed to have survived the ordeal unscathed.

The fog had almost completely lifted, making way for a nice sunny day. For the first time they could see that they were near a rocky coast, with thousands of rocks jutting from the seabed. In the distance a small sandy beach could be seen surrounded by steep cliffs. High above the cliffs a monastery surrounded by large ramparts was visible …

57

Garglethroat and his three companions pulled the lifeboat onto the beach underneath the cliffs, jumped out and lay in the sand exhausted, but also relieved that they had survived the shipwreck.

"We better check out that monastery and see whether they can give us information how to get to Leonidas' mine", said Garglethroat still breathless from their exertions.

"How do we know if it's safe, boss?", asked Ori Fisse.

"We don't!", replied Garglethroat, "but we obviously can't stay here!"

They made their way up the steep cliff. Garglethroat struggled to find footholds as he could not see his feet because of his fat belly. After a while and a lot of swearing by Garglethroat they reached the forest fringing the cliffs and hacked their way through the dense underbrush. Large blood-sucking flies descended upon them, leaving large red boils on their exposed skin. Garglethroat particularly suffered, as he sweated profusely and had no fur or hair to protect him from the aggressive insects.

"I hate this place!", shouted Garglethroat, swatting away a finger-sized fly that had stung him in the leg.

Suddenly Ori Fisse stopped dead in his track. "There is someone sitting on a trunk by a fire straight ahead, boss! He seems to be wearing a monk's robe!"

Ori Fisse motioned to Garglethroat and Skeleto to stand still and be quiet while he carefully moved forward towards the creature. With a swift movement he pulled out his dagger, put his left arm around the creature's neck, and held his dagger to his throat with his right arm.

"Who are you and what is this place?", Ori Fisse asked.

"Don't kill me!", replied the figure. "I am Leonidas and I have just escaped from the monastery up there where I was held captive. Be careful, please, I'm injured", and he pointed at the bandages adorning various parts of his body.

Garglethroat and Skeleto joined Ori Fisse. "Leonidas?", asked Garglethroat. "You mean *the* Leonidas from the goldmine?"

Leonidas looked at Garglethroat. "Yes, how do you know me?"

"We have been told that you purchased a blond human child and I would be interested in buying him from you", replied Garglethroat.

"I am afraid we were attacked by sabrejaws, and the monks from this monastery took the child and his animagi companions away from me", said Leonidas.

"So the child is held in the monastery up there?", asked Garglethroat.

"Yes, indeed", replied Leonidas. "If you promise not to harm me I could help you get to him."

"That's a deal, Leonidas, but we will watch you closely!", said Garglethroat and introduced his companions.

They extinguished Leonidas' fire and followed him to the edge of the forest. The large flies continued to harass them and Garglethroat had to work hard to swot them away before being bitten. Large boils were visible on his body.

From their vantage point they could see several well-tended fields, with animagi monks working in vegetable patches, some harvesting what looked like corn in one field, and others loading a cart with large pumpkins. Just as Garglethroat pondered how to get past the monks and into the monastery unseen, a commotion could be heard near one of the fields. Several monks started running away, shouting to their fellow monks and pointing towards the edge of the forest behind them. Two large sabrejaws had suddenly appeared and jumped after the escaping monks. All monks were now in a panic, threw their tools away and tried to reach the cart where spears could be seen leaning against the sides. But it was too late. The sabrejaws had already reached two of the monks who had fallen behind and started mauling them. One sabrejaw had a monk in his jaw and shook him violently until his head came off. The other was standing on a monk who had fallen to the ground and buried his large teeth into the monk's back. The sabrejaws left their dead victims and jumped towards a group of three monks who tried to fend off the two large cats with just shovels and a hoe. They did not stand a chance. The sabrejaws attacked them, ripping their throats open and mauling them with their deadly sabre-sized canines. The sabrejaws ran towards the cart where at least six monks were hiding, holding their ground with raised spears.

"This is our chance!", shouted Garglethroat to his companions who had watched the killing scene with gruesome fascination. "Let's grab the robes of the dead monks and use the chaos to slip into the monastery."

In a flash they covered the short distance between the edge of the forest and the dead monks scattered in the fields. They quickly undressed them, put on the torn and bloody robes, and hid their faces under the large hoods. All the time they had been watching the stand-off between the monks by the cart and the sabrejaws. They made their way towards the edge of the forest again and continued towards the monastery, straddling the trees for cover. Other monks from nearby fields had come running towards the cart, shovels and picks raised, and they were joined by another group of monks who had emerged from the main entrance of the monastery.

"Now!", shouted Garglethroat and led his companions and Leonidas towards the group of monks by the cart. The monks now wielded their spears and managed to force the sabrejaws to retreat a little. The two cats opened their jaws wide and let out fearsome roars, saliva visibly dripping from their teeth. One of the monks gave a sign to retreat and the group of monks slowly moved backwards towards the monastery entrance. Garglethroat and his companions had surreptitiously joined the group and moved backwards with the others, faking aggressive movements and shouting at the sabrejaws. After a while the group had reached the monastery entrance where they were quickly ushered in by four guards who made sure the sabrejaws where not following them in. The guards closed the large doors with a loud bang and blocked the doors with a large crossbeam.

Garglethroat and his companions stood at the edge of the group of monks who were discussing the death of their companions and how to retrieve the bodies. They gradually moved aside and when they were sure nobody was watching them they slipped away towards the main courtyard in front of the refectory. They were safely inside the monastery without having been seen by anyone …

58

Garglethroat, Ori Fisse, Skeleto, Leonidas and Bunny slipped into the scriptorium in front of them. The building looked empty, as all the monks had gathered in the courtyard to watch the commotion that had ensued after the attack of the sabrejaws. Skeleto spotted an open door leading to a room with a cupboard full of neatly folded monk's robes and they quickly replaced their torn and dirty robes with fresh ones. With their hoods covering their faces they looked like any of the monks in the monastery. They stayed in the room, waiting for the group of monks outside the building to dissipate.

Sebastian and his companions had just left the refectorium when the surviving monks had begun streaming in through the main gates. Erik had been playing football with Sylvester with a leather ball filled with hay. Brother Konrad shouted orders to shore up the large doors, and helped to carry the wounded monks to a small building on the side of the refectory which served as a makeshift hospital.

"My poor monks!", said Konrad walking back towards Sebastian and his friends. "Several dead and so many wounded! These sabrejaws are becoming more and more audacious in their attacks. They have never ventured that close to the monastery during daylight. Maybe they can't find enough food in the forest?"

He led them towards the scriptorium. "My fellow monks can take care of the wounded; we have equally important things to tend to. Come with me. I have to tell you about a disturbing discovery we have made while looking for clues for you as to how to leave Animagana."

They gathered up Erik and Sylvester – and their football – and entered the scriptorium, walking past the half-open door behind which Garglethroat and his companions were hiding.

"I can't believe our luck", whispered Garglethroat with a smirk. "Erik and his mates have just walked past us, and they have another human boy with them whose soul we could extract to escape from this wretched place! Let's follow them carefully."

Konrad led Sebastian and the others up a narrow spiral stone staircase that led to the top floor of the scriptorium. At the top, the staircase opened into a large room full of monks sitting on tables covered with books, parchments and manuscripts. They walked towards one of the tables near the back where a group of monks were debating loudly. They had not realised that they were being followed by five hooded monks.

"Ah, Brother Konrad!", said one of the monks, a large black gorilla, rising up from the table covered with large books. "The news is even worse than we thought, I'm afraid! Can I speak openly in front of our guests?", he asked glancing suspiciously at Sebastian and his companions.

"Yes, of course, Brother Albanus", replied Konrad, "and Sylvester should also hear this as this will concern all of us."

They stood in a circle around the table. Garglethroat and his men and Leonidas and Bunny had placed themselves at a nearby table within earshot of where Konrad stood.

"You need to look at this book, Brother Konrad!", said Albanus and pointed at a small black book covered in dust with a picture of a large white skull on the cover. "This book was hidden behind others in a vellum cloth, and we only found it because we took out other books to look for further answers how to transfer our friends back to their world. Like the 'Chronicles of Animagi Lore', it is partly written in English and pre-English animago language. It is the most disturbing book we have ever seen, and it will mean that an important part of ancient English history needs to be rewritten!"

The monks around the table nodded in agreement and looked at the book with awe. Garglethroat and his companions moved a bit closer, faking interest in one of the bookshelves nearby.

"The book is called 'The book of Death'", continued Albanus. "I think it may be the key explanation after all why Henry VIII, and his henchman Thomas Cromwell, tried to expunge all English monasteries. We all know from history that in the late 1530s Thomas Cromwell was particularly keen to find new weapons to fight the threat from France and Spain. Apart from trying to solicit divine inspiration and help linked to reformist candour associated with the dissolution of the 'papal' monasteries, rumour had it that they were looking for rather strange weapons such as 'Greek Fire', an oil-based liquid that was meant to burn hotter than anything hitherto known and that would also burn when spilt on water – in other words ideal for sea warfare. But when they heard about the possible powers contained in the Book of Death, and that every monastery probably held a copy, Thomas Cromwell's attention seemed to have turned almost entirely towards finding that book. So he used the excuse of Henry VIII's need to divorce Catherine of Aragon to disband the Roman Catholic Church in England to hide the fact that the main reason for destroying the monasteries, and their vast libraries, was to lay his hands on this book with its deadly spell. In the case of St Albans monastery they clearly failed in their main task and somehow the book found its way to here with the monks who managed to escape through the portal in 1537. Nobody knows why the book was kept by our monks, or why it was not destroyed when we fled to Animagana and built this monastery. Now look at this passage in the book which may explain Cromwell's eagerness to obtain full access to the monasteries' libraries", and he turned the book so that Konrad and his companions could see the writing:

The power of the word
Unlocks untold Armageddon
Only to be used by those with wisdom
Or seal the fate of all

"What does it mean?", asked Teddy.

"There is a further passage that explains it", replied Albanus. "If we have translated it correctly it says: 'The following unlocks the power to cast a deadly spell over both animagi and humans. Once uttered those within range of the book will no longer be able to move. They will remain paralysed forever, unless the counter-spell is uttered'. Imagine what Henry VIII could have done to the French and Spanish with this, but they obviously never were able to obtain a copy otherwise history would have probably been very different!"

Sebastian and the others stood still and could hardly believe what they were hearing. Garglethroat and his henchmen had moved closer so as not to miss one of the words spoken by Albanus.

"I can't read out the spell as it would obviously unlock the powers contained in the book, but here it is spelled out loud and clear", said Albanus and pointed at three lines in the book:

GURRAG SHAH FRAHN MARRG
EXARTIUS GORGALKON MOGARAT
RETICULUS MORTIS ETERNICA

Albanus pointed at the next few lines: "And here is the counter-spell:"

MORTATIS RETURNUM VACATRIUM
DESSOLATA NON RETRIBIUM
QUANTOS APPALLY MAGRIBULUS

Konrad and his fellow monks, Sebastian and his companions, and Erik and Sylvester, quietly read the lines that did not make sense to any of them. But they had understood that they should never loudly speak the words of the first three lines while near the book.

"This may be more powerful than the worst weapon we can imagine", said Konrad. "Always bear in mind the warning of the first passage written in English: 'The power of the word unlocks untold Armageddon, and should only to be used by those with wisdom or the fate of all will be sealed'. 'Only to be used by those with wisdom' is the key here. We have to all swear never to reveal the secret of this spell, and it will be best if the book is either destroyed or hidden in such a way that it can never again be found."

"I am sure all of us agree", replied Albanus.

"Thanks, Brother Albanus", said Konrad. "Can I entrust you with the book and its safe disposal. I suggest burning it as soon as possible."

The other monks nodded in agreement and began to disperse. Sebastian and his companions left the table and made their way back towards the spiral staircase, not noticing the five hooded figures watching Brother Albanus clear up the table, tucking the black book under his arm, and making his way towards another staircase at the end of the room.

59

Albanus quickly slipped out of the reading room and went down a narrow corridor towards a small room with a fireplace full of burning logs. He raised his arm to throw the book into the fire when his arm was held back from behind by a strong bulldog paw. Ori Fisse put his dagger against Albanus throat in his usual manner and shouted: "don't move or you are dead!"

"Well done, Ori Fisse", said Garglethroat as he squeezed his fat bulk through the narrow door. "Now give me that book, monk!"

Albanus had been completely taken by surprise and was trembling with fear. He let the book fall onto the stone floor. "Where have you come from and what do you want?", he stammered.

"That's none of your business, monk!", replied Garglethroat while picking up the book. "Boys, we now have a definitive reason to go back to our world and leave this place behind! With the spell contained in this book we will be invincible!"

Ori Fisse and Skeleto had big smiles on their faces. There was no doubt that they greatly enjoyed the new power they suddenly wielded by possessing the little black book.

Bunny meanwhile was becoming ever more worried. *What animagi am I associating with! This is turning from bad to worse! I have to get out of here as quickly as possible!*

"We may let you live if you tell us whether there is a portal to the human world in this monastery", said Garglethroat to Albanus.

Albanus hesitated. *If I tell them about the portal I know they will kill me instantly, but if I do not tell them my fate will probably be the same*, he thought. Ori Fisse pressed the dagger harder against his throat. Albanus started to wretch as he was not getting enough air.

"OK, I'll tell you, please take that dagger of my throat!", he stammered.

Ori Fisse released his grip and let Albanus lead them out of the room. The passageway was empty, they could see the large reading room they had come from in the distance.

"Is there a way other than through that large room?", asked Garglethroat.

Albanus led them deeper into the scriptorium towards a small door that led to a very narrow spiral stone staircase.

"Will you fit through that, boss?", asked Skeleto, immediately regretting his question when he saw Garglethroat's threatening look on his face.

They made their way down the staircase. Garglethroat was indeed struggling to squeeze both through the door and between the narrow walls of the staircase. When they had finally made it down five stories into the basement of the scriptorium, Garglethroat was all battered, dusty and bruised from the tight squeeze. Ori Fisse and Skeleto knew better than to comment on Garglethroat's appearance. Leonidas had equally struggled to wriggle his large body through the staircase and his lion's mane was all dishevelled.

Albanus led them to a simple wooden door that led to a small room covered with bookshelves.

"Are you telling us that this is the room with the portal?", asked Garglethroat. "It just looks like any of your rooms in this library!"

Albanus glanced fearfully back at Garglethroat. He was pretty sure that this was the correct room, but he could, of course, not prove that the portal to the human world was indeed located in the middle of the room.

"I am pretty sure this is the room", Albanus said hesitatingly, "but as far as I know it has not been used since 1537 when we all came over from St Albans monastery."

"So, does this portal lead back to St Albans in the human world?", wondered Skeleto.

"I am no expert", replied Albanus, "but from what Brother Konrad told us recently, each portal is linked to a certain incantation. If you still know the incantation that led you here, then it should lead you back again to your place of origin irrespective of which portal you use in Animagana."

Garglethroat clutched the small leather pouch around his neck in which he had rescued Rigor Mortis' incantation during the shipwreck. He gave Ori Fisse a quick nod of the head and Ori Fisse slit Albanus throat with one clean cut, half severing his head which hung limply to one side. Albanus collapsed to the floor and lay in a puddle of greenish stuffing.

Bunny had witnessed this new ferocious murder with renewed contempt and stared disgusted at Garglethroat, Ori Fisse and Skeleto who stood above Albanus' body with nasty smiles on their faces. *They are enjoying the killing more and more!*, he thought. *Where will it end?* Leonidas also looked rather appalled and worried at how easily killing came to Garglethroat's men.

"We have nearly everything we need to get back to our world, boys!", gloated Garglethroat holding the incantation in his hand. "The only thing we need now is Erik's soul. We know that his soul came back to him in the Jolly Roger pub, so it should be ripe for the picking again! Ha, ha, ha!"

"But I tried the incantation on Erik", admitted Leonidas, "and it did not work. I think the wording of the incantation was wrong! Blackbeard cheated me when he sold me the incantation at the slave market!"

"We know this one works", replied Garglethroat holding up his leather pouch containing the crumpled sheet of paper, "as we used it successfully to come here. And now we also know that this portal will take us directly back to our village. We need to find a glass phial to put Erik's soul in once we have extracted it. Come on lads, we have work to do, but let's clean up this mess first!"

Ori Fisse and Skeleto grabbed Albanus' limp body and swept up the greenish stuffing with their feet as best they could. They left the room carrying the body, checking that the passageway was empty. Skeleto found a small room that looked like a rarely used broom cupboard, and they dumped Albanus' body among the discarded mops, buckets and brushes. On one of the shelves small glass phials were lined up, probably containing detergent or soap. Garglethroat grabbed one, emptied its content on the floor, and put it in the pocket of his robe. "I hope to use this soon and fill it with one of the kids' souls!", he said with a triumphant smile.

60

The monastery had quietened down after the recent sabrejaw attack. The monks had started venturing beyond the gates again and tending their fields, but they were now under heavier guard and back inside by mid-afternoon. All the monks looked on edge.

While Erik and Sylvester played football with a few monks who had rigged up makeshift goalposts made from hay bales in front of the refectory, Konrad, Sebastian and his companions were sitting at one of the tables in the scriptorium.

"I don't understand where Brother Albanus has gone to", admitted Konrad. "I told him to destroy this dreadful black book, but I can find neither a trace of him nor the book. None of the monks I have spoken to have seen him since we met in the large room in the scriptorium earlier. I think something might have happened to him and we need to find him quickly. Imagine that book getting into wrong hands! And Leonidas has also disappeared! I suspect he has left the monastery somehow, but I have never trusted that fellow, so be on your guard!"

"Yes, you are right", said Teddy. "Why don't we split up into small groups. That way we can search a larger area more quickly."

"A good idea, Teddy, but all of you be careful!", cautioned Konrad. "I have the feeling that something strange is going on, although nobody has reported seeing anything suspicious in the monastery lately. Sebastian you go with Teddy and check the top floor rooms of the scriptorium, Ugah and Hagelik you go to the 3rd floor, we will ask Erik and Sylvester to check the basement, while I will go with @@*^# and see if Albanus is somewhere on the 1st or 2nd floor. I must admit that Albanus is sometimes a bit scatty, and maybe I should not have sent him out on his own with this book, but it seemed like such a simple task ... Just to destroy it by burning it ..."

"I am sure we will find him quickly", said Teddy to reassure Konrad, but he was unsure that he believed his own words. *Why would Albanus disappear with that dreadful book?*, he wondered. *It does not make any sense unless someone else has interfered! But all the monks in the monastery should be beyond reproach as they have been together for 477 years!*

They went outside to ask Erik and Sylvester to help them. The two boys reluctantly joined them as they had greatly enjoyed their game of football with the monks. Their team was leading 4:1. It was the first time that Erik had been able to relax a little bit in Animagana and do what boys his age enjoyed most. Sylvester had played well, considering he was 477 years old.

Konrad split them into groups. Erik and Sylvester were sent to the scriptorium basement with clear instructions only to look for brother Albanus and to be very careful. They went down the narrow staircase that led down to the basement. A few monks hurried back and forth carrying large piles of books and manuscripts. Erik and Sylvester looked into several rooms, checking whether Albanus was anywhere to be seen. At an intersection they asked an elderly hedgehog monk whether he had seen Albanus, but the monk only shook his head. Some doors were closed but none were locked, so Erik and Sylvester could systematically check one room after another. They went deeper into the basement where it was much quieter. No monks could be seen in the badly illuminated back passageways.

Sylvester opened the door to a very small room that looked like a broom cupboard. It took him a while to adjust his eyes in the dim light and then he saw it! A body was lying on the floor, greenish stuffing oozing out of a large wound on his throat. "I have f…f…found him!", stammered Sylvester and motioned to Erik to have a look. They both put their hands to their mouths in front of the gory scene. "Quick, let's tell Konrad!"

But as they turned away from the broom cupboard door they were suddenly surrounded by five monks with hoods hiding their faces. They were so stunned that they could not react quickly enough. Ori Fisse threw himself at Sylvester and held his dagger against his throat, while Garglethroat, Skeleto and Leonidas held Erik.

"Come on Bunny, help us!", shouted Garglethroat who tried to pin back Erik's arm, but Bunny stayed back and looked appalled at the scene in front of him.

"Bunny, you traitor!", shouted Erik. "My father trusted you and you betrayed me and my family by selling my soul to Rigor Mortis! I will never forgive you!"

Sylvester was kicking and screaming and had begun to shake off Ori Fisse.

"Bunny, quick!", shouted Garglethroat.

But Bunny moved towards Garglethroat and Leonidas with a determined look on his face. *Erik is right!*, he thought. *I have betrayed everybody who was dear to me for a fanciful dream about another world that turns out to be much worse than the human world we know! I can no longer abide all this killing with dreadful Garglethroat and his men who are the scum of the earth!*, and he hurled himself at Garglethroat, put his small rabbit arms around Garglethroat's throat and tried to wrest him off Erik.

"Bunny! What are you doing you fool!", screamed Garglethroat, trying to push Bunny off. "This is our chance for leaving this dreadful place and take up our rightful place back in the human world. You now know we will have immense power!"

But Bunny held on, squeezing Garglethroat's throat more firmly. A wretched gargle could be heard from the slimy toad as he struggled to get enough air. He began to loosen his grip on Erik.

Ori Fisse had watched Bunny attack Garglethroat and saw that his boss was losing the fight. He let go of Sylvester who scrambled to his feet and ran down the corridor as fast as he could.

In the meantime Ori Fisse had reached Bunny and rammed his dagger deep into Bunny's back. Bunny let go of Garglethroat's throat immediately and put his paws on the gaping wound in his back. Large brown lentils oozed out in what seemed to be a never-ending stream. Ori Fisse wielded his dagger again and in one swift cut severed Bunny's head off his body.

Erik gave out a desperate cry, but did not have enough power to wrest himself away from the four animagi now clinging to his body. Ori Fisse put his dagger to Erik's throat and forced him on the ground.

"The other one got away boss!", said Skeleto, "but it's too late to follow him. He will alert the whole monastery! We need to move quickly."

Garglethroat pulled out the glass phial he had just found in the broom cupboard, opened the leather pouch around his throat, and pulled out the incantation. Ori Fisse, Skeleto and Leonidas pinned Erik down on the floor, while Garglethroat climbed on top of his chest.

UMMM MARISH GRANAFF GANG GOOL

began Garglethroat, gazing directly into Erik's eyes. Erik began to feel the now all too familiar pain in his head.

RAST HEREBDYN IMMORTIS GRATTAN

The pain intensified. Erik tried to shake off Garglethroat who weighed heavily on his chest, but the other three animagi held him down too firmly.

URRR MAJORIM EXORBITUS THYSSUSS

A dreadful pain now erupted in Erik's frontal lobe. It was as if his brain was being sucked out of his head.

DRRAM GARR NON RETURNUM SIC

Erik fainted. A bluish light emerged from his forehead and rose into the air. Garglethroat swept it up with one flick and put it in the phial.

"Quick, to the portal!", he shouted, as they ran down the corridor, leaving Erik motionless on the floor.

Footsteps could be heard coming down the staircase on the other side.

Garglethroat opened the rickety wooden doors to the portal chamber. He opened the phial, the blue ball of light floated in mid-air. He read out the incantation again, while approaching footsteps could be heard just outside the door.

UMMM MARISH GRANAFF GANG GOOL
RAST HEREBDYN IMMORTIS GRATTAN
URRR MAJORIM EXORBITUS THYSSUSS
DRRAM GARR NON RETURNUM SIC

Konrad, @@*^# and Sylvester stood at the door and looked at the scene. Garglethroat had just uttered the incantation, the blueish light was floating in mid-air, Garglethroat and his companions stared expectantly at the space in the middle of the room and … nothing happened! No portal opened, there was no tear in the air, and no swooshing sound to be heard.

For a short moment they all stood flabbergasted, not believing that the incantation had not worked. The blueish light started to move away from Garglethroat who was too stunned with surprise to catch it. It sped up, zoomed past Konrad and his companions who still stood at the door, and sped towards Erik's motionless body. There it hovered briefly above Erik's forehead before gradually sinking down into Erik's head.

Garglethroat, Ori Fisse, Skeleto and Leonidas used the hesitation of Konrad and his companions and hurled themselves at Konrad, @@*^# and Sylvester. The latter were surprised at the sudden attack and had been distracted by the blue light's meandering. Ori Fisse threw himself at Konrad, stretched out his arm with a big cutting motion, but his dagger missed Konrad's large snout by just a few millimetres. In trying to avoid Ori Fisse's deadly blow Konrad fell backwards onto @@*^# who screamed in agony. Sylvester had tried to grab Konrad's arm while he was falling but was also dragged down to the floor. Garglethroat and his men used the confusion, slipped past Konrad, @@*^# and Sylvester who were lying on a heap on the floor, and disappeared down the passageway towards the back rooms of the scriptorium.

Erik had begun to move and peered confused around him, holding his aching head in his arms. *Phew! I think I must have fainted for a short while! Garglethroat must have let my soul slip back into my body?*, he thought.

Erik stared at Bunny's limp headless torso lying next to him. *Maybe he wasn't a traitor after all!*, he thought with immense sadness.

61

Brother Konrad had immediately given orders to all the monks to find Garglethroat, Leonidas, Ori Fisse and Skeleto. They had also buried both brother Albanus and Bunny in the monastery cemetery with a short but evocative ceremony. Although Sebastian and his companions saw Bunny as a traitor who had triggered the chain of events for them being forced to come to Animagana by selling Erik's soul to Rigor Mortis, they still remembered him as a former friend, and felt very sad at his terrible death. In a short speech Teddy had acknowledged Bunny's bravery at attempting to save Erik in the scriptorium basement.

Back in the scriptorium, Konrad, Erik, Sylvester, Sebastian, Teddy, Ugah, Hagelik and @@*^# were sitting around one of the large tables. Erik had recovered from Garglethroat's soul extraction and his headache had gradually abated.

"How did Garglethroat and his men manage to get into the monastery, and how come they have ganged up with nasty Leonidas?", pondered Konrad. "It does not make sense. Where have they suddenly come from? I guess once they met up with Leonidas they knew that he had not taken you to his goldmine but that we all brought you here."

"Maybe Garglethroat's arrival has something to do with the evidence of a shipwreck your monks found on St Albans Beach below the monastery?", interjected Sebastian who had overheard an earlier conversation between Konrad and three monks who had seen debris on the beach.

"That could very well be, Sebastian", said Konrad, "and maybe they just encountered Leonidas by chance? Anyway, it doesn't matter. We now know they are here and are intent on taking a soul to get back to the human world. Worst of all, they are probably implicated in the murder of Brother Albanus and probably have a copy of the little black book with the deadly spell. If they manage to use it we might all be lost!"

"I am sure your monks will find them soon", said Teddy trying to comfort his companions. "The good news is that they do not seem to be well armed apart from one dagger, so your monks should find it easy to subdue them once found."

"Let's hope you are right, Teddy", said Konrad. "But let's now turn to more immediate matters", he continued, peering around the table. "How can we explain that the incantation did not work, although the wording that Garglethroat used seemed to be the correct one?"

"Yet again we need to get back to the original wording in the 'Chronicles of Animagi Lore'", suggested Teddy, and they opened the book at the appropriate page. "There is something we have missed, but thankfully this time it seems to have saved Erik's life."

Konrad placed his finger next to the crucial passage in the book

But behold animagi
Of unspeakable temptations
And no turning back
Without reverse wisdom

"So we know about the first three lines of this paragraph", said Konrad. "'Behold animagi' is the obvious warning all of us should have heeded, 'of unspeakable temptations' refers to the wrong expectations placed on Animagana back in your world which we now all know are wrong, while 'no turning back' rightly suggests that for all of us animagi who have been here in Animagana for very long there is no turning back to your world as our hosts are long dead. So it all rests on the last sentence: 'without reverse wisdom'. We still have not deciphered what this means, and I am sure that the secret for returning to your world lies in that sentence alone."

The six animagi and two humans looked at the passage in the book, each one thinking hard what the sentence could mean.

"'Without reverse wisdom'", repeated Teddy repeatedly. "'Without reverse wisdom'... We somehow gain wisdom from the experience of having come here", he continued thinking aloud. The others looked expectantly at him. "But it is about 'reverse' wisdom...What does 'reverse' refer to here? An action where we need to go 'in reverse', in other words backwards? Or does it relate to something else that needs to be done 'in reverse' ... Wait a moment! I think I have an idea!"

They all looked at Teddy.

"Could it mean that the incantation has to be said backwards?", Teddy wondered.

"You may be right", said Konrad, "especially as the act of going back to the human world would mean 'reversing' your journey."

"Yes, but would that not mean that the incantation should also be said in reverse when extracting a soul in Animagana?", asked Sebastian. "But you obviously witnessed that

Garglethroat had successfully extracted Erik's soul with the incantation said the right way around?"

"I don't know", admitted Konrad, "but the 'reverse wisdom' part might only apply to the portal itself and the act of crossing back into your world. Let's just see what happens if we invert the words. We know we can't read the original without incurring severe damage to all of us, so let's just read the words in silence:

UMMM MARISH GRANAFF GANG GOOL
RAST HEREBDYN IMMORTIS GRATTAN
URRR MAJORIM EXORBITUS THYSSUSS
DRRAM GARR NON RETURNUM SIC

They all felt a strong throbbing in their heads. Most could not complete reading the incantation.

"And here is what it would be in reverse starting with the last word", Konrad said after scribbling down the words on a piece of paper:

CIS MUNRUTER NON RRAG MARRD
SSUSSYHT SUTIBROXE MIROJAM RRRU
NATTARG SITROMMI NYDBEREH TSAR
LOOG GANG FFANARG HSIRAM MMMU

"This sounds even weirder than the original", said Hagelik. "Are you sure you are one the right track?"

"Not sure at all", admitted Teddy, but that is the best I can come up with for the moment. "But we will probably never have a chance to check whether I was right anyway", he said gloomily.

"Whatever happens", said Konrad, "we better prepare for the worst, as your fellow animago Garglethroat is clearly a nasty piece of work! I have asked Brothers Bonifacius and Regulus to look after your fellow animagi from the village, and we have put them into one of the rooms right next to the portal room, just in case we need to evacuate them quickly to your world."

62

Night was falling and it was raining hard again. Garglethroat and his companions had found a place to hide in the monastery stables. After escaping from the scriptorium they had made sure that nobody was following them. Fortunately for them, the monastery was full of passageways, old buildings and alleyways rarely used by the monks. They had climbed up to a landing in the stables where hay was stored above pens where draught horses were kept.

"Everybody knows now that we are here!", moaned Garglethroat. "Why did the incantation not work?"

"I don't know boss", replied Ori Fisse, "maybe the wording is not right?"

"But it's the same one from the same sheet of paper we used back in our world", said Garglethroat. "We killed Callisto to get this paper back! There must be some twist to all this! At least we know the procedure for extracting souls is the same. A shame I could not hang on to Erik's soul, now we have to do it all over again! Anyway, I think we are safe here for the moment, so let's grab some sleep while we can."

They put their robes on the hay which provided them with a comfortable bed. Ori Fisse, Skeleto and Leonidas fell asleep very fast, but Garglethroat stayed awake. When he was sure Leonidas was asleep he pulled the black book with the white skull cover out of its vellum cover. He remembered what Albanus had told his companions in the scriptorium reading room, namely that the spell mentioned in the Book of Death unlocks a power that overwhelms both animagi and humans. Once the spell is uttered within reach of the book those affected will no longer be able to move and will remain paralysed forever, unless the counter-spell is uttered.

I have to try it out, thought Garglethroat. *This may be our passport back to our world, but I need to see first how it works. Albanus clearly said that the words have to be spoken aloud to have an effect and to awaken the powers contained within the book. Let's see ...*

He carefully woke up Ori Fisse and Skeleto, and motioned to them to stand aside. They quickly understood what Garglethroat was trying to do. Garglethroat opened the book on the page with the spell. He shook Leonidas gently. "Leonidas, wake up! I need to briefly speak to you about something important."

Leonidas opened his eyes sleepily and looked at Garglethroat who uttered the spell:

GURRAG SHAH FRAHN MARRG
EXARTIUS GORGALKON MOGARAT
RETICULUS MORTIS ETERNICA

While Garglethroat was reading, Leonidas, in his sleepy state, had not realised what was happening. Only as the last sentence was being read, and when he realised that Garglethroat held the Book of Death in his hand, did he understand, but it was too late: as Garglethroat uttered the last words 'mortis eternica' the white skull on the cover began to glow and the whole book seemed to shine from inside. Suddenly a ray of light shot out of the book, enveloping Leonidas in an eerie green luminescence. Leonidas tried to jump aside but he could no longer move. He closed his eyes and fell to the side. He was lying motionless in the hay.

Ori Fisse and Skeleto who had stood outside of the beam emerging from the book were unaffected by the book's spell, as was Garglethroat who carefully closed the book, thereby extinguishing the green light.

Garglethroat beamed. "Fellows! We have here a very powerful new weapon that will give us mastery of the village back home. Anyone within the beam of light emanating from the book will be affected and can only be saved by the counter-spell. Nobody will be able to stand in our way! Ha, ha, ha! And it seems as if the book itself is the weapon in the end, as the ray of light came directly out of the book, so the spell without the book is of no use!"

Ori Fisse and Skeleto shared in the celebrations, especially as they only had one dagger as a weapon so far.

"We should have no problems extracting another soul now", said Ori Fisse, "either again from Erik or from that other boy! Nobody can prevent us from getting back to our world now!"

"If we apply the spell to Erik or Sylvester we just need to make sure that we can still extract their souls", said Garglethroat. "But in the end it does not matter as we can always wake them up with the counter-spell if need be!"

"Good plan, boss, good plan!", replied Ori Fisse. "Bring on your troops, monks!", he shouted out into the stable, but only the winnowing of the horses could be heard below them.

63

Brother Konrad had convened an extraordinary meeting in the main hall of the refectory for all monks and guests in the monastery. The room was full, all chairs near the tables were occupied, and animagi stood one behind the other all the way up the stairs to the first floor. Sebastian and his companions stood behind Konrad who was perched on a small pedestal so that everybody could see him.

"My fellow monks, dear guests!", Konrad began. "We have convened this meeting as I have to report to you recent events in the monastery which are likely to affect all of us." He told the audience about Garglethroat and his henchmen, how they killed Albanus, stole the Book of Death with the deadly spell that posed a threat to all of them, and how they had tried to escape through the portal using Erik's soul. "Luckily the incantation did not work for opening the portal and Erik could be reunited with his soul."

They all peered at Erik who looked rather embarrassed by all the sudden attention.

"Needless to say that Garglethroat and his men are extremely dangerous and they have already shown that they don't hesitate to kill", continued Konrad. "I therefore urge all of you again to be extremely vigilant and to report anything you see out of the ordinary to me or my fellow senior monks. As a precaution I have also asked Brothers Bonifacius and Regulus to look after our special guests from Erik's and Sebastian's village and to guard them all the time. Most importantly I have gathered thirty of our strongest and best trained monks, and they are already looking for Garglethroat and his men in every part of the monastery. But could I ask all of you not to wander about the corridors alone but only in groups of at least five and to carry weapons with you all the time. We assume that Garglethroat and his men only have one dagger between them, but we don't know whether they may be able to make use of the dreadful secrets contained in the Book of Death. Be therefore prepared for any eventuality!"

An audible murmur went around the monks in the refectorium who were all clearly distressed. Although they had weathered attacks from pirates, brigands and sabrejaws over the centuries, this was probably the worst crisis they had faced in 477 years on Animagana.

"We need to be particularly vigilant about both Erik and Sylvester", continued Konrad, "their souls are particularly vulnerable."

He turned around and looked at Erik again and tried to find Sylvester but could not see him. He stepped down from the pedestal and asked, "Where is Sylvester? I can't see him."

"I think he went off with the thirty monks to fight Garglethroat", replied Erik. "He said he wanted to take revenge for their attack near the portal room."

"The fool!", Konrad shouted angrily. "You all stay here", he said pointing at Sebastian's companions. Addressing three strong monks standing by his side he said: "You, you and you, please go and find Sylvester immediately and bring him back here. We can't risk Garglethroat catching another soul, even if he does not know how to use the incantation to open the portal."

Konrad closed the meeting and dismissed the monks who walked away, armed and in small groups as instructed. A group of monks stayed behind to protect Sebastian and his companions.

64

Garglethroat was still half asleep when he heard a suspicious rustle that did not seem to come from the draught horses below. He opened his eyes and glanced at the space below in the barn. Shapes could be seen furtively moving about, attempting to hide. Garglethroat nudged Ori Fisse and Skeleto to quietly get up when they heard a voice shouting from below: "Garglethroat, we know you are up there! Give yourselves up and we guarantee that we will not harm you! You are surrounded!"

Garglethroat smiled and took out the Book of Death from its vellum cover, glancing knowingly at Ori Fisse and Skeleto. He crawled to the edge of the platform to have a closer look at the monks below. He saw a large group armed to the teeth with pitchforks, sabres, daggers, bows and arrows. He motioned to his henchmen to stay hidden. Suddenly movement to the right of the entrance to the barn caught his eye. A larger shape was trying to hide behind a barrel. *I can't believe it!*, thought Garglethroat recognising Sylvester, *the other human boy has dared come here to confront us! That makes things even easier!*

The monks had planned their attack carefully. A first group was advancing towards the ladders leading to the platform, while another group stayed close to the entrance door awaiting further developments. The draught horses moved about nervously, unused to all this commotion in their usually quiet stable. A few monks had moved towards Sylvester and urged him to leave the scene of the unfolding battle, but without success. Sylvester stood up and looked defiantly at Garglethroat.

"Give up Garglethroat!", shouted a monk at the head of the first group. "We are heavily armed! You have no chance of escape!"

They began climbing up the ladders, arms at the ready. The monks near the doorway put their bows and arrows in position, ready to shoot.

Garglethroat glanced over the edge of the platform. The Book of Death was open at the page with the spell and he began chanting with an increasingly loud voice:

GURRAG SHAH FRAHN MARRG
EXARTIUS GORGALKON MOGARAT
RETICULUS MORTIS ETERNICA

"He is using the Book of Death to cast the spell!", shouted the head monk. "Quickly, grab him before it is too late!"

But it was indeed too late. The now familiar greenish ray of light began emanating from the book. Garglethroat held up the book so that the ray of light began to touch the monks. As soon as they were in the beam the monks collapsed and fell heavily off the ladders to the floor. Garglethroat guided the light towards the monks near the entrance who suddenly looked much less sure of themselves. Some began opening the door to escape, but the beam of greenish light caught them and petrified them instantly. Some tried to hide behind barrels, horses and carts, but as soon as the beam of light touched them they collapsed. After a short while only a few better hidden monks remained. They did not dare move while the green ray of light scanned the stables for any sign of movement.

Sylvester had remained hidden behind the barrel while the dreadful scene unfolded before his eyes. *I can't believe how powerful the Book of Death is as a weapon!*, he thought. *There is no way we can overwhelm Garglethroat while he has such a weapon! I have to get out of here!* He carefully glanced over the edge of the barrel, but immediately Garglethroat directed the beam at him which only missed him by a few centimetres.

"We have to get Sylvester!", said Garglethroat to Ori Fisse. "Flush him out and I'll make sure the beam does not affect you."

Ori Fisse quickly made his way down one of the ladders, dagger between his teeth. He quickly made his way towards Sylvester who jumped up from behind the barrel.

"This is my revenge for your earlier attack on us near the portal room!", shouted Sylvester as he hurled a shovel towards Ori Fisse. The shovel hit Ori Fisse on the shoulder who cried out in agony. Sylvester jumped up and quickly made his way towards the half open entrance, but he stumbled over the body of one of the monks lying lifelessly on the ground … and fell to the floor. Garglethroat directed the beam directly at him. Sylvester looked up and stared directly into the green beam. It felt as if he was gaping into a green abyss, and as if he was sucked into a large tunnel stretching out into eternity. He tried to scream and shield his eyes, but it was too late. He collapsed on top of the monk lying on the floor.

Ori Fisse was still clutching his shoulder but had moved towards the last three monks hiding from the beam behind the horses. One monk tried to put an arrow on his bow, but his hands shook so much that Ori Fisse was on top of him before he could aim his weapon. The Book of Death's green beam paralysed the monk immediately, as well as the horse next to which he was standing, and it only took a few seconds for the last two monks to be stunned by the beam and collapse on the floor. The stable was suddenly dead quiet except for the hushed breathing of the remaining horses.

Garglethroat and Skeleto quickly joined Ori Fisse and walked over to Sylvester's lifeless body. He took out the crumpled bit of paper with the incantation from the leather pouch around his neck and read out the lines to extract Sylvester's soul. Nothing happened.

"OK, here is proof that we can't extract his soul while he has been affected by the beam from the Book of Death", remarked Garglethroat. "Quick! Tie him up and I'll try the counter-spell!"

He placed his face close to that of Sylvester and read out the three lines:

MORTATIS RETURNUM VACATRIUM
DESSOLATA NON RETRIBIUM
QUANTOS APPALLY MAGRIBULUS

When Garglethroat read out the last line Sylvester began to stir. He opened his eyes carefully and tried to remember what had just happened to him. Immediately he saw Garglethroat staring right into his eyes and uttering the incantation for extraction of his soul. As Garglethroat read on, Sylvester felt increasingly dizzy, his head began to hurt, and he felt very weak and numb. A blueish marble-sized light emerged from his forehead which Garglethroat quickly placed into one of the glass phials he had stolen earlier. Sylvester lay again motionless on top of the lifeless monk.

"How will we get through the portal, boss?", asked Ori Fisse.

"They will have seen that the incantation does not seem to work for going back to our world, so we will see if they have found a solution! Take Sylvester with us, we might need him for bargaining!"

Ori Fisse nudged Sylvester to get up. Sylvester felt as if half of his body had been ripped apart – as if an important part of himself was missing. He glanced at the glass phial that contained his soul and wished he could grab it and reunite with the blue ball of light. Ori Fisse pushed him forward and they made their way out of the barn. Only a few monks walked in the passageways as they made their way towards the portal room. Seeing Garglethroat's determined look the monks quickly scurried away.

65

When Garglethroat, Ori Fisse, Skeleto and Sylvester approached the corridor leading to the portal, they could make out an increasing rumble of voices emanating from a large group of animagi. Ori Fisse peered around the corner and saw that the passageway was blocked with monks. He could make out Konrad and his fellow monks, as well as Erik, Sebastian and his friends. The seventeen animagi from Erik's village who had been rescued by the monks, including Barney, Penny and Woof, also stood in the middle of the group. All the monks were heavily armed.

"There are a lot of monks guarding the portal entrance, boss", said Ori Fisse to Garglethroat. "Shall we stun them with the Book of Death?"

"Remember that we don't know the secret to unlocking the portal! So we will have to negotiate. Fortunately we hold a valuable hostage and we have our weapon at the ready", replied Garglethroat brandishing the book.

Garglethroat opened the Book of Death on the appropriate pages, read out the spell and held it above his head as he approached the monks.

"Let us into the portal room or you will all be petrified, never to wake up again!", Garglethroat shouted towards Konrad and his men. "I promise that if you tell us how to open the portal that will allow us to get out of this dreadful world nobody will come to harm. The only thing we will take with us will be this little treasure!", and he held up the Book of Death so that everybody could see it. "But I won't hesitate to use it if you stand in our way! The thirty or so monks you sent to capture us did not stand a chance, and we also hold Sylvester."

Ori Fisse pushed Sylvester forward so that all could see he had no chance of escape. Sylvester felt so weak he could barely stand.

Konrad turned to Erik and Sebastian and his friends. "My worst fears have come true, my friends! Discovering the Book of Death was a dreadful mistake, and allowing Garglethroat to capture it was my biggest error! I should have destroyed the book myself in the scriptorium when we uncovered its dreadful powers. Now we are at the mercy of this ghastly toad and his henchmen, and we have already seen that they don't hesitate to use the Book of Death and kill their hostages if need be. What are we to do?"

Sebastian and his companions were quiet for a moment, observing Garglethroat and his henchmen. They were in a desperate situation and could not see a clear way out of it.

"I don't know what we can do", replied Teddy. "Whatever we do, we will always be at the mercy of the terrible powers contained in the Book of Death, and I can't see a way to save Sylvester. If we let Garglethroat through the portal Sylvester will fall into a terminal coma. If we don't give them the secret to the portal we can't stop Garglethroat from paralysing us all. We have already seen that there is no point in fighting him and we no longer have a copy of the counter-spell. We are in Garglethroat's hands!"

Sebastian was surprised at Teddy's fatalistic view, but he could also not see any way out. *If only I could control my powers to freeze time, then maybe I could buy us some time to think and act accordingly, or I could even try to snatch the book from Garglethroat!*, he thought, but he knew that freezing time had only been possible when his life was directly threatened. *But I just don't know how to control it! I can't be the chosen one the prophecy foretells! It just can't be! I am so weak!*

"I am waiting for an answer!", shouted Garglethroat, and Ori Fisse tightened his grip around Sylvester's neck. The dagger started to draw blood just below Sylvester's Adam's apple. Sylvester was breathing heavily, staring ahead of him but avoided looking at Konrad and his monks.

After a brief whispered conferral, Konrad took a few steps towards Garglethroat. "OK, you win Garglethroat. We have no way of stopping you. We will give you the secret of the portal but only if you promise not to harm any of us with the Book of Death."

Konrad knew that any promise made by Garglethroat could be broken any time, but they did not have anything else to bargain from. Knowledge of the reverse spell to open the portal was their only trump card. "So to even things out a bit we ask you to hand over Sylvester, together with Ori Fisse and Skeleto, and the dagger. We will hold your two henchmen until you are through the portal and then release them to join you."

Garglethroat and his two men discussed Konrad's proposal.

"OK! Deal!", replied Garglethroat. "I will pass you Sylvester and my two men as hostages if you let us through to the portal unharmed."

Konrad quickly looked at his companions and nodded in agreement. The monks reluctantly began to move aside to clear a passage to the portal room. As soon as the room became visible through the throng of animagi, Garglethroat and his men slowly moved forward. Garglethroat held the book high above his head. It was still half closed, but a greenish light could be seen shining through the half-opened pages. They all knew that as soon as he opened it, the deadly beam of light could annihilate any living thing in its path.

The monks, Erik and Sebastian and his companions looked at Garglethroat and his men with deadly stares. Some monks raised their weapons as Garglethroat drew nearer, but Konrad motioned to them to restrain themselves while holding back monks pushing forward behind him with his strong arms. Erik and Sylvester exchanged worried looks. They could all see that Sylvester was very weak and in pain, suffering from the part-severance of his soul and immensely worried about what would happen to him once Garglethroat used the essence of his soul to open the portal.

Despite a few scuffles and loud swearing and shouting by some of the monks, Garglethroat's group made it to the centre of the portal room. Although some monks were also standing near the middle of the small room, they had left a space in the centre where the portal was presumed to be. Garglethroat and his men stopped in the middle of the room and motioned to the monks to stand back further. He then told Ori Fisse and Skeleto to move towards the monks, taking Sylvester with them. Ori Fisse reluctantly passed Konrad his dagger, Sylvester was quickly greeted and embraced by Erik, Teddy and Sebastian. Sylvester was elated to see them again but looked worryingly at Garglethroat holding up the glass phial with his soul.

"We have kept our end of the bargain!", shouted Garglethroat, "now tell us the secret of the portal!"

Konrad hesitated, but stared with great fear at the Book of Death and the shimmering green light lurking between the pages. He just could not risk the death, or at least permanent paralysis, of his fellow monks and friends. "We think that the solution to the portal is to pronounce the secret incantation backwards", he replied hoping they were right. Here it is:

CIS MUNRUTER NON RRAG MARRD
SSUSSYHT SUTIBROXE MIROJAM RRRU
NATTARG SITROMMI NYDBEREH TSAR
LOOG GANG FFANARG HSIRAM MMMU

Konrad reluctantly handed a piece of paper with the reverse incantation to Garglethroat, as there was no way that anyone could remember the jumble of words by heart. Garglethroat raised the phial while still holding up the Book of Death menacingly. He poured Sylvester's soul out of the phial.

Sylvester flinched. *They are willing to sacrifice me!*, he thought looking in despair at Konrad.

The blue shimmering ball of light hovered in the air, stirring in the faint breeze that came through the open door. Sylvester could now barely stand, he felt weaker and weaker ...

Garglethroat began to read out the reverse incantation. At first nothing happened, and Konrad and Teddy already began wondering whether they had been correct in their interpretation of the riddle. But as Garglethroat began reading the third line a faint light began to appear in the middle of the room, rapidly growing into a large tear hovering knee high above the ground.

"Quick Ori Fisse and Skeleto, come here!", shouted Garglethroat and gestured to the monks to release his two henchmen. The monks hesitated to release their precious hostages, but a brief look by Konrad confirmed that they had to comply. Ori Fisse and Skeleto reached Garglethroat and began to climb through the portal. A muted hiss could be heard as their bodies were swallowed up by the hole in the air.

"You have kept your end of the bargain, so I will keep mine and let you live. What do I care what happens to you anyway as I will never see you and your wretched world again!", Garglethroat shouted while laughing out loud.

No, this just can't be right!, thought Sebastian. *We can't just let this murderer escape and let Sylvester fall into a coma!*

Garglethroat had turned towards the portal and had begun disappearing. Sebastian had put his little paws to his head and had started concentrating very hard. *I can do this ... I can do this!*, he shouted inwardly while watching Garglethroat's body being swallowed up by the portal. *I am our last chance to ever leave this place!*

And ... suddenly time stood still. Sebastian had his eyes closed as he was concentrating so hard, but he sensed that something had happened. When he reopened his eyes the room and all the people in it were motionless. Even the dust particles visible against the backdrop of the open portal stood still and suspended in mid-air. *I've done it! I've done it!*, Sebastian shouted. *For the first time I have controlled the freezing of time! But I don't have a second to lose as I don't know how long this will last!*

Garglethroat's body had just disappeared through the portal when Sebastian froze time, so he was unsure whether

Garglethroat was also affected and motionless back in their own world. Sebastian reacted quickly and pulled Ugah and @@*^# towards the portal. It was much more difficult to pull Teddy and Hagelik, who were much taller and heavier than Sebastian, towards the hole in the air. Most difficult were Erik and Sylvester as they were truly gigantic compared to Sebastian. He only managed to make them topple over, hitting the ground relatively hard, but he could not drag their motionless bodies across the cave floor. The task was easier with most of the 17 animagi from his village, as most were small and light. Just when he had successfully dragged the bodies of Barney, Penny and Woof towards the edge of the portal, the room started to turn fuzzy, and suddenly he could see the others moving again.

Konrad and his fellow monks looked astonished at the scene in front of them with Erik and Sylvester toppled over on the floor and a pile of animagi stacked near the portal.

"What is happ…?", shouted Konrad but Sebastian quickly interrupted him. "I have no time to explain, but you all need to help us get through the portal as quickly as possible! I have frozen time for a short while and have piled up most animagi who should come through back to our world, but could not drag Erik and Sylvester closer to the portal as they are too heavy!"

It took not long for Konrad to grasp what had happened. He quickly helped Erik and Sylvester onto their knees and within a few seconds they dashed towards the portal.

"But wait!", said Konrad. "How do we know that Sylvester will survive the portal? He is 477 years old!"

"We can't be sure he will survive", replied Teddy, "but we certainly know that if he stays here he will fall into a coma! So we have to risk it and take him back with us!"

Sylvester held his head, which had started hurting with a sharp and intense pain he had never endured before. It was as if his skull was being wrenched apart, spilling his brain all over the floor. "I ... I... can't stay upright for any longer ...", he stammered.

Teddy did not hesitate one moment and pushed Sylvester through the portal. The 17 animagi from the village had also begun streaming through the hole. Ugah, Hagelik and @@*^# had just gone through when the edge of the portal started closing in.

"It is closing! Quick!", urged Teddy and ushered Barney, Penny and Woof through the hole. "Come Brother Konrad, quickly!"

"But I can't come with you, Teddy!", replied Konrad. "None of us animagi can as our hosts have been dead for over 400 years! It would mean instant death for us!"

In the rush and confusion Teddy had forgotten that animagi could not survive without their hosts and looked with sad eyes at Konrad and his fellow monks.

"I am so sorry", Teddy said, "you are right, we have to leave you here! There was so much more I wanted to tell you, and we never had time to thank you ..."

"The portal is closing!", shouted several monks in unison interrupting Teddy, and Konrad and three other monks rushed towards the hole trying to hold the edges open, wedging their legs against the dusty floor.

"There is no time for melancholic goodbyes!", shouted Konrad at Sebastian, Teddy and Erik who were the last ones of their group still in the cave. "Come on! This is your last chance!"

"How do we know Erik will survive the portal back to our village", Teddy asked. "Won't he fall into a coma immediately when we arrive?"

"We don't know!", said Konrad, "but you can't leave the poor boy here! He would be trapped here forever!"

The four monks now pulled hard at the edges of the portal, their legs beginning to slide. The slit was now barely a few centimetres wide.

"Quick Erik!", shouted Teddy and pushed him through the narrowing entrance. Erik somehow just managed to squeeze through the closing gap shoulders first, followed rapidly by Teddy who struggled to pull his large head through the opening.

"Good bye Sebastian, and best of luck back in your world!", Konrad said with a sad voice. "Thanks to you, your companions and your animagi friends from the village might have been saved!"

The portal was now only the size of an apple, the four monks desperately clinging on to its edges with their feet touching each other on the cellar floor.

Sebastian jumped head first through the small hole and disappeared. A second later the portal closed behind him with a faintly audible hiss. Konrad and his fellow monks looked in awe at the space in front of them. There was no trace or evidence of what had just happened …

PART 3

66

Sebastian opened his eyes. He had fallen onto a large pile of animagi who all peered dazed and confused around them. Ugah was just below Sebastian, partly squashed by Erik who was lying on top of several other animagi.

A bluish glimmer hung in the air at the spot where the portal had been a few seconds ago. Initially it hovered motionless in the middle of the room, but then it started to congeal into a marble-sized ball moving slowly towards Sylvester who was lying still near Sebastian. The ball of light hovered over Sylvester's forehead, seemed to hesitate, then penetrated through the skin and disappeared into his head. Sylvester, eyes still closed, briefly stirred. *His soul has reunited with him!*, thought Sebastian looking at the scene, *that looks promising*.

Sebastian quickly peered around him. As they had all suspected, they were indeed back in the portal room behind the archives in their home village. Thankfully there was no sign of Garglethroat. *Maybe the time it took me to shift the animals while time was frozen, and the minute or so it took to get us all through the portal, was sufficient for Garglethroat to think that we were not following?*, wondered Sebastian. *They must have left the portal room in a rush, thinking that we had stayed behind in Animagana.*

More bluish lights were visible near the entrance to the portal. They seemed to hover briefly about one metre above ground, but then suddenly darted forward through the entrance and the archives, disappearing from view. *Maybe these are the souls of the hosts of the 17 animagi we brought back from Animagana? Maybe they will now reunite with the children who are in a coma?*, wondered Sebastian.

The animagi gradually managed to get up. Everybody seemed to be looking at Sebastian and Teddy.

"Quick! Let's check whether Sylvester and Erik have survived the jump through the portal unscathed", Teddy said looking at both human children.

"I think I'm ok", replied Erik, getting slowly up from the floor and rubbing his head and limbs. "I don't feel any pain and don't have a headache."

"I am also OK, I think", said Sylvester, looking down at his body with great relief. "I seem to have survived the transfer to your world."

Teddy, Sebastian, Ugah and @@*^# gave both Erik and Sylvester a big hug, with big smiles on their faces.

"We have done it!", exclaimed @@*^#. "We have left this dreadful Animagana and managed to get back to our village!"

Sebastian was elated that Erik and Sylvester seemed to be unaffected by their move through the portal. *It is hard to imagine that in Animagana, just a few metres from where we are standing, Konrad and his fellow monks are probably looking at an empty space in their portal room, wondering whether we have all made it alive!*, Sebastian thought with amazement. *We will probably never see them again!*, he thought with sadness. *After all they have done for us!*

Teddy quickly dampened their celebratory mood. "Don't forget that Garglethroat is now on the loose in our village with the Book of Death! Nobody knows what damage he and his henchman will do!"

They all looked towards the portal door. The Bosch painting was clearly visible at its front, reminding Sebastian and his friends about how not that long ago they had struggled to solve the riddle of the portal. Sebastian moved to the door and cautiously looked out to see whether there was any sign of Garglethroat. The archives were almost pitch black, only a faint glimmer of light could be seen coming from one of the corridors between the rows of books.

"I can't see any sign of Garglethroat", Sebastian whispered to the group. "I think we can get out of the portal room."

Teddy led them carefully out of the room. Everybody peered anxiously around them. Suddenly a flash of green light could be seen near the entrance at the other end of the large cave housing the archives.

"That must be Garglethroat!", shouted Teddy. "They have already started using the Book of Death! Quick we must prevent them from doing more harm!"

"But how can we stop them?", asked Hagelik. "We have no weapons to fight them!"

Teddy remained silent. He knew they would not have a chance against the power of the Book of Death. He slowly led them through the seemingly interminable rows of shelves covered in parchments and manuscripts towards the entrance of the archives.

It took them a good twenty minutes of rapid walking to reach the archive shelves closer to the entrance, indicating how much advance Garglethroat and his henchmen had on them. When they reached the entrance area of the archives, a dreadful picture became apparent: slumped over a large table, hunched in awkward positions in their seats, or collapsed on the floor, were Professor Pandanus and his fellow scientists. They looked dead but were still breathing.

Teddy moved towards the limp obese body of Professor Pandanus who was slumped face down on the table. "They have all been petrified by the Book of Death! If we don't stop Garglethroat the whole village – animagi and humans – will be full of petrified bodies. And we don't know whether there is another copy of the Book of Death with the counter-spell here in the archives!"

The whole group stood in silence around Professor Pandanus and his colleagues. So much had happened to all of them in the last days, and they still had not fully adjusted to the fact of being back in their home village. And now they realised that there might be nobody left un-petrified. *Possibly we are already the last living beings in our village!*, worried Sebastian.

"What can we do?", asked Ugah, looking expectantly at Teddy and Sebastian.

"We need to find members of the animagi council and discuss with them what to do next", replied Teddy. "On our own we can't fight the awesome power contained in the Book of Death. I suggest that we stay together for the moment and see if anyone is left. If we see any sign of Garglethroat and his men, I suggest that we scatter as quickly as we can to ensure that at least some of us will survive and are able to call for help. Who knows, we might need to contact other communities for help if there is nobody left here!"

67

It was near midnight in the intensive ward of the large county hospital in the city near Sebastian's village. Like every day since his daughter had suddenly fallen into a coma, Lucy's father was sitting vigil at her bedside, holding his daughter's hand and hoping that his daughter would suddenly wake up. Lucy was connected to various tubes and cables dangling from several medical devices that checked her heartrate, breathing and pulse. Although he was dead tired after a hard day's work, Lucy's father intended to stay for another few hours. His wife would relieve him early in the morning.

Lucy's father had not seen the bluish light that seemed to have appeared from nowhere and was moving towards his daughter's head. Suddenly Lucy opened her eyes. She peered around her with a confused look on her face. Her father had not noticed as he was holding his head in his hands, trying to stay awake.

"Dad ... dad!", Lucy croaked, but hardly any sound came out of her mouth.

Lucy's dad looked up, not believing what he saw. "Lucy!", he shouted, "Lucy, you have woken up!", and he rushed towards her giving her a big embrace. "How are you feeling?"

Lucy was about to answer when they heard a loud shout from the bed in the room opposite Lucy's. "Martin! Martin! Doctor come quickly, Martin has just woken up!"

There was a sudden commotion in Martin's room as they all realised that he had also woken up from his coma.

"Here too!", Lucy's dad shouted. "Lucy is also awake! It's a miracle!"

Apart from Lucy and Martin, five other children from Sebastian's village had just awoken from their comas …

68

After leaving the archives, Sebastian and the group walked through underground passageways littered with petrified bodies. Some were lying on their own, often with distorted limbs as they had fallen when the green ray from the Book of Death had hit them, others in piles of bodies where entire groups had been caught by surprise by the green light.

"This is a catastrophe!", exclaimed Teddy. "There will be nobody left soon! We have to find a member of the council."

They quickly made their way towards Hexybilla's apartment in the caves. At every intersection they carefully peered around the corner to see whether there was any trace of Garglethroat and his men. All they could see were more petrified bodies strewn over the floor. After a few minutes of careful walking they arrived at Hexybilla's bedroom door.

"I hope we are not too late", said Erik while banging on Hexybilla's door.

After a few loud knocks a noise could be heard from inside the door.

"Who is it?", asked a croaky voice, unmistakably belonging to the witch.

"It's Teddy and Sebastian and other animagi, Mrs Hexybilla!", shouted Teddy. "Please let us in, we are in terrible danger out here!"

Hexybilla opened her door a crack. She had obviously been asleep, her frizzy hair looked even more dishevelled than normal, her nightgown was crumpled and had evidently been hastily put on.

"Teddy, Sebastian!", she exclaimed. "But … how …?"

"We will explain everything to you", Teddy replied, "but please let us in."

Hexybilla opened her door and saw the large group standing in front of her room.

"My oh my …!", she sighed, "Most of the animagi who disappeared! How did you manage to get back?"

Teddy and Sebastian did not answer but pushed their way past Hexybilla who made room for all of them to enter her small apartment. Hexybilla stared aghast at four animagi bodies lying just outside her door.

"What happened here …?", she cried out. "What is going on …?"

Teddy again pushed past her, rapidly glanced at the darkened passageway in front of the door and quickly closed the door and locked it.

"We are not safe at all, Mrs Hexybilla", Teddy said to her with a worried look on his face. "It might be safer to go to one of the back rooms so that nobody sees that someone actually lives here."

"But there is only my bedroom!", Hexybilla exclaimed. "I can't let all of you into my bedroom! Look at the state you are all in!"

It was only then that Teddy, Sebastian and the others realised how dirty and grimy they all looked. The various battles with Garglethroat and the transfer through the portal had left them covered in dust and dirt.

"We are so sorry, Mrs Hexybilla", Sebastian interjected, "but we are talking about matters of life and death here! If you don't help us to hide, we might all be petrified in the next few minutes! Please let us into the back room, and let's switch off all lights in this room so that it looks uninhabited. I think that's why they did not get you yet, because they didn't realise that someone actually lived here!"

Hexybilla relented reluctantly and opened the door to her bedroom. The room was very messy, with many clothes, used and unused, lying on the floor, witches' hats of different colours and varying crookedness spread all over the place – some had obviously been trampled on – and dirty socks dangling from the edge of a half-open chest of drawers overflowing with clothes that all seemed to exhale a musty smell. Hexybilla was very embarrassed. For years nobody other than herself had been in her bedroom. It was her own private sphere where she could recover from the exigencies of being an animagi council board member and a teacher. Teddy, Sebastian and the group of animagi did not hesitate and quickly flooded into Hexybilla's small bedroom, while Sebastian switched off all the lights in the front room. They all made themselves as comfortable as they could in the small cramped bedroom.

"Now tell me what this is all about", whispered Hexybilla looking at both Teddy and Sebastian in particular.

Teddy and Sebastian filled her in as best they could, helped in places by Ugah, Hagelik, @@*^#, Erik and Sylvester. Sebastian reminded Hexybilla of their last meeting, before they all had been forced by Garglethroat and the unfolding events to go through the portal to Animagana to prevent Erik from falling into a coma.

"I see …", said Hexybilla. "That explains why you suddenly all disappeared. We never understood how and why you managed to get to Animagana. We were so worried! Erik, your parents have been looking all over for you … the police have been involved!"

Teddy and Sebastian then recounted their adventures in Animagana, they talked about Callisto, Leonidas and Konrad, the monks and St Albans monastery. At this stage in their story they pointed at Sylvester who was sitting next to Erik on Hexybilla's bed.

"I am pleased to meet you, Mrs Hexybilla", said Sylvester.

"Poor boy! Or should I say, poor man, as you are really 477 years old!", replied Hexybilla and they all laughed. "Glad to hear that you seem to have survived the return passage through the portal unscathed."

When Teddy mentioned the discovery of the Book of Death and the dreadful effect its green ray had on its victims, Hexybilla turned very pale.

"Oh dear! That is dreadful news!", she exclaimed. "Now I understand your story about all the petrified animagi lying in the passageways on the way to the archives! I have to admit something dreadful to you: in hindsight it appears that I and Professor Pandanus have made a terrible mistake!"

Sebastian and his friends looked at each other, not understanding what Hexybilla was talking about.

"While you were trapped in Animagana, Professor Pandanus and his team discovered another copy of the Book of Death in our archives. It appears, therefore, that multiple copies of this dreadful book exist."

"But here we have the solution to our problem then!", exclaimed Teddy jubilantly. "We know that the book contains a counter spell that allows us to reanimate the petrified animagi lying outside! And with the book we can fight Garglethroat on an equal basis!"

But Hexybilla looked at them with a distraught face. Tears welled up in her eyes and ran down her wrinkled face.

"Alas! I fear not! When Professor Pandanus and I saw what the book could do we immediately destroyed it. In fact we burned it in the fireplace in the room next door. Had I known that we would need the counter-spell we would, of course, have kept it and written it down, but we just wanted to get rid of it as quickly as possible... Dear oh dear … what have I done", and she held her head in her hands, not daring to look at Sebastian and the others.

Teddy and Hagelik rushed towards Hexybilla who looked faint, and escorted her carefully to the bed where the other animagi quickly made room for her to lie down.

"This is just too much … It's all my fault …", muttered Hexybilla. "This could be the end of our animagi culture now that Garglethroat is free to rampage through our village without us having any means to stop him."

Sebastian and Teddy looked at each other. "There is nothing we can do about it now", Sebastian tried to console Hexybilla. "What is done is done. We now need to focus on how we can prevent Garglethroat from petrifying the rest of the village."

Hexybilla sighed deeply and sat up in her bed. "You are right, we have to be strong now and face this new challenge! But tell me the rest of your story: how did you manage to get back as you obviously had no child's soul to use to open the portal?"

Sebastian told Hexybilla how Garglethroat had extracted Sylvester's soul, how he had managed to freeze time purposefully for the first time just when Garglethroat and his henchmen were going back through the portal, and that this had allowed all of them, including Sylvester, to slip through just in time before the portal closed again.

"You see!", exclaimed Hexybilla looking at Sebastian. "I told you that you are special! Remember what we discussed last time I saw you here related to the prophecy in the *Animagi Book of Lore*? 'There will come a time when a young animago will recognise the power he holds to unleash the control of time'. You've done it! Your special skill might be one way to fight this dreadful Garglethroat! And remember that the prophecy also foretells 'the coming of this animago who will hold the key to Animagana and who will free the beings trapped within'. At the time we did not know what this meant, but you have helped to bring back 17 animagi who had been persuaded by evil Rigor Mortis to abscond to Animagana, leaving their human child hosts in a coma."

Hexybilla looked at the group of animagi huddled on her bed and on the floor, most of whom seemed frightened and disorientated.

"If our theories are correct, I would not be surprised if your human hosts have woken up now that you have come back to our world. Poor Lucy, Martin and all the others …!", Hexybilla said with a sigh. "At least there may be some positive news for our human hosts among this carnage of petrified animagi!"

"What shall we do next, Mrs Hexybilla", asked @@*^# with a worried look on his face.

"We need to contact the other council members as quickly as possible, if it's not too late already", replied Hexybilla. "As we don't have mobile phones down here this will need to be done in person, going from one place to another which will be risky considering that Garglethroat and his henchmen are out there. What do you think are Garglethroat's plans?"

Teddy and Sebastian briefly looked at each other. They had been asking themselves the same question. "I don't think he has a plan as everything just happened so quickly", replied Teddy. "What is evident is that he is petrifying everybody who stands in his way. He will of course also seek revenge, as it is our village and all of us who sent him and his henchmen to prison and have made his life a misery over the last years. I suspect that he will be particularly keen to take revenge on you Mrs Hexybilla and the other council members."

"I am sure you are right, which highlights how urgent it is that we contact the other council members immediately", Hexybilla conceded. *He may also want to take revenge on those humans who sent his host, Andrew Billings, to the maximum-security psychiatric hospital!* she thought, *not daring to divulge this other dark side of Garglethroat yet to the group in front of her. I don't think that this is an imminent threat, but I will need to tell Teddy and Sebastian soon enough!*

"I am not sure what Garglethroat will do about our human hosts and all the uninitiated humans in our village", continued Teddy as if realising what Hexybilla was thinking about. "I suspect that it would be too risky for him to petrify humans, as this would entail a large-scale investigation with all the resources that human society can muster. I haven't thought about this much yet, but I suspect that this would be too risky for him at the moment."

"I agree", replied Hexybilla. "Garglethroat's hatred is probably focused on animagi society, not on humans, although you never know what his warped mind is able and willing to do. The disadvantage we have over human society is also that we are poorly networked with other animagi communities, as there are only few long-distance tunnels and passageways linking our individual communities. And as we have no mobile phone or internet connections other than through those of our human hosts, it is more difficult for us to call for help from outside. We will certainly try to contact the animagi councils in neighbouring villages, but for now we are pretty much on our own, and other animagi groups would be equally powerless to directly confront Garglethroat at the moment."

Teddy and Sebastian nodded. *She is right*, thought Sebastian. *There is just no way at the moment that we can challenge Garglethroat directly.*

"So, first things first", continued Hexybilla. "Your assumption, Teddy, that Garglethroat may not yet target the humans on the surface gives me an idea of how we can proceed. In light of the immense threat to us, I suggest that we temporarily scrap animagi rule number one: not to venture to the surface because of the risk of uninitiated humans seeing us. This will allow us to move through the village above ground without risking encountering Garglethroat with his petrifying ray."

"I know where the nearest escape hatch to the surface is", said Sebastian. "It's the one where I had my nearly deadly encounter with Benny the cat and where I subconsciously used time-freeze for the first time."

Hexybilla remembered when Sebastian told her the story about Benny not that long ago. "It is safest for the moment if most of you stay here", Hexybilla suggested, glancing at the frightened faces in front of her. "@@*^#, if you could look after the group who will stay here, that would be much appreciated."

@@*^# looked at Teddy and Sebastian who nodded in agreement that this was the best course of action.

"I suggest that only a small group of us tries to find other council members", continued Hexybilla, "that way we can also move faster. May I suggest that I, Sebastian, Teddy, Hagelik and Ugah go? We will also take Erik and Sylvester as they can pretend that they are just taking their toy animals for a walk if we encounter any humans on the surface. I also want to introduce Erik and Sylvester to the council as they have played such a crucial part in your return to this world. But be aware, Sylvester, that the world we are in here is not like your former 16th century world. You will have a shock when you see how humans live these days. It is very different from the life you are used to…"

Sylvester had not had time to think about this new human world much. What he had seen so far, the portal chamber, the large archives, darkened passageways and Hexybilla's rooms did not look that different from what he was used to in St Albans monastery in Animagana. But he braced himself for the unexpected.

Erik and Sylvester looked at each other, pleased that they had been 'chosen' to be part of the group that would try to take action against Garglethroat. But Erik was worried about his parents. "Mrs Hexybilla, could we quickly go past my house so that I can tell my parents that I am well? They must be very worried and I miss them immensely." He tried to picture his dad Godfrey and his mum Alathia and how they must wonder what happened to him.

"They are indeed very worried", confirmed Hexybilla. "The police have been around several times, and they searched the whole village and neighbourhood, not understanding what happened to you and how you suddenly vanished. I fully understand that you want to see them as soon as possible, but this is a matter of life or death for our animagi community. If we don't stop Garglethroat our entire community might be gone in the next few days. You must understand, my boy, that every second now counts!"

Erik had to admit to himself that his parents could wait a few hours longer. After all he had been away for weeks, so a few hours here or there should not matter.

Hexybilla nodded when she saw that Erik had understood the urgency of their mission. "Sebastian, lead the way!", whispered Hexybilla, carefully opening her bedroom door.

69

Sebastian led the group of seven through the darkened passageways leading to the trapdoor he had used to get to the surface when he had met Benny the cat. *It just seems like yesterday that I opened the hatch for the first time!*, thought Sebastian, *and yet so much has happened since!*

A few petrified animagi were lying on the dusty passageway floor on the way to the trapdoor, but there was no sign of Garglethroat or his men. Teddy climbed the steps cemented into the wall first, pulled the lever, and carefully opened the trapdoor. "We can go", he whispered down to the others waiting in the gloomy shaft. "I can see a few cars moving about and there is a human walking down the street. It appears that our assumption was right that Garglethroat has not yet dared attack the human world on the surface. It would be teeming with police if he had done that!"

Erik and Sylvester emerged from the trapdoor first in case uninitiated humans were close by who were not allowed to see animagi moving about. They reached down to grab hold of Hexybilla, Sebastian, Teddy, Ugah and Hagelik and tucked them gently under their arms. They all peered around. As Teddy had said, humans seemed to be going about their day-to-day lives as normal, oblivious to the catastrophe that was unfolding right under their feet.

As Hexybilla had predicted, Sylvester stood for a few seconds in awe at the sight. Although this was only a small village, the strange houses, the paved streets and, stranger still, four-wheeled vehicles not drawn by horses zooming past in the distance amazed him. The vehicles made a strange noise, similar to the bees in the beehive near St Albans monastery, just louder and deeper.

"These are called 'cars'", said Erik, noticing Sylvester's wonderment. "There are also flying objects with humans in them called 'planes'", and he pointed at a small shiny object, a jet plane floating through the blue sky high above them, followed by a rapidly dissipating condensation trail.

Sylvester stood with his mouth wide open watching the plane. They all watched Sylvester for a few seconds, allowing him to soak in the impressions of the new world he was now in. *Poor boy!*, thought Hexybilla. *All of this must come as such a shock to someone like him who was trapped in a strange world with a 16th century mindset for so long.*

But they did not have time to linger. Leaving Sylvester to continue gaping at the village with all its mysteries, Hexybilla brought them back to reality. "If humans only knew what is happening this instant right below their feet! They would not go about their day-to-day business so casually!", she sighed.

Indeed, the complete normality of the village stood in sharp contrast to the slaughter with petrified bodies going on in the passageways underneath the posh houses and manicured gardens.

"OK, quickly now", continued Hexybilla. "We will go and see Mrs Moluk first, the chairperson of the animagi council. Hopefully she has not been petrified by the Book of Death's ray yet. Erik and Sylvester, go down the hill and then turn right."

Erik and Sylvester walked down the road and turned right at the next intersection, holding the precious animagi cargo in their arms. They just looked like two twelve-year olds taking their toy animals for a walk. It was around midday and a fine summer's day. The large detached houses with their big gardens looked peaceful on either side of the road. Some humans were on the streets or in their gardens, some looking up and seemingly recognising Erik, although they also looked a bit puzzled at Sylvester's monk's habit. Sylvester still seemed overwhelmed by all the new impressions. As they walked by a parked car he could not stop himself from touching the shiny red-coloured metal, wondering at its smoothness and shine.

"Don't stop Erik!", whispered Hexybilla into his ear. "It is better if your neighbours don't recognise you at this stage, as we need to hurry."

Erik kept his head down and did not look up to people who shouted his name and waved.

After a few turns they reached a large villa overlooking the estuary, with a swimming pool in the front garden bathed by the summer sun. An elderly lady, Mrs Moluk's uninitiated host, was lying in her swimsuit on a reclining chair. Her skin was lathered with sun cream and glistened in the sunlight. She wore large sunglasses and seemed to be asleep. They quickly made their way unseen past her and entered the house through one of the hidden side entrances leading to the maze of animago passageways servicing this property. It was a squeeze for both Erik and Sylvester who just managed to jam their shoulders through the narrow entrance. In the passageways they had to crouch very low, their heads touching the ceiling. They released their animagi friends who were relieved to be able to walk on their own again. There was no sign of Garglethroat or any petrified animagi as they crawled through the passageways.

Hexybilla seemed to know her way around well and pointed towards a small door.

"I suspect Mrs Moluk will be in the room behind this door", said Hexybilla. "This is where she usually stays while her host is in or near the house."

Teddy carefully opened the door and they all entered a large bedroom with a double bed in the middle and a chest of drawers on the side, when they all heard a loud bang. They were under the chest of drawers, the space fortunately large enough for Erik and Sylvester to crawl under. A large object had just fallen from the top of the chest of drawers and lay spread-eagled in front of them. It was Mr Wood, one of the members of the animagi council. Teddy had held them all back, his fingers to his mouth suggesting they should be as quiet as possible.

"My oh my!", they heard the voice of Mrs Moluk above them. She was still on top of the chest of drawers. "Mr Wood! Mr Wood! What happened?"

Sebastian and his friends could hear Mrs Moluk, the large Victorian doll Sebastian remembered well from his first animagi council meeting, awkwardly climbing down the chest of drawers. After a final jump from the lowest drawer she reached Mr Wood. His wooden head and one limb – a branch – had come off and the rest of his body was lying contorted and twisted on the floor.

"Mr Wood! Oh no! How could this happen just now when we need you?", Mrs Moluk muttered.

She suddenly turned around and saw Sebastian and the others crouched under the chest of drawers. She was just about to shout when Hexybilla dashed forward. "Psst! Quiet Mrs

Moluk! It's me and a few other animagi. Not a sound please, as we are in danger!"

Mrs Moluk immediately recognised Hexybilla and breathed a sigh of relief. "Mrs Hexybilla! Thank God! You are still alive! And who do we have here?", she asked pointing at the rest of the group.

They all crawled out from the chest of drawers and Hexybilla introduced each one of them. Mrs Moluk knew Teddy, Sebastian and Ugah from school where she taught maths, but did not know Hagelik yet as he had only recently joined the animagi community. She was particularly pleased to meet Erik, whose disappearance she had heard all about, and the briefly recounted story of Sylvester and his escape from Animagana left her momentarily speechless.

"What a story!", she said when she had recovered her voice. "I can't believe that you survived the ordeal of the portal and that Sylvester is 477 years old! You look just like a 12-year old boy!"

Sylvester realised that he would hear that comment from everybody he was introduced to in this world. *Will I grow again, now that I am back in the human world?*, he wondered briefly.

Hexybilla turned her attention to Mr Wood's remains on the floor. "What happened here? Did he have a bad fall?"

"I fear it is worse", replied Mrs Moluk. "Mr Wood had come to visit me to discuss the terrible things happening in our community, with animagi being petrified in their hundreds by some mysterious green ray. But he also wanted to discuss with me the state of health of his human host who had been suffering from terminal cancer for quite some time. I fear that his host must have just died and that we have witnessed what happens to animagi when their hosts die: they also die!"

They were all speechless and looked at the sad remains of Mr Wood lying on the bedroom floor. Hexybilla and Teddy had seen a few animagi die on the spot when their human hosts expired, but this experience was new for Sebastian, Ugah and Hagelik who had all turned rather pale at the thought of how ephemeral their lives were and how dependent they were on the health of their hosts. The irreversible death of an animagi in front of them came as a terrible shock.

But they did not have much time to dwell on Mr Wood's fate. "Unfortunately, graver matters are afoot, Mrs Moluk", said Hexybilla with a worried frown on her wrinkled witch's face. "With the petrified animagi you already mentioned, you have seen the terrible result of a deadly weapon Garglethroat brought back from Animagana – a weapon that we are unable to fight at the moment, partly because of a terrible mistake I made not so long ago."

Hexybilla quickly recounted Garglethroat's story, her discovery and immediate destruction of the Book of Death with Prof Pandanus, and their journey via the surface to Mrs Moluk's house.

"We were hoping that at least some members of the council like yourself have not been struck down by the green ray", said Hexybilla hopefully to Mrs Moluk, "and that we can discuss a possible solution to this dreadful threat in an emergency meeting. Do you know whether other council members are still alive?"

"I had contact with your human host Suzanne earlier using my host's phone", Mrs Moluk said looking at Hexybilla. "As you know she is our only human on the council. And I hope that Mr Kasperski, the robot toy on our council, is also safe as he lives in a remote house not easily accessible through the underground passageways. I don't know about the others …"

"We need to act very quickly, Mrs Moluk", said Hexybilla. "I suggest that we send out our animagi friends to find the other animagi council members. Erik and Sylvester can go and get Suzanne and check whether we can safely meet at her house. Erik, you may want to go past your house and tell your parents that you are safe, but don't linger. Godfrey will understand as he is initiated and will understand the threat Garglethroat poses. You could then use the phone there to get hold of Suzanne. If we all could meet up again within the next two hours? Use phones to ring this number if possible. Who knows, we may be lucky and Mrs Moluk's uninitiated host might continue sunbathing for a while."

They all nodded and quickly left the room through the hidden entrance under the chest of drawers. In the meantime, Mrs Moluk and Hexybilla started gathering together the sad remains of Mr Wood.

70

"I can hear you again!", Andrew stopped thrashing about his cell, sat down on the rubbery floor and closed his eyes. "My Garglethroat! Where were you? What happened? Why have I not been able to communicate with you for the last month?"

"Hello Andrew, my host", Garglethroat's thoughts streamed into Andrew's brain. "I have been away. I apologise. I made a mistake. I thought that while I was away I could continue the link with you, but for whatever reason the link got severed. But I am back now, and we are stronger than ever!"

Garglethroat told Andrew the story of Animagana, how they got there, some of the adventures and tribulations they had to endure, and how they got back. He missed out the bits that made him look less flattering, for example where he could barely keep up with Mephisto and his brigands when they were rushing through Animagana's dense forest, or when they could no longer control Blackbeard's ship and smashed onto the rocks below the monastery. However, he spent a long time describing his cunning theft of the Book of Death and what the book's deadly ray could do to both humans and animagi. Garglethroat completed his account with a description of the havoc they had caused in the passageways underneath the village where barely an animago was left unpetrified.

"What a story!", Andrew communicated to Garglethroat. "I had not realised what adventures you and your men have gone through. Sorry to hear about Gremlin's untimely death, by the way."

"Yes", replied Garglethroat, "and we were lucky not to lose more! But as you can see, I have the weapon we have always dreamt of. With the Book of Death we can get rid of all those who wish your death and threaten you. And so far there has not been any counter-attack, so I suspect that our copy of the Book of Death might be the only one that has survived the 16th century dissolution of the monasteries."

"That is great, my Garglethroat!", replied Andrew with a big smile.

The two wardens watched Andrew on their monitors and were wondering what was happening. First, Andrew had thrashed around his cell violently like he had done for the past few weeks, and suddenly he sat down very calmly and now he even smiled! *What is going on?*, thought the first warden. *One minute he's all mad, the next he is as docile as a lamb. As if something suddenly happened to him!*

Andrew was aware of the cameras observing him, so he quickly wiped the smile from his face. *I can't let them know that I am communicating again with my animago*, he thought. *I need to carry on as usual, otherwise they will think something is afoot.*

"I am being closely observed here, Garglethroat. I need to be careful how I react, otherwise the wardens will think something is going on. I will need to go crazy again and thrash about my cell. But before I do that … what is your plan? Will you petrify everybody in the village? You know they all hate me and want me dead, so that's what you should do …"

"I know, Andrew, I know", replied Garglethroat. *And I also know that you are raving mad, my friend!*, Garglethroat thought to himself, making sure Andrew could not 'hear' him think. *But you have been good to me, we have formed a good team, and I enjoyed it greatly when you nearly beat the kids at school to death, and especially when you listened to my order to behead your mother with the kitchen knife! I am happy to support your crazy idea that everybody is after you, but there will come a time when I might not need you anymore. Unfortunately I am bound to you through our host-animago link and my life depends on you being alive. But I am working on finding a solution to this little problem ...*

"I know Andrew, and I will, as usual, help you with everything you want", he continued his 'audible' thoughts to Andrew. "But I can't attack the human world on the surface yet as it would create utter chaos, with the police and possibly the army coming in. So let me deal with our animagi enemies in the village first, and then we'll discuss what the best plan of action is. I will also try to get you out of this psychiatric hospital, of course, but again give me a bit of time to work out a plan."

"I was wondering when you would come and get me?", asked Andrew with an impatient tone in his thoughts. "This place is so awful; they treat me like scum here. I don't think they see me as a human being anymore here. Their attempts at 'rehabilitating' me stopped a long time ago. I think they now just want to see me rot in here. So you better get me out of here quick, because if I die you'll also die, and neither of us want that do we?"

So, now you are threatening me, you nasty bastard!, thought Garglethroat with his unhearable thoughts. *I am not surprised they have given up on you mate! You are probably a useless case in psychological terms and probably nobody can help you, least of all myself.*

He switched on his mental connection to Andrew again. "I will help you as soon as I can, Andrew", Garglethroat promised, "as I am also not helped by the fact that you continue to rot in this hospital. Now that we have a weapon we also have a real chance to get you out of there for the first time!"

"That's my frog!", exclaimed Andrew, not realising that he had also said it out loud. He quickly put his hand over his mouth and glanced surreptitiously at the cameras embedded out of reach in the ceiling.

"What is he talking about?", asked Warden number two. They had clearly heard Andrew refer to a 'frog'. "Now he thinks there are animals with him in the cell!", and they both laughed.

"The wardens are getting suspicious, my Garglethroat, I need to stop", Andrew thought. "We'll communicate again soon, but in the meantime think a bit more about how you'll get me out of here!"

"I will, Andrew, I will", replied Garglethroat. "I will see you soon, I promise …"

Andrew leaned against the wall. He was very constrained in his movements by the straight-jacket that tied both his arms and hands together, but for the first time in a long while he was not so bothered. He let his thoughts drift towards his animago, and visions of a daring escape began to form in his mind, the nasty wardens lying petrified on the floor. He would trample all over them, crush their ugly heads with his boots, and slaughter the hospital director in the cruellest way. *I'll get you all! You wait and see. Mark my words!* His head tilted slightly to the side. For the first time in a long time he had fallen asleep very quickly.

71

Sebastian, Teddy, Ugah, Erik, Sylvester and the members of the animagi council were sitting around a low table in Suzanne's spacious house. Suzanne's uninitiated husband was out working and her daughter was still at school, so it was safe to meet for several hours.

Coordinating the meeting had not been easy, as only Mrs Moluk could be accessed by phone while her host was sunbathing in the garden. Erik had gone home to tell his dad, a university academic who was working from home that day, that he was well. Godfrey broke into tears at the sight of his son, rushed towards him and embraced him for a long time. He could not believe that Erik was safe after all the time he had been missing!

Erik introduced Sylvester who had stood aside while Erik and his dad were hugging and told his dad their incredible story. He also explained why they were in a rush to find Suzanne. As a human initiated in the animagi ways, Godfrey immediately offered to help and understood how dangerous the situation was in the passageways for the animagi while Garglethroat was rampaging around with the Book of Death. After ringing Suzanne and checking that the emergency meeting could take place in her house, Godfrey took his car to pick up Mr Kasperski, the robot on the animagi council, and brought him to Suzanne's house.

Erik and Sylvester had gone back to Mrs Moluk's house where Hagelik and Ugah still waited, and together they went to find one of the older teddy-bear council members who lived a few houses down the road from Mrs Moluk. Sadly, they found the animago petrified, lying close to the entrance to his host's bedroom with a mortified look on his face.

They had more luck with the second teddy-bear council member, Arthur McHaggis, who lived half-way between Mrs Moluk's and Suzanne's house. They had found McHaggis huddled in a corner, shaking with fear. He had seen his fellow animagi being petrified by Garglethroat's ray in the passageways just outside his house and had tried to hide. He was immensely relieved when he saw Mrs Moluk and her group enter the room instead of Garglethroat. They had quickly filled him in about the situation. Erik and Sylvester then had gathered the animagi in their arms and had made their way to Suzanne's house via the surface as fast as they could.

"Welcome everybody, and sorry that this has been such a rush", said Mrs Moluk glancing at the group sitting around the table. "It is good to see Mr Kasperski and Mr McHaggis among us, I am so pleased that Garglethroat's ray has not been able to get to you", and she looked with great relief at her two fellow council members. "I would like to inform you that Mr Wood, our esteemed council member, has just died. His host was very ill and must have passed away when Mr Wood was visiting me. Normally I would ask for a minute of silence in memory of Mr Wood, but we don't have time."

They all looked down for a few seconds.

"Although information is patchy, I have also heard through the village grapevine that several children who had been in a coma have woken up. That is excellent news! This shows how important it was for Sebastian and his friends to have brought as many of the animagi trapped in Animagana back with them ... 17 overall if I remember your information correctly?"

Sebastian and Teddy nodded and felt very proud.

"I don't know at this stage how many children have come out of their comas", Mrs Moluk continued, "but I overheard my human host talking to Lucy's mother that she seems fine. Remember that Lucy is the human host for our fellow animagi Barney, Penny and Woof. They are currently sheltering in Mrs Hexybilla's flat and we will need to think about a way to get them to safety in due course. However, I am also sure that several children have remained in a coma, suggesting that there must still be some of our fellow animagi, who had decided to leave our human world for Animagana with the help of Rigor Mortis, who have not returned. At this point, there is not much we can do for them as I can't see a way to extract another child's soul to open the passage through the portal, either on this side or in Animagana."

Those who had been to Animagana nodded in agreement. It seemed as if some animagi from the village would remain trapped in Animagana, possibly forever, and concurrently their child hosts from the village would indefinitely remain in a coma. Sebastian thought about the slave market in Raupenburg on Animagana, and how easy it would have been for several of the village's animagi to disappear forever into the clutches of ruthless slave traders and vicious slave owners.

"I would like to introduce to you Godfrey Wilkinson", Mrs Moluk moved on, and she pointed at Erik's dad sitting at the end of the table. "As you know by now we are very pleased to welcome Erik back into our community, you will have been told on the way here why he disappeared, together with his animagi friends", and she pointed at Sebastian, Teddy, Hagelik and Ugah, "and what adventures and hardships they had to endure to get back to the human world. This here is Sylvester, who comes from Animagana, and although he looks like 12 he actually is 477 years old!"

Those who did not know Sylvester's story looked at him in wonder.

"With their knowledge about what happened, and having witnessed the Book of Death in action, both Erik and Sylvester will be invaluable members of this group trying to fight Garglethroat."

Erik and Sylvester smiled at each other, very proud of being included in such an important undertaking.

"There are two other animagi council members who are not here, but we just did not have the time or opportunity to contact them. So we will have to make do with the group we have here. Anyone who thinks fighting Garglethroat is too dangerous for themselves or their family, including their human hosts, please feel free to say so, as we would all fully understand that what you might be asked to do could end in you being petrified by the Book of Death or, worse, being killed by Garglethroat and his men."

Mrs Moluk peered around the table, but nobody raised a hand or spoke up.

"Many thanks to all of you. I take it from your silence that you are all happy to be involved in one way or another in the fight against Garglethroat and in our attempt to maybe even capture his copy of the Book of Death."

Mrs Moluk let her words sink in for a few seconds. "I would also like to thank Suzanne for offering us her house for this extraordinary meeting. I understand that we have several hours before uninitiated members of your family are coming back?"

"Yes, Mrs Moluk", Suzanne replied. "My daughter will be the first one back, but not until after school is finished."

"Very well then", continued Mrs Moluk. "Mrs Hexybilla over to you …"

Hexybilla stood up and peered around the room. Everybody looked expectantly at her. "Welcome everybody. As you know, the main reason we have come together is that a major catastrophe has befallen our village. Garglethroat and his henchmen have come back with a deadly weapon, the Book of Death, which petrifies everybody who comes into contact with its green ray. We need to find a way to fight them as quickly as possible! The easiest way would have been to use the counter-spell that is also mentioned in the Book of Death. I admit that we had a copy here in our archives, but we destroyed it, not knowing how urgently we would need it now …"

A murmur went through the group, especially among those who had not heard that part of the story before.

"Are you saying, Mrs Hexybilla, that you had another copy of the book and that you destroyed it without taking note of the counter-spell?", asked Mr Kasperski with a puzzled look on his robot face.

"I am afraid that is true", said Hexybilla with an ashamed look. "At the time Professor Pandanus and I did not think that we would need it. I beg you all for forgiveness. In hindsight this was, of course, a dreadful mistake!"

"That is water under the bridge now", said Mrs Moluk, trying to appease the group. "We need to find other means to fight Garglethroat now."

"The most obvious approach would be to use Sebastian's magical skills of freezing time", Hexybilla continued. "If Sebastian could get near to Garglethroat, freeze time, and then snatch the copy of the Book of Death from him, we would be in control of that lethal weapon. But unfortunately …", and she looked directly at Sebastian, "it is not quite that easy. Sebastian, what do you think?"

"Yes, I thought about this since we arrived back in this world through the portal, but as many of you know I have problems controlling this strange power I seem to have. The first three times I used the time-freeze – against Benny the nasty cat, against Garglethroat's men when they had captured me, and against the sabrejaws when they attacked us in Animagana's forest – the time-freeze just happened without me really controlling it. It was slightly different when Garglethroat escaped through the portal in Animagana, leaving all of us behind without much chance of ever getting back to the human world. There I seemed to be able to freeze time by concentrating tremendously."

"But could you do that again when facing Garglethroat holding up the Book of Death?", asked Teddy.

"That's where I am not sure. It might be worth the risk, but if I fail I end up petrified."

"Yes, I realise that this is probably asking too much of you, Sebastian", remarked Hexybilla. "But it might be our only course of action. What do the others think? Shall we have a vote?"

They all felt rather uncomfortable deciding Sebastian's fate through an open vote. Nobody dared look up at Hexybilla.

"I am happy for you to have a vote on this", said Sebastian. "I'll do whatever is best for all of us even if it means sacrificing myself."

"Thanks for that, Sebastian", replied Hexybilla. "It would certainly not be an easy decision to send you to your potential death. Let's have a show of hands then ... yes, you too Mr Wilkinson, and Erik and Sylvester, and Teddy and Ugah and Hagelik ... as we are all affected by this decision. So all those in favour of Sebastian attempting to get close to Garglethroat and freeze time to snatch the book from him, please raise a hand."

Hexybilla peered around the group. Nobody had raised a hand, including Hexybilla. They all looked at each other and smiled. Teddy patted Sebastian on the back. "There is no way we would ask you to sacrifice yourself, Sebastian", he said, "especially as you are unsure how well you could control the time-freeze."

Everybody nodded in agreement and smiled. The tension that had briefly been perceptible in the room rapidly eased.

"Many thanks for that", Hexybilla said, obviously relieved by the outcome of the vote. "We are, therefore, unanimously agreed that Sebastian should not risk his own safety by trying to approach Garglethroat. We need to find other means to fight him!"

They all started thinking hard about other options.

"Well, what about looking for another copy of the Book of Death in the archives?", asked Teddy after a while with his usual clear-headedness. "We know that more than one copy existed, as St Albans monastery on Animagana also had one. The monks might have rescued more than one copy at the time when they put the books and parchments into our archives?"

"That is a possibility theoretically worth pursuing, Teddy", replied Hexybilla, "but how would we find the time to search the entire archives for another copy? Professor Pandanus and his team found the copy we had by chance, while they were looking for a way to get you and Erik back, but you saw that the professor now lies petrified with his team in the archives. I did not ask him at the time where he had found the book. Although I may have an idea broadly in which section of our vast archives another book might be, even without the threat of Garglethroat hanging over us, it would take us weeks, if not months, to find another copy. On top of this, I somehow doubt that our archives would hold another copy. It seems to me that each monastery that was dissolved by Henry VIII's men held one copy of the deadly book ... and for a good reason, judging by its deadly powers!"

They all looked at each other and could see the logic in what Hexybilla was saying. Looking for another copy of the book, and the counter-spell contained in it, was an option, but not a very practical one at this point in time.

"What about fighting Garglethroat outright, without my time-freeze option?", asked Sebastian. "We have fought him before here and on Animagana, with some success, and we could do it again. If we could lay our hands on some weapons ..."

"An obvious thought, Sebastian", replied Hexybilla, "but again I am not sure how practical this is. We have seen how much power Garglethroat holds with the Book of Death, and anyone coming near him will be petrified. This is the reason we will not allow you to go near him on your own. We of course don't know where Garglethroat is at the moment, he might be back in his old lair. He will also need to sleep at one point and could be vulnerable then, but I suspect that his henchmen are then just simply taking over. I think this would be a very dangerous option that could see us all petrified …"

They all nodded in agreement again, realising that it would be suicidal to confront Garglethroat head-on without a magical weapon like Sebastian's time-freeze. They simply did not have the person-power or weaponry needed for such an undertaking.

"We could try and get at Garglethroat's henchmen", said Teddy. "We know that Gremlin died in Animagana and that only the nasty Ori Fisse and Skeleto are left. Is there a way we could persuade them to betray Garglethroat … maybe if we offered them slightly reduced punishment?"

But as soon as Teddy had suggested this, he realised that it was as unrealistic as Sebastian's suggestion. How would they be able to get to Garglethroat's men without being exposed to the deadly ray? They all acknowledged that this would also be a very difficult course of action to take.

"If only I could remember the counter-spell", said Sylvester with a timid voice. They all looked at him. "Back in the stables on Animagana, Garglethroat first petrified me with the Book of Death and then he used the counter-spell to wake me up again. I guess he was testing whether the counter-spell worked, but he also needed me to be conscious so that he could extract my soul. Unfortunately I was too drowsy to remember. All I know is that the counter-spell consisted of about ten words, similar to the spell that petrifies."

"At least we know that the counter-spell works", said Hexybilla. "Don't worry Sylvester. Nobody would have expected you to remember the lines after having been petrified."

Sebastian remembered how difficult it had been on Animagana to remember the spell for opening the portal, and he was fully awake and conscious at the time!

"We could of course try and evacuate the entire village", Mrs Moluk suggested. "But this would be logistically very difficult, as we have seen how hard it is to communicate between a small group like ourselves, but at least it could mean that we would all be out of immediate danger."

"But where would we go?", asked Hexybilla. "We have good connections with other villages nearby, but they are equally vulnerable to Garglethroat's deadly ray. Places we can reach, he and his henchmen can also reach. If you are thinking about going further afield, towards London for example, this would entail a mass evacuation that would be difficult to implement even at a time of peace."

"I agree", said McHaggis, "although this is another obvious idea, I think it would be too difficult and cumbersome to implement under the present conditions. We don't even know how many of us animagi are still alive and not petrified. As far as we know, we might be the last ones left anyway!"

Everybody knew that McHaggis was right. The piles of bodies they had seen so far suggested that a large part of the animagi community had already been petrified. How could they communicate with the few who might have been able to hide, and how could they coordinate an evacuation without Garglethroat realising what was happening?

A glum mood had settled on the group as they realised that none of these proposals had any chance of success.

Suddenly Suzanne stood up and looked at them. "I may have an idea …"

72

@@*^# and the group of animagi who had stayed behind in Hexybilla's apartment were getting restless. It had been hours since Hexybilla and the others had left, and the group left behind was unsure what to do. Several had to go to the bathroom and they were all getting rather hungry.

"@@*^#, we can't stay here forever", said Barney the yellowish Teddy.

"What do you suggest we do, Barney?", asked @@*^#. "We can't just walk out of here. It's too dangerous!"

"But maybe we should just have a look", intervened Penny, the doll with silky white hair. "I'll just have a look", and she opened the door to Hexybilla's living room before @@*^# could stop her. She then stood still for a few seconds and they all held their breath. No sound could be heard from the passageway outside Hexybilla's flat. Penny very cautiously opened the front door and peered out, first left, then right.

"I can't see anything apart from the petrified animagi we saw before", she whispered back to the group. "I think it's safe to go out."

"But where would we go?", asked @@*^#.

"We can try and find our way to our host Lucy's house. It's not too far from here", said Woof, the little brown dog.

"OK, then", said @@*^#, pushing the group gently forward. They quietly sneaked out of Hexybilla's flat and turned left down the dimly lit passageway. Petrified bodies were lying everywhere, some in jumbled heaps, some on their own with surprised looks on their petrified faces.

@@*^# had gone ahead, with the others following. Penny, Woof and Barney were at the back. Barney kept peering behind him, expecting something horrible to lurch from the semi-darkness at any moment. He shivered with fear.

Suddenly @@*^# stopped, but it was too late. They had just rounded a corner, and straight in front of them stood Garglethroat and his two henchmen. The whole group stood where they had stopped, not daring to move.

"Well, well, well!", smiled Garglethroat. "Who do we have here! If it isn't our friends from Animagana! I told you that they had also made it through the portal", he said looking at Ori Fisse and Skeleto, "but you wouldn't believe me when we all landed in a heap in the portal room of the archives. Had we waited another minute or so we could have got them all there and then!", and he looked in anger at his two companions.

Garglethroat composed himself again. "How good to see you again!", he said with a sardonic smile to @@*^# and his group. "You see", and he turned again to Ori Fisse and Skeleto, "I told you it was worth waiting around the passageways for a little longer. I knew more animagi would come out sometime soon. But … where are Teddy, Sebastian and the two human boys?", he asked with a frown on his ugly face. "Have they escaped?"

Nobody answered in @@*^#'s group, too scared to speak.

"I will petrify you if you don't tell me where they have gone!", said Garglethroat holding up the Book of Death.

"You will petrify us anyway!", replied @@*^#. "Come on guys! We have nothing to lose", and he dashed forward, raising his small frog arms towards the three much larger animagi.

Garglethroat lifted the book and closed his eyes. He knew the incantation by heart now:

GURRAG SHAH FRAHN MARRG
EXARTIUS GORGALKON MOGARAT
RETICULUS MORTIS ETERNICA

The Book of Death started gleaming with its deadly greenish light. It seemed to open by itself, and Garglethroat cast the ray at @@*^# who had almost reached him. In an instant @@*^# was petrified and fell forward, flat on his face. Garglethroat directed the ray at the others who had no time to react. They fell like dominoes, toppling on top of each other.

Barney had just emerged into the intersection of passageways when the whole commotion started. But things were happening so fast that he could not react. His fellow animagi were toppling over in front of him and the ray was almost upon him. Instinctively he let himself fall to the ground, just before Penny and Woof collapsed on top of him, petrified. Barney held his breath and lay there motionless, buried under the other animagi. He heard Garglethroat and his henchmen approach, the ray had ceased casting its deadly green light. Ori Fisse and Skeleto prodded some of the bodies lying petrified in front of Barney.

"I think that'll do, boss", said Ori Fisse. "Our magical weapon has done its job perfectly again. And we have finally taken revenge on these animagi who had been with us in Animagana."

"Yeah", replied Garglethroat, "but we haven't got the most important characters yet, Sebastian and Teddy and the two boys. They could be dangerous for us! We have to find them!"

Barney did not dare to breathe. Garglethroat was standing right next to him. A little longer and Barney would have to reveal his presence. *Just hold your breath for a few more seconds! They may go away!*, he hoped.

"What's your plan now, boss?", asked Ori Fisse.

"We continue petrifying any animagi we find. This is part of my revenge after the way they treated me! But we will eventually take our fight to the surface and start annihilating humans. Wouldn't it be much nicer to live above all these dank and dark passageways! But that will need careful planning as humans have vast resources in terms of police and even military. I still need to think about the best course of attack!"

Barney's lungs ached as he had held his breath for too long now ...

"But my immediate task has to be to free Andrew, my host", continued Garglethroat. "Although I have never felt as close to him as he has to me, my life depends on his survival. If he dies I die, and we don't want that do we? As you know, he is currently imprisoned in this dreadful hospital not too far from here, so we will need to get there soon and free him. This should help ...", and he held the Book of Death up in the air.

They all laughed, their chuckles reverberating from the damp passageway walls.

Ori Fisse started moving away up the passageway. After a few seconds Skeleto and Garglethroat followed. When they were out of earshot, Barney inhaled as slowly and deeply as he could. A few more seconds and he would have either revealed himself or fainted. It was hard to breathe with Penny and Woof lying on top of him, so he gently pushed their petrified bodies aside and looked up. He deeply inhaled the rank air. Nobody was in sight.

I was very lucky that they didn't spot me, and that somehow Penny's and Woof's bodies protected me from the deadly ray! I think what I just heard was very important, so I need to pass on this information as quickly as possible to Hexybilla and the council.

He got up quickly and walked in the opposite direction to where Garglethroat and his men had gone. *I can't go to Lucy's house as this is down the passageway where Garglethroat and his men have gone,* he thought in panic. *Maybe I can go to Erik's house which is not too far from here and hide there?*

He hesitated a few seconds and turned towards the passageways leading towards Erik's house. Although he was unsure whether this was the best course of action, he could not think of any other alternative at the moment. He briefly glanced back at the pile of animagi lying petrified on the dusty ground and felt great sadness. *After all we've been through on Animagana together, this is how it ends? No! There must be a way to defeat Garglethroat and his men. I must try and find Hexybilla, Teddy and Sebastian and tell them about Garglethroat's plans!* And with that thought his confidence partly returned, and he quickly made his way towards Erik's house.

73

"Why don't we get to Garglethroat via his human host?", asked Suzanne. "I am not suggesting killing Andrew Billings, I certainly could not do that, as repugnant a human being he might be! But we all know that if we can sever the love a human feels for his or her animago, that animago dies and reverts back to being a soul-less toy. If we could somehow make Andrew forget Garglethroat?"

Hexybilla and her companions thought about Suzanne's idea.

"In theory that could work", said Teddy after a while, "but how would we get to Andrew? We don't even know where he is!"

"I happen to know where he is", replied Suzanne, "and as luck has it, I was planning to do interviews for my psychology dissertation in the South Devon Maximum-Security Psychiatric Hospital where Andrew has been incarcerated. I can easily pretend that I need to talk to Andrew as part of my research, but my real aim would be to persuade him to stop loving Garglethroat."

"That is indeed a lucky coincidence, Suzanne!", said Hexybilla, "and, by the sound of it, well worth a try. But you know that Andrew Billings is a very disturbed human being. Even as a child he showed very strange and erratic behaviour, nobody liked him, and often he was very violent. As many of us know, it all culminated in Andrew killing – or rather butchering – his own mother when he was only 16 years old! I think his nasty personality has rubbed off on Garglethroat, and might explain the hatred Garglethroat seems to feel towards the rest of the world."

"Yes, there have been some studies that have looked at the psychological link between human hosts and their animagi", Mrs Moluk interjected. "Although results are not conclusive, and much more research is needed, several studies I have seen suggest a strong link. This means that nice human hosts, like Erik or Godfrey for example" – at which point Erik blushed but looked at Mrs Moluk with gratitude, while Godfrey looked at the group with large astonished eyes – "usually have nice and friendly animagi" – at which point Sebastian, Teddy and Ugah glanced self-consciously, but proudly, around the room.

"But what about Bunny, Godfrey's animago?", asked Ugah. "His dad is so kind" – Godfrey looked up again with raised eyebrows – "and yet Bunny turned out to be a nasty traitor!"

"Yes", agreed Mrs Moluk, "that example shows that the psychological relationship between human host and animago is not as straightforward as it may seem, and there will always be exceptions to the rule, if such a rule indeed exists ..."

They were quiet for a few seconds, with those who had witnessed Bunny's fate, and eventual sacrifice and redemption, thinking about him with great sadness.

"But how will you persuade Andrew to repudiate his love for Garglethroat?", asked Sebastian.

"That I don't know, Sebastian. As I have learned in my psychology courses, this will require very careful and subtle manoeuvring. I will need to gain his confidence first, find out more about his special bond with Garglethroat, and then try and persuade him that he would act for the common good by helping us get rid of Garglethroat. The fact that Andrew has had such a solitary and violent past will make this particularly difficult, but I am willing to try. In fact I am set up to visit the hospital as the ethics approval for my research has just come through from the university. I can go up there tomorrow, although I will need to juggle visits a little bit around my other commitments."

"That would be excellent, Suzanne", replied Hexybilla. "May I suggest that you take at least two animagi with you? You could easily hide them in a bag and, if you are searched, you could always pretend that they are part of your methodology of gaining your respondents' confidence."

"That is an excellent idea!", agreed Suzanne. "They could also help me with advice there and then!"

"OK!", replied Hexybilla, "why don't you take Teddy and Sebastian. As we all know Teddy is very wise, while Sebastian has shown tremendous courage and adaptability during their adventures in Animagana."

Sebastian and Teddy looked at each other and they immediately agreed that they were keen to accompany Suzanne on her dangerous mission.

"Mrs Hexybilla? Could I also go?", asked Ugah. "I know that I haven't got as much knowledge and wisdom as Teddy, or maybe as much courage as Sebastian, but I have seen Garglethroat and his men in action, and an additional pair of hands and eyes might not go amiss if Garglethroat threatens to scupper Suzanne's plan?"

Hexybilla looked at Mrs Moluk, McHaggis and Kaspersky, and they all nodded in agreement with Ugah's proposal. "What do you think, Suzanne?"

"I think that is an excellent idea, many thanks Ugah! You are not too large, so I can easily hide you with the others in my bag and, as you say, additional help will always be welcome."

"That's settled then!", confirmed Hexybilla. "The three of you go with Suzanne. We will provide back-up from here. The key remaining question is now where we should base ourselves? For obvious reasons we can't go back underground, so we will need to stay in a human house above the surface. But we need to bear in mind that Garglethroat will be looking out for us, so we need to be vigilant all the time!"

"I thought about that", interjected Godfrey, "but I fear that our house would be too obvious a target for Garglethroat as they know Erik, Teddy, Sebastian and Ugah live there. This also means that neither Erik nor Sylvester can go back there either."

"I agree", said Mrs Moluk. "My house might be an option, but my human host is not initiated which makes things tricky!"

"Why not my house?", asked Suzanne. "My son is out of the house, and although my husband and daughter are not initiated, we have plenty of room for animagi to hide. We could use our holiday annex, which is currently not rented out, as our base. My husband never goes in there as I manage our holiday lettings. There is also a phone in there, and I could pass you a mobile phone, so that we can communicate all the time. I would make sure that you would be well stocked with provisions, and our alarm system might help a bit against intruders such as Garglethroat."

"That sounds like a great idea!", said Hexybilla enthusiastically. "Your house is also a bit out of the way and not the most obvious place for Garglethroat to look for us, as long as we all keep this a secret. So we would be very happy to accept your very kind offer, Suzanne."

"I can help with my car if any of you need transport", said Godfrey, keen to help.

"Thank you, that is most helpful", said Mrs Moluk.

"I have my own car", said Suzanne, "so I can take us to the hospital any time, without need for help at the moment. I will ring the hospital immediately and try and make an appointment for tomorrow. If that is possible I suggest we leave as early as possible tomorrow morning."

They all made their way to Suzanne's holiday annex and tried to arrange bedding for everybody. Although it was a large one-bedroom flat, it would be quite cramped in there for them, and older animagi like Hexybilla, Mrs Moluk, Kaspersky and McHaggis were not used to sharing a room with young animagi, let alone with human children. Erik and Sylvester put some mats down near the small kitchen so as not to disturb the others too much.

74

Godfrey Wilkinson was back in his house. He could not sleep because of the turmoil of the last few hours. It had taken him a while to explain to his wife Alathia, Erik's mum, why Erik was not back home, and he had to divulge some of the secrets linked to the animagi world for her to understand what was going on. Only then did she realise what danger they were all in and she stopped insisting on seeing her son for the moment.

It was about three in the morning and Godfrey had gone to the fridge to grab a drink. When he closed the fridge door he heard a faint noise behind him and turned around. A yellowish teddy-bear stood near the door looking at him. "Mr Wilkinson?", the teddy-bear asked. "Are you initiated to the ways of our animagi world?"

"You are lucky, my bear. I am Erik's dad and am initiated. I am host to animagi like Teddy and Ugah … and Bunny who is now dead. Who are you?"

"I am Barney, one of Lucy's animagi. I need your help."

"Yes, of course. I know all about the problems with Garglethroat and your story about Animagana. You are one of the animagi who were rescued by Sebastian and his companions?"

"Yes, indeed", replied Barney with a sigh. "Unfortunately all the other animagi I was with who were rescued were petrified by Garglethroat in one of the passageways not far from here …"

"Oh no!", exclaimed Godfrey. "The others still thought you were safe in Hexybilla's flat."

"We could not stay there much longer, Mr Wilkinson, as we needed to find food and water. I hope you don't mind, but I took some food out of your fridge earlier."

"No problem, Barney, no problem. Have you had enough to eat?"

"Yes, thank you. But the reason I need to talk to you is that, while I pretended to be petrified and lay on the floor, I overheard Garglethroat say that he wanted to free his host, a so-called Matthew … Martin … Andrew …"

"Andrew Billings!", Godfrey confirmed. "Are you sure Garglethroat said he would free him?"

"Yes, that was one of his plans. I don't know when, but Garglethroat was very specific about that. I thought this could be important information."

"Yes, indeed!", said Godfrey, scratching his stubbly chin. "In fact this is so important that we need to tell the others immediately. Follow me", and he grabbed Barney under his arm and walked briskly in his pyjamas to his car parked on the street outside the house.

75

Suzanne steered her small car through the large gates of the South Devon Maximum-Security Psychiatric Hospital. The gates were part of the perimeter fence surrounding the vast grounds of the hospital, and it took her another minute to reach the main building. The hospital had once been a large landed estate, owned by one of the local earls, and had been sold to the hospital trust a few decades ago. It consisted of several rather grand Victorian buildings and a large park that looked almost like a botanic garden with tree ferns, ponds fringed by ornamental plants, and a lot of New Zealand plants introduced to this part of the world in the 19th century. The buildings looked in decent shape and appeared to have been freshly painted recently. As she climbed out of the car with Sebastian, Teddy and Ugah peering out of her handbag, Suzanne nonetheless felt a sense of foreboding as she looked at the large imposing entrance to the main building where an arrow pointed towards the reception.

Now that I am here, I wonder whether I might have taken on too much?, she wondered, *especially as we now know from Barney that Garglethroat is also planning to come here and free Andrew Billings. Although I knew Andrew's mum, I don't think Andrew knows me, and that's good. It's important that he does not realise that there is a link between me and the village, and especially between me and Garglethroat. If he found out, the whole plan could unravel!*

"Remember, guys, that you should stay quiet and not move at all during our visit", she said addressing the three animagi in her bag while climbing the steps towards the main entrance. "As we discussed, I will pretend that showing toy animals to the inmates is part of my methodology for gaining their confidence. Please also remember that Garglethroat could show up here any time. If that is the case all rules are off and our main aim is just to escape. So in that case don't worry about hiding any longer."

Sebastian, Teddy and Ugah nodded in agreement. They huddled further into Suzanne's relatively spacious bag, their heads just sticking out slightly so that they were able to look over the rim.

Suzanne went to the reception where a stern-looking woman with glasses checked her appointment with the director of the hospital in a large diary in front of her. Suzanne knew that she had been lucky to get an appointment at such short notice as there had been a cancellation just before she rang. The receptionist took Suzanne to a security gate where two wardens asked her to place her bag, her coat, and any metal objects such as car keys in a tray. Suzanne walked through a metal detector without the machine beeping and walked over to the wardens to pick up her bag.

"Do you mind if we have a look inside your bag, madam?", asked one of the wardens. "It's part of our security routine."

Suzanne nodded and the warden shook the contents of the bag onto the stainless-steel table. He looked at a notebook, some tissues – used and unused – and grabbed hold of Sebastian, squeezing and shaking him hard. "Just checking there's nothing in there, madam", he said when he saw Suzanne's pained look. Sebastian tried hard not to wince when the warden compressed his chest. The warden did the same with Teddy and then grabbed Ugah. "Hey, look at this one", he said to his colleague. "A gollywog! I had one of these when I was little, I didn't know they still existed!"

"He is quite old", Suzanne tried to explain, hoping the warden would stop squeezing Ugah.

"May I ask why you are bringing toy animals into the hospital, madam?", asked the warden. "You know that you are not allowed to leave anything with the patients?"

"Yes, I'm aware of that", replied Suzanne. "They are part of my approved research methodology to appease the patients and gain their confidence. You may be amazed at what toy animals can achieve to break the ice at the start of interviews with violent psychopaths."

The warden looked at his colleague with a sarcastic smile on his face, but placed the animagi back into the bag and waved Suzanne through. After checking the noticeboard for the hospital director's office, Suzanne climbed the vast and imposing central staircase towards the staff offices. So far she had not seen any signs of patients or nurses. Another receptionist asked her to take a seat while she rang the director.

"What was your name again, dear?", the receptionist asked, while dialling a number.

"Suzanne St Austell. I have an appointment with the director to talk about a research project I'll be doing here for the next few weeks."

The receptionist glanced at Suzanne with a strange look, not hiding the fact that she thought that the South Devon Maximum-Security Psychiatric Hospital was a strange place for a university student to conduct research. After a few minutes, she led Suzanne into the director's office.

The director, a short chubby man with a bald head and large rimmed glasses, stood up from his large old wooden desk and walked towards Suzanne with his hand outstretched. "Ah, Mrs St Austell ... or is it Miss?"

"Mrs, please", said Suzanne, shaking the director's moist and rather limp hand. She took an immediate dislike to the man who seemed like a grovelling, insecure and rather ugly human being. She could see why someone like him ended up working in a place like this.

"My receptionist mentioned that you are from the university and that you are doing a research project on the effectiveness of rehabilitation procedures, using our hospital as a case study?"

"Yes, that's pretty much my dissertation topic. My supervisor, Prof Hedley, thought that your hospital would make an ideal case study."

"Ah, yes, Prof Hedley. I know him and his research well", replied the director, rubbing his greasy hands. "A good man, a very good man! We had a few students like you here over the years, working on their dissertations, so I am reasonably familiar with the needs of research students. You said you would need access to some of our patients?"

"Yes, that would be much appreciated. I have done all the stringent ethical approval procedures", and Suzanne handed the director a copy of the university's signed and approved form, "and am familiar with the dangers and pitfalls involved in interviewing violent psychopathic patients. I have also been told that I will not be allowed to enter the cells of the patients and that the interviews will have to take place in your secure visitor section?"

"Yes, that is correct", replied the director. "Our visitor facility is set up in such a way that you are separated from the patients by a bullet-proof perspex window with an in-built speaker system. You can, therefore, communicate freely with your respondents without danger of being attacked. We will, of course, monitor your interviews with the patients, both for your own and our patients' safety."

I knew that this is the procedure they are using, but it will be tricky to gain the confidence of Andrew Billings with such a set-up, thought Suzanne.

"Maybe once I have gained the confidence of my respondents you would let me visit them in their cells? After all, getting some insider knowledge of the patients' day-to-day life here is an important part of understanding the rehabilitation process?"

"We will see, we will see ...", said the director, while he continued rubbing his hands. "We have indeed had students here in the past who were allowed to see the patients in person, but only after we were pretty sure that there was no danger for them. In the meantime, I have also prepared a little dossier for you", and he pushed a large pile of papers across the table towards Suzanne, "which outlines our policy and practice regarding the rehabilitation of psychopathic patients. You will see from the statistics that we are one of the most successful psychiatric hospitals in the country when it comes to successful reintegration of former patients into the community."

Probably part of the 'famous' care-in-the-community programme which has been such a disaster!, thought Suzanne, but she feigned great interest and thanked the director profusely for the wealth of information.

"Is there a specific patient you would like to see?", asked the director.

OK, now comes the tricky part!, thought Suzanne, glancing briefly at Sebastian, Teddy and Ugah whose heads stuck out slightly from her bag. *I need to pretend that I am not here just for Andrew Billings ...*

"Any patient will theoretically do, Sir, but when your secretary passed me the list of inmates I thought that one particularly stood out: Andrew Billings. I would be particularly interested in talking to him as he seems like an almost irredeemable case."

While he had largely avoided Suzanne's gaze during most of their discussion, the director briefly looked Suzanne straight in the eyes.

Does he suspect why I am here?, Suzanne wondered. *Maybe I should have asked to see another patient first!*

"Andrew Billings…", the director said after a brief pause. "A very interesting case indeed, and one of our most violent patients! You know he killed his mother in the most brutal fashion when he was just 16!"

Suzanne feigned partial ignorance: "I knew he had a violent past, but, no, I did not know that he committed matricide."

"Would you not prefer to see one of our slightly less violent patients first?"

"No, thank you", Suzanne replied with slight hesitation. "I think Andrew Billings sounds like just the patient I need to talk to, and I am sure the safety procedures in place at your hospital you outlined earlier will keep me perfectly safe."

"As you wish, Mrs St Austell. I have no objection, as long as you keep us fully informed what your plans are and when you wish to see him. It will, of course, also depend on Andrew himself. We can't force him to see you. So if he says 'no', then I'm afraid that it will have to be another of our patients."

"Yes, of course, Sir", Suzanne replied. She had of course considered the problem that Andrew Billings might just simply say no to her request to talk to him, but she had to try. "Would it be possible to see him now?"

"I'll see what I can do", replied the director, glancing at his watch and picking up the phone. "We are in between meals, so this might actually be a good time to talk to him."

76

Garglethroat was sitting on a heap of gold and jewellery in the living room of one of the most luxurious animagi flats in the village. He leaned back and tenderly stroked some of the gold coins, humming softly and smiling.

"Look Ori Fisse, how much gold and precious jewellery we have already accumulated, just after a day of rampaging through the village and petrifying any animago that came into sight. And we have managed to secure this wonderful flat for us. Isn't it a step up from our previous cave?"

"Yes, boss", replied Ori Fisse, "it sure is!"

"But our task is far from over, boys", and Garglethroat also looked at Skeleto who was dismantling what looked like a gold-encrusted diadem. "So far I have not seen many members of the animagi council among our victims. Sebastian and his companions must have warned them, and they must be hiding somewhere. We need to find them!"

"Yes, boss", replied Ori Fisse. "But we suspect that they have gone to the surface, flouting the first rule of animagi life not to interfere with the human world. This makes them much harder to find."

"Yes, that's probably what they have done, the bastards! But we will get them! There is not much they can do."

He waved his two henchmen out of the room and continued to fondle his gold. This was one of the few times in his life that Garglethroat appeared entirely happy ...

77

"OK, guys", said Suzanne to the three animagi in her bag. They were sitting in a small room with dazzling neon lighting, in front of a perspex window. They were waiting for Andrew Billings to be let into the cubicle on the other side of the window.

"As Andrew most likely does not know who I am I won't give him my real name", Suzanne whispered, "but it will have to sound similar to my name as the wardens will listen in to our conversation. So don't be surprised if my name will sound funny."

"That's a good idea", whispered Teddy. He was trying to stay as motionless as possible so that the cameras would not pick up the fact that they were alive. "Luckily Andrew seems to have agreed to see you."

"Yes", replied Suzanne, "but wait ... I think here he comes."

A door opened on the wall at the back of the cubicle and a warden brought in Andrew Billings. Andrew was shuffling his feet, obviously they were chained together which impeded his movement. He also had handcuffs on his hands but wore no straight-jacket.

Andrew sat down opposite Suzanne and she looked at him carefully. She knew he was about 25, and that he had been incarcerated in this hospital for nearly nine years since he murdered his mother. His face was angular, he was clean shaven – a hospital policy – and his hair was very short although a brownish blond colour could be made out that stood in sharp contrast to his relatively pasty skin. He was slim and quite tall, but the feature that stood out most was his eyes. Suzanne looked straight at him and immediately felt uneasy. His eyes were a very dark blue, an eye colour Suzanne had never seen before, like a deep pool of ice-cold water. Andrew stared back at Suzanne.

Suzanne cleared her throat. "Hello Mr Billings, I am Susi Snostill." Although Teddy, Sebastian and Ugah had been warned they could not repress a slight laughter, but luckily nobody heard them.

"Call me Andrew, please Mrs Snostill."

"And you can call me Susi."

Suzanne smiled, trying to set Andrew at ease, but was unsure how exactly to proceed. These dark blue eyes staring intently at her were made her fell very uneasy.

"I am not sure how much the director or the wardens have told you, Andrew, but I am studying at the local university for a Masters in psychology. My topic is on rehabilitation processes in hospitals like this one, and I am interviewing a few patients to get their side of the story."

Andrew looked at her intensely. *She is not bad looking*, he thought. *First time I've seen a woman in years! I guess that's part of the reason I agreed to be interviewed ... just for a change really! But she looks really old! I was hoping for someone younger.* With great regret he thought that he had never been intimate with a woman, so he had no idea what it would feel like to be with a woman like Suzanne.

"Rehabilitation, eh?", Andrew replied after a while. "There ain't no rehabilitation here, Susi, as you can see. The only rehabilitation these people know", and he looked up at the cameras, "is solitary confinement in a rubber-walled cell and hardly any interaction with people. I will never be rehabilitated like this!", and he smiled viciously at the wardens who watched every one of his movements.

"I understand", said Suzanne trying to placate Andrew. "But obviously rehabilitation is a long-term process for … emmm… complex patients like yourself."

"Yeah, you can say that I'm complex, although my story is really quite straightforward, as you probably know. I slaughtered my mum when I was 16 and have been in here ever since."

"Yes, I am aware of your case history, Andrew. Do you want to tell me a bit more about yourself? Why did you kill your mother?"

I hope I'm not going too fast here, Suzanne thought. *The last thing I want is to antagonise him!*

But Andrew seemed happy to take the bait. "I killed her because she hated me, and she always wanted me dead! It's all part of a great conspiracy, you know! They all want me dead … including this lot here!", and his dark blue eyes again scanned the room.

"But you must remember times when you did not feel like this, when you were a happy child?"

This question seemed to throw Andrew a little. He brought his hands up to his face and scratched his chin. "Yeah, maybe. But that would go back a long time. I remember that I was always frightened, even as a kid." He again stared Suzanne deep in the eyes, unsure how much he should tell her. "When I was small I had these terrible nightmares … don't know where they came from … of killing people, and enjoying it! That goes back as far as I can remember. Maybe I was just born evil?", and he stared at her with an almost pleading look.

"My psychology studies say that nobody is born inherently evil, but that we are socialised into becoming evil by our surroundings", Suzanne replied. "Can you remember an incident that changed you when you were a child?"

Suzanne briefly glanced at the cameras realising that their discussion had already drifted far off the topic of rehabilitation. *I hope the director does not listen in too carefully! He might realise that I am not really interested in rehabilitation.*

"Well, I remember my dad leaving when I was about 14. That was a real blow, although I also hated his guts. But a dad is a dad, and he just abandoned us!"

"But you had already done some ... nasty things by the time your dad left, hadn't you?"

Andrew looked at Suzanne again. *That woman has certainly read my file!*, he thought. "That is true. It started at primary school when other kids ganged up on me and I beat them up really bad. Parents complained of course and I was made to change school quite often."

OK, thought Suzanne. *So far he seems quite open and willing to talk. Let's try and move the discussion towards why I am really here.* "Was there any occasion where your parents helped you to cope with your anger and bad dreams?"

Andrew scratched his chin again, he was obviously getting slightly nervous. He scrutinised Suzanne's face again, trying to gauge where this discussion was leading to. "I was given a toy frog by my parents when I was about 7. That helped me a lot to deal with my bad dreams and the bad thoughts I was already having."

Here we go!, thought Suzanne. *Now I really need to be careful with my questions not to put him off from talking.* "A toy frog?", she asked pretending ignorance. "Interesting. Tell me more about it."

"Well, it was just an ordinary toy frog, you know like the ones you can buy in any shop. It was quite large and had a nice blue back and a red velvety front, and he had large globular eyes."

Sebastian, peeking out from Suzanne's bag, cringed at this description of Garglethroat. *Here he is describing in all innocence the most vicious creature our animagi society has ever seen!*

"In fact", continued Andrew, "it was similar to the toy animals you seem to have in your bag. Can I see?"

Here comes the moment of truth, thought Suzanne. *I hope he does not recognise Sebastian, Teddy and Ugah being from our village. But maybe my strategy of bringing animagi along might help us.*

She took out the three animagi and laid them out on the table before her. Sebastian and his companions played 'dead' and tried to be as limp and toy-like as possible.

Just like Toy Story!, thought Sebastian, *when Woody the cowboy goes all limp when the adults enter the room!*, and he smiled inwardly.

"Hey, look at these!", Andrew exclaimed, and his face seemed to change from that of a hardened psychopath to one of a normal and caring human being. "And look at the gollywog! I haven't seen one of these for a while! I didn't think they still made them, being politically incorrect and all that stuff", and his hands lurched forward seemingly forgetting that the perspex window was between them. Disappointed that he could not touch the animagi Andrew placed his hands back on the table. "And the two teddy-bears look rather sweet, although one looks rather battered!", he said pointing at Teddy.

"Apart from this one", said Suzanne holding up Sebastian, "they are quite old and well loved. She held up Teddy's foot that still had a bit of white stuffing hanging out. I bring them with me as it might help the patients connect better with their past", she lied, looking Andrew in the eyes.

But he did not notice her stare. He had been completely transformed since seeing the animagi, into a child-like person who could find enthusiasm even in the smallest things. But his face hardened again quickly as he looked away from Sebastian, Teddy and Ugah. "Well, I am sure these toy animals mean a lot to their owners, just like my frog means a lot to me!"

"You said 'means', Andrew ...", Suzanne wondered. "Does this imply that you are still fond of your toy frog, although you must have been separated from him for all the time you have been here?"

For a moment Andrew was completely silent. He glanced from the animagi to Suzanne and seemed to think hard. But as Suzanne had not changed her inquisitive look or made any sign that this was a hugely important part of their conversation he felt reasonably confident that he could answer. *Strange!*, he thought, *this is the first time in my life that I am talking about my special relationship with Garglethroat! And this to a complete stranger! But it actually feels good to talk about it ...*

"Yes", he said while clearing his throat. Thinking about Garglethroat had made him rather melancholic. "I am still very close to him, although I haven't seen him, as you say, for about nine years." He stopped and thought for a while. "Actually ... you could do me a great favour and ask the director whether you could bring me my frog?"

Oh dear!, Suzanne and the three animagi thought simultaneously. *That was not in the plan!,* Suzanne admitted angrily. She thought for a short while about the best possible answer. "I fear that we are not allowed to bring anything to the patients, hospital rules, but I'll talk to the director and see what we can do."

I just hope the director is not listening to this right now!, she thought. *What do we do if he allowed Garglethroat to be brought to Andrew?*

"Tell me more about your relationship with your frog, Andrew", Suzanne continued the conversation, trying to deflect Andrew from the problematic topic of possibly bringing Garglethroat to him.

"To tell you the truth, Susi, Garglethroat ... that's what I called him because ... because I imagined him to have a gargly voice ... Garglethroat was the best thing that ever happened to me. He really helped me through the rough patches when I was a kid, and made life bearable. I don't know whether I would be here alive had it not been for him!"

...but I can't obviously tell you that he's alive with a soul!, Andrew thought. *Who would believe that anyway! And that I can communicate mentally with him even while in this hospital. If you knew, lady, how closely connected Garglethroat and I are, you would be really surprised!*

Suzanne felt almost sorry for Andrew. She had gone to visit him with a predetermined view of a vicious psychopath, inhumane and unable to show feelings. Since they had started talking about animagi, however, a new person had emerged that showed feeling and compassion, possibly in due course even remorse for what he had done.

Maybe we are achieving more with this brief discussion than nine years of so-called rehabilitation in this institution!, Suzanne thought. *Maybe we can get into Andrew's mind after all,* she thought hopefully.

"But what happened when you killed your mother?", Suzanne asked bluntly. "Did Garglethroat not help you prevent that terrible tragedy?"

"Garglethroat helped me alright, Susi", said Andrew looking down at the table, "but not in the way you think …", at which point he suddenly looked up and stared at her with his dark blue eyes. His eyes looked crueller than ever.

"Actually, I don't want to talk to you anymore …", Andrew said suddenly and stood up. "Warden! Take me back to my cell, please. We're finished here!"

"Wait! … I'm sorry Andrew … I didn't mean to make you feel uncomfortable about that dreadful day", and she cursed herself for having interrupted what was, until then, a relatively free-flowing interview that had yielded a lot of information. "Please sit down again …"

But Andrew had already got up and was banging at the door behind him, not looking back. As the warden let him out Suzanne shouted: "Many thanks for the interview, Andrew, that was very informative. If you don't mind I'll be back soon."

Just before the door closed, Andrew turned his head around and glanced back at her. Although it was a look full of hatred and disdain, Suzanne thought that she caught a glimpse of acknowledgement to what she had just said. Maybe there was still a chance to continue the interview sometime …

Suzanne was let out of the room and confirmed with the wardens that she was finished for the day, but that she would be back the next day.

Walking towards her car she looked back and cursed loudly: "Damn, damn, damn … We were getting there and then I messed up with my stupid blunt question about Garglethroat's influence on his mum's death! I should have been much more cautious in how to lead the discussion to that crucial point in his life. I could kick myself! I seem to have forgotten even the most basic psychological training I have received!"

"But he gave us an interesting piece of information in answer to your question nonetheless", said Teddy. "He said that Garglethroat helped him during the murder of his mother 'but not in the way we think'. That means that he pretty much admitted that Garglethroat played a part in inciting Andrew to kill his mum. If he was willing to talk to you again, this might be one way to get into his conscience and to make him realise that Garglethroat is possibly even more evil than himself. Could we use this to persuade him to sever the link to Garglethroat?"

Suzanne still fumed at the botched end of the interview, but she had to admit that Teddy was right. After all, they had received a lot of very useful information.

She started the car and sped off towards the main road.

78

Andrew Billings was back in his cell, sitting in the yoga lotus position on the rubber floor. The wardens had not put on his straight-jacket as he had been calmer the last few days. His hands rested on his knees, his eyes were closed.

It had taken him a few minutes to calm down after the interview with Susi Snostill. *How could she dare pry into my motivations for killing my mum?* But deep inside, after a few minutes of reflection, Andrew had to admit that he had almost enjoyed the interview. *This was the first time somebody had shown a real interest in me and my thoughts!*, Andrew realised with surprise. *None of the sessions I have had with that fat turd of a director, or with any of the other doctors here, has come even close to what I felt while talking to Susi! Although she is old ... maybe she was pretty once when she was younger?... I have to admit that I somehow like her.* Indeed, Andrew looked forward to their next interview.

While he attempted to empty his mind of any thought ... just relaxing and breathing regularly ... a voice tried to penetrate his mind. At first Andrew did not want to react, but then he suddenly snapped out of his semi-trance and realised that it was Garglethroat.

"Hello, my frog!", he thought embarrassed, realising that Garglethroat had probably tried to contact him for a while.

"Hello, my host!", said Garglethroat in the teasing tone they had adopted over the years. "How are you doing?"

"I am much better now that you are back", replied Andrew. "I feel much calmer."

"That is good, Andrew", said Garglethroat. "We have been busy here in the village. Our new weapon is working wonders and we have control over almost the whole village. There are only a few last pockets of resistance we are trying to weed out in the next few days."

"Excellent!", replied Andrew. "You are the true king of the village now. What a revenge on all those who have treated you so badly over the years!"

"Indeed!", agreed Garglethroat. "And I am currently sitting on a pile of gold, snatched from all those rich animagi! You should see it!"

"Hopefully I will soon when you get me out of here", replied Andrew. "What are your plans about the humans in the village?"

"We have left them alone for the moment as we can't risk a massive police and army presence", Garglethroat said. "Imagine what would happen if humans knew about the Book of Death. It would be the ultimate weapon of war. They would try everything to lay their hands on it! But I will need to deal with the humans from the village with animagi connections soon, as they could be a danger to us."

"I understand." Andrew was quiet for a while, letting his mind drift again towards his recent visitor. "I had a visitor today, a student from the university. She is doing a research project."

Garglethroat stayed quiet. *A visitor?* he thought to himself without letting Andrew hear. *What is that suddenly about?*

"She talked about a lot of things with me", continued Andrew, "my childhood, my parents, and the problems I've had.

Initially I didn't enjoy talking to her, but in the end it was interesting and a nice change for me."

"What's her name and where is she from?", asked Garglethroat with a slightly worried tone.

"She is called Susi Snostill. I don't know where she lives."

Garglethroat was surprised at the way Andrew talked about her. This Susi was indeed the first and only visitor Andrew had received since he had been incarcerated in the hospital. "Tell me more about her."

But Andrew stayed quiet.

"Andrew, tell me more about her!", repeated Garglethroat.

After a long time, Andrew replied: "Sorry, Garglethroat, I just don't feel like talking to you at the moment", and he switched off his mind.

Andrew? ... Andrew? ... Garglethroat repeatedly tried to contact Andrew, but there was no reply. Ever since they started communicating by thought, this was the first time ever that Andrew had suddenly cut Garglethroat off. *I better go and get him out of this hospital as quickly as possible!*, he thought to himself.

The director and the two wardens were watching Andrew through the cameras in his cell.

"Look how placid he is, sitting in his yoga position with a smile on his face!", said the director. "Although he ended the interview abruptly, I have the feeling that it did not do him any harm. On the contrary, it seems to have quietened him down. Continue observing him", and he looked at the two wardens, "and keep me informed of his progress, but for the moment I will allow Mrs St Austell to see him again."

79

After their two-hour drive back home, Suzanne, Sebastian, Teddy and Ugah went straight to the Annex in Suzanne's house and reported about their meeting with Andrew Billings. Hexybilla and the group listened attentively and were particularly interested in Andrew's appearance and the information he provided about his childhood.

"Thank you so much for going to see Andrew, Suzanne", said Hexybilla. "We are very grateful to you for embarking on this difficult task. Will they allow you to go back?"

"I was maybe a bit too forceful at the end of the interview when I tried to get more information about Garglethroat's influence on Andrew's decision to kill his mum. As a result, Andrew left the interview in a huff. I hope he will be willing to see me again. As far as the hospital director is concerned, I don't think he will be the problem for the moment. It's strange! Towards the end of the interview I almost felt sorry for Andrew. I don't think he has had many opportunities in his life to talk about any of these issues."

"It shows what a poor job the hospital seems to be doing!", said Mrs Moluk.

"Yes, that also surprises me", replied Suzanne, "especially as the *South Devon* is seen as one of the best psychiatric hospitals in the country. I think they just see him as incurable and use more forceful tactics like restraint and injections rather than one-to-one discussion."

They sat around the room with food on their laps. Suzanne had briefly stopped at the local fish-and-chips takeaway, and the group had indeed been very hungry as they had not dared go back underground to grab food.

"While you were away we had a lengthy discussion about the way forward at our end", said McHaggis munching away at a greasy bit of battered haddock. "Three of us, including myself, Mr Kasperski and Hagelik will venture back into the passageways to find out what Garglethroat is planning. We will also try and find other animagi survivors who might be hiding."

"Is that wise?", asked Teddy. "If you encounter Garglethroat you have no chance against the Book of Death. Believe me, we have seen it in action and it has quite a large radius."

"Yes, we know, Teddy", replied McHaggis, "but we can't just sit here and let you four do all the work. We were already getting very bored and restless just sitting around this room today!"

All members of the group nodded. Teddy could see that this quest would at least give them something to focus on while Suzanne talked to Andrew Billings. "Yes, I understand what you mean. But please be really careful as you could otherwise lead Garglethroat back to here."

McHaggis, Mr Kasperski and Hagelik nodded. They were well aware of the danger.

80

Suzanne had called in sick at her job so that she could spend another day at the South Devon Maximum-Security Psychiatric Hospital. They arrived at about 10am, Sebastian, Teddy and Ugah in the same bag with their heads just sticking out, went through the same security procedures, and were led to the visitor's room.

They had already been waiting for over 15 minutes.

They let us in, so obviously the director has agreed that I can carry on with the interview with Andrew, and they let us into the visitor's room which implies that Andrew might be willing to continue talking to me, Suzanne thought, biting her fingernails. She was very nervous.

After another five minutes or so the door to the back of the cubicle finally opened and the warden led Andrew Billings to his seat behind the perspex glass. At first Andrew did not seem to want to look at Suzanne and just sat there, staring at the table in front of him. Then he looked up with his deep blue eyes.

"I wasn't sure if I wanted to see you again, Susi", Andrew said. "Some of the questions you asked were a bit too personal I thought!", and he stared hard at Suzanne who had to avert her gaze after a few seconds.

"Yes … I'm sorry Andrew if some of the questions I asked were too forward. But I am just trying to get to know you better and to understand what lies behind your story. So please accept my apologies if I offended you yesterday."

Andrew continued to stare straight into Suzanne's eyes. After a few seconds he leaned back and put his handcuffed arms behind his head.

Psychology tells us that this is a position of confidence Andrew is assuming, Suzanne thought remembering some of the material taught in Psychology 101. *That's a good sign! I think he is settling in to continue the interview.*

"Apology accepted, Susi! To be fair, I actually enjoyed our talk yesterday", and he looked intensely at Suzanne.

Wow!, thought Suzanne. *What an admission! That's great!* "Well I am very pleased to hear that, Andrew. I also enjoyed talking to you."

For a moment none of them spoke, they just looked at each other slightly embarrassed at the fleeting moment of intimacy.

"Where would you like to pick up the discussion, then?", asked Suzanne, very aware of the fact that she did not want to seem to be too pushy again.

"I thought about your last question the whole night", admitted Andrew. "You know ... when you asked me about what Garglethroat did when I killed my mother."

Suzanne said nothing and just kept looking him straight in the eyes. *Don't let him get distracted now!*, she thought. *Keep him focused on that key question.* Sebastian, Teddy and Ugah similarly looked expectantly at Andrew.

"Well ...", continued Andrew, bringing his arms forward again and placing them on the desk in front of him. "It was actually Garglethroat who told me to kill her!"

Suzanne and the three animagi were baffled by this answer. *And here we thought that human hosts imprint their personality onto their animagi!*, thought Suzanne. *Maybe it is actually the other way around?* Again, she waited for Andrew to continue without being prompted.

"Garglethroat and I had started communicating long before that. It started shortly after he was given to me by my parents when I was about seven."

That is rather unusual!, thought Suzanne again. Normally our animagi council is quite good at spotting which toy animals are about to be awoken and at then deciding, usually after a while, which human children were worthy of being initiated. In the end it is only a small percentage of children who know that their toy animals have become animagi with speech and souls. In Andrew's case it seems that nobody realised what was happening and that both Andrew and Garglethroat had to work out themselves what was going on. No wonder, maybe, that both behaved differently to what we would normally expect!

"Since then we became inseparable", Andrew continued. "We knew exactly what each other thought, and as I mentioned yesterday, Garglethroat helped me through some very rough times when I was young."

"But maybe Garglethroat was also sometimes the reason why you became quite rough?", asked Suzanne.

Andrew looked back at her and seemed to suddenly realise something. "Yes … maybe …In fact, come to think of it, in most instances where I beat up a kid it was not just me who took the decision … It was as if we were mentally joined together. Often Garglethroat told me there and then what do … how to act …"

I am not saying yet that Andrew may be innocent and that it was all Garglethroat's fault, thought Suzanne, *but it seems that in many cases it was Garglethroat, rather than Andrew, who was behind the attacks Andrew was committing.* "What about the day of your mother's death?"

Andrew was quiet for a few seconds.

Here we are again, Suzanne thought. *Does he trust me enough now to answer that crucial question?*

Andrew stared at Suzanne. Suddenly he moved his shackled right hand forward and pressed it against the perspex glass. Tears welled up in his deep blue eyes. Suzanne did not know what to do, but instinctively she raised her right hand and placed it on the glass opposite Andrew's hand. Only the glass separated them from touching each other.

What am I doing?, Suzanne wondered. *Where is this leading to? Is it just pity I feel or am I beginning to be attracted to Andrew in some strange way? It can't be. He is a psychopathic murderer and I am old enough to be his mum!* She nonetheless kept her hand close to his, looking straight at him. Tears were now gushing from his eyes, he was sobbing loudly.

"They ... they ... were all against me", Andrew sobbed. "But I didn't want to kill her! I loved her! She was my mum! I tried to fight Garglethroat but I couldn't. He told me to kill her ... to cut off her head. I was powerless! It was as if my arms and hands no longer obeyed me! In the end Garglethroat killed her by using my body! When she was dead I was completely numb, nothing mattered any more. First Garglethroat had driven away my dad, then he killed my mum! Yes ... it was him all along!", and Andrew suddenly got up and banged his hand hard against the perspex glass. "Bloody frog! He deserves to die for that ... I want to kill him ...!", and he slumped back into his chair, holding his hands in front of his face.

"Are you alright in there?", a loudspeaker voice suddenly shouted.

Suzanne glanced back at the cameras. "Yes, we are OK, don't worry. ...All part of the interview process", she lied hoping they would let her continue.

What an admission by Andrew!, Suzanne thought. *Maybe we've got him already where we want him! Maybe deep inside he hates Garglethroat for what he has done to him and his family.*

Andrew looked back at her, whimpering like a child. "And you know ... something else ... I can communicate mentally with Garglethroat. I can hear his thoughts and he can hear mine!"

Suzanne and the three animagi were shocked at that revelation.

"Have you told Garglethroat about me?", she asked with a panicked voice.

"Yes, I have!"

"Did ... did you give him my name?"

"Yes I did: Susi Snostill", he replied sniffling.

Hopefully Garglethroat can't put two-and-two together and realise that I am from the village and even on the animagi council!, thought Suzanne hopefully. *If he does he will try and get us immediately.* "What else did you tell him?"

"Nothing ... really ...", Andrew said apologetically, realising that he may have put Suzanne in danger. "I actually blocked my thoughts just after I mentioned you to him. I have not communicated with him since."

Although Suzanne was terribly shaken by the news of Garglethroat knowing about her, or at least about a student with a name similar to hers, she tried to appease Andrew: "That's alright, Andrew. Don't worry. I don't know Garglethroat and he does not know me. I don't think this is of great importance." But she thought Andrew might see in her face that she was lying.

Tears still welled up in Andrew's eyes. "Susi, I somehow like you ... You have talked to me about things nobody has talked to me about before ... I have enjoyed talking to you. I promise that I will not contact Garglethroat again. I have a lot of thinking to do now ... There are a lot of things going through my mind and I feel a little tired now. Could we continue the discussion tomorrow? I would like to see you again soon ..."

"I fully understand, Andrew. Yes ... of course. Let's carry on with our discussion tomorrow."

Andrew looked gratefully at Suzanne. He suddenly looked very small, like a vulnerable child wanting to be cuddled. Suzanne felt immensely sorry for him.

Andrew got up slowly and shuffled to the door. The warden opened the door and let Andrew out. This time he looked back at Suzanne for a long time.

Suzanne had not yet fathomed the strength to get up. The last few minutes had been some of the most intense in her life as a psychology student. She could not believe how quickly Andrew had opened up to her and admitted, also to himself probably for the first time, that Garglethroat had played a key part in his childhood aggression. She glanced at Sebastian, Teddy and Ugah who looked equally stunned.

Suddenly the door to the visitor's area burst open and the director came stomping in, his face red with anger. "Mrs St Austell! What was that all about? I thought you were here to interview patients like Andrew about the rehabilitation programme! Instead you seem to delve into his deepest psychological secrets, which has clearly severely upset him. May I ask where all this is leading to ...?"

You're the last thing I need right now!, thought Suzanne, but she knew she had to keep the director on her side if she wanted a chance to continue seeing Andrew Billings.

"Apologies, director. The interview took a slightly different turn to what I intended." Suzanne paused for a moment, gathering her thoughts. "But as I am sure you are aware, these types of semi-structured interviews can take unpredictable trajectories. You may know the study by McMaster and Tullis, 2010, that discussed ..."

"Spare me that academic mumbo-jumbo!", the director shouted. "I am beginning to doubt whether your dissertation is really about rehabilitation. It is about more than that, isn't it?"

"No, sir, I promise it is not. But to understand the rehabilitation process I first need to understand what drove the patients to do what they did, don't you agree?"

That line of reasoning seemed to be more acceptable to the director, as he markedly relaxed. "OK, Mrs St Austell. I will give you the benefit of the doubt for the moment. I'll give you one more day with this patient, but if your interview continues to go down these strange avenues I will rescind your permit for coming here. Do you understand?"

"Perfectly, sir. I fully understand what you are saying and that the patients' well-being is your foremost concern", Suzanne lied, thinking how pitifully bad the rehabilitation programme in this hospital actually seemed to be. *You certainly have not helped Andrew one iota so far!*, she fumed inwardly.

"Very well then!", the director replied and stormed out of the room. "One more interview, Mrs St Austell ... just one more interview!"

81

Godfrey Wilkinson stopped his car at the last drop-off point. They had left Mr Kasperski at his own house and Hagelik at Josh's house. The aim was for them to get into the passageways and see whether they could find any surviving animagi hiding somewhere and herd them towards Suzanne's house. They should also try and find out whether they could get information on Garglethroat's whereabouts. They all knew how dangerous their mission was, but were determined to do whatever they could to thwart Garglethroat's plans to destroy their village's animagi society.

"Be very careful McHaggis", said Godfrey. "On the surface all seems quiet, no sign of Garglethroat having yet interfered with any humans, but we can't be certain. Either report back to Suzanne's house or give me a ring from your house if possible and I'll pick you up again. I'd better not linger, otherwise Garglethroat might find out what we are up to."

McHaggis quickly left the car. Godfrey left immediately, not looking back. McHaggis walked carefully through the front garden. Like most animagi he had not spent much time on his own in the outside world, but he had no time to marvel at his host's beautiful garden with colourful magnolia trees, effervescent peonies, and lush hebe shrubs. He followed the side of the house until he found the entrance to one of the passageways below.

He climbed down the steps to the passageway which was faintly lit by lamps in the ceiling. It was all quiet, only the sound of dripping water could be heard in the distance. McHaggis knew the passageways around his house well, so if he were to see Garglethroat before Garglethroat could see him, he knew pretty well where the hiding places were.

He carefully walked down the passageway, keeping close to the damp walls. After a few minutes he saw the first body lying on the floor. It was a multi-coloured alien-shaped animago who lay contorted and petrified around a large bag. McHaggis looked up to see whether he could make out anyone further down the passageway but the light was so dim that he could only see about ten metres.

He continued down the passageway towards the centre of the village. He was familiar with the underground labyrinth here, as he had often walked that route from his house to friends or animagi meeting places. At another intersection a large pile of petrified animagi were lying on the floor, some of whom he recognised. He carried on carefully, always looking back as well as in front of him. The passageways were all eerily quiet.

It does not look like I'll find any animagi who have not been petrified down here!, he thought dismayed. *Garglethroat seems to have done a thorough job. We might indeed be the last animagi he has not been able to get to. But of course there could be quite a few who are hiding in their hosts' houses. Maybe I should just randomly go up and have a look?*

Just as he thought about taking one of the passageways leading to one of the houses above him, he heard a noise. It seemed to come from a passageway to the left in front of him. Hugging the wall he moved forward very carefully. No further sound could be heard.

Maybe it was just a mouse or a rat?, he wondered, and started moving towards the next passageway leading up to the house. He turned a corner ... and suddenly stood face-to-face with Ori Fisse.

"Hello!", Ori Fisse said. "Who have we got here? You're a courageous animago venturing out on your own into the passageways. How many more of you are there?", and he peered over McHaggis' shoulder to see whether anyone was following him.

McHaggis was ready to flee and run when he felt a hand on his shoulder. Skeleto blocked his way, dagger in hand.

Damn! Damn! Damn!, cursed McHaggis. *I'm done for!*

"Look what we've found boss!", said Ori Fisse to Garglethroat who was approaching. "There are still some animagi wandering about by the look of it! And we thought that we'd nearly got them all!"

Garglethroat approached with a superior look on his face. He closely scrutinised McHaggis who tried to move his head back to avoid Garglethroat's foul breath.

"I think this one might be a member of the animagi council!", Garglethroat said with a nasty smile. "We'd better keep him alive and see what we can get out of him about his still missing companions!"

Ori Fisse roughly pushed McHaggis forward, his arms pinned at his back. McHaggis was beginning to think that it might have been better to be petrified immediately ...

82

Suzanne was driving back from the hospital. Sebastian, Teddy and Ugah sat next to her on the passenger seat, the seatbelt tied around all three of them. It was getting dark outside and a misty rain, typical for Devon, had transformed the road into a glistening and slippery ribbon winding its way through the sessile oak woods. Suzanne had to concentrate on the driving, but she could not stop thinking about Andrew.

"I am amazed at how much Andrew has opened up, don't you think?"

"Yes, Suzanne", replied Teddy. "You have done a great job so far, gaining Andrew's confidence and letting him talk freely about his relationship with Garglethroat."

"We have achieved much more than I thought we would after just two sessions", Suzanne said glancing with intense concentration at the windy road. "I think we are not far from Andrew being willing to disavow Garglethroat, but it's hard to tell as his mood still seems a bit unsteady."

"We'll have to go back tomorrow", Teddy said, "hopefully the director will not be too awkward."

"Mmmh", Suzanne mumbled.

They were quiet for the rest of the journey. When they reached the village it was pitch black. The street lights were casting a faint yellowish light onto the road. It was raining hard now. Suzanne drove up to her house and looked at the annex.

"Good, you can't see from here whether anyone is in there", she said. "Either they are keeping the lights out as we discussed, or they have made sure that they pulled the double curtains so that no light shines out."

She grabbed hold of the three animagi and locked her car. She half ran up the steps to her house as they were getting drenched by the heavy rain. After a bit of fumbling in her bag for the key she stepped inside. Her husband was sitting on the sofa watching television.

"Hi love", she said, quickly putting Sebastian, Teddy and Ugah down on a chair. She did not want her uninitiated husband to see her carrying three toy animals. As her husband had not moved she quickly ushered the three animagi to the door where they made their way to the annex.

"Anything happened today? How was work?", Suzanne asked her husband.

"Work was alright. Nothing to report, really. I thought I saw a strange light just outside our house earlier, but I think it might have just been lightning. It is really coming down hard now."

A strange light? Suzanne got very worried.

"I'll just quickly get changed ... be right back", she said while rushing out of the room towards the annex.

Please ... please ...no! Let them be safe! she thought as she approached the annex door.

Sebastian, Teddy and Ugah already stood in front of the door. "They're not opening!", Ugah said. "We have told them it's us and that it's safe to open."

Suzanne took out the key for the door, her hands trembling. "I think something might have happened, you'd better stand back while I have a look ..."

She carefully opened the door which creaked slightly. The room was dark, the curtains drawn. Not a sound could be heard.

"Hexybilla ... Mrs Moluk ... Erik?", Suzanne whispered. Are you there?"

There was no reply. Suzanne switched on the light ... and gave out a shriek. "Oh dear!", she yelled, "oh dear ... no ... no!"

Spread in front of the table were Hexybilla, Mrs Moluk and Mr Kasperski ... petrified. On the sofa Erik and Sylvester were lying, also petrified. Sylvester had collapsed on top of Erik, his left arm dangling down onto the floor. McHaggis looked worst. Not only did he seem to be petrified, but he also looked badly injured, yellow stuffing oozing out from both his arm and leg.

Sebastian, Teddy and Ugah had come in, a look of horror in their faces. "How could this happen?", asked Sebastian. "How did Garglethroat find out where we were hiding?", he wondered, tears running down his face.

Suzanne had gone to Hexybilla and lifted up the witch. She lay limp and unresponsive in Suzanne's arms.

"Guys, this is not good at all!", said Teddy. "I think we'd better leave immediately as Garglethroat might still be around. If he also catches us it's the end of our village!"

They all suddenly realised that they were in grave danger. Suzanne gently lowered Hexybilla back onto the floor and they quickly left the room, switching off the light on their way out.

"But where can we go?", asked Sebastian.

"We can't stay in the village. It's just too dangerous now", replied Teddy. "Quick let's go! We can think about where to go once we're back on the road."

They all agreed and ran out of the house, avoiding the living room where Suzanne's husband continued watching TV, oblivious to the tragedy unfolding in his own house.

It was still raining hard and the garden path was wet and slippery. As they reached the steps leading to Suzanne's car a dark shape suddenly blocked their path.

"Watch out!", cried Ugah, but it was too late. The black shape had seen them and swiftly walked towards them.

This is it!, thought Sebastian. *This is the end. We'll all be petrified now!*

The dark shape relentlessly moved towards them and stepped into a ray of light coming from the street. The creature was about Teddy's height, furry, and dripping wet.

"Hagelik!", shouted Teddy. "It's Hagelik!"

"I'm so glad to see you!", said Hagelik, his voice almost drowned out by the pelting rain. "We need to flee as fast as possible. I am sure Garglethroat is on his way back to here!"

They ran down the steps as quickly as the wet conditions allowed and darted towards Suzanne's car. In the distance they could make out three silhouettes running down the road towards them. One was chubby and dog-like, the other skeletal, and the third fat and bulgy with a toad-like gate. Garglethroat and his two henchmen!

The five of them spotted Garglethroat and his men simultaneously. "Quick Suzanne, we need to get away!", shouted Sebastian.

Suzanne fiddled with her keys. *Why did I lock the car?*, she fumed. In the dark it was hard to find the right key. Suddenly the key slipped from her fingers and fell into a puddle of rainwater at her feet.

"Quick! Quick!", said Hagelik, "I can see Garglethroat raising something in his hands. The Book of Death!"

Suzanne was on her knees, sifting through the brown murky puddle with her hands. "Help me guys! I've lost the keys!"

They all crouched down, feeling the cold water. After a few seconds Sebastian pulled out the keys and passed them to Suzanne.

Garglethroat was now only about 50 metres away. The Book of Death glistened wet above his head, he was mumbling the incantation.

Suzanne finally managed to open the car door and they all squeezed in as quickly as they could. The car started immediately as it was still warm from their earlier drive. Suzanne slammed the gearstick into reverse, jammed the accelerator and rushed back, hitting rubbish bins on the other side of the road. The bins crashed onto the road, emptying their smelly contents across the pavement like a gutted animal spilling its insides.

Garglethroat and his men were now only 20 metres away and the Book of Death started to glisten in a greenish light.

Suzanne slammed the gear into first and stood on the accelerator. The small car was slow at gaining speed, but after a few seconds she changed into second gear. A green ray was forming behind them. Hagelik peered out of the rear window, his head above the back seat. The green ray hit Hagelik face on and Hagelik collapsed onto the seat petrified.

"Heads down, heads down!", yelled Teddy. "Go Suzanne go!"

The whole car seemed to be enveloped in the green ray when suddenly the car went down by a few metres as it entered a dip in the road. The ray was no longer reaching them but was illuminating the sky just above them. Suzanne hit the brakes hard.

"What are you doing?", Sebastian, Teddy and Ugah shouted.

"We have reached the dip in the road behind our house. The ray can't reach us here for the moment!", Suzanne tried to explain her actions.

"But they'll catch up with us in a second!", shouted Ugah.

Suzanne watched the ray which fanned out above them. As Garglethroat could not see them in the dip he waved the Book of Death from side to side, so that the ray was not always above them. Suzanne waited a few seconds until the ray had passed them on its way to the right and then she stepped hard on the accelerator. The car sped forward, out of the dip ... second gear ... third gear ... the ray came back towards them, but then the road turned off to the left, leading towards the main road out of the village. The ray stayed on the right, unable to follow them. When they reached the intersection to the main road, the ray could no longer be seen.

"Phew! Well done Suzanne!", said Teddy. "That was quick thinking!"

They looked back at the village which was disappearing fast from view in the dark and rain.

"We need to get away as far as possible from Garglethroat", said Suzanne, still breathless from her daring driving. "But at the same time we need to make sure that we can get back to Billings tomorrow morning. He is our last chance now that pretty much the whole animagi community in our village has been wiped out!" She thought again about their companions lying petrified in the annex. "So I suggest that we try and find a place to stay near the South Devon Maximum-Security Psychiatric Hospital, what do you think?"

"Yes, that makes sense", replied Teddy. "The only advantage we have is that Garglethroat has no means of transport out of the village. He obviously can't drive a car himself and he will find it hard to force a human to drive him. But I bet that he will want to get to the hospital as quickly as possible now and bring Andrew back under his control. Andrew is now really the only weak point for Garglethroat, and he knows that."

The others knew Teddy was right. Getting back to Andrew Billings as quickly as possible was their last and only chance.

83

"Did ya sleep well, love?", Suzanne was sitting at breakfast in a Bed-and-Breakfast, just a kilometre from the entrance to the psychiatric hospital. The owner was pouring her another cup of strong black tea. Sebastian, Teddy and Ugah were in her bag on the neighbouring chair.

"Yes, thank you", lied Suzanne. In reality she had barely closed her eyes all night. Images of the dreadful scene in her annex kept coming back. In the middle of the night Sebastian had also jumped up from a nightmare shouting "The green ray! The green ray!" The animagi had clearly also not slept well and all looked rather tired. Petrified Hagelik was still lying in Suzanne's car.

It was still early, but Suzanne was keen to be at the hospital as soon as visiting times allowed, i.e. nine in the morning. She parked her car outside the main entrance to the hospital. But this time she had a good look around the garden before going up the steps. Suddenly the lush vegetation of New Zealand trees, ferns and bushes did not look quite so alluring, but rather were potential hiding places for Garglethroat and his henchmen.

"I hope Garglethroat has not been able to organise a ride to here yet!", she whispered to the three animagi as she walked up the steps. After going through the security routine she was led straight to the visitors' room. The director was nowhere to be seen. There was no sign of Garglethroat.

This time she did not have to wait long for Andrew. He almost rushed through the door the warden was holding open, and immediately sat down smiling at Suzanne. He immediately held up a hand towards the glass and Suzanne did the same, their hands only separated by the thick perspex glass. They said nothing for a while and just looked each other in the eyes.

One reason Suzanne had not slept well was that she had thought through her strategy of questions for the day. As Garglethroat could threaten to petrify them all and snatch Andrew at any moment, she had decided to be absolutely honest with Andrew. But she knew that this was also a great risk, now that she seemed to have gained his confidence.

"Andrew", she said, continuing to stare into his dark blue eyes. "I have to admit that I have not been entirely honest with you." She waited for his reaction. A slight frown appeared on Andrew's face, but he continued to hold his hand against the glass. "My real name is Suzanne St Austell and I am from the same village as you." Andrew looked puzzled, questioning wrinkles had appeared above his eyes. Still he held his hand towards the glass. "These three toy animals", and she pointed at her bag, "are like your frog Garglethroat. They are alive and conscious just like your frog."

Now Andrew removed his hand. He glanced at Sebastian, Teddy and Ugah. "You mean to say that they can speak like Garglethroat?", he asked with an incredulous look.

He does not know anything about animagi, their culture and their life in the village!, Suzanne thought. *What a secluded life he lived as a kid! But maybe that was all part of Garglethroat's ploy. To keep him totally isolated from everything!*

"Yes, they can speak", and she looked at the three animagi.

"Hello Andrew", Sebastian whispered.

"H…h.. hello", Andrew answered not knowing what to make of this.

"Please don't worry, Andrew. My intention was not to mislead you. But if I had told you who I am and where I am from, and that I have three animagi with me, you might not have wanted to talk to me at all. I had to take the risk. Please forgive me", and she pressed her hand hard against the glass.

Andrew sat there staring at her, saying nothing.

Don't lose him now!, Suzanne thought. *This is too important.*

"Have you recently had contact with Garglethroat about what is happening in the village?", Suzanne asked to keep the flow of the conversation going.

Andrew cleared his throat. He was clearly puzzled by Suzanne's revelations. "I mentioned yesterday that I would not contact Garglethroat again after our discussion", Andrew revealed, "but I know exactly what he has been up to in the village. He has told me about the weapon he brought back from Amig… Anag …"

"Animagana", Teddy whispered.

"Yes, Animagana", Andrew replied with a thankful look towards Teddy. "This Book of Death with a deadly ray. Garglethroat was very proud of it!"

"He is indeed!", said Sebastian. "And he has wiped out pretty much every animago in the village. We might be the last ones left!"

"He is taking revenge for what the village has done to him in the past", Andrew replied, trying to defend Garglethroat.

"But he was put in prison for murder of two councillors a few years ago", said Suzanne. "And then he killed prison wardens to escape. He also killed animagi so that he could escape to Animagana. I think we should take revenge on him, not the other way round!"

But Suzanne immediately regretted her severe attack on Garglethroat. *Gently,* she thought, *gently! He has to be persuaded himself that Garglethroat is evil.*

"Everybody in the village has always been against Garglethroat ... and against me", said Andrew with more conviction. "We have only tried to protect ourselves!"

Damn!, thought Suzanne. *He is still strongly defending what Garglethroat is doing. We won't have a chance of swaying his opinion of Garglethroat like that.* She was at a loss as to how to continue the argument.

Just as she opened her mouth again to speak, the door to the visitor room opened with a loud bang and the director came barging in, followed by two wardens. The director was, again, red in the face.

"I warned you, Mrs St Austell, that if your interview continued along the same lines as yesterday I would have you barred from coming back. The questions you are asking of this patient are very personal and have nothing to do with the rehabilitation process you claim to be analysing. In fact, you are working against everything we have tried to do with Andrew!"

Oh dear! That's the end!, thought Suzanne. *He will kick us out! And what a hypocrite he is! We have done more good for Andrew than the whole nine years' worth of so-called 'rehabilitation' you have tried Mr Director!*

"I ... I...", but Suzanne could not find the right words. In the end, she knew the director was right. She had cheated her way into the hospital to get to Andrew Billings.

Andrew looked at Suzanne with pleading eyes. He had placed his hand back on the glass. Tears welled up again in his eyes.

Suddenly noise could be heard from the corridor outside the visitors' room. Loud bangs and yells ... and a green light that rose in intensity shone through the door's glass window.

"Garglethroat!", Suzanne and her animagi shouted simultaneously.

The director did not understand what was happening. He and the two wardens turned around, but it was too late. Garglethroat had stormed into the room holding up the Book of Death. As he was running he was chanting

GURRAG SHAH FRAHN MARRG
EXARTIUS GORGALKON MOGARAT
RETICULUS MORTIS ETERNICA

The green ray shot out of the book and hit the director and the two wardens who were immediately petrified. The director still had his angry look on his face as he crashed hard onto the floor, his broken glasses flying towards Suzanne's feet.

Sebastian, Teddy and Ugah had jumped out of the bag and ran towards the far end of the room. But there was nowhere to hide. Garglethroat skilfully manoeuvred the ray towards them. He hit Teddy who was immediately petrified, and then Ugah while he was still running. Ugah crashed petrified against the legs of a nearby chair.

Sebastian stood with his hands against the wall, facing Garglethroat. *Now is the time for the time-freeze!*, thought Sebastian. *Come on! You did it when Garglethroat vanished through the portal in St Albans monastery, so you can do it again here. As the prophecy says: you are the chosen one! All depends on you now!* He closed his eyes and concentrated harder than at any other time in his life. He focused and felt something happen, but when he opened his eyes Garglethroat still stared at him with a nasty and knowing smile.

Garglethroat held up the book above his head, the green ray swerved towards Sebastian who was so scared that he could no longer move. The ray hit Sebastian who fell petrified to the floor ...

"Ha, ha, ha!", shouted Garglethroat. "Look how they are falling like dominoes! Nobody can stop us now!"

Suzanne had watched the scene in horror. She was leaning against the desk on her side of the cubicle, with Andrew behind her on the other side of the perspex window. Garglethroat could not direct the ray at her from his position, for risk of also hitting Andrew. He moved a bit to the side, still holding up the book.

Andrew had also gaped at the scene unfolding in front of his eyes in horror. *So this is how effective Garglethroat's weapon is! It is indeed deadly and unstoppable!* He was at a loss about what to do. Should he support Garglethroat or should he try to stop him? He was utterly confused. *I can't stop him from here anyway, I can't get through the perspex glass!*

Garglethroat had moved to the side of the room where he had a better angle for aiming the ray at Suzanne. Gradually be brought the ray into position, it edged ever closer towards Suzanne's face.

No! No! Garglethroat!, Andrew thought, and he tried to open his mouth but he could not utter a word. *Not her! She has helped me! She has helped me more than anyone ... She has helped me more than you have helped me!*

And it suddenly dawned on Andrew what he could do to stop Garglethroat. *You have been part of my life Garglethroat, I thought you helped me through the hardest times when I was a child. I believed and trusted you entirely. I loved you!* Tears welled up in his eyes again as he fought his deepest inner emotions.

But it was you who told me to harm these kids in the playground! And it was you who told me to kill ... to butcher my mum! You made me do it. It wasn't me who did it ... it was you who did it through me!

Andrew's look at Garglethroat changed from one of bewilderment to sheer hate, as Garglethroat's bad influence on Andrew's life had suddenly become clear to Andrew. Watching Garglethroat enjoying the carnage he was causing in the visitors' room further reinforced Andrew's sudden hatred towards his frog.

The ray was now just a metre away from Suzanne. She had closed her eyes, expecting the inevitable. There was no way she could stop Garglethroat now. The village and the animagi community were lost forever!

I hate you, Garglethroat! I hate you!, thought Andrew and stared intensely at Garglethroat.

Garglethroat's grin was gone. He still held the Book of Death above his head, but his hand had started shaking.

"Boss! Boss!", Ori Fisse shouted. "What's happening? We have to finish this now! There's only the lady to go! We've got them!"

But Garglethroat looked increasingly ill at ease. His grin had turned into a frown and then into a grimace of pain. His hand shook more and more, he could barely hold the Book of Death. The green ray was darting back and forth but kept missing Suzanne. For the first time, a look of immense fear appeared in Garglethroat's bulgy eyes. He peered around him, puzzled at what was happening. He could no longer hold the Book of Death above his head, his legs began to give in and thick beads of sweat started covering his entire body.

Suddenly his legs gave way and he went down on his knees. His arms sagged, the Book of Death dropped to the ground in front of him in such a way that it closed itself. The green ray immediately stopped. Garglethroat then seemed to deflate in front of everybody's eyes. He looked like a balloon whose air was gradually being let out, he seemed to diminish, his previously shiny eyes glazed over and lost focus ... He crumbled to the ground like a thin rag. He was dead ...

Ori Fisse could not believe his eyes. He darted towards the book of Death.

"No you don't!", shouted Suzanne, and although she was still stunned about what had just happened, she threw herself forward towards the book lying on the floor. Ori Fisse and she reached the book at the same time, but Ori Fisse had no chance against the power of a grown adult. Suzanne was enraged now. She pulled the book hard towards her, making Ori Fisse let go and stumble. Ori Fisse pulled out his dagger, but Suzanne was already up and kicked him hard with her foot. Ori Fisse flew right across the room and smashed into the opposite wall. He lay motionless on the floor, his dagger in the opposite corner of the room.

Skeleto had not reacted as quickly as Ori Fisse to Garglethroat's death. He was still stunned when Suzanne briskly walked over towards him, raised her foot, and stomped down will all her force on Skeleto. His brittle plastic skeleton frame burst into a thousand pieces upon impact of Suzanne's heavy shoe. Bits of plastic skidded all over the floor.

But Suzanne did not stop there. She walked over to where Ori Fisse was lying, still breathing but unconscious. "Take this, you little shit!", she said, crushing him under her foot. "This is for all the misery and agony you three have caused!" A loud 'plop' could be heard as Ori Fisse burst open under Suzanne's shoe. His head rolled one way, his arms another, and an ugly orange-coloured fluffy and smelly filling oozed out of him. Suzanne grabbed the filling and ripped it apart, strewing it all over the room.

She then moved over towards Garglethroat's limp body on the floor. She raised her foot but hesitated. She glanced over at Andrew. He nodded. Suzanne let her foot crash down on Garglethroat and the ugly toad burst open like a bag of crisps. In his case the stuffing was small greenish plastic beads that spread all over the floor. Garglethroat had completely burst open and was now as flat as a pancake. Nobody would ever be able to revive him again!

Only when the last green bead had settled on the floor did Suzanne catch her breath. She looked at Andrew who stood behind the perspex glass, stunned at the scene that had unfolded in front of him.

Suzanne walked towards him and placed her hand on the glass. Andrew hesitated a few seconds, but then also raised his hand and placed it against Suzanne's. "Thank you", she said in a warm voice. "Thank you."

Andrew felt something he had not felt for a long time. He felt liberated! Like a large weight had been taken from his shoulders. He smiled at Suzanne, happy that she was there.

"Andrew, I promise that I will get you out of here as soon as possible. I think my professor at university can use his influence to have your case re-evaluated. But this will take a little while. Will you trust me?"

He smiled at her and looked into her eyes. "I will trust you Suzanne. As you can see", and they both looked at the carnage of bodies lying dead or petrified all around them, "you have changed my life. I will wait."

"There are a lot of things I need to do now", said Suzanne, "including reviving Sebastian, Teddy and Ugah, but also the hospital staff. Just be aware that they will want to lock you up again for the moment."

"I am aware of that, Suzanne. Hopefully you can unpetrify all these poor people and the animagi back in the village."

Suzanne looked gratefully again at Andrew. They could not have done it without Andrew Billings! In the end he had realised that Garglethroat had just used him, and it was Andrew stopping his love for his frog that had killed Garglethroat.

Suzanne quickly flicked through the Book of Death. As she had never seen it before it took her a while to find the right chapter. She recognised the important part by seeing the incantation Garglethroat had uttered when he started the green ray. *OK, I certainly don't want to read that one out aloud!* The counter-spell was just a few lines below. *I hope that is the right one!*, she thought. *I'll try it out on one of the wardens first.*

She walked towards the nearest warden lying on his back on the floor. She started reading with the book open in her hands:

MORTATIS RETURNUM VACATRIUM
DESSOLATA NON RETRIBIUM
QUANTOS APPALLY MAGRIBULUS

At first nothing happened. *Damn! It didn't work!*, Suzanne thought. But then the warden started moving a finger, then a hand, then his whole right arm. He raised his upper body from the floor and rubbed his eyes with his hands. "What happened?", he asked, but Suzanne did not reply, she just hugged him.

While the warden was still recovering, Suzanne walked over to Sebastian and repeated the counter-spell, and then to Teddy, Ugah, the director and the other warden. They all got up, still half stunned from the petrification.

"Well ... I was saying ...", muttered the director, but when he saw the three squashed animagi bodies and their stuffing all over the floor he realised that something had happened.

"It's all right, director", said Suzanne. "We are finished here. I apologise for the way the interview has gone and for the mess on the floor. You can sweep all this into the rubbish bin. You are right, we should better go now", and she smiled at Andrew who still stood behind the perspex glass, smiling back at her.

She put the still rather groggy Sebastian, Teddy and Ugah into her bag and stepped out of the room with a broad smile on her face.

84

Suzanne was still in a daze. The events had unfolded so quickly over the last twenty minutes or so. She still could not believe that Garglethroat, Ori Fisse and Skeleto were dead and, indeed, that she had crushed them all to death! She felt immensely proud, but she also knew that she could not have done it without Andrew.

They had revived all the petrified wardens and staff at the hospital, with most of them not understanding what had happened. She walked down the steps near the main entrance when she saw a large car parked right in front of the hospital. The driver was slumped over the steering wheel, in the back a young boy of about four lay petrified.

"This must be how Garglethroat got to here so quickly", said Teddy.

Suzanne used the counter-spell to revive the man and his son. Although still dazed from the petrification, the man confirmed that Garglethroat and his men had somehow managed to get into his car and that they had threatened to kill his young son if he didn't take them as quickly as possible to the hospital. Suzanne told the man to go into the hospital and rest a while before driving back, and then she walked over to her own car where she first of all unpetrified Hagelik.

About ninety minutes later they arrived at her house. They all found it eerie that the village appeared to be completely normal, human adults and children going about their usual business, enjoying the warm sunshine. The human world was still completely oblivious to the tragedy that had befallen their animagi community.

They rushed into Suzanne's annex as quickly as they could. Suzanne opened the curtains and let the sunshine in. Their companions were still lying the way they had found them the previous evening. They looked peaceful as if they were sleeping.

Suzanne took out the book, opened it at the appropriate page and read out the counter-spell. One after the other woke up from their petrification, dazzled by the bright sunlight and rubbing their eyes. After a few minutes they had all settled down and sat around the table. Erik and Sylvester were on the sofa, still looking rather groggy, but Erik was already on his iPhone ringing his parents and telling them that he was ok. Barney rubbed his eyes and let out a huge yawn. Only McHaggis was still lying down, too injured to sit up, but at least he was alive and awake.

"I am so sorry!", McHaggis said with a raspy voice. He cleared his throat. "Garglethroat and his men caught me, but instead of petrifying me they... they...." Tears welled up in his eyes. "They tortured me! I could no longer stand the pain and told them where we were hiding and that Suzanne, Teddy, Sebastian and Ugah had gone to see Andrew several times. Garglethroat looked really shocked when he heard that we were trying to get to Andrew. Maybe it was at this point that Garglethroat realised that he was in real danger."

"That's alright, Arthur", said Hexybilla and put her arm carefully around his shoulder. "We all made a mistake letting you three go out to look for Garglethroat and other animagi who had not been petrified. We should have known better! But let's hear from Suzanne what happened at the hospital and how she came into possession of the Book of Death."

Suzanne, Sebastian, Teddy and Ugah recounted what happened, how Andrew had softened up more and more, and how his trust of Suzanne was growing. They vividly described how Garglethroat and his men had suddenly burst in, petrifying everybody except for Suzanne, and that it was Andrew who severed his link to Garglethroat and thereby killed him.

Hexybilla and her companions were stunned by the story. They particularly enjoyed the bit where Suzanne recounted how she had stamped on Garglethroat and his henchmen and how they burst, spilling their ugly fillings all over the floor. This eased the tension a bit and most of them managed a tired smile. But they were all still too exhausted to be in a real mood for celebration.

Sebastian also mentioned how he had tried to freeze time, but that, despite immense concentration, he had not managed to do it. "It shows how right we were a few days ago not to send me in to intercept Garglethroat!", he said. "They would have petrified me immediately, or tortured me …", and he looked at poor McHaggis who managed to respond with a smile.

"I think this also shows that I am not the chosen one from the prophecy, Mrs Hexybilla", Sebastian continued. "I always doubted that I would be the one, and my inability to save us at the direst time of need only confirms that it's not me the 'Chronicles of Animagi Lore' refer to."

"Maybe, maybe, Sebastian", replied Hexybilla. "I still haven't lost my faith in you …", and they all laughed.

While Suzanne, Teddy, Sebastian and Ugah told their story, Hexybilla had grabbed the Book of Death. She opened it to the page with the spells. "If only I had kept our copy of the book!", she said with a sigh. "How things would have been different!"

"That is water under the bridge, Mrs Hexybilla", said Mrs Moluk. "Thanks to the courageous intervention of Suzanne, Sebastian, Teddy and Ugah our story has a happy ending after all. We just need to make sure that this book never again falls into the wrong hands!"

"I'll make sure of that!", replied Hexybilla, clutching the book to her chest.

"I'm afraid we still need the book, Mrs Hexybilla", said Sebastian. "We need to wake up all those petrified animagi lying in the passageways below our village. There are so many, that will take quite some time!"

"You are absolutely right, Sebastian!", said Hexybilla and passed the book to him.

Although they were all deadly tired and most of them still stunned from being petrified, they immediately left the room and walked into the passageways below Suzanne's house. McHaggis was left behind and was looked after by Mrs Moluk.

Every time they found a petrified animago Sebastian opened the book and uttered the counter-spell. They gradually fanned out from Suzanne's house to cover most of the passageways in the western part of their village. After a brief dinner break at Erik's house – where Erik's mum hugged him and was over the moon for finally being able to see her son – they continued using the counter-spell until late in the evening.

At around midnight, Barney led them to the passageway where @@*^# and the other animagi who had returned from Animagana were lying in a pile of petrified bodies. One after another was unpetrified, there were hugs and cheers, and they all thanked Sebastian, Teddy, Ugah, Erik and Sylvester for not only having saved them from Animagana but also from Garglethroat's petrifying ray. After several weeks of absence, the seventeen animagi, who had been duped by Rigor Mortis to sell their host's souls, could return to their hosts.

I bet there will be a lot of discussions, regrets and reconciliations with their hosts, if they are initiated!, thought Sebastian looking at the group dissipating in all directions.

"I think that's it!", said Hexybilla. "These might have been the last ones. We will have everybody check their houses, hosts and the most remote passageways, and there might still be some petrified animagi we haven't found, but I am sure the bulk of our work is done. Well done everybody! I am so dead tired now, I can only think of my nice bed, and I am sure you are all thinking the same!"

They all nodded, tiredness visible in their haggard faces. Erik took Sylvester home with him, followed by Sebastian, Teddy and Ugah. Hagelik went to be reunited with Josh, while Barney said goodnight and walked into the passageway leading to Lucy's house.

For the first time in a long while we should all be able to sleep easy tonight, without worries about children in a coma or Garglethroat's petrifying ray!, thought Hexybilla as she opened the door to her flat.

85

One week had passed since Garglethroat's death and the re-awakening of the petrified animagi. Sebastian, Teddy, @@*^#, Ugah, Hagelik, Erik and Sylvester were walking back through the passageways – as usual Erik and Sylvester had to bend down in many places – towards Hexybilla's flat. They had just come back from a big celebration in the Great Cavern where many speeches had been given, Sebastian and the others were praised for their courage, Suzanne was mentioned specifically for her bravery, and everybody just celebrated to be alive and well again.

"That was a great celebration!", said Sebastian. "I think almost every animago from our village was there!"

"Yes, even McHaggis made it although he was on crutches and his doctor had said he should really stay in bed!", replied Teddy.

"I thought the minute of silence for all our dead fellow animagi was particularly moving and really important", said Sebastian. "I saw that many cried."

They all agreed and walked on in silence for a while.

"I particularly liked it when the disc jockey played Deep Purple, that really got the crowd rocking and dancing!", said @@*^#.

"Deep Purple!", replied Erik. "But they are ... like ancient! It was much better when they played more modern stuff like Coldplay and Arctic Monkeys. What do you think Sylvester?"

Sylvester cleared his throat and tried to speak, but only a croak came out with high pitches intermixed with low ones. They all looked at him. "What's going on Sylvester?", asked Erik.

"I don't know, the last few days my voice has gone all funny!", replied Sylvester.

"I know what is happening!", said Teddy, as ever so wise and knowledgeable. "Your voice is starting to break, mate!"

"You mean ... you mean ... that my voice is changing to that of a man's voice?", Sylvester asked astonished. "But ... but ... that means that ..."

"Exactly!", said Teddy, "it means you are actually ageing and growing up. Your body is changing! You are no longer immortal!"

"Wow!", said Sylvester with a big smile on his face. "I am growing up! I have been waiting for this for at least 465 years! Ever since I turned 12!"

"I'm afraid it also means you will die one day, just like all of us!", said Erik with a slightly more serious tone.

"But that's fine!", said Sylvester. "As many told you on Animagana, you can't believe how tedious it can be to be immortal. That's why there are so many suicides on Animagana!"

They all went silent for a while, thinking back at their adventures in Animagana and how long ago that all now seemed, although only a few weeks had passed since they came back through the portal.

"I wonder how Brother Konrad and the others in St Albans monastery are doing?", asked Erik, expressing what they all thought.

"They'll be alright", said Sylvester. "They have muddled through successfully since 1537, so they will continue to survive. Hopefully all of you will have helped a little bit, with your interventions at the slave market and against the pirates, to make Animagana a better place."

"Hopefully", said Ugah, "but the sad thing is that we will never know. There is just no way we can ever go back!"

"That is true", said Teddy. "Remember what Mrs Moluk said at the celebration: although we helped to reanimate the kids who were in a coma by rescuing the seventeen animagi we brought back with us, after all the counting and de-petrifying we still know that six animagi who went to Animagana through Rigor Mortis' dark scheme are still trapped somewhere in Animagana, probably never to return. Sadly it means that four human children from the village are still in a coma and will probably never wake up, the essence of their souls lost forever during the transition of their animagi through the portal."

Again, a deep sadness overcame the group. They all realised that despite the great outcome in the fight against Garglethroat, there were still some dark shadows overhanging the animagi community. But they also knew that their community had also come out more resilient than before by having to tackle Garglethroat and his dreadful deeds.

They arrived at Hexybilla's flat and knocked on the door. Hexybilla knew they were coming and let them in. Professor Pandanus had also been invited and greeted them all, thanking them again for what they had done and for unpetrifying him. They sat around the table in the living room, a big roaring fire was burning in the fireplace behind them.

"So, here we are for the final act of the Book of Death!", said Hexybilla solemnly. The book was lying in the middle of the table, dark and threatening. "This time Professor Pandanus has already copied the counter-spell from the book, in case anyone else ever uses the deadly green ray again." She pointed at a sheet of paper lying near the book. "In the next few days we will make hundreds of copies and send it to all animagi communities around the world, so that the darkness that befell our community will never affect anyone again."

"I am so sorry that we did not do this the first time we found a copy of the book here in the archives", said Professor Pandanus apologetically. "At least with this present action we will make sure that such a mistake will never happen again."

They all nodded and looked at the book, still in awe of its dreadful powers.

Hexybilla slowly stood up, grabbed the book and walked towards the fire. "So, as we all agreed, let us destroy this book forever and hope that no other copy will ever be found again. Imagine if Henry VIII and Thomas Cromwell had laid their hands on that book in the late 1530s! How different the world would be from now, and I am also sure it would not have been a better world at all!", and she tossed the book into the fireplace.

Similar to when they had burned the first copy of the Book of Death they had found in the archives, for a short moment nothing happened. The book was lying on the burning logs, seemingly unaffected. But again after a while a terrible green smoke began to ooze from the book and a ray of green light was visible between the pages. The animagi ducked instinctively as they did not want to be accidentally hit by the green ray. But the book suddenly erupted into flames and a faint hollow scream could be heard emanating from the book.

"It's almost as if it's alive!", shouted Sebastian.

They all stood up and moved closer to the fireplace to look at the book lying in the embers. The book was finally consumed by large flames, disintegrating into smaller lumps that burned with an intense green flame. The whole room filled with green smoke and the smell became unbearable. They all moved away from the fireplace and held their noses. Hexybilla quickly opened the front door wide to let the smoke dissipate into the passageway, and gradually the smoke eased. Only a pile of greenish ash was visible in the fireplace.

They all looked each other and uttered a great sigh of relief.

86

Erik and Sylvester were sitting on the sofa in Erik's house, watching TV. As Alathia, who was still not initiated, was working, Sebastian, Teddy and Ugah had joined the boys on the sofa. Erik was holding Sebastian on his lap, not embarrassed at all to show his affection to his teddy-bear in front of the others. They had all gone through too much together to worry about little things like that.

Godfrey, who was again working from home, came in with a big smile on his face. "I have excellent news, guys!", and he particularly looked at Sylvester. "After a whole week of haggling with the British Adoption Agency, they have finally allowed us to go ahead and apply for full adoption of Sylvester!"

They all cheered loudly and looked at Sylvester who was very happy.

"There is still a long way to go, and the fact that you just came out of nowhere, with no papers like a passport or birth certificate has not made matters easy, but they have agreed to look into your case, and I think the chances are good that you can stay with us."

"That is great news, Godfrey! Thank you so much!", said Sylvester with his croaky breaking voice. He looked at Erik who smiled at him and tapped him on the back. Not only were they good friends now, but they were also likely to become brothers!

Godfrey left them to enjoy the moment.

"What movie are we watching, guys?", asked Erik, picking through their vast collection of DVDs.

"We've got to start with Toy Story again", said Sebastian. "That's what we watched before the whole catastrophe started unravelling, and we never finished watching it. I want to see Woody and the other toys and how they have to go limp when adults enter the scene. They are really unlucky that they don't have initiated humans like we have."

"I then want to see 'The Golden Compass'", said Teddy. "I like the story about humans having 'daemons' – animals that can talk – and have a really strong relationship with their human hosts. Like us, daemons can't survive without their humans although their bond seems a bit stronger and intense."

"Yeah", said Ugah, "but that is just a story, whereas our link to our human hosts is real!", and they all laughed. "I certainly want to watch all the Harry Potter movies again", he continued, "I particularly like the house elves, like Dobby, who are a bit like us."

"I quite enjoyed the one we watched the other day", said Sylvester, "with the lion and the four school kids …"

"The chronicles of Narnia", Erik said. "Yeah, that story is alright, but it's maybe more of a kid's story."

Sylvester did not quite yet understand these subtle nuances in the modern world. "OK, what about 'Eragon'? There you have humans talking with dragons!"

"OK, what about 'Ted' with Seth McFarlane's voice?", asked Sebastian, and they all looked at him in astonishment.

"I'm surprised you know this one!", said Teddy. "It's 15-rated and contains some rather raunchy scenes which are not really suitable for little animagi like you!"

But they all agreed that this was also a good story – especially as it had a speaking teddy-bear as the main character

– and they mentioned several other movies where humans and animals had special relationships.

"I bet you that all the authors of these great stories – J.K. Rowling, Pullman, Paolini and C.S. Lewis – are or were initiated humans who played an important part in their animagi community", Teddy wondered. "I can well imagine J.K. Rowling going off regularly to her local animagi council meeting, C.S. Lewis knowing all the secret animagi passageways in his old Oxford chambers, and Pullman sitting with all his animagi discussing the plot to one of his great books!", and they all laughed at the thought of these eminent writers surrounded by their animagi, chatting away about the intricacies of human-animagi relationships.

There they sat, huddled together, talking and laughing and enjoying each other's company. A typical group of friends, joyful, teasing each other, and with a strong sense of friendship, at the intersection between the complex worlds of humans and animagi …

Acknowledgments

This book could not have been written without the help of many people who provided inspiration for characters and ideas.

First I wish to thank my wonderful son Erik who has provided inspiration for the main human character in this book. Although Erik is now an adult I have adapted his character to a 12-year old, an age where surprise, wonder and curiosity are still hugely important. Erik has also supplied the animagi characters of Sebastian and McHaggis, although I have to admit that in real life Erik never showed much interest in his toy animals and 'make-believe' play. The only exception was his whale Ferdinand who always had dreadful accidents while (pretend) swimming, which resulted in him ending up with a completely crushed and crumpled face. Erik could not get enough of this story and Ferdinand's accidents always made us laugh. Erik also provided very useful comments on an earlier draft of this book.

The second person I wish to thank is my wife Olivia for very useful critical comments on several drafts of this book and on its characters, and for constant encouragement while I was working on this book.

The third person I am immensely grateful to is my brother Peli. The story of Animagana is loosely based on a childhood dream world we had developed over many years which was similar to that described in this book. Most importantly, Peli supplied the inspiration for the character of Garglethroat who was a real and important (and nasty) toy animal in our make-believe stories. During a discussion over a pizza Peli also provided the impetus for setting the key scenes in Part 3 of the book in a psychiatric hospital. Peli and his daughter Zina also provided the inspiration for the character of the witch Hexybilla, although in their game Hexybilla is rather wild(er) and has a motorbike with 28 exhaust pipes (!) – a feature which unfortunately could not be built into this story.

I myself feature only as a lesser character in this book (Godfrey, Erik's dad), although the Professor of Psychology Hedley comes closer to my real-life character as a university academic. But many animagi in 'Sebastian' have their real counterparts as my toy animals: Teddy, Bunny, Ugah, Hagelik, Mrs Moluk (who actually is Mr Moluk in my world). We also had a whole group of self-made crudely stitched-up frogs with rice fillings (which often spilled) who provided the inspiration for @@*^# (although where this name comes from I haven't got a clue). All other animagi featuring in this book are fictional characters but I am sure that somewhere in this world there is a toy similar to Barney, Mr Kasperski and indeed Mr Wood (hopefully not nasty Ori Fisse, although Skeleto I suspect will be a common toy).

Suzanne, a key human character in 'Sebastian', is loosely based on a good friend of ours from the village – a true heroine in our own world.

Geography is also an important inspiration and our real village on the South Devon coast provided an important inspiration for this book, with its slightly sleepy atmosphere and content inhabitants not realising what lies beneath their houses and streets.

Parts of the story in this book have been inspired by other children's fantasy writers (both books and films) whose writings and story-telling I greatly admire. I am hoping (like many authors I guess) that the book has a bit of a Harry-Potterish-feel to it, with glimpses of magic through Sebastian's time-freeze, the friendship between Teddy and Sebastian, and the atmosphere at animagi school and meetings, but I never would claim to come even close to J.K. Rowling's magical writing skills. The notion of animagi (used as a plural; singular 'animagus') also appears in Harry Potter, although in a different context from that used in 'Sebastian'. The movie 'Toy Story' (Pixar Studios,) which features several times in this book, also provides a fantastic template for developing an imaginary world that lies just behind that of humans. The idea of the portal to Animagana, although not dissimilar to Pullman's book 'The subtle knife' in the sublime trilogy 'His Dark Materials' or to the movie 'Stargate', was already used as an idea in our own childhood play in the 1960s and 1970s, probably also influenced by Star Trek's notion of 'beaming'. The pirates on Animagana and the story about the pirate ships have been inspired by one of my favourite French childhood comics, 'Barbe Rouge' by Victor Hubinon. The story about St Albans monastery was inspired by the fact that our family lived in St Albans for ten years, a magical town with an awe-inspiring cathedral (but no longer with a monastery), if it wasn't for the dreadful traffic choking the town centre.

In addition, I wish to thank … ooopps, I have to go now. Teddy is getting bored again of watching me write and wants to play chess.

Printed in Great Britain
by Amazon